# LONG JOURNEY HOME

Also by Michael R. Lane

<u>Mysteries</u>
*The Gem Connection*
*Blue Sun*
*The Butcher*
*Six Weeks*

<u>Fiction</u>
*Emancipation*
*UFOs and God*
*The Family Stone*

<u>Poetry</u>
*A Drop of Midnight*
*Sandbox*
*Mortal Thoughts*
*Love & Sensuality*
*A Leap Year of Haiku*

# LONG JOURNEY HOME

Michael R. Lane

BARE BONES PRESS
P.O. Box 9653, Seattle, WA 98109

ISBN: 979-8-9891948-2-7



Published by Bare Bones Press, Seattle, Washington.

The characters and events in this book are fictitious. Any similarity to real persons, living or dead is coincidental and not intended by the author.

Design: Bare Bones Press
Production: Bare Bones Press
Cover Art: Michael R. Lane

Bare Bones Press
P.O. Box 9653
Seattle, WA 98109

www.michaelrlane.com
www.barebonespress.com

First Edition: March 2024

*"How was your journey?"*
*"Lonely."*
*"Find many lights?"*
*"Some."*
*"Ends your story as begun."*

— Michael R. Lane "Welcome Home"

# CONTENTS

# CASE 121

The town coupe station wagon rolled along the winding mountain road known as Serpentine Pass. Wilson Stork preferred Serpentine Pass to the main highway because The Serpent cut an hour off their commute to his parents' house, despite The Serpent's sinister reputation for treacherous curves, poor visibility, and dense fog.

The Serpent made Carma Stork uneasy at night. The heavy stillness was one reason. The dismal isolation was another. Lastly, it was the silence—a bone-chilling silence that at times made Carma shiver with fear.

Carma held her breath in a silly attempt to mute her heart while she strained to listen for extraneous sounds. She heard nothing aside from the soothing hum of the car engine. Mission failed. Carma released her breath with a nervous sigh.

*Tonight isn't as bad as all the other nights we've traveled The Serpent*, Carma thought. A full moon added visibility. The fog was wispy, almost dreamy; as if they glided through an ethereal mist.

Carma turned her attention from Serpentine Pass to the lone small figure curled comfortably beneath an earthen brown woolen blanket in the back seat of their car. Victoria was the pubescent twin of her mother at that age, her tiny hazelnut face a visage of peace. Her daughter at rest consoled Carma.

"She's still asleep," Carma whispered to her husband. "Not like the last time we made this trip."

Wilson Stork said nothing. He smiled, glanced at Carma, and then nodded his head in agreement. Wilson was a quiet man. After more than a decade of marriage, Carma knew which buttons to push to alter that circumstance. Her husband's silence was comforting to Carma, in contrast to The Serpent.

Carma observed Wilson. Her attentive gaze found him comelier than when they married. His tan face shimmered from the moonlight. No one would have guessed Wilson Stork was an accountant, to look at him. He was a powerfully built man with broad shoulders, a barrel chest, and a thickly muscled neck. Their only child had described her father's hands as being as big as shovels. Carma watched his manicured fingers, the size of frankfurters, casually grip the shimmering black steering wheel, gracefully guiding their station wagon along at a steady pace. While his hands were short of the metaphor their daughter had used to describe them, those were the same hands that were mighty enough to wield a sledgehammer single-handedly, yet gentle enough to massage her breast. His strong, compliant hands best expressed how and why she loved Wilson. They were hands Carma entrusted with her life.

Carma laid her head upon her husband's hard shoulder. Wilson lofted a strapping right arm about Carma's shoulders and gave her an adoring squeeze. Wilson kissed her forehead. Carma smiled. She was at peace.

"I love you, Wilson." Her words were just above a whisper. There was a moment's delay before Wilson replied, "I love you too, sweetheart."

Lifting her head from her husband's shoulder, Carma found him gazing down at her. His smile was affectionate and warm. They kissed a brief but sensual kiss before Wilson reluctantly pulled away.

Carma had settled her head back upon Wilson's shoulder when she saw something flash across their windshield. A nude woman was standing in the middle of the road. Wilson snatched his arm from about Carma while jerking the steering wheel away from the woman with his other hand. The car violently swerved to the right, missing her. Carma felt a second of relief. Then the sight of the gray metal guardrail erupted in front of them. Wilson desperately attempted to steer the town coupe away from disaster.

The station wagon burst through the barrier, catapulting down over the side of the mountain. Carma's screams pierced the cool empty night air as the car toppled end over end through space, crashing into jagged rocks some two hundred feet below.

*   *   *

Carma eased open a tall, wood-stained door, stepped inside the office of Dr. William J. Adams, and quietly closed the door behind her. It was a tidy, well-organized, spacious corner office modestly furnished, blessed with an abundance of natural light streaming from two picture windows along the north and east walls. Three mediocre paintings and a pair of unimpressive sculptures passed for obligatory art. A couple of mature floor plants and several junior hanging plants stretched for the sun. Centered between two eight-foot-tall oak bookshelves along the south wall was an ornamental grandfather clock of equal stature. Made of finished oak and shimmering from polished brass and beveled glass, the clock stood unchallenged as the jewel in the room. One could see its heart through its oval glass chest. A brass gridiron pendulum smoothly swept back and forth, making a soft tick-tock as if each precious second were a gentle kiss from time.

Carma was late. Her alarm clock's gnawing electronic noise had awakened Carma from her nightmare. Reality resuscitated her mind. Carma lay still as a corpse, breathing heavily, staring at the flat white ceiling as if it were something to fear. Perspiration dampened her face and her supple green nightgown. It was a nightmare which had frequented her for the last four years. Still, it took time for its effect to diminish.

The alarm clock had turned itself off, the final signal that her nightmare had ended. Carma rose from her bed and staggered to the bathroom. She plucked loose the shear nightgown clinging to her sweat-drenched hazelnut skin, average breast, hourglass waist, washboard stomach, muscular hips, and legs. Carma was a tall woman with feet and hands regarded as small for her height. She used her hands as bumper guides against the walls on her way to the bathroom.

She settled her unsure steps on the firm carpet as if someone had littered her path with thumbtacks.

Gingerly crossing the cool tile bathroom floor to the pallid sink, Carma turned the pearl handled spigot. Cold water sapped the warmth from her face, leaving in its wake the frigid wetness of undeniable consciousness.

Carma dabbed her face dry with a black cotton hand towel from the brass towel rack to her right. The towel absorbed most of the wetness, but did little to replenish the warmth the icy liquid had stolen. She replaced the towel, only to find herself taking notice of the woman in the mirror.

A face of soft round features and pouty lips stared back from clover-honey eyes. Her jet black, mid-sized Afro was unevenly matted. She dismissed its condition as par for the course. Carma was often told that she was beautiful. While Carma placed little emphasis on physical beauty, she was not blind to the fact that she may not have had a chance to marry Wilson Stork without it.

Dr. Adams had not moved. He stood erect at the office center, gazing at the distant snowcapped northern mountain ranges, his caramel hands clasped behind him.

A drop of cold water had formed a tributary from Carma's widow's peak to her right eye, breaking the trance of the mirror. Carma made her way from the bathroom to the bedroom closet. She glanced at the alarm clock on the pinewood nightstand. Glowing white numbers read 9:16. The numbers struck Carma like a teacher with a wooden ruler across the palm before the abdication of corporal punishment in American public schools. Carma had forgotten to reset her alarm. She had a doctor's appointment at ten.

Carma showered and dressed as quickly as she could. Her hair and makeup were done to perfection within minutes. Carma slipped into an Analise beaded silk dress, a gala of colorful tropical flowers with an arresting asymmetrical ruffled hem that swirled from her left knee across her lower right calf. Her shoes were open black leather slingbacks with two-inch heels.

Carma did not notice the lattice of sunlight illuminating everything it touched with a pleasing radiance. She did not feel the mild spring breeze wafting in from the open bedroom window. She had no time to give gratitude to life. Carma was late for her appointment, and nothing else mattered.

Carma had made a hurried inspection of herself in the full-length bedroom mirror. Satisfied with her appearance, one spray from her crystal perfume atomizer was the final touch.

She hurried across the room, grabbed her Gucci handbag from the maple wood dresser nearest the bedroom door, and sprinted from her condominium to the elevator down the hall.

Carma had no difficulty locating her emerald Lexus in the spread of pre-assigned parking spaces in the private garage of high-security Morning Glory condominiums. Within seconds, she raced toward her appointment.

"Doctor Adams," Carma said in a hushed voice, as if she were disturbing a meditating priest.

Dr. Adams turned to face her. "Mrs. Stork, so good to see you again," Dr. Adams said in his silky bass voice, extending his right hand as he crossed the room to greet her. His hand engulfed her delicate fingers with a firm but tender grip. His hospitable handshake was accompanied by a goateed smile of the straightest whitest teeth Carma had ever seen. Carma detected a hint of something. Was it cologne or aftershave? No—milder, more subtle, more alluring, Carma concluded. A faint seductive musk that beckoned Carma to move close enough to exchange body heat.

As though statuesque lovers taking stock in each other after a long separation, they remained standing in the middle of his spacious office. Dr. Adams was dressed in his tailored dark blue herringbone suit which exploited his long, lean, tapered body. Carma was dressed in casual apparel that garnered appreciative stares from would-be admirers.

Carma enjoyed his touch. She always prolonged their handshake beyond what many would deem appropriate. Carma would cross that same line staring into his luminous dark brown eyes. *Aesthetic union born of criminal circumstances*, Carma thought. A phrase she had read somewhere, but she could not recall its origin.

"Sorry I'm late," Carma said.

"That's quite all right, Mrs. Stork."

"I would rather you called me by my maiden name, Doctor."

"That being?"

"Davis."

"As you wish, Miss Davis."

"Let's make it Carma. I think it's time for us to be on a first-name basis, don't you, Doctor?"

Dr. Adams fidgeted before answering. "If you feel comfortable with that, Carma, then so do I."

Carma had hoped the doctor would reciprocate, extending to her the same familiar courtesy she had just relinquished. Carma decided to press further when he did not respond in kind.

"Do you mind if I call you William?"

"I'd rather you didn't," Dr. Adams said, his smile diminished to a warm grin without dulling the light in his eyes. Carma managed to conceal her disappointment.

"Won't you have a seat?" Dr. Adams waved a hand toward two bland brown leather chairs with solid wood arms haphazardly arranged in front of his plain maple wood desk. "Or would you prefer the couch?" He waved this time at the chairs' cousin, an equally bland brown leather analyst couch across the room.

"I'll take the chair," Carma said.

They shared a smile at a clear inference to the electric chair. Dr. Adams moved one of the leather chairs out of the way. He positioned the other directly across from the wing-backed brown leather armless swivel chair behind his desk. Dr. Adams helped Carma into her seat and then sat across from her on his side of the desk.

"Is there anything in particular that you would like to talk about today, Carma?" Dr. Adams asked.

"Not really."

"I see," Dr. Adams said, pausing for thought. "How is everything—in general?"

"Everything's fine."

"Work is okay?"

"Work is fine. No problems aside from the usual."

"How's your personal life, Carma, if you don't mind my asking?"

"Boring. How's yours, Doctor?"

"I lead a full life."

"Are you seeing anyone?"

"No, I'm not, but let's remain focused on you."

They smiled. Carma had gathered a slew of background information on her handsome doctor by such queries. Dr. William Adams was divorced with two children: Abayomi, seven, and Nabila, four. His favorite colors were red and green. His favorite foods were beef stew and sweet potato pie. He enjoyed basketball, football, tennis, reading, teaching, skydiving, hiking, fishing, and Kung Fu. He loved spending quality time with his children. He loved his work. He despised politics and television. He preferred boxers to briefs. He slept *au naturel* in the summer and spring, and he expected to retire by age fifty.

"Precede, Doctor," Carma said, making a mental note to pursue, at her earliest opportunity, what William meant by leading a full life.

"Have you given any thought to Chester, lately?" Dr. Adams asked.

Chester was Carma's last boyfriend, the sixth in just under three years. He was the third man to ask Carma for her hand in marriage. Her third strike, as Carma jokingly put it. Chester loved her. Like all the rest, Carma did not love Chester. Only her ex-husband, Wilson, had captured her heart. That was, up until now.

Carma met Wilson Stork at a medical convention. Wilson was there to learn more about health care accounting practices. Carma was there keeping pace with the latest breakthroughs in pediatric and obstetric nursing. Carma noticed Wilson the first day. Wilson took notice of Carma at the formal dinner later that week. He was not alone in his recognition. Her tomato-red backless gown turned many heads, that night.

Wilson came over, politely introduced himself, and from that moment on, Carma knew he would become her husband. Physical beauty was her bait. Her mind and personality were the hooks. Her barrenness cut the line.

"What Chester and I had was nice while it lasted, but that relationship is over," Carma said. "He still calls on occasion to see how things are going."

"Do you ever call him or any of your other ex-boyfriends?"

"Once it's over, it's over. I don't believe in backtracking. Do you, Doctor?"

"Do I what?"

"Do you ever call any of your old girlfriends, or backtrack, as I call it?"

Dr. Adams replied with a smile. "We're talking about you, remember?"

"But of course," Carma said, allowing herself a mischievous grin.

"When I asked about work," Dr. Adams said, "you said 'no problems aside from the usual.' Would you care to elaborate?" Dr. Adams leaned forward, interlacing his fingers on top of his desk with an expression of deep interest. Carma hesitated for thought.

"Some of the routine problems are when a child is prematurely born or has a treatable illness of one type or another," Carma said. "Those situations can be administered to as needed. But when an infant is stillborn, drug-addicted, mutilated, or physically deformed—in short, saddled with a condition that is beyond our control—those are the days that rattle me."

"Why is that?"

"Isn't it obvious?"

"How many years have you been an obstetric nurse?"

"Need I remind you, Doctor, that I am a Registered Nurse who specializes in pediatric and obstetric care," Carma said with a haughty air and a bemused smile.

"I knew that," Dr. Adams said, returning her smile. "Forgive me. I meant no disrespect. Which do you enjoy most?"

"You mean, between pediatrics and obstetrics?"

"Yes."

"I enjoy them equally. Chimera Hospital has assigned me to obstetrics for the past two years. Almost fifteen years now, combined, in answer to your previous question regarding my years of medical service."

"The point I was attempting to make earlier—albeit rather badly— was: have you not experienced your share of misfortunate births throughout your profession?"

"I don't know what my share of misfortune births are. One is too many for me. However, the short answer is yes. Even so, it doesn't make it any easier to deal with."

"How do you normally handle one of those stressed-filled days, Carma?"

"Exercise and meditation. They help me relieve stress and any pent-up grief or anxiety. They bring me back to my center."

"Very good," Dr. Adams said with a grin. He knew what Carma meant. Kung Fu, fishing, and hiking had the same effect on him. Sensing she had struck a favorable chord, Carma returned his smile. Clearing his throat, the doctor adopted a serious demeanor before continuing. "Did you recently have one of those days?"

Carma's body became rigid. Her hands played nervously in her lap. She stared directly into the doctor's eyes as she answered him with a brief nod.

"When?"

"Yesterday." Her voice was low and tense.

"Something happened?"

Carma nodded.

"Can you tell me about it?"

Carma let out a deliberate breath and closed her eyes for a moment before she spoke. "I was involved with three births yesterday. All went as expected. By that, I mean there were no complications. I had worked twelve hours, and with the weight of Shepherd's death on my soul, I was feeling every minute."

"Shepherd?"

"I never told you about Shepherd?"

"No, you haven't."

"I was there when he came into the world. Six pounds, eight ounces—a baby boy with eyes so big, they could take in your entire office at a glance. His parents did not want to give him a name until they knew if he would survive. A wise choice on their part—naming a child makes it even tougher to let go, if you have to. One of the nurses said he reminded her of the shepherd boy in the animated TV special *The Little Drummer Boy*. No one could remember the child's name in the story, so we all agreed to call him Shepherd.

"There was nothing physically wrong with Shepherd. He simply lacked a will to live. He wouldn't eat, sleep, cry, or even move. The only part of Shepherd that exhibited life was his eyes. Those big, sad, gray eyes seemed to absorb everything. It was as if there was an ancient spirit in that infant body—the reincarnation of an old man who had seen it all. I don't mean, like a generation of experiences. I mean, as if he had witnessed the beginning and end of time and all that was in between, and not one moment had fazed him.

"Shepherd appeared to want nothing to do with this perpetuating myth we called life. He seemed to be biding his time. He knew his flesh would yield and he could return to wherever it was he either desired or needed to be.

"We did everything we could to keep Shepherd with us. The entire obstetric and pediatric staff volunteered time, hoping to bring him around. No matter what we did, Shepherd would stare at us with those big gray eyes as if we were the ones to be pitied.

"I stopped in to see Shepherd during a break between my second and third deliveries. He died in my arms. His last breath was like a contented sigh. I could have sworn he smiled at me, leading into his death. We were instructed by the attending physician that if Shepherd passed away, to let him go, because there was nothing more we could do for him.

"I laid Shepherd in his crib next to his Koala bear, closed his eyes, kissed his forehead, and said goodbye. The desk nurse cried when I told her Shepherd had died. I understood. We had all been holding out for a miracle."

Dr. Adams' first impulse was to tell Carma how sorry he was. Experience informed him that would be counterproductive. He needed to press forward if they were going to continue to make progress in her therapy. "Did you cry, Carma?"

"No."

"Why not?"

"I wanted to," Carma said with a sigh. "I felt the same depth of grief the desk nurse felt, who did cry, but I couldn't muster a tear."

"How did you handle Shepherd's death?" Dr. Adams unconsciously titled his head to one side, trying to discern the compelling undercurrent in her voice.

"Not well, I'm afraid," Carma said. "I tried prana, yoga breathing, in the nurse's locker room, but that wasn't cutting it, either. So I went to my backup plan."

"Which is?"

Carma gave Dr. Adams a nervous smile before answering. "I go to the maternity ward to look at all the healthy babies that have come into this world, when I'm severely stressed. That always makes me feel better."

"Do you ever hold or play with any of the infants?"

Carma eyed Dr. Adams as if the question held ominous overtones. "Of course, all of the time. They are so adorable. How could anyone resist?" Carma concluded with an exuberant smile that lit her entire face.

Dr. Adams paused for a moment to gather himself. While he had noticed Carma's mistrust, at the same time, he was losing his professional edge. Carma's smile had forced to the surface a feeling he kept at bay. A feeling their patient-doctor relationship could not survive. A goading fire prodded his desire to hold Carma and help soothe her doubts. Even if it were just for a flashbulb moment, he wanted, more than anything, to enlighten Carma about this deep-rooted emotion. *Maybe one day*, he thought. *She needs my help. I must maintain a strict professional rapport.*

Dr. Adams unconsciously righted his head. He carefully formulated his next question before he spoke. Keeping his voice level and calm, he asked, "Is there anything else that has happened on your job lately that you would care to discuss?"

Carma's smile vanished. She stared at Dr. Adams with dispirited eyes. Dr. Adams realized he had touched a shadowy, sensitive place. Carma often withdrew when forced to reflect on matters she would rather forget. She rose from her chair and made her way toward the eastern picture window behind him. Dr. Adams paid close attention to Carma's every move, pivoting in his swivel chair to assure he had a full view of her at all times.

Her steps were like those of a self-condemned woman who looked toward the window as a possible means to her end. Dr. Adams watched with studious care as Carma stood before the window, gazing up at strands of cottony clouds floating beneath a powdery blue sky. While the window was shatterproof, Dr. Adams was ready to restrain Carma in the unlikely event she tried to harm herself. Carma stood still and silent for a few minutes. It seemed much longer to the doctor.

"It is a beautiful day." Her quiet voice was drained of all anxiety.

"Yes, it is," Dr. Adams said. "It's supposed to be even lovelier tomorrow, according to the weather report." The latter comment was not flippant conversation by the doctor. It was intended to instill hope for the future.

"I expect he's right," Carma said, as if resigned to the fact.

"He was a she," Dr. Adams gently responded. "In any case, I believe she is." The doctor heard the comforting tick-tock of his grandfather clock. He listened and waited.

"When I left the hospital yesterday," Carma said, "I saw something that disturbed me."

"What was it?"

"I decided to leave the hospital by way of the ER. I don't usually go that way. Usually, I leave through the main entrance. Yesterday was different. I was compelled to take that route."

Carma drew in a long breath and let it out slowly.

"I heard cries from sick and injured children awaiting medical treatment while anxious parents tried calming them with consolatory comments. Suffering children and worried parents seemed to be all there was in the ER when I left. The medical aromas were stronger, more potent than usual. The lighting was brighter, too.

"With my eyes straight ahead as I marched down the corridor, a medical team rushed toward me with a patient on a gurney. The patient was hooked to an IV. I could tell that the patient was in critical condition, judging by the expressions on the attending team's faces. I kept my pace—and as much as possible my distance—bound and determined to march by that unfortunate soul without as much as a glance.

"My head jerked in their direction as soon as they were within five feet of me, as if someone had grabbed my face and forced me to look. That's when I saw her: limp, unconscious, with lacerations and deep bruises all over her face, neck, shoulders, and upper chest. She couldn't have been more than ten. That child was about the same age as Victoria when she died. *God*, I couldn't believe it.

"I asked the attending nurse what had happened. She said the girl had been in a terrible car accident. I managed to pull myself away from the sight of that battered child long enough to make it the rest of the way down the hall and get on the elevator.

"I wanted to leave Chimera as fast as possible. I just stood in the center of that elevator, trembling as if I were trapped in a freezer, paralyzed, unable to perform the simple act of pressing a floor button. My breathing quickened. I felt myself on the edge of hyperventilating.

An all too familiar odor invaded my lungs—a putrid decay that brought with it remorse and fear. It's stench I despise with all of my being, yet it represents each person's inevitable plight. It intermingled with the powerful disinfectant smells of hospital cleaners.

"Death had recently been aboard that elevator in the form of a fresh corpse on a gurney, no doubt. That realization fueled my recovery. I focused my mind on something you told me, Doctor, in one of our earlier sessions: 'During your darkest hour, you can find light by focusing your thoughts on something uplifting.' I focused my mind on the babies I had enjoyed earlier. My breathing leveled off and the trembling stopped. I knew my panic attack was over once I pressed the lobby button. I got out of Chimera Hospital as fast as I could."

There was an uneasy pause.

"I remember tripping over my shoulder bag. I must have dropped it in front of me," Carma said in a voice weighted with exhaustion. "At least I managed to pick it up before I ran out of there."

Tears welled in Carma's eyes while she stared out of the window at an impassive sky. Dr. Adams offered Carma tissue. She extracted two, carefully dabbed around her eyes and about her cheeks, and then tossed them away before taking two more. The doctor let a few moments pass before asking his next question. "What do you think brought on this episode?"

"The child on the gurney brought back painful memories of Victoria."

"Do you think anything else might have caused it?"

"Like what?"

"Like something associated with your current physical condition?"

"What current physical condition are you referring to, Doctor? In case you haven't noticed, I'm in excellent shape."

Dr. Adams peered closely at Carma. He could see her reflection in the window. Carma was in a fragile state. This was a critical juncture in her therapy. It was his duty to determine whether she was strong enough for him to deliver unto her the truth, or continue to lead her down a path of self-discovery. Dr. Adams opted for the latter. He asked himself whether he had based his decision on sound judgment, or if his better nature had overtaken him.

"What did you do when you left the hospital?" he asked.

Carma took a deep breath before answering. "I hurried to my car, got in, and rushed home. I have to laugh, though." Carma forced a nervous grin.

"About what?"

"I didn't run a single red light or stop sign even in my haste to get home. I obeyed the speed limit all the way. I obeyed the rules of the road even in times of distress."

Carma turned to look at the doctor with a teary-eyed smile and said, "Traffic safety is something Wilson always preached. I was a real terror on the roads, before him. He kept lecturing me about my dangerous driving habits, hoping I'd change.

"What he failed to realize was that no amount of lecturing in the world was going to change me. The love I had for him and our daughter is what did it." After a stilted pause, Carma said, "I always thought I'd be the first to go."

"Why would you think that?"

"Isn't it obvious? No mother should have to bury her child."

Dr. Adams nodded. "Did you think you would die before your ex-husband?"

"Wilson?" Carma thought for a moment before she continued, as if mentally conferring with outside counsel on the matter. "Yes, I did."

"Why?"

"I'm not sure. It was just a feeling, like it was my fate or something."

Her smile departed, leaving a depressed expression on her beautiful, tear-stained face. Her eyes dimmed, dropping from the doctor's analytical stare. Dr. Adams was glad they had. The soft glow of her skin was mesmerizing in the natural light.

Carma Davis stared out of the window. The doctor found himself fighting mixed emotions of compassion and desire. He wanted desperately to help Carma in the way a man wants to help the woman that he loves. Again, Dr. Adams had to remind himself of how he could best serve his patient. Dr. Adams relented. He gave Carma time to compose herself before asking his next carefully crafted question.

"Going back to the incident at Chimera, I'd like to ask you another question about that, if I may?" His voice was low, soothing, and accented by the soft tick-tock of the grandfather clock. Carma gave him a slow nod to proceed.

"What brought on this sudden urge to exit the hospital by way of the ER?"

"Shepherd had died, as I said. My mind kept wrapping itself around his final moments. Then, a man's voice echoed in my head out of nowhere."

Dr. Adams heard a new note in her voice when Carma answered his question. It was a portent that she was regaining her strength. "What did the voice say?"

"A child is born. A child must die."

"Did you recognize the voice?"

"Not at first. I did once it became louder."

"Who?"

"My father." Carma turned from the window to face the doctor with an expression of intense concentration. Dr. Adams could see her fire returning—a signal for him that it was safe to proceed.

"Was your father a poetic man?"

"Not really."

"Why do you suppose he would cryptically speak to you?"

"I don't know. Maybe because my father knows I'm fond of poetry."

"Did your father's voice say anything else?"

"He did," Carma said while returning to her chair. "He said, 'The tide is high. You must make your rounds and hope the face of blood denounce.'"

"What do you think your father meant by that?"

"I thought he was referring to Shepherd, at first. Then I began thinking that maybe it had something to do with a place in the hospital that is almost as tragic as infant mortality. That is always the question. Which is worse: dying at birth, or after having sampled a full life?"

"And that philosophical question is what led you to the ER?"

Carma shrugged. "I suppose. Anyway, I was frightened."

"Frightened of what?"

"I had a sense that something terrible was about to happen."

"Then why did you go?"

Carma paused, pensively considering her answer. "I had to. There was something, or someone, there I needed to see."

"The child on the gurney."

"Yes."

"Did your father say any more?"

"No. Dad just kept echoing those same lines. The closer I got to the ER, the fainter my father's voice became. His voice went silent once I saw the girl on the gurney."

"Do you think your father led you there for a reason?"

"Yes, but for what reason?"

"I was hoping you could tell me."

Carma squirmed in her chair for a moment while attempting to discern what logical reason her deceased father may have had for marshaling her to the ER. The doctor awaited a response with only the comforting tick-tock of his grandfather clock in the background.

"I can't think of any reason for it, Doctor."

"Let's move on. What did you do when you got home, Carma?"

"I went to the bathroom to splash cold water on my face. Then I took a few minutes to calm down. After that, I did some yoga, showered, and then went to bed."

"Did you have any dreams you can recall?"

"Yes."

"Would you like to share them with me?"

"There's not much to tell. It's the same nightmare I've been having for the past four years."

"You mean, the one about the fatal car accident?"

"Yes."

"Was there anything different about the nightmare, this time, compared to any of the other times?"

"No—wait! Yes, there was! This time, Victoria was asleep under a brown woolen blanket in the back seat of the car, not jumping around like the other times I've had the dream. The fog wasn't dense, either. There was a full moon. It illuminated everything."

"How did you know the blanket was woolen, Carma?"

"I just did."

"Did you touch the blanket in your nightmare?"

"No."

"You personified its existence in the way people embody objects in dreams?"

"*Exactly.*"

"And what more did you see?"

"I could see the scenery—what little there was of it. The road was more visible."

"Did any of those elements strike you in any particular manner?"

"What do you mean?"

"Did anything new that you saw, or experienced, release an emotional response of any kind from you, in your dream?"

"Emotional response?" Carma thought for a moment. "I felt no different than any of the other times."

"Tranquil feelings such as serenity, love, and the security of family."

"Yes. The biggest change in the nightmare was I was able to see things that, before, I could only sense."

"Your sense perceptions manifested themselves, in essence."

"Yes."

"Have you been able to recall any details about the nude woman standing in the middle of Serpentine Pass?"

"She was only there for an instant."

"Can you remember anything about her, like her hair, her face, shape, or skin?"

"No."

"How about her height or posture?"

"Not a clue. I've tried. I have been racking my brain for years, trying to remember the slightest detail about the woman who cost me my daughter. I don't even know if she is alive or dead."

"Do you still get angry when you think of her?"

Carma thought for a moment. "No. Now, I'm more curious."

"How so?"

"Who was she? And why was she standing in the middle of Serpentine Pass with no clothes on?"

"Why do you think she was there, Carma?"

"Could be she was mentally ill. Maybe she had been attacked and abandoned. Maybe she was lost or confused, miserable, feeling hopeless—who knows?"

"Maybe one day we will." Dr. Adams waited for Carma to respond. He wanted Carma to chew on what she had just bitten off regarding her mystery woman. Dr. Adams moved on when Carma remained silent.

"Did you always call your daughter Victoria—never Vicky?"

"Always Victoria, like my mother did with me. My mother always told me, 'Carma, if I wanted you called something other than Carma, I would have named you something different.' Guess I picked up that attitude about my child from her."

"Why do you suppose Victoria was asleep, unlike—"

"The way it happened."

"You can put it that way."

"I don't know, Doctor. Maybe my subconscious needed a change." Carma didn't smile. Dr. Adams took that as a signal that she was serious.

"A change from what?"

"The gory reality of the truth."

"That being?"

"The car accident that cost me my daughter!"

"Of course." Dr. Adams paused to take in Carma's state of mind. She sounded irritated. That meant she was vulnerable again. The last thing Dr. Adams wanted was to have Carma withdraw into a state of depression. He needed to continue to delve deeper into the shift in her ongoing nightmare, at the same time. "Why do you think these alterations occurred in your dream, Carma?"

"I don't know. The nightmare was the way it happened all of the other times. This is the first time it's ever changed."

"Let's approach the change in your nightmare from a different perspective." The door eased open enough for an elegant, middle-aged woman with tanned skin and haunting green eyes to poke her head inside and wait to be recognized.

"What is it?" Dr. Adams said, perturbed by the disturbance.

"I'm sorry to interrupt, Doctor, but it is ten-fifty-eight," his admin said, giving Dr. Adams the two-minute warning he had requested for back-to-back appointments.

"Thank you, Jackie," Dr. Adams said. Jackie nodded and removed herself from the office, closing the door.

"I'm sorry, Carma, but that's all we have time for today." Dr. Adams noticed that Carma appeared relieved.

"I'm sorry, too," Carma said with a coy smile. Carma thought it best to give Dr. Adams a graceful way out when he did not respond to her flirtatious behavior. "I meant, I'm sorry I was late."

"No worries, you're usually early. Is there anything you would like to discuss, in parting?"

*You*, Carma, thought. *I'd like to know if you would have a candlelight dinner with me tonight.* "Nothing comes to mind," is what she said.

"I feel we've had a breakthrough today that I would like to explore. Would you be willing to bump up our sessions to twice a week?"

"If you think it would help. I'll do anything to keep from reliving that nightmare almost every night."

"Good."

"Do double sessions mean twice the cost?"

"For you, Carma, we'll make it two for the price of one."

"I'm honored."

"You caught me at a good time. My cabin in the woods is paid for." Dr. Adams was only half kidding. He did have a cabin in the woods that was paid for, but he could not justify in his mind why he felt compelled to share that information with Carma.

"Cabin in the woods," Carma said, glowing. The very thought of her and the doctor alone in a secluded cabin was one of her romantic fantasies. "Sounds cozy. Any chance I might join you sometime?"

Both remained silent as they stared into each other's eyes. They tenderly smiled like two people in love. Carma was not going to give her doctor a way out of this one.

"Drive safely, Carma." Dr. Adams felt it necessary to say something to sever the towline of his illicit yearning, least he took Carma in his arms and kissed her.

They rose simultaneously from their chairs. Dr. Adams managed to whittle his affectionate smile down to a pleasant grin by the time they shook hands. Carma prolonged the handshaking experience. She once again apologized for having been late. Dr. Adams assured her that it was not a problem and then playfully scolded Carma not to let it happen again. Carma promised she would not, with a laugh.

"See Jackie on your way out to schedule your next appointment," Dr. Adams said.

"You never answered my question in regards to your cabin," Carma said with sensual inflections to her voice.

"I know."

Carma nodded her understanding, grinning as she left.

Dr. Adams escorted Carma to his office door, watching her leave with regret. They never seemed to have enough time together. He could not help but reflect on the warm softness of her hand in his as he closed the door behind her. He, too, had detected a delicious fragrance on Carma, reminiscent of a rose in replete glory. Had she seen the burgeoning longing in his eyes to kiss her? Dr. Adams restrained himself, not allowing his emotions full will.

Sitting in his chair, he removed a digital recorder he kept inside the top drawer on the right-hand side of his desk.

"Case 121," he spoke into the recorder. "The case of Carma Stork, who has requested to be called by her maiden name, Davis. We've had major breakthroughs today on three counts. First is the request to be called by her maiden name.

"Second, a traumatic experience she recently suffered while at the hospital that spurned a panic attack strongly suggests that her subconscious is attempting to break through to her conscious mind with the truth.

"The third is the change in her dream. In her dream, the child, Victoria, lay asleep beneath a brown woolen blanket in the back seat of their station wagon. Less fog and a full moon allowed Carma to see more of her surroundings.

"Unfortunately, there is still no information on the nude mystery woman in the middle of the road. However, I must assume the remainder of her dream was unaltered. The aforementioned variations represent significant steps in the right direction.

"I will elaborate on all counts later."

Dr. Adams paused for a moment to gather his thoughts before continuing.

"Carma's case was referred to me a year ago by a retired colleague and former professor of mine. I have had improper feelings toward Carma from the start. I reasoned then that those feelings were no more than infatuation, and they would pass.

"They have not. My feelings have amplified. I fall deeper in love with Carma with each session. Compartmentalization has saved me, thus far. By separating my emotions from my intellect, I have brought to the forefront all of my skills to stave off any misconduct."

Dr. Adams paused again, inhaled deeply, and then slowly released his breath before continuing.

"My love for Carma Davis has become such a distraction that each time I look into her eyes, I struggle to maintain the professionalism in which I take so much pride. It has always been my policy not to become personally involved with my patients. Nevertheless, Carma is everything I want in a woman: beautiful, intelligent, strong, and resourceful. This glaring fact can no longer be ignored.

"Should my feelings ever override my ability to be objective in my assessment of her mental state, I will have no choice but to refer Carma Davis to another psychiatrist."

The doctor paused again to gather his thoughts before he continued.

"Miss Davis continues to suffer from the delusion of a daughter she has never had. Carma has exhausted every possibility of reversing her sterility—a condition she suffered as a child, due to a fatal car accident that occurred under similar conditions as the one in her nightmare. Her father was killed while driving their family station wagon in which Carma lay asleep in the back seat.

"Wilson Stork filed for divorce almost immediately after discovering Carma's irreversible condition. That was the trigger mechanism—I believe—that shattered her already fragile mental state, since Carma's fantasy family life emerged precisely at that time.

"I have not been able to convince her ex-husband, Mr. Stork, to aid in Carma's recovery, as of yet. In short, Mr. Stork wants nothing to do with his 'crazy ex-wife' (as he refers to Carma). Therefore, there is nothing further to report on Case 121 at this time."

Dr. Adams completed his informal report and eased back into the spongy folds of his soft leather chair. He felt compelled to glance out of the window behind his chair, for some strange reason. He stepped over to the picture window and gazed east, out over the wonder of a beautiful summer day in the city. He witnessed a diverse spread of people navigating their way through an immense parking lot that his office building shared with the Miracle Mile Mall.

Dr. Adams could pick out Carma's beauty from the crowd, even from a distance. He watched Carma stroll to her car, get in, and drive out of the parking lot onto Charles Drew Blvd. He continued staring until the emerald Lexus disappeared amongst a sea of other vehicles down the long gray boulevard into oblivion.

The sound of a buzzer severed Dr. Adams from his thoughts. He walked over to his speakerphone and responded to the inhuman interruption.

"Yes." His voice was calm, as if he had just awakened from a peaceful nap.

"Mr. Anderson is here to see you, Doctor. Shall I send him in?" Jackie's voice came through the speakerphone like the clear, sharp tone of reason.

"Please do," Dr. Adams said.

Slipping into his professional decorum, Dr. Adams moved to greet Mr. Anderson at the door. His heart was not as quick to dismiss Carma Davis. Dr. Adams reflected on the warm light in Carma's beautiful clover-honey eyes before the dull click of the doorknob snapped him out of his trance.

# LETTERS

We normally give our tattered and outdated clothes to the neighborhood Goodwill. All weekend we rummaged through our bulging closets, deciding what to discard. Threadbare jeans, moth-eaten sweaters, old shirts and pants that no longer fit, a couple of young-man-sized bright colored Sir Jac jackets I hadn't worn in over fifty years, and my eggshell-white, two-piece high school graduation suit that fell into the jackets category (pledged every year by me for recycling) were the lot I planned to bid adieu.

Lorraine had made her choices with equal resolve. Between the time that we gathered our items into our arms and made the determined march to our SUV, my graduation suit, both jackets, and a woolen plaid sweater given to me by my father were plucked from the litter.

Lorraine was smarter. She had placed her nostalgic clothes aside before making the hike. That was why I went up to the attic. Neither of us wanted the job of finding a place to hibernate our memories.

Lorraine flipped a coin and I lost. Knowing my wife, I should have checked the coin.

Warding off cobwebs, navigating over and around a variety of forgotten items, creeping through a carpet of dust, and trying not to inhale too much dry stale air, I determined that our treasured belongings would be safest in a brass-trimmed wooden trunk my grandparents gave me when I went away to college.

I found it settled in a shroud of thick dust, decorated with a few cobwebs behind a ratty recliner and beside a cracked full-length mirror. I seemed to remember there was nothing in that trunk. Fortunately, it was unlocked, because I had no idea where the key was.

I dropped the armload of remnants onto the recliner seat, sending a puff of gray powder into the dim attic light. Flipping open the trunk, I reached for the clothes to toss them in when I noticed a dingy yellow shoebox tucked in one of the corners. Carefully, I lifted the box. I tugged at the rotted rubber band wrapped around it. It snapped and fell away like a dehydrated earthworm.

There were a fistful of time-tainted envelopes inside, with handwritten names and addresses and canceled postage still affixed to them.

'Angela Morris, 2212 Lexington Road, Latrobe, PA 15571', the top return address read. I thought aloud, "Why does that name ring a bell?" Then it dawned on me.

*Angela, Angie* ... my ninth-grade girlfriend. That's where those letters had gotten to. I'd assumed they were lost years ago. I was glad Lorraine hadn't discovered them. If she had, Lorraine would've said something about it by now. There are two things my wife can't keep: a secret, and her temper. Before I realized it, I had sat on top of the clothes on the recliner and read a few of the letters.

*

Hi, Davey:

You don't know me, but I've been checking you out for some time. I wish I had the courage to walk up to you and talk, but I don't. I think you're fine, and if you give me a chance, you might feel the same about me.

Please meet me at Skibo's at seven o'clock this Saturday. I guarantee you won't be disappointed.

See you later (I hope),
Madame X

*

Madame X, my foot. If Angie had wanted to remain anonymous she shouldn't have put her name and address on the envelope.

Angie was right. I wasn't at all disappointed. How could I be? Every dude in high school wanted her. I remember walking into a locker once, watching her walk down the hall. It was embarrassing as hell. Chester never lets me forget it. Too bad her family moved to Chicago. We were quite a couple.

Each letter pulled me a step closer to being a teenager again. Not wanting to mow the lawn, clean out the garage, wash the dishes, dump the garbage, or do my homework; spending endless hours on the telephone; playing football, baseball, and hoops. Shooing away my baby brother, Melvin, who would pester me about one insignificant thing after another; rapping with "the fellows" on the front porch well into starlit nights. (Rapping meant conversation back then not making music.)

Blue lights in the basement; getting down to the happening sounds of soul, R&B, funk, disco and pop blasting off limestone basement walls. Ballads that murdered you softly, asked 'have you seen her?' and crooned of love that mellowed the moments so boys with girls could slow dance and whisper sweet or naughty things into their partner's ear.

A little wine, a couple of joints, and the night belonged to us.

*

Dave:
What's up, man? This army shit is fucked up. Boot camp was more bullshit than one of Principal Kinkenstein's morality speeches. Is that old eagle still squeezing the tenth-grade science teacher? What's her name—Miss Charmin (yuk, yuk)?

Anyway, this is a quick note to say howdy and let you know I'll be shipping out to Vietnam in a couple of days. It's supposed to be some heavy shit. It can't be any worse than fighting cave man Willie Wilson.

Many thanks for the photo. You and the fellows are looking good; spill a little wine for me.

Be glad you got flat feet, Blood. I sure as hell wouldn't be here if I didn't have to. Gotta go; tell your folks I said, hi—and tell that silly little brother of yours, too. Could you do me one other favor? Tell Christine not to worry. I'll be back before she knows it. Thanks. A head squeeze and double noogies, good brother.

Later,

Kevin

P.S.

Are you getting any from Marcie yet? You can't keep going solo forever (yuk, yuk).

*

I wonder what happened to Kevin? I thought he was killed in combat. Mr. Parsons got word his son made it back to the States in one piece, but he never came home. I wish I had been over there with him. I don't know what I could've done, but I should've been there.

*

Dave:

What's happening, man? Just wanted to drop you a line to let you know how proud I am of you. Also, to let you know that no matter where you are or what you do, I'll always have your back. We're partners. That goes deeper than friendship. I don't have to tell you that. You already know.

Seems like our partners are all over the map, these days. You're out in California. Ray and Kevin are in the Army, Soup's in the Air Force, Ty's in the Navy. Sam and Kettle are away at college, like you.

I'm the only brother who stuck around Latrobe. If I hadn't dropped out, maybe I would've gone to college like you, but you know me. School's never been my thing. All I ever wanted to do was make money. I'm working at the steel mill, now. Something we promised none of us would ever wind up doing. Sorry I didn't hold up my end of the bargain.

I can't complain about the money. It's ball-busting work, but I'll get used to it. If nothing else, it'll give me a chance to figure out what I'm going to do with my life. Any suggestions? Don't give me any of your smart-ass answers, either.

I miss you, partner. I miss all of the fellows. I know you're doing well. You always did have a knack for the books.

I gotta go. Stay in touch.

Easy,

Sparrow

*

Marcie Anderson
Morrison Hall, Room 304
Chatham College
Pittsburgh., PA  15221
Dear David:

How are you? I hope you're doing well. Chatham is a very good school, in a scenic part of Pittsburgh. The people are friendly, but the food could use some help. I'm sorry I didn't write sooner, but school has got me bogged down. You know how that is.

How is Cal Poly? Are you having any problems adjusting to California life? Or are you kind of laid back, now?

I hope you're keeping your hands off those California girls.

David, there is something I have been wanting to say to you. Now is as good a time as any.

For the two years we went together in high school—and still going strong—I fantasized about us making love. When it finally happened, I can't honestly say it was how I'd dreamed it would be, but it did get better—much better, in fact!

Do you feel the same?

I wish we had done it before choosing schools. I'd probably be with you in California right now, fighting off the competition.

Thinking about you makes my whole body tingle with anticipation for the next time we'll see each other. Are you coming home for Thanksgiving? I hope so. I am! Please let me know.

Love you,

Marcie

*

Dearest David:

It was great seeing you at Thanksgiving and the day before and the day after and the day after that. Time away from you seems so long, while time together so brief. Thank you for the lovely birthday card and sweater, and don't worry about not writing. I understand. So, don't be so hard on yourself.

My roommate Velva says "Hi!" I hope you don't mind my telling her about us. Have to go, David. Class starts in a few minutes.

Take care,
Marcie

*

My Obsession:

Sharing the Christmas break together was fabulous. I will always cherish it. I awoke this morning with your name whispering in my mind. Your smile danced through the closed curtains and shone tenderly on my face. Clutching the pillow, I searched for comfort, but it made me want you more. Your scent curled about me. Delicious thoughts of you made me warm all over. If you were here now, I wonder what I'd do. It surprises me how rapidly the answers surfaced.

First, I'd lightly roll my fingers over your skin, one at a time. Then I'd bathe you in moist, gentle kisses. When I felt your heart racing beneath my touch, only then would we make love. Yet, all the love my body could give could only be a fraction of that from my heart, and that, a fraction from my soul. What I am trying to say is: I miss you, and love you very, very much. Please take care for both of us.

Love,
Marcie

*

Dear Peanut Head (your brother told me to say that, smile):

Don't you love us anymore? I realize your sophomore year is more challenging than your first, but it's been a whole month and we haven't heard from you. We miss you a lot around here.

Things are pretty dull without you to stir things up. Melvin tries, but he doesn't have your catastrophic touch. When you have a chance, drop us a line and don't *call*. Write. It's not because of the long distance charges because, I would love to hear your voice. It's because a letter stays with you a lot longer than a telephone call. So, drop us a few lines when you have a chance.

In the meantime, eat right, get plenty of sleep, study hard, and *leave those girls alone*. Remember my motto: if you make it, you take care of it. So, don't forget your raincoat. Comprender? Besides, you have a good woman in Marcie. Don't mess it up.

Melvin wants to know if he can borrow some of your records. I told him to ask you. By the way, your dad says "Get a job!" I have to go before my tears stain this letter. Miss you.

Love,
Mom
P.S.
I was just kidding about your father. Melvin's request was genuine.

*

Dearest:
I can't stop thinking about you. It's a wonder I get any homework done. It's as if you're in the air I breathe, constantly filling me with life. Do you have the same problem?

David, I'm not very good at poetry, but here's something I conjured up just for you:

Yes, it is true
my depth of affection
shallows ocean floors
defies gravity's force
constrains times' hands
alters fates' destiny
weaned by the lucid embers
of your honeyed abysmal eyes
transcending me deeper
into the place of your beginning

and mine,
suspended in a universe
dimensionless and infinite.
I … well—you know.

I guess you can tell we're studying The Romantic Period in English Literature right now.

I'm calling it "Rapture," in your honor. I hope you like it. More to the truth, I hope you love it as much as I love you.

Bye,
Love
P.S.

Your mom tells me you may not be home this summer. Is it true? I hope not. Please let me know.

*

Hey, Dave:

What's happening? Mom says you said no way on my borrowing some of your records, but here's the deal. With Dad's help, I started doing a little part-time disc jockeying around town, and I was wondering if I could rent some music from you? Some of my friends dig that old stuff.

Don't worry, I promise to take care of your albums. Mom and Dad will make certain I do. I need to know soon. I'm D-jaying a set next weekend. It would be nice to mix in a couple of golden oldies with some of my newer cuts.

Mom and Dad offered to let me use some of their records, but I told them no thanks. I was looking for old, not ancient.

Why did I say that? Dad went off on one of his 'how we kids today don't know anything about good music' speeches. You know how he gets. Anyway, name your price.

Remember, I'm just a kid. Don't take advantage of me.

Later, Big Bro',
Mel

*

Sweetheart:

I miss you. I'm working a summer job at the public library. It doesn't pay well, but it's cool, comfortable work that allows me a lot of time to read. Not many people come in, though. I guess they have better things to do than read books this time of year.

How do you like being an electrician's apprentice? Be careful—that's dangerous work, I hear. I'd thought I'd send along a recent picture of me, this time. It's been so long since we've seen each other. As you can see, I have my hair styled differently. Everyone says it looks great. I like it, too. What do you think?

Send me a picture of you. While I can't touch or hold it like the real thing, I'll take what I can get … for now.

I was glad you called on Sunday. Your voice melted in my ear. I hope you were able to solve that problem you were having, although I'm still not certain what it was. I cried a little when we hung up because I miss you so much. Call again anytime—collect, if you like—my parents won't mind. I'll pay for the calls myself, if they say anything.

I almost forgot. Everyone from the library says, "Hi Dave!"

Bye, love,

Marcie

*

Hey, Dave:

Thanks for the use of your records. Special thanks for waiving your fee—leaves more money for me. Did you know dad charges me for gas, pick-up, delivery, and setup fees? He says it'll help prepare me for the real world, where you get nothing for free.

Too bad you're not studying law. I could use a good lawyer to get Dad out of my pocket.

I really like D-jaying. It's got me thinking about going into radio or TV. Do you think I can do it? Believe it or not, my record collection has gotten bigger than yours. Mom didn't think that was possible.

We're going to miss you around here for the summer, Peanut Head. Until I see you again, stay cool.

Easy doings,

Mel

*

David:

I received your letter on June 22, but it's taken me a month to think of a response. At first, I went into shock. Then I cried. Eventually I grew angry, until finally I just ached from the inside out. I felt used and betrayed, like an old pet that's outlived its usefulness and been given away. Nothing seems to matter anymore. How could you do this to me?

You say you've met this girl, Lorraine, and you think you may be in love with her. Would this have happened had I been there?

Didn't you love me?

What difference does it make now? I've lost you. From my heart, I wish you the best, although I will admit that if the two of you were here right now, I'd kill both of you. Does that sound bitter? Damn it, you son-of-a-bitch, I hope so!

You say that in time I will forget you. Maybe that's true. Until that time comes, I am going to allow myself the anger and grief usually reserved for widows.

I guess it is true what that song says: "If you can't be with the one you love, then love the one you're with." Only romantic fools like me believe "Absence makes the heart grow fonder."

As civilized as your offer of friendship was, I must fiercely reject it. For, in truth, I could never relinquish myself to such a role. I will miss you like I would miss a limb or a lung removed, but this is goodbye.

Please don't attempt to telephone, write, or stop by my home when you return to Latrobe. You are an unwelcome stranger here. I am returning the bracelet you gave me when we went to the prom. I don't need to tell you what you can do with it. I would have sent the sweater, too, but somehow it was destroyed in the fireplace.

Farewell, My Love,
Marcie

*

Lorraine's voice drifted up the steep stairs like the low moans of distant ghosts through dense mist.

"What?" I hollered down, both annoyed and grateful for her intrusion.

"What are you doing up there?" Lorraine said. "I've been screaming my head off for five minutes!"

"Then you should be hoarse by now!" I yelled back.

"When are you coming down? We need to make our Goodwill drop and get back!"

*Never* is what I thought. "In a minute" is what I said.

"How long does it take to drop off a few clothes in an attic?"

"There's lots of stuff up here! I was just looking for the right spot!"

"We've got a lot of work to do around here today! The grass needs cutting and the hedges need trimming!"

"I know, I know, I'll be down in a minute!" With that, Lorraine went away.

Of the young men who were my partners growing up, only Sparrow and I have managed to stay in touch. Sparrow, whose real name is Chester Gates, found his knack as an assembly line supervisor for Ford Motor Company. Mel changed his mind about radio. My little brother has gone on to make documentaries, instead.

Then there was Marcie. As corny as it sounds, time does heal all wounds. Lorraine and I were present at Marcie and Xavier's wedding.

They reside in Philadelphia now with their three children. Marcie is an English professor at Temple University, having graduated magna cum laude from Chatham College with a B.A. in English and earned her doctorate in English from Yale. On those rare occasions when we talk, we never bring up that dark moment of our shared past.

If I had it to do over again, I would have done things differently. I would have made a conscious effort to keep alive close ties with all of my partners.

Regarding Marcie, I would have told her I loved her more, wrote more often, sent flowers, candy, and sentimental gifts, and maybe even went to college closer to home. At the very least, I would have told her about Lorraine face-to-face.

I would have gone on to explain that Lorraine could never replace what we had. "It was a once-in-a-lifetime special, Marcie," is what I would have said. "The type of love that burns brightest before it dies."

That would, of course, have been her cue to strangle me. I would have taken it like a man. For what Marcie and I shared, enduring her outrage would have been the least I could have done. It's what I *should* have done.

I gingerly placed each letter back in its envelope and returned them to the shoebox with their unread cousins. The shoebox I set reverently in the same corner of the trunk I had found it. Piling the clothes inside the trunk, I eased shut the lid. If I could have remembered where the key was, I would have locked that thing.

# SILVER ANNIVERSARY

Addae Wade stood askew in his midnight blue terry cloth bathrobe and matching slippers beside the king-size brass bed in which his wife lay. His hulky brown, fifty-five-year-old body slouched forward. His jaws sagged like a boxer's, giving him a hangdog look that only his smile could overcome.

Piteously, his misty dark brown eyes roamed, from stem to stern, his wife's paralyzed frame. The wrenching sight of Nadia Wade in so uncharacteristic a position brought forth the deepest, most nauseous anguish he had ever experienced. It had taken him two years to digest the finality of her criminal situation. His wife would be that limp shell before him for the remainder of her life.

Addae could not phantom why Nadia had suffered such a fate. His wife had a zeal for life. Nadia was a regular at Sunday worship who made certain Addae was by her side. She didn't smoke at all or drink alcohol to excess. Her personal habits were impeccable. Rarely did Nadia complain. Her integrity was without repute, as was her character. Yet, all of her spirit and dignity had been eradicated in a few brief months. Without warning, the baffling disease struck and brought with it a downward spiraling sickness, acute pain, and severe disability in precisely that order.

Addae watched Nadia sleep. The deliberate rise and fall of her flattened breasts beneath the floral cotton granny nightgown gave grateful evidence of life within. Addae studied her mocha face, hoping to gain some clue as to whether sleep gave his wife peace. Her flat, petite nose did not twitch, as it had so often done when she was healthy and she dreamed.

Her round, short, lashed, evenly spaced eyes—one of three voluntary muscles Nadia still controlled (the others being her jaw and her ability to swallow)—lay still beneath the faintest hint of eyebrows. Silvery gray flowed into hair black like fertile soil, blossoming out onto the white pillowcase. It formed a thick, lush halo about her head, giving her face a majestic appearance. All that was absent was her smile. Although her teeth were not perfectly straight or gleaming white, they were all present, and completed a smile of grace and charm—a smile that occasioned far too little for his liking.

His eyes strayed from the splendor of her face down the inviting length of her neck to pause at her sheltered bosom. Addae could see her breasts in his mind's eye. The gentle rhythm of her chest caused shameful feelings to surface. Erotic tingling rustled through his body. *Unthinkable longings, for a woman in her condition*, Addae thought, attempting to calm himself.

It had been over two years since last they made love. More than anything, Addae missed making love to Nadia.

His hungry eyes rolled over her body, burning away the cloth obstruction and unveiling the woman beneath. Even in her dormant state, her body was a work of feminine art that Addae had come to know well over the years. Every curve, bump, and crevice of her smooth glowing form was etched in his beefy hands—hands he had used to massage, stroke, caress, and at times playfully abuse her skin. It was velvety, supple skin that flowed like mocha waters beneath the firm coaxing of his gliding touch.

Nadia's body had become more familiar to him than his own. He was the one who exercised Nadia, changed her diapers, bathed and lotioned her skin, manicured her nails, pedicured her feet, washed and tended her hair, cleaned her teeth, and cared for her face.

As innocently as a father would have cared for his infant child, he did all of these things for Nadia and more. That knowledge, that precise understanding, more than anything made Addae ashamed for having thought of his wife in sexual terms.

The melodic ding-dong-ding of the front doorbell interrupted his self-persecution. He wiped his sweaty hands across his tear-filled eyes and glanced at Nadia. Her eyes were closed. They were the only indicator as to whether she had awakened.

On his way to answer the front door, Addae stopped by the upstairs utility closet to grab a clean washcloth to dry his eyes and hands. The doorbell rang again. Addae took a deep breath, steadied himself, and then stuffed the washcloth into his bathrobe pouch pocket before making his way downstairs. Without hesitation, he turned the crystal doorknob and opened the front door.

"Good morning, Addae. How you doing, bro?" a plump, bronze-skinned man with iron gray cornrows asked. His mail carrier was wearing a short set uniform that showed off his strong legs.

"Fine, Isaiah," Addae said. "And you?"

"Never better, never better," Isaiah said with his usual toothy grin. The mail carrier stood directly in the doorway. Isaiah never immediately handed Addae his mail. It was his way of insuring conversation.

"If you don't mind my asking, how's Nad doing this morning?"

In typical American fashion, Isaiah condensed everyone's name. Nadia instantly became Nad. The only person he had never heard Isaiah call by a nickname, pet name, or an abbreviated version was Addae. He dreaded the day Isaiah might decide to call him Add, demoting him from a person to a mathematical function.

"No change, I'm afraid."

"Don't give up on Nad. Your wife's a fighter; spirited! Never known a woman like her excepting, maybe, my wife Pumpkin." Isaiah rubbed his chin, as if giving his statement serious thought. A dry sandpaper sound accompanied the action. "They cut from the same cloth, your Nad and my Pumpkin," Isaiah concluded.

Pumpkin's real name was Elouise. Addae had never heard Isaiah call her anything but by her affectionate pet name. Nadia and Addae used to muse that they doubted Isaiah remembered his wife's real name. They never had the courage to ask Isaiah if he did. It would have been too embarrassing if Isaiah had actually forgotten.

"Don't worry, they'll find a cure for Nad," Isaiah said. "When they do, she'll be back on her feet in no time. You just keep the faith and things will work out, mark my words."

"I wish I had your optimism, Isaiah."

"Optimism is what faith scrapes off the bottom of its shoes. Faith is what I have, and so should you. It was faith that brought Moses out of bondage. It was faith that set Dr. King ablaze. No sir, you put that word 'optimism' right out of your head and fill your heart with faith. That's the house God built in each of us. And you know The Lord will never lead you astray."

Aside from the mandatory once-a-week visit from Nadia's doctor, Isaiah and Pumpkin were the only regular visitors he and Nadia had. Victor, their oldest son, lived in Baltimore with his wife and their three-year-old twin boys. Their baby, Gloria, was on her first archeological dig in Kenya. Both children saw their parents when time and circumstances permitted.

The same could be said of Addae's two sisters and Nadia's four brothers. Their parents had passed on years before Nadia's infirmity.

"You know, I was telling my wife just this morning..." Isaiah continued.

Nadia always believed Isaiah should have been a preacher. Addae agreed. When they brought up the subject with Isaiah, he'd discard it with a smirk and a dismissive wave of his hand. Isaiah said a preacher's hours were too long, his responsibilities too great, and all for far too little money. That always brought a smile from him and Nadia, and a hearty laugh from Pumpkin.

When Addae and Nadia argued that spiritual fulfillment far outweighed any earthly measure, Isaiah had a patented response: "If that's the Heavenly Father's will, then he'll show me the way. Until then, I'll keep delivering mail."

Addae was in no mood for one of Isaiah's pep talks. His fondness for his best friend of thirty years gave him the patience to listen. Addae realized a long time ago that Isaiah had the best of intentions at heart, even if it didn't always work out that way. Addae hunkered down to give his full attention to what he knew Isaiah regarded as an uplifting sermon.

"I said, 'Pumpkin,'" Isaiah preached on, "'I got a strong feeling something good is going to happen today. That something is going to be the blessing Nad and Addae have been waiting on.' I just know it—

and it will, too! I know about these things. I've never been wrong in over forty years. Not since lighting struck Percy Sumpter over in Callal County. Remember that?"

Addae nodded, even though he had no recollection of what Isaiah was talking about.

"All you got to do is keep faith in your heart," Isaiah said. "God will do the rest."

Addae kept silent about why God had allowed the love of his life to be struck ill in the first place. "Thanks for your concern," he said. "I appreciate all you've done for Nadia and me."

"Ain't that what friends are for?"

"You're not my friend, Isaiah," Addae said. "You're my brother. I just wanted to say thanks for everything you and Pumpkin have done for us over the years, especially during these trying times."

For once, Isaiah was speechless. He smiled, then gave Addae a hug. Addae hugged Isaiah back.

"I love you too, bro," Isaiah said. As they released their embrace, Isaiah added, "In a manly man sort of way, you understand."

Both men laughed.

"Now, what would Pumpkin say if we became more than friends?" Addae said.

"She wouldn't say nothing. She'd kick me out of the house, and I'd be coming to live with you."

"Then people would really talk."

Isaiah laughed. "You still crazy. I've got to finish my route." Isaiah handed Addae the small bundle of assorted envelopes suspended in his ashen hand.

"Give Nad my love," Isaiah said as he headed down the cement path. Addae recalled something he had wanted to mention to Isaiah, and called out to him. Isaiah stopped midway down the path and turned his body to face Isaiah.

"Today's our twenty-fifth wedding anniversary," he shouted to Isaiah.

"Twenty five years already! Congratulations! We're expected at my son's for dinner tonight. I'll bring something by with the mail tomorrow. Then, later, me and Pumpkin will help you two celebrate!"

"No need, on both counts."

"It'll be our pleasure!

"Meaning, Pumpkin will pick up something this afternoon," Addae said in jest.

"You got it!"

"And you'd like any excuse to party!"

"Right again!"

Both men smiled broadly.

"Give Pumpkin our love!"

"Will do. See you tomorrow!"

Addae watched Isaiah leave. The sun shone brightly, glaring off the dry, gray path. As Isaiah moved farther and farther away, the air appeared hazy about him. His feet seemed not to touch the ground, as if he were simply drifting along. Addae squinted in an effort to bring Isaiah into focus.

As Isaiah veered right, onto the sidewalk, his appearance became ghostly before vanishing into the celestial sunlight. Addae assumed his eyes were playing tricks on him, especially since he wasn't wearing his glasses. That, more than anything, must have contributed to the affect, he concluded.

Addae eased the door shut—much like a mortician would close a casket lid upon the deceased—and sauntered toward the kitchen, leafing through the mail along the way. The doorbell rang just as he was opening the third envelope. This time, he found a tall, tan, distinguished-looking man with natural waves, a black satchel, and a fidgety manner awaiting him on the other side.

"Hello, Dr. Pressman," Addae said matter-of-factly.

"Hello, Addae. I'm afraid I'm in a bit of a hurry. Mind if I head up to see how our patient's doing?" the doctor said as he brushed past Addae for the stairs.

"Go right ahead," Addae said. "You know where the bedroom is. I'll be in the kitchen if you need me."

Dr. Pressman had already disappeared into the bedroom by the time Addae finished his statement. Addae felt no need to accompany the doctor, since he knew the entire weekly routine and had no reason to believe that this time anything would differ.

First, the doctor would examine Nadia, checking her for bedsores and the like. The doctor would stick Nadia with a pin in her limbs and body, looking for any physical response. There would be none. Then Dr. Pressman would examine his wife's eyes, ears, and throat, would give her vitamin shots, and then bid her adieu with a synthetic, reassuring smile.

On Dr. Pressman's way out, he would mention how fit Nadia looked and would report on how close they were to 'pinpointing the disease that devastated Nadia' before hurrying off.

Addae could not relive those depressing events—not at this time; not on their silver anniversary. He was too weak. Hope was all he had left, and it had begun to fade into the fiery canyon of despair. Depression crawled lazily upon his shoulders, weighing him down like an ocean liner anchor. It took everything he had to pull himself up.

*I must be strong*, Addae thought. Once again, he was. For an uncountable time, he wrested despair from his shoulders as he wearily sauntered into the kitchen. Nadia would be hungry. Addae began preparing breakfast. The good doctor could and would let himself out.

*　　*　　*

It was an exceptionally muggy August afternoon. Adults shuffled about at a measured pace, as if to hasten would exhaust him. Children who normally disregarded climate changes moved only when necessary. Animals took refuge wherever they could find it. All but a few pesky insects did the same. There were no cooling breezes bringing periodic relief. The country air was much too thick to allow for that.

A lilting hush, unlike motion, traveled everywhere along the sweltering airways. Forced stasis instigated introverted thought—not perplexing, intricate contemplation such as the creation of the universe or the origins of man, but simpler, generic ones. Men considered fishing, camping, shooting pool at the nearest air-conditioned bar, or taking a leisurely drive while women fancied picnics, afternoon lovemaking, a dip in nearby Bennett Lake, or reading a novel in the shade of a large tree. Children daydreamed of skateboarding, rollerblading, bicycling, swimming, ice cream, and daredevil acts.

Nothing was gained by such idle ponderings, except for perhaps the biding of time; for all knew that with the blue blackness of night would come a cool softness that would allow them unrestrained movement. Until that time, life was simple in their sleepy town: a slow deliberate existence for this time of year, at this time of day, for the inhabitants of Somerville.

The blood-red brick two-story house appeared docile in the early summer evening beneath a powder blue sky. It was an old house, with most of its windows on the north and east side. This made it hard to heat in the winter. Conversely, it was a blessing in the summer. Inside, instead of being molten with heat and humidity, it was balmy.

Addae was grateful. He had not cared for the summer heat since his wife had become ill.

Summer had been their ally in times gone by. He and Nadia had spent many a sultry summer day strolling hand in hand about town. Her playful kisses, unexpected caresses, and easy way of resting her head upon his shoulder would draw warm responses from passers-by, not to mention his own fondness for such treatment.

Life was beautiful, then, much like a lazy summer's day. It was dreamy and bright, and Addae loved it that way. He yearned for their return, but in his soul, he knew those days were lost forever.

Forever—how horrible that word sounded to him now. Addae had always understood it to mean how long he and Nadia would have together, the way it was. Never would he have suspected their lives would end up this way. With all of his being, Addae wished for the rapid return of winter. At least, in winter, he would be safe from those dreadful, irretrievable summer memories.

His heart felt heavy as he placed the domed lid atop the silver chafing dish. He'd decided to use the Swiss-crafted silver serving set just that afternoon. Addae had always considered it an elaborate but useless wedding gift until now. Only their twenty-fifth wedding anniversary made its possession practical.

Addae checked to make certain everything he desired was upon the silver tray: chafing dish, ladle, soup spoons and bowls, white lace napkins, goblets, a champagne bucket filled with ice and a pricey bottle of champagne, and, lastly, a lone black rose rising majestically from a white porcelain bud vase. All was perfectly arranged upon the tray.

Addae stared uneasily at the tray for a long time before lifting it from the kitchen table. Something made him uneasy, and he was compelled to believe that the answer to his uneasiness was somewhere upon that tray. No matter how hard Addae stared, all he saw were his hangdog, fun mirror images in the polished silver of the serving set.

Swallowing hard, as if the deed required courage, Addae hoisted the tray from the kitchen table and walked toward the stairs. Aside from the faint brush of his steady footsteps upon the carpeted stairs, the house was filled with a viscous silence.

It had been that way since the beginning of Nadia's illness. For him and his wife, it had become a way of life … or a way of survival.

Balancing the silver tray between his steady hands, Addae slipped through the partially open bedroom door. Inside the bedroom, he donned a bright smile. He had even taught himself to put a twinkle in his eyes—at least, he believed he had. Addae was never certain, since he was the only judge on the matter. A loving smile, with cheerful words, was all part of a sad charade to mask the deep remorse he really felt.

Addae had changed Nadia into a romantic pearl white stretch lace tricot long gown with a coordinating long tricot robe. The color of the gown brought out the shimmer of her mocha skin. Her majestic halo was in full glory. Nadia wore no makeup. Her face was clear and glowing. Addae had given her a pedicure and manicure that day, after her bath. Her fingernail and toenail polish matched her nightgown.

Addae wore a charcoal gray, two-piece linen suit, a paisley print silk tie, and an ivory dress shirt with silver cufflinks engraved with his initials. His footwear was the same midnight blue terrycloth slippers he'd had on that morning.

"Well, how's my lovely lady doing on this fine day?" Addae asked while easing the serving tray upon the tray table near the foot of her bed. The disease had robbed Nadia of her voice.

When she felt strong enough, she mouthed her words. Otherwise, Addae could decode her response by reading her buckeye-colored eyes. The glint in her eyes and a valiant smile indicated she was feeling fine.

"You do know what day it is, don't you?"

Nadia gave Addae a deliberately long blink that indicated no. Her smile relaxed to a grin. Addae knew that her mouth would slacken to a half-open gape. Her jaw muscles were not strong enough to sustain any other position. In time, Dr. Pressman predicted that Nadia would lose all control of her jaw muscles. From what Addae had witnessed over the last three months, he knew that time was drawing near.

"I don't believe it," Addae said with pretend disbelief. "You've forgotten! Well then, I'll have to refresh your memory, won't I? On this day, some twenty-five years ago, you and I became husband and wife. Now do you remember?"

Nadia slowly blinked twice, indicating yes.

"Good. Now that that's settled and I have your undivided attention, allow me to present to you a meal fit for such a grand occasion."

Removing the lid from the chafing dish, Addae unveiled a warm brown broth spotted with bits of carrots, peas, potatoes, celery, and corn. Everything Nadia ate had to be easy to swallow. It reduced the possibility of her choking on her food. Addae passed his nose near the pottage to emphasize its pleasing aroma.

"Dee-licious. I hope you're ready to eat, my dear?"

Nadia blinked once. Addae was stunned—so stunned in fact that he stopped smiling. The warm glow in Nadia's eyes indicated to Addae that she was amused. A brief mischievous smile confirmed that fact.

*Why doesn't she want any of our anniversary dinner?* Addae thought. He pondered the question for a moment before managing to force a smile upon his bewildered face.

"Aren't you hungry, love?"

Nadia blinked once.

"I see. Well—I'll tell you what. Why don't we... ah..." Addae looked nervously around the room, searching for something that might give him an idea as to what to do or say next. Upon seeing the silver tray, an idea flashed.

"Why don't we have a little champagne? That should get your appetite going."

Nadia blinked twice, followed by a wink.

With a bit of pomp and circumstance, Addae popped the cork on the bottle of champagne, filling two silver goblets halfway. Raising both goblets to shoulder height, he toasted. "Here's to our twenty-fifth wedding anniversary!" He wanted to say more, but the words that came to mind, for one reason or another, didn't seem fitting.

Addae finished one goblet in two quick gulps. He did not taste the champagne, but he knew he would shortly feel its affects. Addae put both goblets down on the tray. He filled the goblet from which he had drunk and set both of them on the nightstand near the head of the bed, on the side that had been his before the pre-illness years.

Bending over the bed, he gently worked his left hand behind Nadia's head and eased her forward. Addae titled the half-filled goblet into her waiting mouth, making certain to maintain an angle that made it easy for Nadia to swallow. Nadia permitted the effervescent golden liquid to trickle down her throat, not spilling a single drop.

Addae eased back Nadia's head upon her pillow after she finished. He then placed her goblet on the tray next to his, filling it as he had done his own. Standing erect with his arms folded across his chest, Addae watched Nadia.

His smile once again disappeared. This time, he didn't care. All Addae wanted was to observe Nadia for a moment. He could see happiness radiating in her eyes. Nadia managed a full smile—one that reminded Addae of the young woman who had captured his heart at first glance.

Despite her cheerful mood, Addae could sense himself slipping toward depression. His will seized depression by the throat and wrestled it into submission. This time, there would be no place for sorrow. He would not allow it.

His eyes wandered over the entire structure of the bed. It was the same bed they'd once shared; the bed that possessed countless hours of passion within every spring. It was a bed that had known many joys, and few sorrows, and which now served as his lovely wife's sad resting place.

Repeatedly, his eyes staggered over the bed and then Nadia, pausing only for him to reflect on what he saw. His stomach had been churning all the while, when suddenly it ceased. Soothing warmth spread through his entire body. It came as such a pleasant surprise that Addae, without realizing it, recovered his smile. For the first time since the crisis, Addae was experiencing elation.

Addae kicked off his slippers and eased himself in beside Nadia. Tenderly, Addae worked his left arm behind Nadia's limp shoulders. Addae maneuvered Nadia upon her right side with great care, gently tugging her body close and resting her head upon his massive shoulder.

For the final touch, Addae laid Nadia's left arm comfortably across his stomach. He could feel her warm, steady breath upon his cheek. Calmness settled within him, and he sensed its existence in his wife, as well.

"I'll love you from now to eternity, Nadia. Our souls are always meant to be together no matter what our bodies dictate."

Addae continued to speak to Nadia with the delicate reassuring voice of a patient lover. He repeatedly told Nadia how much he loved her and how all would be well in the end, concluding each statement with a gentle squeeze of her shoulders or a soft kiss upon her face.

"Yes, baby, it's like Isaiah said," Addae said in a gentle tone befitting the moment. "Everything will work out fine. Yes, Lord. Mark my words on that."

*　　　*　　　*

Isaiah rang the doorbell of the Wade home at his usual hour the next morning. As promised, along with the mail, he had nestled in the crook of his right arm a silver-papered package with a white envelope loosely taped to the top.

After repeatedly ringing the doorbell, Isaiah began to feel uneasy. It had never taken Addae more than three rings to answer the door. With Nadia ill, Addae rarely left the house. A queasy sensation rumbled in the pit of Isaiah's gut, a clear sign to him that something terrible had happened.

Isaiah went around the house looking through the downstairs windows wherever possible. There was no sign of his friend. Isaiah called the police from his smartphone.

*　　　*　　　*

About thirty minutes after Isaiah telephoned, two county officers arrived at the Wade home. Isaiah was there to meet them. He quickly informed the officers of his concern. Although the officers were from a neighboring county (Somerville was too small to afford its own law enforcement), they labeled Isaiah a worrier. Both had heard, from fellow officers who had prior dealings with him, of Isaiah's tendency to exaggerate the slightest problems. Being duty-bound, they had to investigate his suspicions.

The tall, wiry officer with a Jimmy Durante nose rang the doorbell twice. He tried the door and found it unlocked. Isaiah immediately commented on the oddity of that situation. The county officers entered the home with their hands settled on the grips of their unlatched service weapons.

The shorter, stocky officer ordered Isaiah to remain outside. The officers split up and searched the house. Like a cat on the prowl, the tall officer climbed the stairs two at a time. At the top, he noticed that all the doors were closed except for the one just off to his right. Removing his weapon from its holster, he warily approached the door. He cautiously eased inside and surveyed the room.

Instantly, the tall officer discovered the whereabouts of the Wades.

Isaiah heard the upstairs officer yell downstairs to his partner. The stocky officer darted upstairs. The tall officer had already moved in to examine the lifeless figures on the bed. His partner joined him.

Isaiah waited a few moments, then tiptoed up the stairs. He stood just outside the bedroom door, staring at the lifeless bodies of his friends. Tears spilled from his eyes as he choked on his own saliva.

Had it not been for the silver package falling to the floor, the officers would not have known he was there. The tall officer moved to usher Isaiah downstairs. Isaiah had already seen too much. Isaiah dashed down the stairs and out the door, spilling mail in his wake.

The tall officer picked up the silver package and made his way out of the house to the parked cruiser near the end of the walk. The remaining officer didn't touch anything. He merely observed. The short officer noticed the silver serving set and the open bottle of champagne cocked to one side inside the bucket. Leaning over the champagne bottle, he sniffed. An acrid odor caused him to jerk away. He didn't recognize the odor, but reasoned it must be poison mixed in with the champagne.

Turning his attention from the champagne, the short officer stared stoically at the deceased couple. He noticed their positions. The woman's head was resting upon the man's shoulder, her arm strewn across his stomach. The man's arm held her body close to his, while his legs were stretched and crossed.

It was the same position one might find in a contented couple who had fallen asleep while watching television in bed. The man's free hand held aloft a black rose, as though he were presenting it to an invisible suitor. He could not unravel the mystery of how the man's arm remained frozen in that position. He had raised his arm while still alive—that fact rang true. Once he'd died, though, the rose should have fallen.

The short officer dismissed the puzzling arm and moved in closer to the bodies to see what else he could discover. He found their facial expressions odd, for people so recently deceased. Most stiffs he'd encountered had sported grotesque expressions. This couple defied the norm. There was serenity in their faces—due to what factors, he was uncertain. Maybe it was their docile grins or the set of their eyes. Their eyes were open, calm, and even sedate, staring at something that brought them peace.

The officer put their eyes in the same category as the raised arm puzzle and moved on with his investigation. He prowled the bedroom for clues and deduced theories until his partner returned.

"The coroner's on the way," the tall officer said as he stepped next to his partner, who was once again studying the dead couple.

"Did you catch that old man?" the short officer asked.

"Nah," the tall officer said. "The old geezer runs pretty fast."

"We all do, when we're scared."

"I wonder what the package was for," the tall officer asked.

"What package?"

"The one the old man dropped."

The short officer shrugged. "Don't know. Could've been somebody's birthday or something."

"I'll tell you one thing," the tall officer said, "those two went in style."

"Yeah."

"Any clues?"

"My guess is poison," the short officer said. "The champagne's got a funny smell to it."

"Looks like suicide," the tall officer said.

"Yeah, it does, but I didn't find a suicide note."

The tall officer let out a sad sigh. "We'd better wait outside. The meat wagon will be here soon."

The two officers waited outside, beneath the hazy blue sky of a stifling hot day, for the people who handle death to arrive.

# THE JAZZ DEAL

Smoky and Winston walked into Cavanaugh Investigation Agency with no fanfare. Normally, they would snap at me and hit on my beautiful professional partner as soon as they opened the door.

Renita was out sick. They didn't seem to notice. That was another bad sign. Smoky and Winston stepped into my office. They sat across from me with grim faces and heavy moods.

"CJ, we want to hire you to help out a friend," Smoky said. He was a mocha-skinned man with a white beard and a Pittsburgh Crawford baseball cap. His real name was Holland Jenkins. He'd earned the nickname Smoky because of the silky smooth way he played jazz.

"What, no hello?" I said, trying to lighten the mood. They stared at me as if I were the worst comic they had ever seen.

"What's his name?" I asked.

"His name is Bass Plate," Winston said. Winston Davis had a deadpan expression and fervid eyes to go with a stern, handsome, tan face. They were musical comrades.

Winston and Smoky could play any instrument. They had an ear for music that you had to born with. While they had known their share of industry success, these days, they were content doing studio work.

Occasionally, they did their own recordings. They had an arrangement with a local jazz label to handle all of the art and business dealings for a portion of net sales. Their music never failed to garner domestic and international acclaim. Their only live performances were in the summer at Pioneer Courthouse Square. Large crowds always formed, forcing police to break up their concerts. They sold and autographed their CDs during those concerts and encouraged cash donations that they would turn over to the rescue mission on Burnside Avenue.

"His real name is Paul Yarder," Smoky said.

"How'd he get the nickname 'Bass Plate'?"

"He was one of the baddest players that ever hooked the bottom," Winston said. "Standup or electric, Bass Plate held down the fort."

"Amen," Smoky said.

"What's he done?"

"He ain't done nothing," Winston said.

"You heard about that theft at the Portland Art Museum?" Smoky asked.

"Who hasn't? That hot new artist had one of his paintings stolen, 'Dreaming in the Desert'."

"Bass Plate is head of security at the Portland Art Museum," Smoky said.

"My, how the mighty have fallen."

"Save your sarcasm, CJ," Winston said. "Bass Plate's doing alright."

"At least, he was," Smoky said.

"Meaning?"

"The PAM people are blaming Bass Plate for the theft," Smoky said.

"You mean, they're accusing him of stealing the painting?"

"No, but they need a scapegoat and it don't get any better than head of security, in this case," Winston said.

"I see."

"May cost him his job," Smoky said.

"He's been working that gig for almost twenty-eight years," Winston said.

"Two years away from retirement," Smoky said.

"I'd like to help you, gentlemen, but theft really isn't my forte."

"Catching criminals *is* your forte, CJ," Smoky said. "You're good at it."

"Damn good at it," Winston added.

"Of course, we'll pay your going rate," Smoky said.

"Plus expenses," Winston added.

Smoky and Winston nodded in agreement to the last statement, as if it were a truth served to them on a platter. I looked back and forth at the faces of my friends. They didn't rattle easily. And they didn't go out on a limb for just anybody.

"Bass Plate means that much to you two?"

"He's like family," Smoky said.

"We grew up together."

"How could Bass Plate have grown up with you, when the two of you didn't grow up together?"

"We mean musically," Smoky said. "Bass came along around the same time we did."

"He just didn't get the break. Hard times hit, you take what you can get."

"Does he still play?" I asked.

"Can't," Winston said.

"Lost use of his left hand," Smoky said.

"Smashed it laying rails for the railroad."

"That's too bad."

"So you'll take the case?" Smoky asked.

"Don't make us beg, CJ."

"I hear you, and I feel your pain—"

"Here comes the bullshit," Winston said. "Don't mess with us, CJ."

"I'm serious—so serious, in fact, that I don't want your money."

"Thanks, CJ. We knew we could count on you," Smoky said. "Lunch is on us." Both men were set to leave.

"Not so fast," I said. "I said I didn't want your money. But there is something else I would like."

Both men sat. They eyed me as suspiciously as if I were a thief in their candy store. I waited.

"What?" Winston said after a long silent pause.

"I want ten albums each from your vintage jazz collections."

Winston erupted out of his chair. "*Have you lost your mind?* Any one of those albums is worth more than you make in a month!"

"A week, maybe. A month: no way," I said.

"I'm not giving you ten of my babies," Winston said.

"No albums, no CJ."

"I can't believe you're treating us like this," Smoky said to me. "We're your friends."

"Yes, you are," I said to Smoky.

"You've got a hell of a way of respecting friendship," Winston said.

"I buy your music. Any time I need special favors from you two, I'm willing to pay. Now you want something special from me, and I feel the two of you should be willing to do the same. Let's call it an exchange of good faith."

"Let's call it what it really is—extortion," Smoky said.

"You say extortion, I say finder's fee."

"We offered to pay you," Winston said.

"I don't want your cash. Those LPs would mean more to me than anything money can buy."

"They mean a lot to us, too," Smoky said.

"Albums, or no deal."

"One album each," Smoky said.

"*What?*" Winston said, glaring at Smoky.

"Don't make me laugh," I said.

They looked at each other. Both men headed for my office door.

"Nine," I said. They turned and walked back to my desk. There was a glint in Smoky's eyes. He was in a bargaining mood. Winston's eyes told the opposite story.

"Two," Smoky said.

"Eight," I said.

"Three."

"Seven."

"Four."

"Six."

"Five, and that's our final offer."

"My choice?"

"Your choice of two, we pick the other three."

"I don't know where you're getting this *we* nonsense from," Winston said. "I'm not giving up my LPs."

"Fine. I'll give you ten of mine, CJ," Smoky said.

"Five each, or no deal."

"What difference does it make?" Winston asked.

"Yeah, what difference does it make?" Smoky echoed.

"You came here together, wanting to help a mutual friend. Your commitment should be mutual. You're either both in, or no deal."

Smoky and I stared at Winston while he agonized over his decision, as if trying to decide between death by jumping off a cliff or a bullet.

"Guaranteed results?" Winston said.

"Meaning?"

"If you don't find the painting, no albums," Winston said.

"If I don't find the painting, no albums."

"Alright, I'm in," Winston relinquished.

"Gentlemen, you have yourselves a deal."

Smoky and I shook on it. Winston gave me a low grunt and a weak slap of five.

*    *    *

The next morning when I walked into PAM, a bass voice asked from behind, "Can I help you, sir?" I turned to face a uniformed security guard. A deep brown man with a prominent paunch, narrow shoulders, and suspicious brown eyes walked up to me. He was well groomed and tall. His uniform was typical of PAM security personnel: a dark blue blazer with gray slacks, polished black leather shoes, white shirt, and black tie. He appeared to wear it with pride. In all of the times I'd been to PAM, I hadn't noticed him. That told me he knew how to blend into the background.

His left hand lay limp by his hip. It was gnarled and discolored. It was at that moment I knew the man addressing me was Paul Yarder, his left hand being the obvious result of the tragic accident Winston had mentioned.

I felt compassion for Yarder. I had never heard him play, but if what Smoky and Winston said were true, then life had cast another twisted turn of taking the beautiful and making it grotesque. Nonetheless, I followed protocol.

"I'm here to see head of security," I said.

"That would be me," Yarder said. "And you are?"

"C. J. Cavanaugh. I'm a private investigator." I showed him my ID. Paul Yarder took a moment to size me up. His eyes narrowed to a laser focus on my face.

"You're here about Dreaming in the Desert?" he asked.

"Yes."

"Did the PAM board hire you?"

"Nothing like that. I'm a friend of Smoky and Winston. They asked me to look into the matter to see if I might be able to help out."

Yarder's eyes went from mistrust to pleasant surprise. "They're good men, like brothers to me. And as much as I appreciate your wanting to help, I'm not sure there's anything you can do."

"Can't hurt to try."

"True," Yarder said with a nod. "With the board looking to fry my butt, I can use all of the help I can get."

"Anything on the surveillance footage?"

"Negative. The painting was stolen between 5:32 and 6:04. That's the difference between the last time it appeared on the surveillance footage and the blackout."

"Blackout?"

"There was a power outage during that time. The backup generator kicked in to maintain lighting and atmospheric controls.

"What we didn't know was that the surveillance equipment was not tied in to it. Turns out that the backup generator was installed before PAM had electronic surveillance. When the surveillance equipment was installed, our current backup generator was supposed to be updated or replaced. It didn't happen. That one slipped through the cracks."

"Apparently, someone was aware of that loophole." I asked to see the surveillance footage from that night. Yarder filled me in on everything else he knew on the way to the surveillance room.

"It happened just after closing," Yarder said. "The security person noticed a blank spot on the wall where a painting used to be. She notified me."

"What did you do upon notification?"

"I ordered all exits locked and contacted the police."

"Good work, Mr. Yarder."

"Standard procedure." Yarder would have been amazed at how

often standard procedure was neglected during a time of crisis. "And you can call me Paul," Yarder went on to say. "Any friend of Smoky and Winston is a friend a mine."

"Does that mean I can call you Bass Plate?" I half-jokingly asked.

"Are you a musician?"

"I wish."

"Then you can call me Paul," Yarder said with a wry smile.

"Paul it is," I said, appreciating his having turned the tables. "Were there any patrons lingering in the museum at that time?"

"No," Paul said. "We keep a roaming security force. A security presence helps deter would-be criminals. At least, that's usually the case. During first closing rounds, the security staff checks security risk areas and remains on the lookout for dawdling patrons."

We watched the digital surveillance of that night together. I was searching for the obvious within the obvious. I made some mental notes about activities worth investigating.

"I'll show you where the painting was ripped off to give you an idea of what we're dealing with," Paul said after we finished viewing the surveillance footage. Yarder pointed the way like an usher leading a tour group.

I looked around the Wilson Payne exhibit. Police had cordoned off the area. PAM security was posted at each entrance.

"Were those guards stationed there when the painting was stolen?" I asked.

"No. They were on patrol," Paul said. "We do, however, keep a security person posted at all building exits."

"Have you ever had any daylight thefts before?"

"We've never had any thefts at all before. There have been attempts, but we caught them all."

I looked at the positioning of the security cameras. They covered every square inch of the crime scene. There was the distant sound of hammering coming from inside PAM. I asked Paul about it.

"That's the construction crew," he said. "PAM has acquired a larger warehouse for their arts properties. That left them with more museum space. They decided to turn it into exhibition halls. The construction crew is getting things ready."

"How long have they been at it?"

"About a month."

"I'd like to talk to the security person who discovered the theft."

"No problem. Normally, she's on swing shift. This week she's working days to cover for a vacationing employee."

Paul got on his walkie-talkie and arranged a meeting. The young woman was professional and succinct. She had nothing new to add to resolve the mystery. I asked Paul if he minded if I had a look around the museum.

"Not at all," he said, "if you don't mind buying a ticket." I smiled and showed him my PAM membership card.

"I hope you have better luck than me," Paul said. I wondered if he was only talking about the stolen painting.

*　　*　　*

Yarder radioed ahead that I would be coming. I entered the construction site through a clear curtain of thick plastic strips, as if I were entering a CDC quarantined site. The musty combinations of drywall, plywood, and wood tickled my nostrils. Construction supervisor Ed Davis met me at the mouth of the construction site wearing the laborer's uniform of work jeans, a flannel shirt, work boots, and a hard hat. You could tell he was in charge because he carried a thick stack of official-looking multicolored forms secured by a clipboard. His handshake was firm and his eyes were steady.

"How can I help you, Mr. Cavanaugh?" he asked in a voice accustomed to being at the helm. "Let me start by saying none of my people are thieves. I've worked with this crew on a number of projects and I'd be willing to bank on their characters."

"Maybe none of your people are thieves, but they might hold clues as to who is. Mind if I talk to them?"

"I suppose. Don't take too much time, they're on the clock."

"Thanks. Who was working at the time the painting was stolen?"

"A skeleton swing shift crew," said Davis as he leafed through the paperwork on his clipboard. "We have six weeks to complete this project and PAM wants us to keep our costs down. I asked for volunteers to work swing shift for a couple of weeks to help defray any overtime pay. You'd be surprised how much overtime labor elevates cost."

There were moments filled only by the sounds of shuffling papers and a full construction crew at work until Davis found what he needed.

"I remember that we didn't have any volunteers for that week, so I made the choices based on work that needed to be done. An electrician, a plumber, and a carpenter were on swing shift."

"Were they supervised?"

"No need. I've worked with them long enough to know I can trust them to do the work they're assigned. They don't get it done, then they're out of a job."

"An electrician?"

Davis paused and gave me a sideways glance before responding, "Yeah, so?"

"I'll talk to the electrician first. Where were you when Dreaming in the Desert was stolen?"

Davis's face reddened. "You're not suggesting I had anything to do with stealing that painting?"

"I'm not suggesting anything, just asking a question."

"I was having dinner at my in-laws with my wife and three kids."

"Easy enough to check out."

"Well, check this out," Davis said. "The next time you have questions for me about this crime or any other, you can talk to my lawyer."

For some unknown reason, the smartass in me leaked out. "Do you have an attorney?"

"You'll find out when you meet him."

"I look forward to it. In the meantime, could you send me the electrician? I'll be waiting for him over there." I pointed to the stacks of plywood, 2x4s, and drywall near a newly erected drywall. Ed Davis looked as though he would rather kick my ass, but marched off to do what I asked.

"Thanks for your cooperation, Mr. Davis," I said as he was walking away. Davis kept walking and never looked back.

*     *     *

"Where were you between 5:32 and 6:04 Thursday night?"

"What's it to you?" Judy Fernandez was between five-four and five-five, sported an average build for a woman in her early forties, and had short dark hair, a deep tan skin, dark brown eyes, and a raspy voice.

"I'm a private investigator working with PAM security trying to solve the painting theft," I said. "Now, you can talk to me, or you can talk to security. If that's not good enough for you, then you can talk to the police."

"I've already talked to the police, so what's your point?"

"This time, I'll be present and asking the same questions I'm going to ask you now."

"You have that kind of clout?"

"I do."

Fernandez grumbled before she answered, "I was here."

"Doing what?"

"Knitting a sweater for my grandmother, what do you think? I'm an electrician; I was running wire from the central fuse box to the local grid."

"Anyone vouch for that?"

"You want an eyewitness. Look, friend, it don't work that way during swing shift. We're a skeleton crew with plenty of work to keep us busy. Sometimes we work in the same area, other times we don't."

"The short answer is no, then. Did you cut the main power for any reason, that night?"

"Yeah, I cut the power that night around 5:30. I'm not sure about the exact time. I needed to tie in some lines to the main fuse box."

"How long did that take?"

"About half an hour. I cut the power back on as soon as I was done."

"What happens to the surveillance equipment when the power is cut?"

"The backup generator kicks in."

"Instantly?"

"Things power down, then up, so there's a delay. I'm not familiar enough with the backup generator here to be certain about the time frame, but they're usually fully operational within a few minutes."

"Did you know PAM's backup generator is only tied into the lighting and atmospheric controls?"

"What are you trying to say?"

"I'm saying the surveillance equipment was inoperable during your power outage."

"I didn't know."

"Isn't it your job to know?"

"Yes, but I assumed the backup generator was tied into the security cameras."

"Who did you ask about the backup generator?"

"Nobody. I checked it out for myself. It worked fine."

"But you didn't know the security cameras would be offline during your power outage?"

"No, I swear."

"And there is no one to confirm your whereabouts between 5:32 and 6:04 on the night the painting was stolen?"

"I told you, we do our work where and when we need to. We don't keep tabs on each other."

I had heard enough. I thanked Judy Fernandez for her time, and asked her to send in the carpenter. She couldn't leave fast enough.

*   *   *

A man in his mid-twenties (between five-seven and five-eight with long dark blonde hair, medium brown eyes, an athletic build, and a thick, trimmed mustache) approached with caution. "You the guy asking questions about what happened on the night somebody stole the painting?" he asked.

"That would be me. And you are?"

"Jeff Nelson."

"Where were you between 5:32 and 6:04 on Thursday night, Jeff?"

"Right here, working—mostly nailing 2x4s and plywood and stapling drywall."

I leaned on the stack of plywood near where we were standing. "Anybody confirm your whereabouts between the times I mentioned?"

"I don't know. You keep your head down and do your work, in construction."

"If you want to keep your job."

"Exactly."

"So you don't have anyone to confirm your whereabouts between the times I mentioned?"

"Like I said, I don't know. Are we done here?"

"Just one other thing." Nelson warily eyed me. "I'm thinking about building an extra room onto my house. How would I approach something like that?"

Nelson relaxed. "First, you figure out what you want. Then talk to contractors who do that kind of work."

"Couldn't I just talk to a carpenter like you?"

"You could, but you would need to bring in more than a carpenter to build an addition."

"What about building materials?"

"The contractor will handle that."

"What do contractors do with excess materials?"

"Return them, sell them, store them, or, as a last resort, scrap them."

"Sell them to whom?"

"Anybody who wants to buy them. Take that plywood you're leaning on. We're only going to need about half of that to complete this job. I bought some 2x4s and a few sheets of plywood and drywall myself for a shed I'm building in my backyard. They're high-quality materials, and it's cheaper than buying them from a store. Ed gets them at a discount, since he buys in bulk. He sold it to me at cost."

"Did you buy any materials that night?"

"Ten sheets of plywood."

I patted the stack of plywood. "It must be difficult handling this stuff on your own."

"Two sheets are not so bad. Any more than that, you need help."

"Did you have help loading it?"

"Yeah, two of the guards gave me a hand."

"Do you remember their names?"

"Charlie and Mat." Charlie and Mat worked swing shift, so they were unavailable for immediate questioning.

"You'd met them before?" I asked.

"I'd seen them around. We had small talk; introduced ourselves."

"You'd seen them just around PAM, or elsewhere?"

"Just around PAM."

"And they helped you move the plywood all the way from here to the loading area?"

"Of course not. I stacked the sheets on a cart then took it from here to the freight elevator and down to the loading area. Pushed the cart right up to my truck, and they helped me from there."

"How long would you say that took?"

"Not long. There were three of us, so we did the whole stack at once."

"Was this before or after the power was cut?"

"It was after the power was turned back on. My shift ended at midnight, so it was somewhere between midnight and 12:30."

The surveillance footage had confirmed what Nelson said. Charlie was at his regular post, guarding the loading dock, when Nelson showed up with a cartload of plywood. Mat was making his rounds. The tape showed the three men loading the plywood into Nelson's truck at 12:14 a.m. There was nothing suspicious about any of their movements or behavior.

"Hey, Nelson!" the construction supervisor yelled from across the site. Nelson acknowledged him with a nod. "Chit-chat's over, let's get back to work!" Nelson turned back to me and asked, "We done here?"

"For now."

Nelson grabbed a sheet of plywood from the stack I was leaning on and left.

*　　　*　　　*

Bill Langit was a thin Filipino of average height with short dark hair, tan skin, and dark eyes. He was about 45 and had a placid expression that made him look as though he were bored with life. "Mr. Cavanaugh?" he said in a voice so soft I could barely hear him over the construction noise. I suggested we speak on the other side of the plastic curtain. Langit looked concerned. I told him I would clear it with his boss. He agreed with some reluctance.

I opened with my 'where were you at when' question.

"Right here," Langit said.

"You mean, right at this exact spot," I half-jokingly said.

"No," Langit said with a brief smile. "I mean, I was in the north end of the construction site."

"Doing what?"

"Installing PVC pipe to run electrical wiring through."

"Can anyone vouch for your whereabouts?"

"I doubt it."

"Don't electricians usually install their own PVC pipes?"

"Sometimes they do. Judy has a lot to do on this project, with nobody helping her. The boss asked if I could help out."

Langit kept cutting his eyes back through the plastic curtain. He was nervous about something. My first impression was that he was concerned about his boss getting upset with him for spending too much time with me. My other impression was he didn't want someone else to see us talking.

Judy Fernandez walked by, carrying her toolbox. She put her toolbox down near the curtain. While Fernandez adjusted her work gloves, she took a long, hard look at Langit. Langit stared back for a moment, then looked away. Fernandez picked up her toolbox and walked away.

*Opportunity was knocking,* I thought.

"Did you see anything suspicious on the night Dreaming in the Desert was stolen?" I asked.

"No."

"Are you certain?"

"Yes."

"What if I were to tell you that someone on your swing shift told me they saw you hanging around the Wilson Payne exhibit shortly before Dreaming in the Desert was stolen?" It was the oldest trick in the book, but worth a try.

"She's lying." Langit raised his voice to a normal speaking level.

"Why would she lie about something like that?"

"Because *she* was the one hanging around the Wilson Payne exhibit around the time it was stolen."

"How do you know that?"

"I had run out of glue, and went to the supply truck to get more. On my way back, I saw Judy hanging around the Wilson Payne exhibit. I asked her what she was doing. She said she was taking a break. She said her hands were cramping up and she needed a few minutes to stretch out her fingers. I told her if she didn't fulfill her work quota, the boss was going to fire her."

"What did she say when you tried to hustle her back to work?"

"She waved me off. She told me to quite my bitching, and she'd have her quota done for the night."

"About what time was it when you saw Judy taking her break?"

"5:53. I remember because I saw a wall clock on my way back to work."

"Had she cut the power?"

"Yes. I was in the process of cutting and installing the first of three pieces of PVC to complete my quota. The boss had given me permission to leave at seven. I couldn't leave until Judy gave her approval to my PVC installations. She was holding me up."

"Why seven?"

"My oldest daughter had a high school music recital," he said with pride. "She plays the violin. It started at eight. I didn't want to miss it. If I left here at seven, I would have had time to shower and change clothes. I'd already missed her last two performances because I was working."

"How many swing shifts have you worked so far?"

"All of them. I like the hours."

"Did you make your daughter's recital?"

"No," Langit said with regret. "The police investigation held me up. By the time I was allowed to leave, it was too late."

"Sorry," I said, and I meant it. Once a moment like that is gone, it's gone forever. Langit clearly knew that. "How'd your daughter take it?"

"She told me not to worry, Papa—that there would plenty more chances for me to see her perform," he said with a proud smile. "My wife recorded the performance. We all watched it together. It wasn't the same as being there, even though my family tried to make it seem that way. I'll make it up to her somehow."

"She sounds incredible."

"She is."

"When did you next see Ms. Fernandez?" I asked, getting back on track.

"No more than five minutes later," Langit said, his smile running away from his face. "She passed me on her way to wherever she was working. That's all I know. Can I get back to work now?"

"You can go, Mr. Langit. Thanks for your time."

Langit left with the same placid, bored expression he'd had when I met him.

*　　*　　*

I took a moment to view the paintings of Wilson Payne on my way back to Paul Yarder. Payne's work initially reminded me of the renaissance period in northern Europe.

It made use of both linear and aerial prospectives, coupled with a delicacy of color and treatment. Yet, there were Cubist ingredients mixed with bold spots of modern that stood out without disturbing the other carefully-crafted elements.

The way he utilized light and textures, colors, and tones and shapes, made one first take in the whole, then dissect it, only to return to the completed work. Without intending, I found myself gazing, for a couple of hours, at his paintings. They were fascinating and beautiful, yet disturbing enough to keep you out of utopia and anchored in reality. Wilson Payne was a very gifted artist on the doorstep of greatness, in my opinion. I regretted not having seen his masterpiece.

I asked Paul for the names and telephone numbers of the police detective and insurance investigator handling the crime, along with the address of the artist. Paul had the telephone numbers of the detective and insurance investigator stored on his cell phone. To get the artist's address, he had to telephone the main office. He gave me the requested information only after I agreed to keep him posted on anything I turned up.

Sergeant Kyle Bedford was the police detective working the case. He and I had worked together on numerous cases when I was doing freelance insurance investigative work, the staple of my practice. The insurance investigator knew of me by reputation. Both were glad to help.

Unfortunately, neither had a clue as to how the theft happened. I thought it couldn't hurt to have a talk with the artist.

*     *     *

Wilson Payne lived in Alameda in a high-end condominium. He buzzed me in after I convinced him I wasn't a solicitor or reporter, and that I was working to solve the case of his stolen painting.

The housecleaner obviously had the year off. The furniture was so ratty donation centers would have rejected it. I looked around at what was a spacious luxury condo with hardwood floors, a large fireplace, and vaulted ceilings that had been reduced to a biohazard. There were rumpled clothes, crumpled newspapers and food bags, and old pizza and takeout boxes strewn about as if a tsunami had hit; and the *smell* ... a nauseating combination of rotting food and turpentine?

"Surprised?" Payne said after closing the door behind me.

"A little," I said as I took it all in.

"Your face says differently."

"With all of the attention you've gotten lately, let's just say that I anticipated something different. As an investigator, I should have known better."

"The attention hasn't changed my starving artist status. Now I'm a starving artist with acclaim. You should have seen the rat trap I lived in before. They don't pay you to exhibit your paintings. You only make money if you sell them. So far, it's been a lot more talk than cash."

He'd missed my point. I'd meant that he could have kept up the place. Poverty had nothing to do with him being a slob.

"You're doing well in the critics department. The Oregonian had a great write-up on your paintings. That must count for something."

"Words don't pay the bills. Artistic pursuits cost money."

"Don't you have a patron?"

"Yes—hence, the condo."

"Who's your patron?"

"They prefer to remain anonymous."

"These anonymous people pay your room and board."

"Yes."

"Have they seen this place lately?"

"I take it you're referring to the clutter. I'll get around to cleaning up."

*You're going to need disinfectant, a backhoe, and a dumpster to clean this place.* I kept that remark to myself. It wasn't my business.

Payne was 48 according to his online bio. Bald on top, his thin white ponytail hung like a frail dying vine, a match for his scruffy beard. He wore old torn, paint-stained jeans and a paint-stained orange short-sleeved sweatshirt that barely covered his paunch. His clothes had so much paint on them, I wondered how much he got on the canvas.

Payne cleared away a spot on the couch and invited me to have a seat. He had uncovered a large stain on the couch that I couldn't identify. I said I preferred to stand, but thanked him anyway.

"Can I get you anything?" he asked.

I was thirsty. I couldn't see the kitchen from where I was standing. My estimation was that it was as bad as what I could see. "I'm good, thanks. How long have you been an artist?"

"I started drawing and sketching in high school. I've been painting and sculpting since I was twenty-four."

"Did you study art?"

"At The Art Institute of Seattle and Reed College."

"Good schools, both local. Were you born and bred in the Northwest?"

"Vancouver, Washington. I've visited a number of places and lived in a few, but the Northwest keeps calling me home."

"Your work is good, from what I've seen of it," I said with genuine praise.

"'Good' don't pay the bills."

"Two ingredients that make for great art are 'embittered' and 'talented'—or so I've heard."

"More like twenty-plus years of frustration." With a sigh, Payne changed his tune from contempt to playful. "So, you're the bloodhound hoping to track down Dreaming in the Desert."

"Yep. Can you tell me anything about the thief?"

"The thief had good taste, is all I know. They stole my best work at that exhibit."

"I might add: before I had a chance to see it."

"I have color slides of Dreaming in the Desert, if you're interested."

"Not the same as the original."

"Agreed."

"Do you have any enemies who might want to bring you down?"

"I guess. Jealously, envy—they're all part of the human condition. Sometimes it's obvious; other times it's submerged. Who knows?"

"I'm looking for anyone who might be out for revenge."

"Do you really think this was anything more than greed?"

"Stolen artwork rarely surfaces. Sometimes sordid wealthy collectors purchase them then stash the art away in secret private collections. A professional thief will only take the risk if they have a buyer or buyers already lined up. Even those unscrupulous customers are not interested in someone new. They prefer vintage properties. So, there is a possibility this might be someone with a grudge."

"I can't think of anyone capable of stealing anything more than a pack of gum."

I looked around the condo. Payne had an easel setup near the far eastern living room window. The easel had on it what appeared to be an unfinished canvas.

"Can you think of anyone who might be out to get you?" I asked.

"Nope."

"What about ex-lovers or rivals?"

"All of my ex's—including my two ex-wives—have found better men. I know this because they rub my nose in it every chance they get. I don't have any rivals. You've either found success or moved on to other careers, at my age, in this profession. I'm the never 'say die' type who finally got lucky. I've lost contact with all of my peers."

"Pissed anybody off lately?"

"Could be," Payne said nonchalantly. "When I'm in one of my moods, I exhibit what some might call an artistic temperament. I still can't think of anyone I might have pissed off, as you put it, to the point of wanting to do anything more than punch me in the nose."

"What was that painting valued at?"

"I don't know and I don't care. I just want it back."

"Are you insured?"

"With what? My biting wit and leading-man good looks?" Payne sarcastically said. "My agent tells me some blanket PAM insurance policy covers the paintings. I don't get caught up in the business end."

"Yet, earlier you kept bringing up the issue of money."

"Artist have to eat, too."

"Museums insure their exhibits against damage and theft," I said. "You'll be compensated the appraised cost minus your agent's commission if they can't recover your painting."

"Do you have any leads?"

"None," I said. I was lying. I had a couple, but I didn't feel comfortable sharing that information with Payne. "I've taken up enough of your time, Mr. Payne. I'll let you get back to painting."

"I hope whoever stole Dreaming in the Desert appreciates it," Payne said.

"We may still recover it."

"Do you honestly believe that?"

"It's possible."

"Like winning the lottery is possible."

"The odds are a bit better than that."

"Well, I'd better get back to work to see if I can create another masterpiece. If only it were that simple. I'm working on reproducing Dreaming in the Desert.

"It's difficult. Inspiration is often linked to a specific time, place, and state of spirit and mind. I painted Dreaming in the Desert back in 2011. I was in a different place mentally, spiritually, and artistically.

"You pour a piece of your soul into some of your pieces. Dreaming in the Desert was one of those rare, clear visions that seemed to create itself. To reproduce the brush strokes are challenging enough. To journey to that place again is almost impossible."

"I understand," I said.

"Do you?"

"On the periphery."

"Honest answer. Thanks for listening, just the same."

I noticed something on the floor sticking out from beneath a pile of crumpled newspapers. Curiosity drew me over to have a closer look. I tossed aside some of the crumpled newspapers. There was a stack of plywood underneath. I squatted to get a closer look, straightened and tapped the stack with my foot in a couple of places.

"Plan on doing something with plywood?" I asked.

The artist casually smiled and said, "My nephew dropped that off. He wants to see what he can create from it. I said I'd help him. I've never worked with plywood before, so it'll be a learning experience for me, too."

"Is he an artist?"

"I've been teaching him wood sculpting. He did those pieces over there." Payne pointed in the direction of the mantel over the fireplace. To my surprise, the mantle looked clean. There were five woodcarvings. They weren't bad, and I said so.

"He has potential," Payne said. "He's one of the few people I know who understands my unrelenting passion. I hope he has better luck than me if he decides to become a full-fledged artist."

"When did he drop it off?" I asked.

"What?"

"The plywood."

"I don't remember exactly. Sometime last week."

"He gave it to you?"

"More like left it here for us to work on."

I had a good view of the kitchen, from where I was standing. I witnessed another surprise. It appeared spotless.

"Plywood, huh," I said.

"Art is where you find it."

Payne walked me to the door. I wished him well on his recreation. He wished me good hunting on finding Dreaming in the Desert.

*       *       *

I parked my car where I could inconspicuously watch Payne's condo.

The more I thought about the condition of his condo, the more things didn't click. Not only did the crumpled newspapers covering the plywood appear orchestrated, but so did the smells and chaos.

All of it was done to mask the existence of that stack of plywood. The ratty furniture, on the other hand, was probably legit. A strong suspicion had gathered in me, and I was searching for something to give it a spark. The flame ignited when Jeff Nelson showed up.

I telephoned Sergeant Bedford and filled him in on my hunch. The sergeant and his partner, Doug Perry, arrived on the scene shortly after Nelson. I rushed over to join them.

"Who is it?" Payne said to the sergeant over the intercom.

The sergeant identified himself, his partner, and me, followed by, "Mr. Payne, we have a few follow-up questions that won't take long."

"You can ask your questions over the intercom," Payne said.

"I prefer we did this in person, sir."

"Do you have a suspect?"

"I can't tell you that, sir."

"Come back when you can."

"Mr. Payne," Bedford said, "your lack of cooperation is suspect. It might be misconstrued that you had something to hide. I could take you down to the precinct for questioning, based on that suspicion."

"I know my rights. You can't enter my premises without a warrant."

"We either do it here, or at the precinct. You make the call, sir."

There was a pause. "Just a moment," Payne said. It took a couple of minutes before Payne buzzed us in.

A pile of crumpled newspapers marked the area where the stack of plywood was. Payne appeared flushed and slightly winded. "I hope you know you're disturbing my creative process," Payne said. "I was in the middle of painting."

"Does painting always make you so flushed?" I asked.

"Art is sometimes as much a physical experience for me as it is an intellectual and inspirational one."

"We apologize for disturbing your muse, Mr. Payne," the sergeant said, "but we'll make this as quick as possible."

"Do you have any leads on who stole Dreaming in the Desert?" Payne asked.

"Mr. Cavanaugh has a theory on that," Bedford said. "Perhaps it would be best if he explained."

"Mind if I use your bathroom before I get started?" I asked. "I work better on an empty bladder."

"Down the hall—wait! The toilet's stopped up. It's pretty foul in there right now"

"Maybe I can fix it," I said. "I'm pretty good at unstopping toilets."

"Maintenance will handle it. There's a gas station a block west of here. I'm certain they would let you use their bathroom, if you can't hold it."

"Is there a reason you don't want Mr. Cavanaugh to have a look at your toilet, Mr. Payne?" the sergeant asked.

"No. I just didn't want Mr. Cavanaugh to go through all of that trouble when professional help is on the way. Are these the questions you have for me?"

"Then you won't mind if Mr. Cavanaugh has a look?" Bedford pressed.

Payne sighed. "Past the kitchen, first door on your left."

The first door on my right past the kitchen was closed. I opened it. It was the master bedroom. There, at the foot of the made king-size bed, was the elusive stack of plywood.

"Back here, Sergeant!" I yelled from the bedroom doorway. The sergeant, followed by Payne, then Perry, saw what I saw.

"I told you the bathroom was the first door on your *left*," Payne said.

"I got lost."

"You have no right to barge in here like this."

"Mr. Payne," Bedford said, "you invited us in. We didn't barge into anywhere."

"After you threatened to take me down to the precinct."

"You do have the right not to answer my questions, Mr. Payne," Bedford said. "And I still have the right to take you down to the police station and ask you questions there."

"Based on what?"

"Suspicion of burglary," Bedford said.

"I haven't stolen anything!" Payne protested.

"Mr. Cavanaugh believes different."

"Who the hell is he?"

"Only one of the best investigators I've ever known," Bedford said. Detective Perry nodded in agreement with his sergeant's positive testimony.

"Thank you, Sergeant."

"Whatever," Payne said.

I walked into the master bedroom to get another look at the stack of plywood. Hiding behind the bedroom door was Jeff Nelson.

"Jeff what are you doing back there?" I said. "Don't be shy, come out and join us."

Nelson scowled at me. He stepped out in plain sight of everyone. "What's going on?" he said, unsuccessfully trying to sound innocent.

"Detectives Kyle Bedford and Doug Perry, you've met Jeff Nelson, the nephew of Wilson Payne."

"Nephew?" the sergeant said. Detective Perry herded Payne and Nelson together inside the master bedroom.

"You didn't know, Sergeant? I suppose that little tidbit wasn't important enough for Nelson or Payne to mention when you interviewed them."

"And why would it be?" Nelson said indignantly.

"Ultimately," I said, "your familial relationship makes no difference, although I would imagine you two are very close. More like father and son, than uncle and nephew. There's not much a good son wouldn't do for his father."

"Yeah, I stepped in to help raise Jeff. His real father abandoned him. My sister, his mother, did her best, but it's hard working full-time and raising a child alone. I think of Jeff as my son. You can connect him to the theft of Dreaming in the Desert from that. That's quite a leap, Cavanaugh. You should consider becoming an artist, with that kind of an imagination."

"Maybe one day, Mr. Payne. Today, I'll focus on summarizing the facts of this crime."

"The only crime I see is you and these cops harassing me and my nephew," Payne protested.

"What were you doing hiding behind the door?" Bedford asked Nelson.

"I wasn't hiding," Nelson said. "I was having a look at my uncle's door frame. He said he thought it was coming apart."

"That's right," Payne said. "I asked Jeff to look at my door frame. Is that a crime?"

I squatted down beside the stack of plywood. "No," I said, "but stealing your uncle's painting is."

"Don't be ridiculous," Payne said. "My nephew hasn't stolen anything."

I pointed to the plywood. "That was your fatal flaw."

"What the hell are you talking about?" Nelson said. "It's nothing but a stack of plywood."

"Then you won't mind if I have a closer look," I said.

"This has gone far enough," Payne said. "I'm calling my lawyer."

"I doubt you have a lawyer," I said to Payne. "You may call your agent or one of your patrons, and they will contact an attorney. By that time, Sergeant Bedford will have secured a search warrant, leaving this discussion for not."

"A search warrant for what?" Payne said.

"As I said before, Mr. Payne: suspicion of burglary," the sergeant said.

"And I told you before, we haven't stolen anything," Payne said.

"Then you won't mind if Mr. Cavanaugh has a closer look at that plywood," Bedford said.

Payne and Nelson looked at each other. Nelson was clearly waiting on Payne's lead. Payne looked indecisive.

"Mr. Payne, anyway you cut it," the sergeant said, "we're going to have a look. It'll go easier on you two if you cooperate now."

Neither Nelson nor Payne said anything.

"Let me see if I can help," I said. "This stack of plywood is glued together, but you couldn't tell by just looking at them. I figured it out when I tried nudging a couple of pieces earlier, and they wouldn't budge. I asked myself, why glue so much plywood together? Maybe Payne or Nelson had an artistic vision for those sheets of glued plywood; or maybe they had a more practical purpose in mind."

I knocked on top of the plywood near the edges. It sounded dense. I knocked near its center. It sounded hollow. I felt around the edges until I found what I was looking for. There was a cut piece, big enough for a handhold, slid into a notch near the middle of a long side of the stack.

Detective Perry found a screwdriver and I was able to pop out the piece. I lifted what amounted to a lid. The center of the glued plywood was hollow, forming a large pocket. The pocket was padded with thick white foam and lined with pearl-colored satin. Door hinges were recessed and screwed into the interior of the plywood. Perfectly placed in its nest was Dreaming in the Desert. It was stunning.

"Somehow, you found out about the backup generator, didn't you, Nelson?" I said. "It could have come across in some idle conversation you had with one of your construction buddies. You may have casually mentioned it to your uncle without the slightest notion of committing a crime. You saw an opportunity, didn't you, Payne—the chance to get out of the poorhouse and gain some financial breathing room. The life of a starving artist isn't like those romanticized movie versions, is it. The reality is that most struggling artists live hand-to-mouth. Some are even homeless."

"I would never let that happen to my uncle," Nelson said.

"I'm certain your uncle appreciates that, Nelson," I responded. "But your uncle is, first and foremost, a man. Like most men, we have this deep abiding need to take care of ourselves. It's a male ego thing. Now that your uncle was approaching fifty, he had an eye on a safe haven where one could rest his head. That's when you began concocting your plan, didn't you, Payne? You knew your nephew would help because he trusted you. After all of these years, to finally be free of money worries and liberated to focus all of your energies on your art— it was your way out of the desert, so to speak."

"But I have patrons, believers in my work. They are more than happy to foot the bill."

"For how long?" I said. "I'll wager you didn't have them before your museum exhibit. It had been decades before you were awarded that opportunity. You said so yourself: they don't pay artists to exhibit their work. Not one of your paintings had sold. What if your big break turned into heartbreak? It was too much temptation not to take that chance.

"Payne, per your instructions, Nelson fashioned a plywood portfolio case for your painting. You worked out the plan and your nephew took it from there.

"Nelson, you knew what guards would be where and when, from

casual observation. You also knew from experience that at some point the electrical power needed to be cut. You managed to find out in advance when that would be.

"Fernandez may have given you the head's up. After the day shift construction crew punched out, you and a couple of the security staff were seen on surveillance footage unloading plywood from your truck.

"I'm willing to bet it was that same plywood portfolio case sitting right over there. To anyone who asked, you were returning the plywood because you had bought too much.

"Like the construction crew, there was a changing of PAM guards from day shift to swing shift later that day. The day shift security staff that helped you unload the plywood portfolio case never made the connection with the swing shift security staff that helped you load the same item onto your truck. The construction supervisor never questioned it because he didn't know.

"You stacked the plywood portfolio case next to the rest of the plywood that would be used on the job and waited.

"You're on surveillance footage wheeling in the plywood portfolio case, Nelson, and leaving it near the painting at 5:16. The day construction crew and your boss had cleared out.

"Seeing construction workers' tools, equipment, and supplies lying around the museum had become commonplace for PAM security. When you left a cart of plywood near your uncle's painting, security staff thought nothing of it. All you needed to do at that point was return to work and wait.

"The cart of plywood was on tape before the power was cut. It was gone, along with the painting, when the surveillance taping resumed. That's why I grilled you about building materials at PAM with that phony addition to my house story. I needed to be certain who was responsible for that cart of plywood. You became my prime suspect from that moment on."

Payne eyed his nephew. "I knew you were full of it," Nelson said to me. I continued as if he hadn't spoken.

"With the first flicker of lights, you knew the power had been cut. That meant there would be no electronic surveillance until mainline power was restored. Patrols weren't due for at least ten minutes, from what you had observed.

"You lifted the painting, placed it into your homemade portfolio case, and closed the lid. Then you pushed the cart back to the construction area, where there were no security cameras and the stack of plywood would look even less conspicuous. Out of sight from everyone, you put in the wood plug for the handhold using just enough glue to make certain it held, but not enough you would have trouble prying it out later.

"The plumber and electrician didn't notice your activities because they were too busy doing their own thing. Mainline power was restored. The alarm sounded. The police were summoned. People were questioned and properties and vehicles searched, but to no avail.

"After you finished your shift and the chaos died down, two security guards helped you load what appeared to be a stack of plywood into your truck, never realizing that Dreaming in the Desert was nestled inside. What better alibi than security cameras capturing it for all to see? You drove home where your uncle was waiting. The two of you brought the painting here.

"That's where things went wrong, didn't they, Nelson?"

"I told you to get rid of that painting," Nelson said.

"Shut up!" Payne said. "We're not saying another word until we speak to an attorney."

"Your nephew's partly correct, Payne," I said. "You wouldn't have been caught if you had destroyed the painting. By the same token, if I hadn't discovered that stack of plywood, I would have walked away leery, but empty-handed. Both needed to be obliterated to destroy any trail of physical evidence.

"Dreaming in the Desert was your masterpiece—perhaps your one and only. You loved that painting in a way you had never loved anything or anyone. How does one destroy a portion of one's soul, especially if you could resurrect it?

"You were planning just that, weren't you, Payne? You knew you couldn't chance resurrecting the original and trying to pass it off as a recreation. With the kind of testing they can do today, any art expert worth his salt would discover that it was the original. A few years from now, when the theft of Dreaming in the Desert had become little more than a trivia question, you could claim to have recreated your masterpiece after many painstaking efforts.

"Except for one thing—you were finding it more than difficult to recreate; but impossible. Even with it right at your fingertips, you still could not find that place in yourself from where Dreaming in the Desert had emerged. It would have been easier for you to commit suicide rather than destroy your masterpiece.

"On to Plan B: sell Dreaming in the Desert on the black market. That way, your original masterpiece would live on and you would have had the insurance money, to boot."

"How did you know Jeff was my nephew, Cavanaugh?" Payne asked.

"Ten sheets of plywood," I said. "That's what I counted earlier when I looked at that portfolio. Nelson said he bought ten sheets of plywood the night Dreaming in the Desert was stolen. Was it a coincidence, maybe? When Nelson showed up here, that kind of chance could not be dismissed."

Neither Payne nor Nelson said anything.

"A shame, really," I said. I looked around. The master bedroom was tidy, but had more of the decrepit furniture, as did the rest of the condo. "You did it for the money. If you could have held out a little longer, buyers would have lined up to pay top dollar for your work. You are a very good artist."

"So say you, so say my agent, so say the critics, and yet I have not a damn dime to show for it," Payne said with disdain.

Payne stared at his painting as if it were God granting him salvation. Nelson clenched and unclenched his jaw as he stared at the floor. They were taken away in handcuffs in those dissimilar states of mind.


*     *     *


The Chai tea was delicious. The honeydew melon and cantaloupe cubes were divine. Topping it all was the sweet, wistful, soothing instrumentals of 1965 vintage jazz.

There is nothing like music on vinyl. They say it is because there is a continuous, uninterrupted natural flow to the recording rather than digital bit streams that are too clean and restricted. I don't know if that's true. I do know my ear can tell the difference between digital and vinyl. Vintage jazz on mint condition vinyl is near as good as it gets. The only thing better is hearing it live.

The arrest of Wilson Payne and Jeff Nelson made front-page news in the Oregonian. The article spelled out how Security Chief Paul Yarder resolved the masterful theft with help from private investigator C. J. Cavanaugh. It also went on to say that, in gratitude, Mr. Yarder would be retiring with full benefits and salary for the rest of his life.

I didn't care who got credit for solving the case. All that mattered to me was that Dreaming in the Desert was returned to PAM, and that Smoky and Winston delivered on their part of the deal, even though I had to pry Winston's albums from his vice-like grip.

The stodgy photograph of Yarder shaking hands with the PAM CEO had the men looking toward the camera, standing in profile at arm's length. Yarder, of course, was shaking with his good hand. Both men were in uniform: Yarder in his PAM security livery and the CEO in an expensive suit, shirt, and tie.

I put down the newspaper. The adagio music took the moments away. Smoky was on piano. Winston was on snare drums. The saxophonist was a mystery man to me. The upright bass came up for a solo. The bass sounded effortless and spontaneous, yet clean, as if rehearsed a thousand times. The band dived back in. The ensemble moved like a lazy river over the piano notes.

Smoky and Winston were right. Bass Plate held the fort. He was also one of the best bass players I'd ever heard. I looked at the newspaper photograph. There was a gleam in Yarder's eyes. He looked happy and proud.

# COMA

Where am I?

Who am I?

My vision's so blurred I can't see a thing. It's dark. I can tell. Even with my eyes closed, I can feel the oppressive weight of darkness. My throat's as dry as dust. My tongue feels like sandpaper. Tastes like sandpaper. There's a strong antiseptic odor in the air. Something's attached to my chest. Something's attached to my head. What's that blipping noise? My head is killing me. I feel weak, too weak to move. If this is death, the afterlife is not all it's cracked up to be.

Last thing I remember was a blistering cold day. Frostbite warnings had been broadcast all week. Eleven people had frozen to death due to the weather. Snow had fallen all the previous night, becoming gelid heaps on every object from parked cars to barren trees to stoplights shrouded with icicles. I remember the sound of useless road salt ricocheting off car wheel wells in synchronized intensity to their speeds. Evening had keeled over like a ubiquitous gloom, releasing dour melancholy to dominate the world.

Robinelle had telephoned me from her mother's earlier that day. It was four-fifty-three a.m. on a Wednesday. I remember the time because my bedside clock's digits glared at me from next to my retro-styled desk phone on my nightstand.

Robinelle said she had just flown in from Atlanta and was anxious to see me. Her voice sounded distant, as if it were coming out of a dream. Robinelle apologized for having awakened me, saying she "remembered me being an early bird."

"That was years ago," I muttered into the dream.

I floated between sleep and consciousness during a quiet pause. When Robinelle asked if I were still there, I snapped awake. It was pitch black outside. Robinelle asked if we could get together. I jumped at the chance.

It had been four long, loveless years for me since Robinelle had married and moved away. We stayed in touch—somewhat—if a birthday and Christmas card once a year can be considered staying in touch.

Work was an absolute bust for me that day. I paid no attention to the V.P.'s game plan on landing the Algra-Flemming seaweed account. I had nil appetite at lunch. (Maybe the seaweed presentation destroyed it.) The Robinelle Dempsey fog—formally Robinelle Taylor—had cleared by late afternoon. By then, I was home readying myself for our grandiose reunion.

I was giddy as a teenager going on his first real date, inspecting my appearance at every stoplight. I was constantly questioning myself: should I brush my hair? Are my eyes red? Are my teeth white enough? Would Robinelle notice the new wrinkles in my forehead or the slight bags under my eyes? The self-doubt train raced along greased rails of disparaging questions, not to mention the answers did nothing to alleviate my agitated state.

Just before Liston Avenue, I was at a stoplight inspecting myself for the umpteenth time in the vanity mirror when the driver behind me honked his horn. The man was fat and bald. He looked irritated and uncomfortable.

Come to think of it, he was sweating. I could see perspiration on his face because I remember thinking how peculiar that was. Somehow, seeing his discomfort helped relieve my edginess. I took him as a sign to relax. After a few deep breaths, I left the mirror alone and forged ahead.

Robinelle's mom was a military widow who still cherished her deceased husband, holding fast to his last name. If there were any other way to get to Mrs. Taylor's house, I would have taken it. Having to make a running start on ice in order to climb a hill nicknamed *The Slalom* ain't my idea of fun.

For twenty-four passionate months we savored life, evolved together, seduced and wrapped ourselves into one another, and shared a private glass cocoon submerged in a pool of ceaseless amour. Hard to believe it ever ended. Every woman I've met in the post-Robinelle era, I've compared to her. Not one ever came close to the woman she was, in my estimation.

When I arrived at her mother's house, anxiety leaped on my back like a terrified monkey. I'd been in high-level board meetings involving multimillion-dollar contracts and didn't bat an eye, but the thought of seeing my ex-girlfriend, ex-lover, and ex-life again, made me as nervous as a prospective son-in-law about to ask a disapproving father for his daughter's hand in marriage.

Cameron answered the door. Robinelle's nephew was taller, better looking, and much more mature than I remembered.

"Hello, Craig. Nice to see you again," Cameron said with a smile. Cameron and I had always gotten along. He was as disappointed as I was when Robinelle and I split. He looked me in the eyes and firmly shook my hand. His voice had gotten deeper.

I could remember when Cameron stuttered. Had so few years made that much of a difference? There was confidence and pride in him that didn't exist before. After Robinelle and I parted company, I fell out of touch with her family, but the last time I saw her mom, she had mentioned that Cameron had joined the Air Force. His enlistment clearly had a positive effect on him.

Cameron offered me a seat in the dining room. He left me seated to inform Robinelle that I had arrived. I became nostalgic once alone with my thoughts.

Nothing had changed in Mrs. Taylor's house that I could tell. The small dining room was lit by soft, inviting light from the quaint chandelier. All other downstairs lights were off, except for those on the Christmas tree in the living room blinking red, yellow, green, orange and blue, casting dotted light patterns on the ceilings and walls in a synchronized dance to a mute accompaniment.

The fresh scent of pine was dominant. The house was its usual spotless. I could see my pensive reflection in the deep polished surface of the oak dining table. The dark green carpet appeared as though someone had combed every fiber.

Serenity. I'd always felt at home in Mrs. Taylor's house. Centered, as if it were where I belonged.

Out of my view, I heard Cameron descend from the upstairs to the basement. He was talking to an incessantly giggling young child. From upstairs, I heard the faint, distinguishable voices of Robinelle and her mom. Muffled footsteps casually descended the stairs. My body tensed. I clasped my hands in front of me atop the unyielding table. My palms were damp. I must have looked like a dutiful schoolchild putting on his best behavior for his favorite teacher.

Robinelle and her mother entered the dining room. For me, time froze. Her mom smiled pleasantly and said a gracious hello, and then she seemed to cease to exist. I can't remember what her mom was wearing, her hair, her face—not even the texture of her hand when I stood to shake it.

All I saw was Robinelle. All I knew was Robinelle, leaning against the wall, hands behind the small of her back, smiling that delectably seductive smile of straight, pearly teeth and full, smooth lips. The brightness of her beautiful brown face left me weak at the knees.

Her mom said, "Haven't seen you for awhile, Craig; looks as though life is treating you well" (or something of that nature). I was so tuned into Robinelle that her mom's words were like background noise. When Robinelle said, "Sure does," was when I realized that I was returning her smile.

"How are you, handsome?" Robinelle's voice was like a cold margarita on a hot summer day, stoking my desire and igniting my passion. I moved toward her like a child drawn to a hypnotic flame, questioning my senses, needing confirmation she was real. The mere fact that she was there in the flesh was disorienting, like a vision or a dream. Any minute, I was going to awaken alone, sobbing, clutching a pillow wet with tears, experiencing that familiar anguish that brought with it remorse, drunkenness, and reclusion.

I don't know how long it took me to say hello, gazing down at her as she continued to radiate, not touching her for fear she might dissolve. Her gentle fingers caressed my face. When she kissed me—or maybe I kissed her—my eyes were closed. Just like old times. Her lips were soft, wet, warm, and delicious. The spell was broken. I had returned to heaven. I heard Mrs. Taylor say she would leave us alone to talk, emphasizing the word 'talk' as if someone made her spit it out by slapping her on the back.

"Can I get you anything?" Robinelle asked. Her mother disappeared up the stairs. Robinelle grinned, a mischievous smile. She had that way about her—a coy, bewitching playfulness that made you crave her more. I wanted like hell to say *you*, but thought better of it.

"No thanks," was all I could manage.

I asked Robinelle where Leon was. She explained he could not tear himself away from his office furniture supply business. Sadly, she added that Leon was always busy with work, these days—far too often too busy for his own family.

A child's momentary giggling scrambled up the basement stairs, followed by Cameron's hearty laugh. "Would you like to sit down?" Robinelle asked.

"Love to," I said—perhaps with a bit more vigor than I should have, but my insides were volcanic with excitement.

Telling her how great she looked didn't make matters better. She smiled and thanked me, returning the compliment with that devilish gleam in her big, dark eyes. Did she know that turned me on? Of course she did. We were together for two years. How could she not know?

She looked even better than her photographs, and she'd looked fabulous then. Was it married life or the baby that made her a more beautiful butterfly than the one that flew away? Maybe it was just my imagination, seeing the woman of the past and not the present.

Whatever the reason, I didn't care. I still loved her, probably more than ever before.

I didn't hear Cameron ascend the stairs, or the giggling little boy he had perched on his shoulders. Robinelle and I stopped holding hands just as Cameron caught sight of us. A blush of guilt passed over Robinelle's face.

"Mom-mee, look at me! I'm flying!" the child said.

"I see, honey," Robinelle said. "Now, fly down here and give Mommy a great big hug." Cameron eased the child into Robinelle's wide-open arms. "Mmm, sugar hug, sugar hug. Yum," Robinelle said.

The child giggled and repeated after his mother. He was a bright-faced boy who looked nothing like Leon. He was a scaled-down version of his mother except when he smiled. He looked different, then. Sticking his thumb and forefinger in his mouth, he rested comfortably in Robinelle's lap.

When he looked my way and gave me a wondering stare, followed by absolute quiet, I felt uneasy; as if I were at a party of strangers and had attempted to interject myself into a convivial conversation of which I had no business.

"You know who that is?" Robinelle's voice was as soothing as a cup of warm cocoa on a cold day. The child shook his head no, not taking his eyes off me.

"He's a friend of Mommy's. His name is Craig." The child did not change expression or move a muscle. I sat there with my forearms propped on the table, smiling foolishly, not knowing what to say or do with myself. Out of the corner of my eye, I could see Cameron standing in the kitchen entrance, his arms crossed, feet shoulder width apart, observing the scene with mild amusement.

"Why don't you go over and say hello to Craig," Robinelle said, placing the child on the floor and adjusting his pants seemingly out of habit more than need. Unsteadily, he walked up to me (a little afraid, I could tell) and said a muffled hi, his fingers still lodged in his mouth.

"Hello!" I said, giving him my hand to shake that he shook limply with his free hand while still staring.

"Mighty glad to meet you, young man," I said.

"Tank you," he said.

"How old are you?" I was desperate. I love children, but I never know what to say to them when they're that young. *Just talk to them*, people say.

About what? How about those Steelers, and did you hear the one about the priest, the rabbi, and the minister? What do you think about WMDs, nuclear power, the financial markets, domestic politics, unemployment, global warming, international trade, capital punishment? Somehow, I don't think toddlers are ready for that sort of dialogue, and I can't seem to regress to Dr. Seuss, so there's the rub. Asking a child their age is the only icebreaker I know.

The child said something I couldn't quite make out. He still had his thumb and forefinger in his mouth.

"Take your hand out of your mouth, honey," Robinelle said. She was smiling with obvious pride. I wasn't sure if it was at him or the both of us.

"Three," he said.

"How many is that?" I said using my best adult to child's voice. He looked back at his mom. "One, two, three," Robinelle said, putting up her index, middle, and ring finger; her ring finger a reminder of loss hooped with her gold diamond wedding band.

"One, two, three!" he repeated, doing the same, grinning triumphantly and swaying back and forth.

"And what is your name?" How adults maintain that infantile dialogue on children's shows is beyond me. I felt ridiculous.

"Ryan!" he blurted out. His confidence emerged in a rush. "What's yours?"

"Craig," I answered, ignoring the fact that his mom had previously mentioned it. "Do you like flying, Ryan? Way up there?" I asked, pointing to the ceiling.

"Yes," Ryan blurted out.

"Then let's fly!" Grabbing Ryan firmly but gently by his waist, I swept him up and away. I laid his body flat across the palms of my hands and flew him around the kitchen, the dining room, and the living room, making airplane engine noises and saying *you're a plane* repeatedly all the while.

He laughed and stuck out his arms like wings, dipping and climbing over things that were clouds, mountains, or towers until his engine ran out of fuel. Landing him securely in his mother's arms, he wanted more. After refueling, I made a few more passes before Robinelle ordered all Craig Bastion flights cancelled and asked Cameron to operate the controls. I was grateful for her intervention. My reserves were running low.

Robinelle ordered Ryan to give me a hug before he and Cameron departed. The kiss on the cheek surprised me. It may have showed. I watched, somehow proud, as Cameron propelled a squealing Ryan airborne back to the air force base code name: Basement.

"He's great," I said, swelling with joy for Robinelle.

"Yeah, he is," Robinelle said. "I love him a lot. He means the world to me." The way she spoke and then looked deep into my eyes with an insightful, steady stare, as if she were trying to tell me something she couldn't possibly say, left me puzzled. I let it go. Knowing Robinelle, she would tell me in her own time.

We made that gradual transition from fantasy to reality, once again holding hands on top of the table and talking about the changes in our lives over the past few years.

*Why did I ever let her go?* I asked myself.

*You know damn well why!* The voice of reason bellowed inside my head. *The green-eyed monster, that's why! Any woman who tried to stab you three times, threatened you with a baseball bat, punched you in the eye while you were sleeping, and vowed to kill you before letting you go while watching the romantic dramatic-comedy "Same Time, Next Year" can justifiably be considered dangerous.*

The voice was right. That part of our Eden, I continually blocked. I couldn't recall how many arguments Robinelle and I had over fictitious affairs. My reputation as a player didn't help matters any, despite the fact that it was true—before I met her.

Robinelle was the only woman I ever considered being one-hundred percent faithful for. Yet, she trusted me the least. By her own admission, she didn't trust men, but not due to personal experience. She'd been lucky that way.

Robinelle's distrust came by way of her girlfriends. Or, should I say, her girlfriend's boyfriends and the way they would come on to her, not caring that they were seeing her friends. This led to her viewing most men as dogs.

I wish I could have found a way to persuade her I was different. Giving her my undivided attention, flowers, gifts, compliments, and dedicated love were not enough. It seemed the harder I tried, the less she believed me. Her jealousy became so intense that even my friends and family began to fear for my life.

At first, I had thought her death threats were a joke—until I looked deep into her eyes. Robinelle had a mind like a Rottweiler's bite. Once she sank her teeth into something, she did not let go. Being loved to death was my vision of our lives together. I chose separation and life.

The treacherous part had been convincing Robinelle that it was her idea we part company. That was where Leon came in. Robinelle and

Leon had been an item before I stole her away. Leon was infatuated with Robinelle. As much as she hated to admit it, Robinelle had strong feelings for him, as well.

Robinelle and I had one of our knock-down drag-out arguments about a fictitious affair I was supposed to have had with a long-time female friend of mine. Robinelle stormed out of my apartment. That was always my queue to rush after her and convince her that none of it was true.

I restrained myself. I let her go. There were two things Robinelle and I had in common: we were both stubborn and prideful. I didn't call her for a couple of days, knowing she wouldn't call me. My expectation was that Leon would be there to console her. One thing would lead to another and I would find myself the odd man out. It worked, and I felt dreadful.

Every rose has its thorns. I had been pricked by Robinelle and wanted more. My family and friends encouraged me to stay away. They were all convinced I had done the right thing. I buried myself in my career to keep my mind off my love. At a low point, I called Robinelle, if only to hear her voice. It didn't matter if it was only for a brief moment. That moment would be the shot I needed to right myself for a while.

On the day I realized it was truly over between us, her mother answered the phone. When I asked for Robinelle, she was pleased to tell me that Robinelle no longer lived there. She and Leon had eloped. Not only that, but they had moved away—to where, her mom would not reveal.

It wasn't until after the birth of their child that I heard from Robinelle. She sounded happy. Her joy ironically pleased me a great deal, as if her happiness was all that mattered—all that was ever important. The birth of her child never stopped those clawing questions from echoing from my soul. *What if I hadn't let her go? Could we have found a way to extinguish her flames of jealousy in a pool of trust?*

Perhaps I should have told Robinelle about her sister Leslie, my most vehement and vocal detractor. About the time she came to my apartment and asked to use the bathroom; about how she had the gall to come out of my bathroom nude.

"Is there anything you see that you like?" she'd asked. After I ordered Leslie to put on her clothes and get out, she had the audacity to ignore me and continue her attempts to seduce me. It was unreal—like a bad surrealistic movie you couldn't turn off. She left me no choice but to throw her out, tossing her clothes out the door behind her.

That's when Leslie started feeding Robinelle lies about me and other women. Guess I should have told her about her rotten older sister. Maybe she would've believed me. I doubt it. Robinelle looked up to Leslie. Too bad Leslie didn't have the same respect for Robinelle.

The hours blew past, that night at the table, sweeping us through time and space and back to a place when romance between Robinelle and me was second nature. It was indeed the best of times we'd enjoyed.

The hour grew late. I had to be at work early the next day. Everyone else in the house was sound asleep. Robinelle walked me to my car. I was glad I'd parked just outside. It was frostbite weather, and she was only wearing a sweater. The cold air felt as heavy as a glacier and moved just as slowly. I felt its pinch in spite of the furnace stoking full force inside of me.

"We'll get together tomorrow for dinner to pick up where we left off," Robinelle said. "About seven? There's something I need to tell you." Robinelle gave me that insightful stare again.

"Why can't you tell me now?" I asked.

"Tomorrow will be soon enough, Craig," she said. "Trust me."

"Fine," I answered. For a brief moment, I drank Robinelle in with my eyes before it happened—a long sultry kiss, the kind that leaves you gasping for air.

"Talk to you tomorrow," Robinelle said. "Drive careful."

*Honey, for you, anything,* I wanted to say. "Get inside before you catch pneumonia," is what I said. She stood inside the glass outer door, waving as I pulled away. I did not want to leave. It took all of my inner strength to press on.

I was on automatic pilot, driving home. The years Robinelle and I had been apart hadn't dulled my memory on how to do so. For some odd reason, I kept replaying seeing Ryan for the first time. Man, could that kid laugh. What a smile…his smile…his smile…that smile…there was something about his smile that kept eating at me, gaining the vortex of my attention.

Halfway home, the reason leaped into my mind. Ryan's smile—I knew that smile! That's when I pulled over and looked into the vanity mirror. It took a while to manage a genuine smile, but after I did, there was no question. Ryan had my smile, dimples and all. That was our child. Robinelle and I had a son!

For months before our break-up, Robinelle had talked about having a baby. She even went as far as to say I didn't have to concern myself about any financial or parenting commitments. I bet she stopped using the pill. She'd always been adamant about not wanting me to use condoms. She said she didn't like the way they felt.

Was I crazy? Was it my imagination running wild because I loved her so much? Had the craving to create a permanent bond between us made me delusional? There was only one way to find out. I turned the car around and headed back.

I believed that was why Robinelle looked at me the way she did. She was telling me, *the secret is in my eyes—can you see it? Can you see it in the glowing face of your child? Can you hear it in his unbridled laughter? In him, can you see yourself as I do?*

What if it was true, then what? Should I ask her to get a divorce and marry me? Demand that the child know I'm his real father? If necessary, fight for my legal rights as his biological dad?

That's when it happened. I hit The Slalom moving much too fast. My car spun out of control like a merry-go-round gone berserk. I remember the first two collisions, both with parked cars. The nauseating sounds of metal colliding and glass shattering cut me to the core. I felt a sharp tearing in my neck, then a blunt pain in the right side of my head. There were blinding lights shining in my face. I heard a few indistinguishable voices attached to indistinguishable faces, coming from what seemed like a great distance. Then things went black.

My vision is clearing, now. What little light there is hurts my eyes. I can make out that I'm in a hospital room. My saliva is as thick as cold pea soup. I wonder how long I've been out. Except for that blipping noise, it's quiet. It's deathly quiet. Seems like it all happened moments ago.

Where's the nurse?

Where's the doctor…my family…my friends…Robinelle…my son?

I feel so weak. I can barely move.

Was it all just a fairy tale dream turned nightmare in the end?
Where do I go from here?
What do I do now?

# FEAR

It was Friday. The after-work twenty-one-to-thirty-something crowd had piled into the trendy, non-smoking, brownstone Pilgrim Lounge to hook up or relax before heading home to whatever awaited them. The Lounge—as it was referred to by most—offered semi-private, flexible front, center, and back elegant dining rooms with a separate, spacious lounge area and fully staffed L-shaped bar. Self-described by the owners as contemporary posh, polished hardwood floors and gleaming sputnik chandeliers, blended seamlessly with soft rounded furnishings replete with bold colors in harmony with neutral elements.

The middle-class mingled alongside millionaires in this stylish environment. Feelings of inferiority didn't exist because no one acted superior. This was not a place for the haughty or ostentatious. Personality and intellect paid high dividends in an atmosphere of modern sophistication and casual comfort. While the achievement of a vigorous bank account was respected, it mattered not if your personality was a dud or fraud. That was because everyone frequenting The Lounge was content financially, and none saw any reason to masquerade.

Mason Williams, Joaquin Ruiz, Kalpen Modi, and Japheth Silverman had been friends since grade school.

Mason was a lean, stoic, clean-shaven man with a short fade and calm brown eyes that remained transfixed on his object of attention.

Tall and boisterous Joaquin, who often led the topics of conversation, sported a tight goatee, expressive brown eyes, and short black hair, combed back and held in place with a dab of gel.

Kalpen had the beginnings of a well-nourished belly. He was a small, neat, regal-looking fellow with collarbone-length, dark wavy hair, a stubble beard, and laughing brown eyes.

Spirited and slightly chubby, with curly blonde hair, a chin curtain beard, and skeptical blue eyes, Japheth had a mischievous smirk as his normal expression and representative mindset.

They were born and bred Americans who, through hard work, focused determination, and a few fortuitous breaks along the way, managed to pull themselves up from the bottom of the economic ladder to the middle.

By day, they were an accountant, an air-traffic control specialist, a college professor, and a software developer. Their respective ethnic identifications were African American, Hispanic, Indian, and Caucasian.

Upbeat instrumental music rained down as background noise, keeping The Lounge energy-sparkling and buoyant. The Lounge served great drinks, quality bites, and world-class service, and everyone in the city knew it.

The creators of Pilgrim Lounge took full credit for cultivating the economic diversity of their clientele. In truth, it was not their conscious doing. People from varied pecuniary walks of life discovered them through word of mouth and social mediums. It was an organic revolution that was still going strong.

During happy hour it was first in, first choice, when it came to seating for all but the back dining room area, which was exclusive for dinner patrons.

The four men had lucked out and scored a window seat table at the far end of the center dining area. They elected to close the venetian blinds enough to curtail the glare of the relentless summer sun without losing its natural light. Joaquin sat on the outside next to Kalpen. Mason sat on the inside next to Japheth. The four friends were still on their first bourbons on the rocks. Even though they were taking either the subway or a taxi home, none of them saw that as an excuse to get drunk, which meant they took their time and savored their hard liquor.

Work venting dominated the first few minutes of their conversation. All but Mason participated. Mason enjoyed everything about being an accountant, so he had nothing to contribute.

Joaquin did not feel like cooking when he got home. He had talked the group into ordering the happy hour Buffalo Special, when normally they would have the vegetable platter. Everyone understood.

Joaquin's wife, Liana, and their children, Sancho and Isabella, were away visiting his in-laws. A surprise visit by an aunt and uncle from Spain, whom his family had not seen since their wedding (video conversations excluded), had brought about the spontaneous trip. Unfortunately for Joaquin, his supervisor had already scheduled his vacation during the same period. Joaquin became acting supervisor in his absence, making it impossible for him to get the time off. Not that he didn't try.

While none of the others wanted to spoil their appetite for dinner, they couldn't let their friend eat alone. Joaquin filled his plate. One-third from the heaping platter of crispy, spicy, boneless Buffalo wings, half with mini-carrots and cauliflower, and the rest with cheese quesadillas, staying clear of the basket of baked corn tortilla chips.

Joaquin ate as if it were his last meal. The others occasioned a nibble of everything but the Buffalo wings, dipping their choice in a divided server bowl of hummus, guacamole, or salsa (depending upon the appetizer).

"You think you own something," Joaquin said, taking a breather from his gluttony. "What do you own? I mean *really* own?"

"My house, my car—well, I'm still paying on both, but—" Kalpen said.

"You own nothing! All those things and more belong to nature."

"You're telling me my big screen TV belongs to nature?" Japheth said skeptically

"Damn straight."

"How do you figure?"

"Fire comes and destroys your house, or an earthquake or a flood or a tornado, storm, lousy power surge, or even a meteor strike happens. Nature, buddy, don't bow to nobody. It even owns your ass."

"A power surge is not nature," Kalpen said with a grin. "It's manmade."

"Meteors are from space," Japheth said.

"Meteors are natural occurrences," Kalpen said, clearly enjoying the debate. "They are literally forces of nature."

"Thank you, my friend," Joaquin said, wagging an approving Buffalo wing at Kalpen. Japheth looked at Kalpen and nodded in acceptance of his explanation.

"We are all friends at this table," Mason said. Mason had been tracking the conversation, and had believed there was no need for his input until now. He felt compelled to clarify that obvious fact.

"Right you are, my friend," Joaquin said to Mason. Kalpen and Japheth laughed, a masculine sort of chortle. It was their way with laughter.

Mason unblinkingly stared at Joaquin. Acknowledgement for his friend's sarcasm did not show on his face or in his eyes. He continued to stare at Joaquin as if observing a specimen he did not want to disturb. Joaquin would have been uncomfortable were it not customary Mason behavior.

As a child, Mason's parents took notice of what they termed his 'unusual behavior.' Doctors found nothing physically wrong. He had no chemical imbalance they could detect. Psychological testing proved Mason had an exceptional IQ and no behavioral issues. His personality assessment revealed some anomalies in the area of emotional stability. While his emotional responses were normal in every test, how he processed them was not.

For some reason the psychiatrist was unable to determine, Mason's mind would tamp down or stamp out feelings before they ever reached fruition. Every emotion was logically processed. Instead of being acted upon, his feelings were treated as a condition in need of a solution; a riddle to be dissected. While Mason had no trouble recognizing emotions in others and acknowledging them within himself, he rarely *felt* any necessity to exhibit them. The psychiatrist explained that the human brain was possibly the most complex element in the known universe, and was equally unpredictable. In short, Mason was simply wired that way.

As his psychiatrist correctly predicted, Mason learned appropriate emotional responses not by his own genesis, but mostly by closely observing others. Even then, he rarely displayed what he learned. The psychiatrist cautiously suggested medications to his parents that might help Mason achieve an emotional balance.

A definite "NO" was their answer. Their only concern was for the wellbeing of their only child. As long as he was healthy and happy in his own way, they saw no reason to gamble with his condition.

"OK. Lightning, then," Joaquin said, putting the conversation back on track.

"That's stretching it," Kalpen said.

"I agree with Kalpen," Mason said. "The chances of any of us being struck by lightning within a year are about ah-million. Our chances of being struck by lightning in our lifetime are about one-in-twelve thousand, factoring in a life expectancy of eighty."

"Still, being struck by lightning *is* a possibility," Joaquin said. "Tomorrow isn't promised to any of us."

Mason nodded his agreement. Kalpen gave a slight shoulder shrug, as if to say he remained unconvinced. Japheth's smirk only widened.

"You live, you die," Joaquin said.

"Yeah, but—" Joaquin interrupted Japheth before he could finish.

"Oh, and you think you can control those factors?"

"Somewhat, sure—"

"Like you can guarantee you won't die from a heart attack in the next week."

"Yeah, I can guarantee that," Japheth said with a confident smile and dismissive shake of his head.

"Did you hear about Gilley Carson?" Joaquin raised his eyebrows when he spoke. The glint in his eyes brightened. Everyone at the table knew that meant he was about to arrive at the zenith of his argument.

"The long-distance runner?" Kalpen said with calm anticipation.

"That's the one. He kicked the bucket from none other than a heart attack, and his doctor doesn't have a clue what caused it."

"That's an unusual case," Japheth said. "Tragedies like his are rare, not common."

Joaquin took a moment to dip a carrot into the community hummus and shove it into his mouth, savoring the moment. Interesting conversation and banter stimulated appetite for this group.

The others could no longer resist the mouthwatering sights and aromas of the Buffalo special. They half-filled their plates, Mason making the same selections as Joaquin, but on a smaller scale. Kalpen and Japheth chose vegetables and substituted chips for Buffalo wings. Joaquin added a few more Buffalo wings and carrots to his near-empty plate.

Their server stopped by to check on them. She was a young, fresh-faced brunette and wore horn rimmed glasses. "Is everything alright, gentlemen?" she asked with an ingratiating smile.

"Everything's fine, thank you," Joaquin answered. Kalpen and Japheth nodded their agreement. Mason simply stared at her.

Mason had noticed earlier that their server was new. As she refilled their water glasses, Mason thought, *she looks young enough to still be in high school.* Immediately, he dismissed such foolishness. *No reputable establishment would risk losing their liquor license by being idiotic enough to hire someone underage.*

"Can I get you anything else?" she asked everyone at the table.

They ordered another round. She politely moved on to fill their order.

"It happened," Joaquin said, after wiping his mouth clean with a cloth napkin, "and I can guarantee it'll happen again."

"Bottoms up," Japheth said.

The friends raised and clinked their cut crystal whiskey tumblers together. Without further ceremony, they quaffed their drinks.

"And for those random and inexplicable exceptions, you cite nature," Japheth said, not hiding his doubt.

"Yep." Joaquin's eyebrows relaxed. He appeared satisfied he had proven his point. The server returned with fresh drinks, clearing the table of its empties.

"Will there be anything else?" she asked.

"No thank you," Kalpen said, speaking for the group.

Mason continued to observe their nameless server. She was short, and her body was lean like that of a ballerina. She spoke with a hostess's confidence, as someone who enjoyed not only her job but the company of people.

*Her voice and manner are perfect examples of professional courtesy,* Mason thought. *How has she mastered them so young?*

Mason was curious. He considered asking her age. His friends would openly chastise him if he did. Asking a woman her age was a cardinal sin, even of someone clearly as young as their server. *What if I asked how long she has been doing this kind of work?* he thought. *No one would be offended by that.*

"Let me know if you need anything else," she said. Her smile was a permanent fixture as she stepped away to offer her services to the table in front of them.

"I'm not convinced," Japheth said, giving Joaquin another dismissive head shake, "and to prove it, I'll meet you here next week," Japheth tapped his forefinger twice on the table, "at the same time. First round is on you."

Mason had returned his attention to their conversation.

"I'll try," Joaquin said. "Don't know if I'll be alive that long."

Kalpen swallowed the cauliflower and hummus he had been chewing and wiped his mouth clean with his cloth napkin before speaking. "If you're trying to be funny, Joaquin, it's not working."

"No joke," Joaquin said, pointing a Buffalo wing at Kalpen. "None of us know when our time's up." Joaquin concluded by eating the Buffalo wing.

"It's a wonder you've made it this long, the way you're carrying on about nature," Japheth said, pointing back at Joaquin with a carrot.

"Not carrying on, bro— relaying the facts." Joaquin wiped his hands clean on his cloth napkin, dropped it on the table next to his plate, and stood.

"Where are you going?" Kalpen asked, chewing a cauliflower dipped in hummus.

"To the bathroom."

"Nature calling?" Kalpen asked. The four men roared with laughter.

"That's one way of putting it," Joaquin said, walking away with a broad smile.

Unlike the lounge and bar areas, in the dining areas, standing was not allowed. To get to the bathrooms, you had to pass through the lounge. Joaquin waded through the vibrant lounge crowd to the bathroom. Everyone eyed the devastation that remained of the generous servings of the Buffalo special. They all knew from personal experience that Liana was a helluva cook. For their friend to wolf down as much as he did of the special meant that he was starving.

"What will meeting here next week prove?" Mason asked in a flat, dry tone.

His friends knew Mason well. Mason could be quiet, at times, to the point of introversion. Other times, you couldn't shut him up. They had learned over the years not to pressure Mason into being one or the other. Their friend had an odd personality. He seemed to lack a certain insight when it came to social interaction. They suspected it was a condition akin to the emotional disconnect of autism, but none of them had the heart to explore the matter further.

Mason could and did feel emotions—of that they were certain. What Mason lacked was that developed skill, the intrinsic knowledge of how to connect with people on a visceral level as his personable friends did.

His condition was particularly distressing when it came to women. Mason didn't seem to have a problem getting laid. He was physically attractive, and women often found his personality quirky and appealing, at first. That was before they realized his impassive behavior and unfiltered comments were engrained, and that it didn't change with familiarity. Mason had failed to hold onto a woman for more than a few months since college. Even then, it was more pity that lengthened his college relationships rather than love or even fondness.

Japheth, Kalpen, and Joaquin were family. A family who accepted each other for who they were. His friends were concerned that Mason would never find true love, as each of them had done. Every time they and their spouses had tried to play Cupid, Mason's indifferent behavior doused any hope of a romantic flame. Even their wives admitted that to know Mason was to love him. The challenge was getting past his idiosyncrasies.

At first, most women found his unflinching candor and spot on observations endearing. Some even regarded the challenge of changing Mason an experiment they believed ready to pursue. Once they discovered his odd ways were cemented into his character, the thrill of the personality makeover dissolved into an acid bath of frustrations and coarse reality.

Mason was literally a person who defined 'what you see is what you get.' While life never deals in absolute certainties, Mason was not likely to change. As the wives of his friends had learned over the years, from their interactions, Mason had as much to give to a committed relationship as the best of men. It was having patience and a willingness to embrace his peculiarities that rarely seemed to survive the liftoff stages of dating.

"We meet here almost every Friday for drinks after work, so what's the big deal?" Mason observed.

"It's Joaquin's way of attempting to prove that nature rules," Japheth said. "My showing up next week—alive and well—is my way of proving to Joaquin that we have some control over our mortality and thereby our lives."

"Actually, you're both right," Mason said. "At times we do, and other times we don't."

"Like when?" Kalpen asked.

"When you have a medical checkup, and some terminal disease or condition is diagnosed early. You take control over your mortality by going to that checkup."

"That only means your time's not up," Joaquin said to Mason upon his return.

"I think you're confusing fate with nature," Mason said.

"I see Mason's taking your side on this nature issue, Japheth," Joaquin said, sounding pleasantly amused.

"Yes, he is," Japheth said. Japheth held up his hand to receive high-fives. Mason and Kalpen delivered. Joaquin playfully rejected his friends' victory gesture.

"I'm not taking anyone's side," Mason said. "I'm merely addressing the facts as I see them."

"It all ties into life," Joaquin said. "And let me tell you something about life. You never, ever experience the same moment twice."

"Then how do you explain déjà vu?" Kalpen asked.

"Thinking you've experienced something and actually having done so are two vastly different matters, my friend."

"Thought and experience are not polar opposites," Kalpen said. "If anything, they are children born of the same parents."

"I agree," Japheth said.

"Care to weigh in?" Kalpen asked Mason.

"Thought and experience feed into each other, in my opinion. Like learning that if you touch fire, you're going to get burned."

"Aha!" Japheth said.

"They can also operate independently, as in cases of inductive reasoning— understanding that if A plus B equals C, then B plus A also equals C—which doesn't require any prior experience to speak of."

"There you go," Joaquin said, raising his hand to get a high-five from Mason.

"What's with the high-five?" Kalpen said. "Mason's saying you're both right."

"I'll take 'em when I can get 'em," Joaquin said. Everyone laughed, giving each other high-fives all around.

"I'll be glad when Liana and your children return," Kalpen said, "to bring you out of this life-is-half-empty funk."

"I second that," Japheth said. "They've been gone less than a week and you're already behaving like it's the end of the world."

"I can't imagine what he would be like if they left him alone for any extended amount of time," Kalpen said.

"Therapy would probably be in order," Japheth said. His sly grin was on full display.

Everyone chortled. Joaquin waited until the laughter settled before he spoke.

"You only live once," he said, referencing back to his topic on life. "Might as well make the most of it."

Mason believed that Joaquin had posed an intriguing concept he felt compelled to address.

"It's interesting that you should declare we only live once, Joaquin, when most religions believe in some form of perpetual existence."

"True," Kalpen said. "As a Hindu, I believe in reincarnation and transmigration of the soul until one has achieved perfection."

"As a Jew," Japheth said, "I don't believe in reincarnation or transmigration or resurrection, as some of my faith do. Death, to me, means the separation of soul and body; leaving the soul free to transition into a spiritual world liberated from all earthly bonds."

"As a Roman Catholic," Joaquin said, "I don't believe in reincarnation or transmigration or resurrection, either. It is man's fate to live and die once during his earthly pilgrimage. His deeds during that time will determine his judgment in the hereafter."

"I'm a Christian," Mason said. "It is the religion my parents have embraced, and I have accepted it. It brings them comfort, knowing I share in their belief. Religion, as I see it, is a roadmap to the philosophies of your life. It offers guidelines to aid us in becoming better human beings, when practiced honestly and absent of malice, arrogance, and ego. That is how I accept the role of Christianity in my life.

"Personally, I don't know if God or spirits or afterlives or anything exists after death. As for myself, I don't care if it does. It seems to me we spend far too much time preparing to die than we do appreciating life."

His friends nodded.

"People have faith for a wide variety of reasons, Mason," Kalpen said. "It brings us comfort and hope when all else fails. Have you not called upon God for help in your darkest hours?"

Mason thought for a moment. His friends patiently awaited his response.

"No, I can't say that I have. I always try to reason my way through a situation or accept it for what it is."

"I heard you pray to God to accept your Uncle Julian into heaven at his funeral when we were kids," Joaquin said.

"We all heard you," Kalpen said.

"You were crying and everything," Japheth said.

"My tears were in earnest. My prayer was not. I was doing what was expected of me, in that regard. My Uncle Julian believed. He was a devout Christian. If I was mistaken and heaven and hell and spirits and souls do exist, who was I to endanger his ascension? While I'll accept that religious risk for myself, I won't do it for the people I care about."

"You don't believe in God?" Japheth asked.

"I'm undecided."

"Or souls, or spirits, or the afterlife in any form?" Kalpen asked.

"Again, undecided."

Mason looked around at his friends. They appeared stunned by this revelation. All of this time, they had assumed that Mason's religious faith was true. He was a regular at Sunday services. He showed genuine respect for the rights and customs of not only his own apparent beliefs, but those of his friends, as well. Had they been deceived? Was he telling them it was all an act?

Their eyes moved away from Mason, finding other places to rest amongst the energetic crowd. An impromptu silence fell upon the table. Mason realized that his revelation was the source of their unease, raining doubt on a cherished connection they had shared for years. Mason felt it best to elaborate.

"I loved my Uncle Julian very much when he was alive. He was gone, and I missed him. I still do. That was why I was crying. Thinking of him makes me happy, then sad, knowing that he's no longer present in body."

His friends gave curt nods of understanding, but kept their gaze away, remaining lost in thought. The crowd noise and music filled in for their collective silence. Mason could extrapolate the general theme of their ponderings from years of close observation of their habits.

At a moment like the death of his Uncle Julian, Mason appeared to be exactly like them. Not weird or odd, but normal in his grief. That made him one of them in spite of his condition. Which he was, in actuality. Was it only moments like that which allowed them to fully embrace him for who he was? If so, was that still the way his friends perceived him?

Mason quickly reasoned *no* as the appropriate response to his last doubt. They had been friends for over two decades. Pity doesn't last that long.

"It's common to declare we only live once," Mason said, attempting to bring the conversation back to an earlier theme. "That being an accepted truth by many, then it would be logical to extrapolate that we only die once, as well.

"During our unique existence, if we are fortunate, we can control how we live intellectually, physically, and even spiritually, if you believe in such a thing. Most of us are not granted such good fortune. Doing their best, as opposed to making the most of their opportunities, seems to suit most people's taste."

"You know, sometimes I think you're too smart for your own good," Joaquin said to Mason with an empathetic shake of his head.

"Nobody's too smart for their own good," Mason said.

"Hear, hear!" Kalpen said with a chuckle. The four brothers from different mothers raised their tumblers high to toast Mason's last statement, finishing their drink. Joaquin was ready to order another round. Kalpen checked the time on his phone.

"As much as I enjoy our time together, I have to leave," Kalpen said, getting to his feet.

"Me too," Japheth said, doing the same. "My in-laws are coming over for dinner tonight, and I promised Edra I'd help out. My wife wants everything to be perfect."

"I promised my daughter I'd help her prepare for her latest role," Kalpen said.

"That's right, Kavita got the lead in *Hansel and Gretel*," Joaquin said. "Good for her."

"Do you do character voices?" Japheth asked.

"Yes."

"Sound effects?" Joaquin asked.

"The whole nine yards."

"I could see you as the wicked witch," Japheth said. Everyone but Kalpen laughed.

"Very funny," Kalpen said.

"Kavita must be excited," Mason said.

"She can hardly contain herself."

"You might have a professional actor on your hands," Joaquin said.

"Kavita is a good actress," Mason said. "She was exceptional in *Peter Pan* and *Sleeping Beauty*. It wouldn't surprise me if she was successful in the field."

"Thanks," Kalpen said. "I'll tell Kavita you said that." Mason nodded his consent.

Children did not have a problem with Mason. They readily accepted him for who he was, with little judgment and no pretense. Kavita was a bright and spirited child who was proud to call Mason her uncle. When she did, it made Mason feel warm inside. The same could be said of Joaquin and Japheth's children when they enlisted him into their families.

Mason knew the feeling to be love. Love in the same protective sense he had toward his young cousins. The root of this merry emotion confused him. Psychiatrists and sociologists explained it as an evolutionary adaptation—a primitive instinct for the survival of the individual and species. Those were means that Mason could cognitively digest.

Yet, there was no denying the rock-hard validity of love. There was also no fighting its magnetic pull. Mason would do things for people he loved that he would not consider doing for anyone else. He would even fight to the death to defend them or keep them from harm.

What eluded him was the *why*? Why shelter a select group of people from all others in regards to this safeguarding commitment? The concept both perplexed and fascinated him.

The check arrived. There was no quibbling about who'd ordered what and how much it cost. As was their custom, they divided it four ways, paying in cash and leaving a generous tip.

Their server came to collect. She politely thanked them, bid them a good evening, and was on her way. Mason observed her all the while.

Unlike most male friends who at most shook hands when they parted company, the friends good-naturedly hugged. After Kalpen and Japheth left, a young couple came over and asked the two remaining friends if they would be willing to trade their table for two seats at the bar. Joaquin and Mason agreed. The couple, joined by another young couple, enthusiastically thanked them for the swap.

Mason and Joaquin made themselves comfortable at the pleasantly crowded, L-shaped lounge bar. Bright conversation danced all around them. Joaquin ordered another round from a fortyish clean-cut bartender named Hal that Mason had evaluated a few months before.

"What's your plans for the rest of the evening, Mason?"

"I have a dinner date."

"A dinner date!"

"You sound surprised."

"Astounded is more like it. Did you come into a fortune I don't know about?"

"No. Why do you ask?"

"I'm just yanking your chain, bro. A dinner date; that's great!"

"Why's it great?"

"It just is, that's all. Good luck. And I mean that in every way."

"If you're still being sarcastic, it's escaping me."

"No, I mean it. Anybody I know?"

"No. Would you like to meet her?"

"Why don't we hold off on that for the time being."

Joaquin looked down at his bourbon on the rocks and swirled the contents of his tumbler. He didn't want Mason to read what he was thinking, which was, *this is probably another dead-end attempt at a relationship that won't last. Could they even call what Mason was experiencing as a relationship anymore? Isn't it implicit that, when referring to a relationship, you're referencing something that has lasted more than a few months?* That was most certainly not a debate he was going to have with Mason.

As far as Joaquin was concerned, Mason had enough problems with women without chipping away at what must be, by now, his brittle confidence.

"What's her name?" Joaquin asked, looking up from his drink at his friend.

"Maxine Wilkerson."

"Is she hot?"

"I take it by 'hot' you mean physically attractive?"

"Yes, *of course.*"

"While beauty is relative to individual tastes, I would say yes, she's hot to me."

"How long have you known her?"

"Eight days."

"This your first date?"

"Yes."

"Tell me about her. How'd you meet? When? Where? Don't leave me hanging, bro."

Mason was accustomed to being grilled about his dates by his friends and family. He knew why. Everyone in his close circle didn't think he was aware of his failings with women. Every time there was the slightest possibility of a serious relationship brewing, his friends became excited and hopeful that she might be *the one.* He never let on that he felt the same. What good would it do?

"We met at my Aikido dojo," Mason said. "Shihan Yamamoto asked me to take over his intermediate class due to a family emergency. After class, a group of us were headed to the subway, and Maxine and I started talking. She landed here by way of a job promotion which required her to transfer from Chicago. Maxine is a marketing executive. She doesn't have any family or friends here, so I offered to be her chaperon. Before I knew it, Maxine suggested we have dinner and asked me to pick the restaurant. And that's that."

"Cool," Joaquin said, nodding with approval. "Wait, you said you met her eight days ago."

"Yes."

"Why so long for the dinner date?"

"It took us this long to coordinate our schedules."

"I see. What do you think?"

"We'll have dinner and talk. I'll try to help her get acclimated to our city."

"Do you like her?"

Mason thought for a moment before answering, "Yes."

Joaquin, like the rest of his friends, worried about Mason ending up alone. "Mason couldn't keep a woman under lock and key," Japheth once told Joaquin and Kalpen. Mason's longest-running college relationships found his resigned brilliance uniquely charming … initially. They also used him for his immense brain.

There's a thin line between cute and annoying. While not a conscious effort on his part, Mason often crossed that line sooner rather than later, with women.

"What are your plans for the rest of the evening?" Mason asked.

"Go home and straighten up the place. Liana and the kids are coming home on Sunday."

"Do you miss your family?"

"You have no idea how much."

"I believe I do, based upon your earlier bleak topics of conversation."

"Our house is not a home without them," Joaquin said. The men drank in silence for a moment, soaking up the warm and cheerful atmosphere.

"What's your biggest fear?" Joaquin asked.

"I fear nothing."

"Everyone fears something. Mine is ending up alone," Joaquin nonchalantly said. There was no evidence of concern in his eyes, expression, or body language. If anything, Joaquin appeared at peace, as if he had long ago accepted that truth about himself.

"I fear nothing," Mason repeated.

"None but a coward dares to boast that he has never known fear," Joaquin said.

"Ferdinand Foch."

"Who?"

"The French general you just quoted."

"Really? Where did that come from?"

Mason shrugged. "Maybe you were paying closer attention in your history class than you realized."

"Guess so."

"Courage is resistance to fear, mastery of fear—not absence of fear. Mark Twain."

"You've mastered your fears."

"Kalpen told me something that summarizes how I address fear. He said, 'What is needed, rather than running away or controlling or suppressing or any other resistance, is understanding fear. That means: watch it, learn about it, and come directly into contact with it. We are to learn about fear, not how to escape from it."

"Deep."

"I'm sure Kalpen was quoting someone, but I couldn't tell you who."

"And that's how you handle fear."

"I don't know that I handle fear at all, Joaquin, but that's my process of dealing with it when it occurs."

"'In time, we hate that which we often fear.'"

"Shakespeare."

*"Seriously?"*

Mason nodded. "Antony and Cleopatra, Act 1, Scene 3."

"I've got to stop doing that."

"'To conquer fear is the beginning of wisdom.' Bertrand Russell."

"The Welsh philosopher."

"One in the same."

"I don't know if I buy into the wisdom part. I do believe that it's through the conquest of fear that we come to know courage."

"You've touched upon a topic that is difficult to define, Joaquin. Courage is a virtue that can be inspired by a range of factors, overcoming fear only being one of them.

"There's physical, moral, and psychological courage. A person acting rashly due to a situation that requires immediate action may be motivated out of self-preservation—a natural instinct we all share—although his actions could be construed as bravery. Someone else's impulse in the same situation might be to protect the welfare of others.

"Most people, I believe, would agree that the second statement is more of a true testimony of courage. However, is incapacitating one's personal fears in order to survive any less courageous?"

"Now that you put it that way, I'm not so sure."

"I'm certain some of the choices you've had to make as an air traffic controller have involved courage."

"If you only knew! It does get hairy up there, sometimes."

"There's Darah!" Mason said.

"*Where?*"

"Over near the entrance."

Mason pointed at her reflection in the mirror opposite the bar. He looked over his shoulder at a well-built, baby-faced woman of average height with bright brown eyes, smooth caramel skin, and a lustrous mane of natural curly black hair. Darah Davis was a talented corporate patent attorney. The little black dress she was wearing told Mason she wasn't coming from work.

Darah was funny, brilliant, tough, and sexy; a ferocious professional who hid her soft heart well. Darah and Mason had met at a fundraiser for adult literacy programs. Mason was most attracted to intelligent women as much as they were, at the start, attracted to him.

The two of them dated for a little more than a year and regarded themselves a couple three months into that. Darah was, by far, Mason's longest serious relationship. There was sincere talk of marriage between and surrounding them.

His friends believed that Mason had finally found *the one*. Try as they might, his friends and their crew (as they sometimes referred to their families) were unable to keep the two of them together. When it ended, it ended with a crash.

Darah had telephoned Mason at his office earlier in the day. She said she had something very important to discuss with him. They agreed to meet at his place after work.

"Mason, we can't see each other anymore," Darah said with an attorney's resolve. They stood in the middle of his living room. Darah had marched in when Mason opened the door, bypassing his attempt at a hello kiss.

"You're breaking up with me," Mason said in a nondescript voice.

"Yes."

"Is this about the partner's dinner party last night? I could tell you were upset. Want to talk about it?"

"She was the senior partner's wife, Mason. The very same senior partner who is about to retire."

"I understand."

"Do you?"

"Yes, you've explained it to me before. Once the senior partner retires, the other partners are bumped up and a junior partnership becomes available. A partnership that you and James Logan are top candidates for."

"Exactly, which is why I needed you to schmooze with me at the senior partner's dinner party last night."

"Schmoozing is what I was doing."

"You told the senior partner's wife that she looked fat in her dress."

"I did not. She asked me if I *thought* she looked fat in her dress."

"You said yes."

"She asked me to be honest. I qualified my answer by being more specific. I mentioned she looked chubby in her dress, not fat."

"*Big difference, Mason,*" Darah said, frustration taking precedence. "She was fishing for a compliment. She wanted reassurance from someone other than her loving husband that she looked beautiful."

"She did look beautiful."

"Why didn't you simply tell her that?"

"That's not what she asked. She asked if she looked fat."

"And therein lies our biggest problem."

"I don't understand."

"Mason, you don't possess the basic social filters normally employed in polite company that most people have. Sometimes even I think you're an automaton."

"I am not an automaton. I'm a human being."

"Mason, baby, most people would have known to play along with the senior partner's wife—or any woman, for that matter—under similar circumstances. It's a part of our adult social skill set. A behavior quality that I'm afraid you sorely miss."

"You mean, I should have lied."

"Yes! I mean, no! Certain situations require us to bend the truth a little. In order for us to function as a civilized society, sometimes a thin lie is what's needed."

"I'll bear that in mind."

"That can't be the first time you've heard that?"

"No it isn't. I'll work harder on instituting that adult skill set."

Darah let out a heavy sigh. "I've tried and tried and tried and tried repeatedly to help fill in that gap, but nothing is working. Sometimes your rampant candor and unflinching insights are like a foot-in-mouth disease. And I can't find the cure."

"I understand."

"What is it you understand?"

"You're breaking up with me."

"I don't see us having a future together."

"That's not true."

"What's not true?"

"You love me. You could see us being married and raising a family. But I'm not a logical fit for your career aspirations. Appearances are as vital as courtroom acumen, legal knowledge, and talent, in your profession. In order to achieve your goal to become a full partner one day, you will need a spouse who compliments that purpose."

"That's not the only reason."

"It's the primary reason. I've heard what people have said about me when we're at your social functions and they think I'm out of earshot. They call me things like dweeb, weirdo, oddball, strange, and retard, to name a few. The ones who try to be kind call me things like Rain Man, Spock, Data, or simply 'unusual.' They think I need help or medication just because I place a high premium on logic and don't wear my emotions on my sleeve."

"Why didn't you say something?"

"Why didn't you?"

Darah looked down. She had stood up for him countless times in the beginning of their relationship. As time went on, she found it easier to laugh with them about Mason rather than to continue a battle with no apparent end.

"I didn't say anything because I'm used to it," Mason said. "Being insulted and belittled doesn't bother me. I've been called those names and worse for most of my life. It's typical behavior for people who don't understand me. But it clearly bothers you."

Darah was speechless.

"You've tried to change me. Coax me into someone you and your friends and family and associates and colleagues regard as normal. If happiness is the freedom to be oneself, then I am happy. I may not laugh or smile or joke a lot. I may not make small talk or possess a polite social filter, as you've aptly pointed out. I may take some matters too seriously for most, but that is who I am. Those who truly love me have accepted me as I am, as I have accepted them. As I have accepted you."

Darah compassionately stared at Mason. Every word he said rang true. What bothered Darah was his delivery. There was no passion or anger or bitterness or remorse or sense of urgency behind his words. Just cold, hard, stated facts.

"I'm sorry, Mason," Darah said, her voice reflecting the regret she felt. "I wish I were stronger or more audacious or something, because I do love you.

"For me, being in love has stipulations. One of them is: it has to fit snugly into my career goals. To be perfectly honest, to make that work, I'll settle for companionship over love. I'm not the falling-head-over-heels-in-love type of woman. Never have been; never will be. That's who I am."

Darah unwaveringly stared into Mason's eyes. Suddenly, her strength drained from her. She felt exhausted. Tears pooled in her eyes. To her surprise, she began to weep.

Mason reached down and gently rubbed away her tears with his hands. Not a thought, but a reaction. His thought was to offer Darah the crisp, clean, white handkerchief he kept quarter-folded in his back pocket, which he did.

"No thank you," Darah said, waving his offer away.

"It's clean," he reassured her.

"Since you put it that way," Darah said, not receiving any reaction to her sarcasm. She took the handkerchief and wiped away her tears, only to have them replaced by new streams from the wells.

"I know," Mason said. "I'm not your first love and I won't be your last. I sincerely hope you find the man you deserve. Can we still be friends?"

"That's supposed to be my line," Darah said, still wiping away her tears. "I'm the one initiating the breakup."

Mason stared at Darah, not moving a muscle, not saying a word.

"After what I've said and the selfish reasons I have for ending our relationship, and you still want to be friends."

"Reason. I only heard one reason—that being your career—and yes, I would like to remain friends. As you said, you're being true to yourself. I respect and appreciate your honesty."

"Even if it means breaking your heart," Darah said with a quiver.

Mason thought for a moment before answering, "Yes."

Darah was speechless. She gazed at Mason. Darah wiped away more tears with his now-damp handkerchief. New tears flowed free to replace the old ones.

"I do love the cool, calculating way your mind works, Mason. What attorney wouldn't? You're also kind, thoughtful, and considerate to people you care about, even if you rationalize the behavior. But your candor is like that of an unbridled juvenile. When you are in a situation that requires tact or diplomacy or a delicate hand, you seem incapable of navigating those waters."

"I understand."

"Do you?"

"Yes."

"Do you understand how much telling you this is breaking my heart?"

Mason nodded. "You love me. What did you expect?"

Darah shook her head with a weighty sigh.

"It's my mind that you love," Mason said.

"Mason, you have one of the most brilliant minds I have ever known."

"I was hoping it was my body."

Darah laughed. "That's funny."

"You don't love me for my body. I work out regularly, you know."

Darah laughed her tears away.

"You do have a nice body, Mason, but if I had to choose, I would definitely say I love you most of all for your mind."

Mason observed her with a forced grin. He knew what he'd said was funny. Sarcasm often was. What he had done was a logical ploy, a trick he had picked up by osmosis from his friends—a subtle effort to break the tension.

"I don't want to lose you, Darah," Mason said after Darah's laugh settled into a smile. His smile vanished.

"I'm already lost, Mason."

"Darah, I love you, and I only want what's best for you."

"Maybe I'm not what's best for you. Did you ever think of that?"

Mason gave her question serious thought. "That's not possible," he firmly said.

With one hand, Darah petted his cheek, pulling his face down to press his other cheek against her own. Mason felt her trembling; her warm dampness; the feathery brush of her eyelid against his skin. Mason moved to put his arms around her. Darah released him and pressed a hand to his chest. Mason stopped. Darah gently cupped his cheeks. Her kiss was soft upon his lips. Mason thought, *if there be a God with a kiss this tender, this sweet, let me die today and rise up to greet her.*

"Goodbye, Mason," Darah said, her voice barely a whisper.

Mason watched Darah leave. Something inside of him burst as the door closed behind her. Agony filled his core, but he felt as if a vacuum had sucked the life out of him. He didn't make a sound. Mason stood stock still, paralyzed in the spot where Darah had abandoned him. A Buckingham Palace guard would have been proud of his discipline.

He felt he should run after Darah. Declare he would change. Make some great, sweeping, symbolic gesture of love and plead for another opportunity to prove himself worthy of the partner she needed him to be.

After all, that was what men in his situation did in those romantic movies. It usually worked. The rocky couple were resolutely set upon the joyous path of happily-ever-after, after weathering the trials and tribulations of romance. But his feet wouldn't move. An avalanche of emotions suffocated his thoughts—shock, denial, sadness, and anger. His mind plowed through them as quickly as possible, beating down desperate pleas from his heart to take action.

His vision blurred. Mason felt something warm and wet on his cheeks. How long had he been weeping? He wiped away his tears with his hands. The warm wetness returned. He left it alone. The battle waged on.

Deductive reasoning took a foothold. Logic joined the ranks. A throbbing pain like he had never experienced before made his head feel as though it were about to explode. Mason stood there for as long as it took to will himself to regain control, internally battling the harrowing demons tormenting him.

His will knew what his heart could not accept. He wouldn't change. He couldn't change. Mason tasted his salty tears until night replaced the light and the door by which Darah had exited his life had been swallowed whole by feral darkness.

"I should go over and say hi to Darah," Mason said to Joaquin.

"No!" Joaquin blurted.

"Why not?" Mason looked confused.

"Let her go, Mason. Darah is never coming back to you. It's over."

"I'm aware of that. She made that quite clear. That doesn't mean we can't be friends—or, at the very least, civil toward one another."

Joaquin took a sip of his drink. He stared into his tumbler. He needed to speak truth to Mason. Stated bluntly, it would work. That didn't mean it wouldn't leave an emotional scar no matter how deeply Mason buried it.

"How does Darah react when you talk to her, since your breakup?" Joaquin had witnessed a couple of those encounters. 'Awkward' was how he would describe them.

Mason thought for a moment. "Civil."

"Does she appear uncomfortable at all?"

"As a matter of fact, she does. Standoffish and reserved, which is not at all like her."

"That's probably because being around you *makes* her uncomfortable, Mason. She still has feelings for you."

"I still have feelings for her. In fact, I still love her."

Mason had filled in his family and friends on their breakup scene, excluding the part about how he reacted after Darah left. His exclusion was not due to shame. He simply deduced it would not further clarify a disastrous situation.

"That's all well and good, but Darah doesn't want to love you anymore. She wants to be rid of you, Mason, so she can get on with her life. You make her feel ... uneasy. It's not only because she still loves you. It may be that she still harbors guilt about how and why she ended your relationship."

The first date between Mason and Darah was sexual. It was a Saturday night. The first week in September. They had been out drinking and dancing. Mason saw Darah home. Both were buzzed. Dancing the night away had kept Darah from excess.

Mason did not get wasted. Once had taught him a lifelong lesson. Kalpen, Japheth, and Joaquin had taken Mason out to celebrate his twenty-first birthday. From ceaseless encouragement by his friends, and in typical rite-of-passage fashion, Mason binge drank. The staggering, reeling, head spinning, and vomiting came over him like shockwaves, plunging him into a crash and burn tailspin. The excruciating hangover and general fallout such excesses entail made the day after a living hell.

Mason adopted two drinking policies after that embarrassing and agonizing experience: to drink responsibly or not drink at all.

Darah snatched Mason by his suit jacket lapels the moment they crossed the condo threshold and yanked him to her for a steamy kiss.

Mason could taste the merlot on Darah's soft lips. When she thrust her tongue into his eager mouth, the plummy, chocolaty flavor overpowered the woody bourbons he had nursed that night. It was not their first kiss, but was by far their most passionate to date. It was a sputtering affair of fervent kissing interrupted by graceless stripping of each other as they whirled through her condo to her bedroom; objects and shadows a blur, undressing each other down to their underwear, leaving their tossed clothing settled wherever they landed.

Darah prepared her extra-firm king-size bed for what was to come before disappearing into the adjoining bathroom. Mason hastily searched for his suit jacket. He found it contorted at the foot of the ladder bookcase in the living room. Quickly, he retrieved a condom from its right pocket and dropped the jacket where he found it. Darah emerged in all of her feminine glory. Mason was nude, as well. His erection needed release from the uncomfortable restraint of his restrictive boxers.

"I'm wearing an IUD," Darah said, first noticing Mason's appealing erection, then the golden condom packet Mason dangled by the corner in front of his chest.

"You can't be too careful," Mason said. Darah smiled in agreement.

Darah volunteered to help with his condom. Mason massaged her breasts while she rolled it on. They scrambled into the enormity of Darah's prepped king-size bed like anxious teenagers. Their first time together was lust—panting and grunting and sweating; hastily responding to ardent, instantaneous pleasure commands. Satisfying primal urges was not as gratifying as making love, as they would soon discover.

When they did make love for the first time one month later, it was more mind-blowing than anything Mason had ever experienced.

They took their time. He savored Darah's body with his hands, his lips, and his tongue. Darah relished his body in the same manner. As in lust, they were oiled with sweat and her muscles were hard, but her voice and touch were tender. Mason gasped her name in hunger; whispered her name in fulfillment. He called her sweetheart, baby, honey, and more—endearing terms that rolled off his tongue like satin on skin.

"Every time she sees you, Mason," Joaquin said, "she's probably experiencing guilt."

Mason heard every cautionary word Joaquin delivered. He did not respond. Joaquin knew what Mason was doing: rationalizing.

Joaquin looked around at all the people having a great time. Happy hour was nearing an end. The after-work crowd was vacating to a populace of dinner patrons. With their departure, the energy had changed. The din had transformed into a pleasant hum.

Darah's breakup argument had been cogent. Joaquin's interpretation regarding Darah having scorn for her feelings toward him made perfect sense. That did not dismiss how he felt, or the fact that, in private, he still pined for Darah. It did not erase the emblazoned memories of their passionate lovemaking, sex being the only time he seemed capable of fully abandoning logic. For whatever reason, his mind allowed him to fully experience the uninhibited cauldron of amatory pleasure that two fiery bodies entwined in erotic harmony could generate.

Mason had lovers after Darah, returning to what had become his pattern of one-night stands and short stints in libidinal gratification with women he neither loved, nor who loved him. With Darah, he had gone to carnal heights like none other. He equated their love as the fuel for their dazzling ascent.

"Bumping into each other by chance," Mason said, "was not premeditated on my part."

"I don't think that matters in the end, bro."

"It would be impolite not to at least acknowledge Darah with a hello. It's been over a year since we split. The last time I saw her was three weeks ago. We spoke for a few minutes without any problems. I think she can handle a simple greeting and a question or two about how her life is going."

"You might only be pushing her further away, Mason. If you really want to be friends with Darah, let her come to you."

"I'm willing to take the chance of 'pushing her further away', as you put it, Joaquin. I think you're underestimating Darah's resiliency."

"In matters of the heart, we're all weak in the knees, Mason."

Mason had been watching Darah in the bar mirror. Seeing her made him ache. As much as he hated to admit it, Mason wanted to be a part of her life again, even if only for snippets like this. He privately chastised himself for not presenting his case on why they should not have given up on their love. Sometimes love requires tenacity. He had become accustomed to amiably bowing out.

Had he ran after Darah, pleaded for another chance, or allowed her to witness the solitary tidal wave of emotion he had experienced, perhaps Darah would have been persuaded to grant him a reprieve. Maybe Darah would have been the catalyst to force a change in him that he seemed incapable of by any other means. A few stolen moments in her presence would be food enough to nourish his yearning for reconciliation. It was a thread of hope twinkling in the midnight of despair.

"Thank you for your concern and advice," Mason said matter-of-factly to his friend.

Mason pivoted on his barstool. He was about to step into the crowd and wade his way over to Darah when a tall, handsome, successful-looking brown-skinned man in a designer suit with top-shelf grooming hugged and kissed Darah on the lips. He didn't recognize the man. The couple smiled at each other in the way Mason and Darah once had.

Mason couldn't hear their conversation, but he remembered the timbre of Darah's voice ranging from commanding to sensual, depending upon the circumstances. Given Darah's behavior toward the kissing man, it was no stretch for Mason to imagine Darah was speaking in sensual tones as much as the hum allowed. The couple's conversation was brief and cheery before they left.

In that moment, his hopeful thread was snipped. Mason felt queasy. It was the collapse of their relationship all over again. This time, Mason knew what to do. He quickly turned back to the bar. He took a sip of his bourbon on the rocks, followed by another. Looking down at the bar, Mason breathed deeply.

Joaquin noticed the crushing wave of heartbreak roll across his friend's face as Mason watched Darah and her mystery man walk out of the door. The pain in his eyes would have made water weep.

Joaquin had never seen Mason react in that manner towards to any of his former girlfriends. Most times, Mason had appeared aloof and analytical, in reflection. "Short-lived, physical, superficial relationships" was how Mason had described them, even when that was not true.

His friends and their crews knew Mason loved Darah. For the first time, Joaquin realized how much. Mason loved Darah as much as he loved Liana. Joaquin sympathetically patted his good friend on the shoulder, as if to stay his grief.

Mason continued with his deep breathing. *Alter your focus*, Mason thought. *Emotions are triggered thoughts, no matter the primitive effect they have upon us. Deflect the negative thought with a positive one—one of equal or greater power. That will dictate my physical response.*

Joaquin looked on with concern. Mason appeared ready to implode. His eyes were brimming with hurt. Anguish devoured his face. From his years of knowing Mason, only tragedies such as the death of someone dear wrenched from him this expressed level of feelings.

Hal looked on, as well. Joaquin shook Hal off as he was about to come over and ask if Mason was okay. Mason continued to breathe deeply, allowing himself to rapidly fall into a meditative state. Mason reflected upon a happy memory. The Lounge atmosphere gradually washed away like surface waves returning to the sea.

His parents had given him a border collie puppy for his ninth birthday. Mason named him Chester May after the two people he loved most, his dad and mom. At that time in his life, the men he now called brothers were only beginning their journey together. Chester May gave him unconditional love. Aside from his parents, grandparents, and a small handful of blood relatives, no one else did.

Chester May became his best friend. Warm memories of his best friend calmed Mason—memories that begged the question: why he had not had a pet since Chester May died?

His breathing steadied. Anguish melted from his face, giving way to serenity. Had Joaquin not witnessed Mason quickly compose himself a number of times before, he would have been bewildered at his rapid metamorphosis. Instead, he accepted what Mason did as his norm.

"Are you alright, amigo?" Joaquin asked.

At thirty-six, Mason had begun to question whether it was in the cards for him to have the family life his friends had so easily achieved. Seeing Darah seemed to make erratic destiny more absolute. Mason glanced at his friend and then looked back over his shoulder at the area where Darah had stood.

"Yes," Mason said, turning back to the bar. "I'm fine."

*Once again, meditation worked,* Mason thought. *Ultimately, I will need to find closure from Darah, as I have with every tragedy in my life. Healing my broken heart is going to take time and effort. How much of both, I have no idea.*

*It is said that forgiveness is a big step toward closure, in these situations. What is there to forgive? Darah was only being honest. That leaves time healing all wounds, or finding another love. Here's hoping the latter comes first.*

"I'm going to get a dog," Mason said, taking a sip of his drink as a toast to his last thought. "Maybe two."

"What brought that on?" Joaquin incredulously asked. Joaquin glanced at Mason. His stoic demeanor had returned.

"I love dogs," Mason said with a shrug of his shoulders.

Joaquin could not fathom how anyone could go from gut-wrenching heartbreak to calmly considering adopting a pet. Except for Mason. This was the emotional history of his friend. He had that ability to exercise some weird mind trick that would rescue him from the barrage of anguish. Exploring the matter would only lead them back to misery for his bro. Joaquin decided to go with the flow.

Hal gave Joaquin a furtive glance while waiting on a customer two stools down from them. Joaquin answered Hal with a quick nod.

"We got our dogs from a shelter," Joaquin said.

"As good a place as any."

Mason recognized the pining love song playing over the sound system. It was a smooth jazz saxophone instrumental of a Motown classic, "My Cherie Amour," by Stevie Wonder. His parents loved Stevie Wonder. Mason did, as well. The irony almost made him smile.

*Perhaps Darah was onto something,* Mason thought. *Is it time to stop trusting in love, save the memory of it? Maybe I should seek a compatible partner for marriage, career, family and future. What could it hurt? Love hasn't worked out for me.*

The problem for Mason, with accepting that philosophy, was that he had loved, and was loved by people willing to accept him for who he was.

There was no denying the overwhelming power the feeling evoked. Love gave people the strength to endure what would cause them to crumble under normal circumstances.

For him, that was the flaw in Darah's thinking. He witnessed, almost daily, how amazing a life built on a foundation of love could be, through his family and friends. To settle for less was illogical and unworthy of a lifelong commitment.

"I keep having this recurring dream, Joaquin—or nightmare, dependent upon your point of view," Mason said, sounding like his old self.

"What is it?"

"I wake up in a strange bed in a strange room, alone. The room is well lit—bright, in fact—but I'm compelled to leave. I open the door and walk out into a dark hallway. The further I walk down the hall, the darker it becomes, until pitch-black swallows me up like a starless night devouring the sun."

"Poetic."

"Thank you," Mason said matter-of-factly. "I'm talking about the kind of encompassing darkness where you literally can't see your hand in front of your face.

"Even though I can't see anything, I keep walking until I come to what I sense is the end of the hall. I blindly reach out and my hand finds a doorknob. I turn the doorknob and open the door. In the inky blackness, I see something. I'm not talking about how we see in the light. I mean, I see something in the dark in the same way we see in the light."

"What do you see in the darkness?"

After a long pause, followed by a deliberate sigh, Mason looked up at Joaquin. With eyes both distant with the light of himself and near with the note of recognition, he said in a soft voice, "I see myself."

"What do you think it means?"

"I don't know."

A somber moment passed as the men quietly pondered the significance of Mason's dream.

"Ready for another?" Hal asked, breaking their contemplation.

Joaquin looked at Mason. "No, thank you," Mason said. Joaquin nodded his accord. The young brunette server with horn rimmed glasses gained Hal's attention with a wave from the server section of the bar. Mason and Joaquin noticed. She smiled and waved at them.

Joaquin raised his tumbler and returned her smile. Mason simply stared, wondering if her flirtatious behavior was motivated by their generous tip. Hal excused himself with a nod, to assist his coworker.

"I'd better get going," Mason said. "I don't want to be late for my first date with Maxine."

"Right," Joaquin said. Both men knocked back their drinks and left the Pilgrim Lounge together.

Mason and Joaquin stepped out into a clear summer evening. The concrete jungle still clamored with hectic energy. Humans manufactured its life blood. The twilight heat hovered in the low eighties. Humidity had plummeted from a suffocating eighty percent to a manageable fifty. Intermittent breezes moved heat and humidity and sound along, as well as noxious vehicle fumes and restaurant exhaust aromas ranging from delicious to nauseous. Starlight sparkled on the dusking blanket of a looming night sky. All went unnoticed to the two friends heading south.

Joaquin successfully managed to steer Mason's mind away from Darah and his dream during their walk by talking about sports and politics. Once Joaquin felt he had diverted Mason's mudslide of depression, Joaquin refocused their attention onto his friend's impending dinner date.

"Where are you meeting Maxine?"

"At Jadis."

"Pretty high class for a first date. You must want to impress her."

"The restaurant's close to where she lives. She'll feel safe and secure knowing that no matter what happens this evening, she won't be far from home."

"Thoughtful and considerate," Joaquin said, a quick jerk of his head the only indication that he was amused by his friend's rational. Mason ignored the gesture. "You're off to a great start."

"I'm hoping she doesn't walk out on me during dinner like most of my dates seem to do these days."

"I keep telling you, you need to change your game. Loosen up, have some fun. Women dig that."

"I feel loose and fun."

"You could've fooled me."

"That doesn't take much."

"Good one. See, that's what I'm talking about. Be more playful and spontaneous. And try not to be so … analytical and brutally candid all the time."

"I'll consider it, but I can't promise anything. I am who I am."

"Don't consider it, Popeye. Put it into action."

"I want a relationship, Joaquin. One that's going to lead to marriage and children."

*"And you tell them that on the first date?"*

"Yes."

"No wonder they walk out on you."

"I don't understand."

"A first date is an opportunity to start to get to know someone."

"I understand that, but—"

"It takes time to build a relationship, Mason. Especially one that will lead to the altar."

"I've heard of people getting married within a month or a week— even on the day they meet."

"That's true, amigo, but it doesn't happen that often. And, I'll wager you, most of those marriages don't last. You just need to be patient. The right woman will come along."

"Darah was the right woman, and now she's gone. I'm running out of patience. I want love now."

Mason stared at Joaquin for a response. Joaquin took a moment to get over Mason's confession.

"You can't order love, Mason, like you can a pizza. It comes to you in its own time; in its own way."

Joaquin and Mason reached their crossroads. Joaquin and Mason hugged. Joaquin walked away. When he looked back over his shoulder, he saw that Mason hadn't budged. Mason stared down the street leading to Jadis as if it would be his final march.

Joaquin walked back to his friend. He didn't have to ask what was wrong. While it didn't show on Mason's face, it pulsed in his eyes. For the first time since he'd known Mason, he knew his friend was afraid.

"Listen: after all of those Buffalo wings I put away, I could use a little more exercise to work it off."

"We could go to the gym. I have a membership at one not far from here."

"What about your date?"

"Right," Mason said with a determined nod. "You're right, of course."

"Come on."

The two men strolled down the street with Joaquin dominating the conversation. Mason quietly listened, disturbed by a foreign feeling. What was it, exactly? Mason considered the puzzle during brief lapses of silence. His friends always had a way of making him feel better about himself no matter the situation. Joaquin was accomplishing that goal, and Mason was grateful.

They arrived at the front entrance of Jadis as Joaquin concluded his story about his youngest, Sancho, having gotten his head stuck between the bars of his baby crib when he was one. It was a story Mason had heard a number of times before. Joaquin waited for Mason to go inside. Mason didn't move.

"Don't let me keep you," Joaquin said.

"You're not."

"I'm just yanking your chain, bro."

"You mean, being funny."

"Yeah, as many times as I've used that expression, I thought you'd have that figured out by now."

"Just checking," Mason said, uncomfortably eyeing the restaurant.

"I'll catch up with you later. When I do, I want to hear all about your date with Maxine."

Mason surprised Joaquin with a sudden hug. Joaquin was taken even more off guard by its intensity. He hugged Mason back as if he were one of his children in need of consoling.

"Go on now, Mason. You can do this."

In dusk and streetlight, Joaquin walked east toward the nearest subway station. Mason stepped inside Jadis.

The maître d' informed Mason that his date had arrived. She had been seated at their table. Maxine was early. Mason didn't know what to make of that. Most of his dates were late.

He strode toward Maxine, shoulders back, chest out, as was his way. Maxine stood and acknowledged him with a sincere smile. Mason had seen smiles like hers before in the first light of some of his relationships. He relished those moments. They were the jewels in the crown of possibilities. The dream crept back into his mind like an icicle up his spine, crawling across the belly of his skull. Darkness enticed his soul as Mason reached for the hand Maxine earnestly extended in gracious greeting.

# DEATH BEFORE THE ALTAR

Each time the ringing peeled away a layer of unconscious vision and tugged me into a conscious reality. The sound was distant and familiar, penetrating an indistinct dream. It echoed, then stopped; echoed, then stopped. The more distinct the vibration, the more distant the dream and the more concrete the reality.

"Hello?" My response was reflex. My conscious mind trudged through my subconscious fog. I don't do drugs, don't smoke, and rarely drink. When I have a nip, I prefer scotch, neat.

David Tenderloin was Glen Meadows' best man. Dave had organized the bachelor party. Dave made certain I had a bottle of premium scotch to nurse, with my name on it. I drank half the bottle. Even though I made it a point to drink water along with my scotch, I was feeling the effects.

"Marshall, help."

"Rosie?" I managed to say.

"They think Glen murdered somebody." Rosie Collins' normally silken voice was hysterical. It dragged me all the way back. I bolted upright in bed. My action made the room spin.

"What? Murdered who?" My cotton mouth made the words stick to my tongue.

"Candy."

"Who's Candy?"

"One of the strippers at Glen's bachelor party," Rosie said.

"What?"

"A stripper named Candy was murdered at Glen's bachelor party, and they think he did it. You've gotta help us."

The room stopped spinning. My thoughts felt like they were wading through mud. I closed my eyes tightly and focused. "Where are you?"

"39th Precinct, where they're holding Glen," Rosie said.

"Have you called Harold?" Harold Penshaw was the finest criminal defense attorney in the state, and part of our circle of close-knit friends.

"No darn it. I should have called Harold first," Rosie said in a voice spilling over with frustration. "When I discovered what was going on, you were the first person I thought of."

"Don't worry, I'll call Harold. Don't say anything to the police about anything."

"Please hurry, Marshall."

"I'll be there as soon as I can."

"Thank you."

I hung up and called Harold. A drowsy baritone answered after the fourth ring. "This better be good."

"Glen's been arrested."

"For what?" Harold sounded coherent.  Obviously, he knew when to quit drinking.

"Murder," I said.

"If this is one of your practical jokes, Marshall, it isn't funny."

I filled Harold in on the particulars. I could imagine his keen brown eyes narrowed to slits, his sharp mind zeroing in on the facts. Harold immediately took charge.

"I'll call the 39th and speak to the arresting officer to find out exactly what Glen is being charged with. You get down there and calm Rosie. Did you tell her not to talk to the police?"

"I did."

"Good. I'll meet you there—and, Marshall..."

"Yeah," I said.

"Try not to piss anybody off."

"I'll be on my best behavior."

"Do better than that."

"Right," I said just before we hung up.

I got out of bed, my head reeling as much from the news as from the adverse effects of the scotch. I drank as much water as I could stomach. I don't know if it helped or I simply believed it did.

I took a moment to gather myself. In the bathroom, I massaged my scalp to get blood to my brain, and to give the water more time to dilute the toxins in my stomach.

The man looking back from the mirror did not appear to have suffered from overindulgence. He could use a shave, but other than that, he was the same dashing, brown-eyed, bald-headed, six-one, one-eighty (in good shape) with the tiny plum-colored, egg-shaped birthmark on his right brown cheek fellow as the day before.

The teakettle was boiling and I felt about sixty-five percent by the time I got out of the shower. While my tea brewed (I prefer tea to coffee), I downed a couple of B-vitamins with a cup of tomato juice. I sipped steaming hot peppermint tea sweetened with clover honey and wolfed down a nuked bowl of leftover homemade chicken noodle soup without feeling nauseous. That added another fifteen percent to my recovery. It was good enough to get me on my way.

*        *        *

The 39th Precinct was bustling with law enforcement activity. Rosie was nowhere in sight. I emptied my bladder in the public bathroom before walking up to the front desk to inquiry about Glen and Rosie.

"Well, well, well, if it isn't the hotshot private dick Marshall Freeman," Desk Sergeant Jerry Sikes greeted me with his crooked sarcastic snarl. "What brings you to our fair station?"

"Why, your beguiling wit, of course, Sergeant," I said with equal sarcasm.

"And here I was thinking you were here on behalf of your murdering friend."

Sikes was a good cop, once upon a time. Walking a beat had soured him. It was on the streets that he developed his 'us against them' mentality. Those same streets had dulled his blue eyes and thinned and prematurely grayed his hair. Impartiality had become an inconvenience to him, not an obligation.

"I'm here to make certain my friend has a fair chance to defend himself," I said. "Guilty until proven innocent, I believe is your credo."

Sikes hated me. As far as he was concerned, there were too many times where I had proven his police department wrong in their rush to judgment on so-called rock-solid cases. It didn't occur to him that the service of justice and not egos are something we should both have in common.

"We'll see about that." Sikes' snarl tightened into a self-righteous sneer.

"Where is he?" I asked.

"You're not family," Sikes said. "I don't have to tell you nothing."

"He's my client," I said.

Sikes checked Glen's visitors list. "I don't see your name here. Guess that means he forgot to tell us about you, or you're making it up."

"What about his fiancé?" I asked. "Where's she?"

"None of your damn—"

"Your client is in conference with his fiancé and his attorney." I turned to find Homicide Detective Aaron Powell standing tall and strong as an oak, and just as broad. He was a man who exuded a quiet confidence behind his disarming baby face and piercing hazel eyes.

Hard to believe he had been doing homicide for eight years, twelve years total, on the force. Aaron and I shared the same views on justice. His only interest was capturing the people responsible for the crime, not padding his collars at anyone's expense.

"Let's talk, Marshall," Powell said. Sikes' snarl went from me to the detective. I walked with Aaron. I could feel Sikes' eyes burning holes in our backs.

"What's the deal with you and Sergeant Sikes?" I asked the detective.

"Whattaya mean?" he asked.

"I know why he hates me," I said. "I have a history of showing up the police."

"That you do," Powell agreed.

"I don't apologize for my vigilant pursuit of justice," I said.

"Nobody's saying you should."

"What's your story?"

"Remember the Halsom case?" Powell said.

"Yeah, you did a good job tracking down the killer."

"Glad it met with your approval," Powell sarcastically said.

"I would have solved it sooner," I retorted in kind.

"The case wasn't originally mine," Powell said. "The detectives assigned the case had a man in custody they made for the murderer. As usual, the desk sergeant was bragging about how great those detectives were for closing the case so fast. The detectives sucking up the limelight as if they were the latest reality show celebs.

It didn't smell right—not only to me, but also to other veteran homicide detectives. Our captain was on board with similar gut feelings, and he pressured the investigating officers to dig deeper. The detectives went through the motions and swore they had the right man.

I couldn't just stand by and do nothing, so I took it upon myself to do some off-duty investigating."

"Good for you," I said.

"You're not the only one obsessed with justice in this city."

"So I see."

"Anyway," Powell said, "I found out my colleagues had taken some shortcuts on their way to a conviction. They ignored a couple of vital clues and leads for the sake of expediency, which is not unusual for those guys."

"In short, they're lazy," I said.

"Right. I let my captain know what I'd found. He reassigned the case to me and my partner. We caught the real killer. The detectives in question were reprimanded, and the sergeant was made to look a fool."

"Sikes doesn't need any help in that department."

"Since then," Powell said, "I've been on Sikes' shit list."

"He must have one hell of a long list by now," I said.

"I'm sure he does," Powell said.

We found an empty interrogation room, closed the door, and sat at ninety degrees of each other.

"Penshaw is a damn good defense attorney," Powell said, "but I doubt he'll be able to clear your friend of homicide. We have him dead to rights."

"I don't believe it."

"The vic was strangled with his tie."

"Everyone was wearing a tie at Glen's bachelor party when they walked in," I said. "No one was wearing one long after that, because the strippers tossed them away during the erotic entertainment."

"Only your friend's fingerprints and those of the vic were found on the murder weapon," Powell said.

"Who else's fingerprints would you expect to find on his tie?" I said. "Someone could have worn gloves."

"Actually, someone did," Powell said. "Forensics found evidence on the tie that a pair of black leather gloves were worn when the vic was strangled. I'll bet the lab will be able to find a match to a pair of black leather gloves we found in your friend's home and which, by his own admission, he wore to the party last night."

"I'm sure there's a rational explanation for all of this."

The detective paused as if working out something in his head. "There's something else."

"Do I have to guess, or are you going to spill it?"

"Your friend and the stripper had consensual sex," Powell said.

I was stunned. "You're sure," I said.

"We'll be sure when the DNA results come back, but yes," Powell said.

I knew the detective was being straight with me. Despite common misconceptions, most strippers are not hookers. "Did he confess to it?"

"He did," Powell said.

"Does his fiancé know?" I asked.

"My partner and I didn't tell her, is all I can say."

"What's your bottom line?"

"Your friend had sex with our vic. He realizes what he's done. He knows if his indiscretion gets out, his marriage is over before it's begun. He panics. In a knee-jerk reaction, he strangles Candy (aka Julia Persons) with his tie. He kills Julia to keep his infidelity a secret from his wife-to-be."

"Putting on his gloves first," I said.

"Alcohol clouds judgment," Powell said. "It probably seemed like a good idea at the time."

"Did you find the tie at the murder scene?" I asked.

"Yes," Powell answered.

"Glen had the presence of mind to put on gloves, but he was so drunk, he left the murder weapon behind that would connect him to the vic."

"He's obviously not a professional," Powell said. "Like I said, he panicked. Once he saw what he'd done, fear took over, and he bolted."

"Who saw him leave?" I asked.

"You were there," Powell said. "Did you see our perp leave?"

I didn't like the detective calling Glen a perp, but kept my cool. "No."

"What time did you leave?"

"Eleven thirty-two," I said.

"Was Glen still there when you left?"

"Yes."

"Who else was with him?" Powell asked.

"There were the strippers: Candy—Julia, Kitten, and Magic," I said. "Harold, Dave, Clifford, and Doug were there too. I'm sure any of them can alibi Glen."

"Apparently, everyone but Dave," Powell said. "Glen and Candy left shortly after you did. Dave made Glen promise to take a cab home and call him as soon as he got there. Dave left Glen and Candy alone. He said that if something happened between them, he didn't want to know about it. Were Candy and Glen clicking?"

"All of the women were paying special attention to Glen," I said. "He was the star of the show; they were supposed to."

"You know what I'm asking," Powell said.

"There were no licentious fireworks between Glen and Candy," I answered.

"Humph," Powell said. He didn't believe me. He was smart not to. Candy was very attractive. In fact, all of the women were. I'm sure Glen wasn't the only man in that room having sexual fantasies about them. The detective moved on.

"When Dave didn't hear from Glen after a couple of hours, he became concerned," Powell said. "He called Glen at home, and there was no answer. He tried the hotel room, and there was no answer. Dave went back to the hotel to check up on Glen, expecting to find your client passed out from too much drink. Imagine his dismay when he found a dead stripper instead. Like a good citizen, he called the police. The rest of the physical evidence speaks for itself."

"Where did you arrest Glen?" I said.

"At his home," Powell said.

"Was he sleeping?" I asked.

"Like a drunken log," Powell said. "Dave let us in with a spare key that Glen had loaned him. Even when his house alarm went off, our perp didn't wake up."

"I know my friend. There's no way he could take a human life and be able to sleep. The only thing Glen is guilty of murdering is a song."

"Suit yourself. Thought you'd like to know what you're getting yourself into."

Powell was being straight with me, and I appreciated it. "Thanks," I said.

"Don't thank me. I'm going to do my job. And right now, my job is to follow the evidence and do everything I can to put your friend away for murder," Powell said with resolve.

"Not when I prove he's innocent," I said with equal tenacity.

"Good luck with that," Powell said. "You're going to need it."

*　　　*　　　*

Glen and Rosie were in the lobby when I returned from the public bathroom. Harold was wrapping up the details on Glen's release with the desk sergeant. I joined Glen and Rosie, who were waiting near an egress. They were holding hands as if they were still in love.

"How're you doing?" I asked Glen.

"Been better," Glen said. From the looks of him, I couldn't agree more. Glen looked haggard. It was clear he was having a hard time processing what was happening. His clothes were rumpled, his eyes were bloodshot, and his knuckles had a few minor cuts—disconcerting images for a man who took great pride in his appearance. His wide shoulders slouched, making him look softer and smaller than his ripped five-ten. His coolly confident demeanor was streaked with doubt and confusion. Typically, a fire burned bright in his light brown eyes that matched the fire in his belly. It had dimmed, although not to the degree of Sikes.

My friend and I briefly shook hands and hugged. Rosie and I hugged and planted friendship pecks on each other's cheeks.

"Thanks for your help," Glen said. Rosie added her appreciation with an agreeing nod. She looked more composed than Glen.

We all loved Rosie. She was smart and strong, with nutmeg skin and big brown eyes. Her cheeks appeared narrow until her broad smile rounded and lit up her face. At five-eight, her figure was perfect for a man of my taste: narrow waist, full hips, small-breasted, and a dancer's legs. Her natural hair was woolen, but she wore it straight in the American definition of good hair.

Harold joined us. Harold Penshaw reminded everyone of a young Sidney Poitier with a Pele body he still had from his college soccer playing days. His fashion sense was immaculate conservative professional while working, as he was then, and casual conservative when not. His was the definition of dignity in both manner and speech.

His presence, while unobtrusive, commanded respect. For those who disregarded that message, Harold was quick to rectify the situation.

"Let's get out of here," Harold said. Harold led the way. Rosie and Glen followed, holding hands. I brought up the rear.

"Don't leave town!" the desk sergeant yelled at Glen.

"We'll be shacking up with your wife like everyone else," I yelled over my shoulder. I didn't know Sikes' wife, in any respect. I didn't have to. I knew the statement would infuriate him.

"*You son-of-a—*," was all I heard as we stepped into daylight. Mission accomplished.

"I'm glad you waited until Glen was released," Harold said to me with a knowing smile.

"Told you I'd be on my best behavior," I said as we walked to my car. I asked Glen what had happened, in reference to his cuts.

"Some dude in the holding cell tried to take my shoes," Glen said. "I taught him that wasn't a good idea. A couple of his homeboys wanted to teach me a lesson afterwards, and I took them down, too."

"He put them in the hospital," Harold said, not sounding pleased.

Glen was a part-time tae kwon do instructor with some training in judo and jujitsu. He'd tried his hand at professional kickboxing until he discovered that the time, sacrifice, and hours of training did not literally pay off in the cash column. Since street fighting didn't appeal to him, Glen settled on being a highly paid CPA.

"Kicking ass is not a strong step toward proving your innocence," Harold said.

"Why?" Glen said. "I didn't kill anybody."

"Let's get you home," Rosie said, her silky voice returned. I wondered if Rosie knew the whole story about what had happened with Glen at the party. A furtive nod from Harold signaled to me that she did. Rosie was still there, treating Glen like the man she wanted to marry. That made her all the more amazing, in my eyes.

"Good," Glen said to going home. "Give me a chance to wash the prison stink off."

Harold sat in the front with me, Rosie and Glen snuggled in the back. Glen apologized repeatedly for dragging us into this mess. We tried reassuring him that it wasn't his fault and that we were going to help him clear his name. Based on the worried look in his eyes, I don't think our comforting words helped much.

We chaperoned Glen to his house. Rosie and I prepared a breakfast of Greek omelets, sausage links, tomato juice, toast, and coffee. I would drink tea instead of coffee. Harold called his wife, who had dropped him off at the 39th, to reassure her all was well. Then Harold phoned his office to pawn off and rearrange his caseload with his associates so that he could devote himself to Glen's case.

Once Harold was done wheeling and dealing, he offered to help in the kitchen. Instead, we made him set the table and wait. Three was a crowd.

Harold gave me a furtive look while he waited. We both knew some questions had to be asked of Rosie. There was no tactful way to do it. I gave Harold the nod that I would.

"Rosie, dear," Harold said just as I was about to speak.

"Yes?" Rosie said.

"Where were you between ten and about one last night?" Harold asked.

"Home. Why?" Rosie said.

"Can anyone verify that?" Harold asked.

"My parents and two of my bridesmaids," Rosie said. "You can't possibly think I had anything to do with this?"

"These are standard questions," Harold said. "They have to be asked of everyone involved in an ongoing investigation."

"Really," Rosie said. "Where were *you* during ten and about one last night?"

"I was at Glen's bachelor party until midnight. I took a cab, which the door attendant hailed for me, from the hotel to my home. I arrived at about twelve-twenty-two, after which time my wife can vouch for my whereabouts."

Harold's response was stoic. It seemed to fluster Rosie. "What about you, Marshall?" Rosie asked.

I told Rosie what I had told Detective Powell.

"I can vouch for the fact that Marshall left before me," Harold added.

"Will anyone verify what time you got home?" Rosie asked me.

"My neighbors, Mr. and Mrs. Gorski, were returning from their rounds as part of our neighborhood watch patrol, of which I am a member. We spoke briefly before wishing each other a good night."

"You can't honestly believe I'm capable of murder?" Rosie looked back and forth between us.

"No, we don't," Harold said.

"Everyone is capable of murder," I said.

Harold gave me an exasperated look that let me know I had said the wrong thing.

"You think I could murder that poor woman," Rosie said, "and then turn around and try to pin it on the man I'm about to marry?"

"I'm just saying—" I started to say.

"What kind of a woman do you think I am?"

"It's more of what kind of man I am," I said in a docile voice.

"Excuse me?" Rosie said.

"In my line of work, I'm in the company of people who cheat, lie, steal, and murder so often that I sometimes take things too far with decent people like you. I'm sorry." Harold raised a deft eyebrow to show he approved of my apology.

Rosie stared at me for a hard moment. "Maybe you should change your line of work."

"Maybe I will," I said. "But not before we've cleared Glen."

"I know this a difficult time for you," Harold said to Rosie in a reassuring voice. "You have every right to be upset with Glen. God knows, your wedding day should be the happiest moment of your life— and one day, it will.

"For now, there's a greater good that needs to be considered. A man's future—your fiancé's very life—hangs in the balance. Our questions may seem insensitive and an affront to your character. We ask them with earnest intentions. These are questions police detectives and the DA are going to ask you, just as they are going to ask me, and Marshall, and everyone else associated with Glen.

"These inquiries are part of how our system of justice works. I promise you that when the smoke clears, Glen will be a free man. And you will be a free woman."

Harold's words relaxed Rosie and refocused us on the bigger issue. Glen emerged from his bathroom showered, shaved, and wearing Crocs, a casual shirt, and slacks. While he hadn't completely detoxed from the bachelor party, he looked and smelled a whole lot better. We sat down and ate, somehow managing to tiptoe around the murder charge and a postponed wedding in our polite breakfast conversation.

Glen insisted on cleaning up after breakfast. Harold and I insisted on helping. Rosie called her parents to let them know she would be home soon to tell them all about the situation. Rosie left shortly thereafter. Glen had no such concerns. Glen was an orphan. We were his family.

Harold, Glen and I gathered in the living room. They drank coffee. I drank hot tea. Glen was looking more like his old self even as his predicament loomed large in his eyes. "What happened?" I asked Glen without preamble.

Glen spent the next hour telling us everything he could remember about last night around the time of the murder. Harold listened and took notes. Glen couldn't remember anything from around midnight until the time the police arrested him. It was as if he'd blacked out.

Hearing Glen say he had blacked out was surprising to me. I had seen him drink a fair amount of his favorite tequila at the party. Glen was known for his drinking prowess. Getting buzzed, not drunk, was his thing. Maybe he got carried away, like me, because it was his bachelor party and I'd missed it.

*    *    *

I had already begun the investigation in my head before I left Glen and Harold. I sat in my parked car going over possible scenarios of how the murder had gone down. Unfortunately, the most plausible was the one Detective Powell had laid out involving Glen.

First things first. I called Dana Carter, my personal assistant.

"Primo Detective Marshall Freeman's office. If we can't solve it, it can't be done. How may I help you?"

"Dana, what did I tell you about ad-libbing?"

Dana Carter was forty-three, short, and plump, with cinnamon skin and big brown eyes. She was a sharp, conscientious worker who kept my office in top shape (and me, sometimes, along with it).

Her husband's pet name for Dana was Bubbles—an appropriate nickname for her personality. We had been together for twenty years. I don't know what I would do without her.

"I know, I know," Dana said. "I'm just trying to give the same old worn-out greeting some pizzazz."

"Stick to the old script."

"Old script. Got it. Dry and boring."

"Let's hear it."

"Freeman's Investigations; how may I help you?"

"Perfect."

"Blah," Dana said.

I had to chuckle. "I'm going to have to cancel my appointments for the next few days. Notify my clients. If they're in a hurry, refer them to Dan or Teri."

"What's up?"

I told Dana about Glen. Dana let out a short whistle. "Did he do it?" she asked.

"Of course not! Take care of that for me, will you?"

"No problem, boss. Is there anything else I can do to help?"

"If there is, I'll let you know. Thanks for asking."

"Stay safe."

"Don't I always?"

"No, you don't. That's why I said it."

"I'll do my best, Mom."

"Mom, I like it. You do behave like one of my children sometimes."

"See yah." I hung up on what I'm certain was a playful smile on Dana's youthful face. When I started the car, I knew where my investigation would begin.

*     *     *

The bachelor party for Glen was of the old-fashioned kind: women and booze. I questioned Clifford and Doug face-to-face, both of whom were friends of Glen, Harold, and me. They'd drank heavily at the party and were fuzzy on the details, but there was one thing they were clear on—they had left before Glen and Candy.

I stopped by Thorndale's, the retail drugstore where Dave worked as a pharmacist. Dave took me to their break room, where we could talk. He looked shook up.

"I haven't gotten a thing done today," Dave said, as if he were in shock. "I can't get this murder business out of my head."

"It's still early, yet," I said. "You'll get there."

"How's Rosie?"

"Doing her best."

"This thing with Glen has to be eating her up inside. I'll check in on her later—if you think that's wise?"

"I'm sure she'll appreciate it."

I wasn't surprised at Dave's concern for Rosie. The two of them had been close friends since childhood. He'd only known Glen for a couple of years. Rosie was the one who talked Glen into allowing Dave to be his best man. Glen would have otherwise chosen Harold or me.

"You and Glen were the last people to see Candy alive," I said.

"Yeah. I was beat," Dave said. "Between work, planning, and attending the bachelor party, I was determined to see Glen had a good time. I tried hanging in there with him, but that guy can go all night."

"Tell me about it."

"I thought if I could get him to promise he'd take a cab and let me know when he got home, we'd be good. I even tipped the doorman to keep a lookout for him and make certain he put Glen in a cab. I gave the doorman a slip of paper with Glen's name and address written on it in case Glen was too hammered to remember."

"The police said you became worried when you didn't hear from Glen."

"I did."

"What'd you do?" I wanted to compare Dave's answer to the information Detective Powell had volunteered. It was a cruel trick of the trade to pull on the best man, to test his honesty, but it had to be done.

"After I didn't hear from Glen, I called his house. There was no answer there, so I tried the hotel. There was no answer in his room, and that got me worried.

"I decided to check the hotel room first, expecting to find Glen passed out from too much to drink. When I got there is when…" Dave breathed deeply, looking down at the floor as if seeing Candy's body before him. I thought he was going to lose it. "I found her."

"Relax," I said.

"One reason I became a pharmacist instead of a doctor is because I couldn't handle human suffering. Especially the end result of the direst cases. I didn't have the nerve or stomach for it."

"Not many do." Dave took a moment to compose himself and then nodded to let me know he was okay to continue. "What did you do next?"

"I was in shock. I didn't know what to do. It must've taken me at least five minutes to pull myself together enough to call the cops."

"After you called the cops, what did you do?"

"I couldn't stay in the same room with Candy, so I went down to the lobby and waited for the cops. I tried calling Glen at home again and again while I waited for the police."

"Why?"

"To hear his side of the story; to find out if he knew what had happened to that poor woman. I'm sorry about getting Glen into trouble."

"It's not your fault. You did the right thing by calling the police.

Did you notice anything suspicious or out of place in the room?"

"God, I don't know. The room was a mess from the party. You know. You were there."

"Yeah, I know."

"If there was something missing or out of place, I couldn't tell. To be honest, I was still drunk myself when I went back to check on Glen."

"Did you drive or take a cab when you returned to the hotel?"

"Drove," Dave said. "I know it was stupid, but I had to know if Glen was safe. Rosie would never forgive me if anything happened to her fiancée on my watch."

His dismissing my friend's predicament was becoming annoying, but I had the big picture to bear in mind. Confronting Dave on that issue would have been counterproductive.

"Where did you find the strippers for the party?" I asked.

"The Runway on Broadway."

"I know the place."

"You do?"

"Yes, I do."

"I'm surprised."

"Why's that?"

"You seem like such a straight-laced guy, I wouldn't expect you to be familiar with a gentleman's club."

I didn't explain to Dave that in my line of work, you had at least your toe in all sorts of lifestyles. As far as strip clubs were concerned, to each their own. I was of the mindset to save my money for the special women in my life rather than squander it on a fantasy.

"You obviously don't know me as well as you think," I said.

"You can say that again."

"Do you remember anything else about last night?"

"Only that I wished it never happened."

"Thanks for your help."

"If there's anything I can do, anything at all, please let me know."

"I will."

We shook hands. I left for my car, leaving Dave to try to find his way back to work.

*　　　*　　　*

I returned to the site of our bachelor party, hoping to get lucky. Luck greeted me at the front door of the Maple Leaf Hotel, albeit not the kind I'd hoped for. The night door attendant was pulling a double shift. He remembered me and my friends. He remembered Dave giving him the tip and note. He also remembered Glen being sloppy drunk when he poured him into a cab.

Through the door attendant, I was able to track down the cab driver, who I talked to by phone. The cabbie remembered Glen. The cabbie remembered Glen being so out of it that he practically had to carry him into the house.

I didn't have clearance from the police to check the murder scene, so I stayed clear of the room. It's a rule I had taken with a grain of salt in the past, but I didn't want to take any chances of making things worse for Glen.

The hotel swing, then night shifts, were on duty at the time of our party. The swing shift started at four, the night shift at midnight. I would be back to talk to them if the case was still floundering by then.

*　　　*　　　*

Tony Pirelli was the owner of The Runway, a five-star gentleman's club and a happily married man. He wore an expensive suit, shoes, shirt, and tie. His grooming was impeccable and his manner sophisticated and polite.

To look at Tony, one would regard him as a successful businessperson. And you would be right. Beneath his sophisticated exterior lurked a man who could get down and dirty with the best of them.

I had worked a few investigative jobs for Tony, two of which exonerated him of murder charges. While Tony would break a few bones, he was by nature not a murderer. He was quick to assist when I asked for his help.

"Good to see you, Marshall," Tony said. We shook hands. My hand got lost in his paws. Tony was a big man, six-six and a solid two-sixty. An ex-pro football player, he had kept himself in good shape. His wife said Tony was vain regarding his appearance, a fact she alluded to that she loved about her man.

"Likewise," I said. "Only I wish it could've been under better circumstances."

"You're welcome anytime, Marshall."

A few dancers were working a sparse afternoon crowd. The crowd appeared more interested in their drinks than the sexy woman lobbying for tips. Tony led me to his office in the back. The woman I needed to talk to were gathered there.

"I remember you," Kitten said when I walked in.

"You were at that bachelor party last night," Magic said.

"That's what I'm here to talk to you about."

Fantasy, Kitten, Diamond, and Magic were the names I knew them by. I elected to work with their stage names, at least for the time being.

"Big Daddy, I can't stay long," Fantasy said. "I've got a tort exam tomorrow and I really need to study."

"And I'm due to start my shift in half an hour," Diamond said.

"I'm sure Mr. Freeman won't keep you ladies long," Tony said. "Answer his questions directly and honestly and you'll be out of here in no time. Isn't that right, Marshall?"

"Absolutely."

The woman who worked for Tony called him Big Daddy because he was just that. He looked after them. He paid a decent wage, the dancers kept all of their tips, and they had health insurance and a 401K plan.

What he expected in return was professional behavior. That meant no drugs, fitness, good hygiene, punctuality, and no hustling or prostitution. Nothing went on at his club except stripping, drinking, and dining. If anybody got out of hand, it was remedied with extreme prejudice. If Tony discovered any of his employees were involved in illegal activities, even outside of his jurisdiction, he'd place them on notice. If they didn't clean up their act, Big Daddy saw no choice but to terminate their employment.

"I'll leave you in Mr. Freeman's capable hands," Tony said. "Be nice, Marshall."

"Aren't I always?" I said.

"No, you're not," Tony said. "That's why I said it."

Tony left with a smile, but we both knew he meant what he'd said. From the looks on their faces, the woman knew it, as well. Even dressed in casual clothes, these women were striking. If a straight man were to see them on the street, in a mall, at a grocery store, or at a dance club, they would, at the very least, look twice to admire what they had to offer.

The strange thing about me is that all that goes by the wayside when I'm on a case. Especially a case that was as close to home as this one.

"I get the gist that stripping isn't the only thing you ladies do," I said.

"I'm studying for my law degree," Fantasy said.

"I'm studying to become a nurse," Diamond said.

"Still searching," Kitten said.

"Three more months and I'll be a licensed electrician," Magic said.

"All of you are single?" I asked.

"I am," Diamond said.

"Why are you interested?" Kitten asked. They laughed.

"I'm interested in establishing a motive on why Candy was murdered." My statement established a somber mood. I wasn't sorry.

"How well did you know Candy?" I asked.

"She was one of our sisters," Magic said.

"Know if anyone might want her dead?" They all shook their heads.

"Candy was a sweetheart," Diamond said.

"She'd give you the shirt off her back—no pun intended," Kitten said.

"If you needed a favor, Candy came through more than most," Fantasy said.

"Did she have any enemies?" I asked.

"If she did, I couldn't tell you who they were," Magic said. The other women nodded their heads in agreement.

"How did you ladies come to work the bachelor party last night?" I asked.

"Candy asked us if we were interested," Kitten said.

"Obviously, we said yes," Diamond said.

"Did you know any of the men at the party before last night?" I asked.

"I knew Dave," Fantasy said.

"Yeah, he's a regular," Diamond said. "Big tipper."

"I've seen Clifford and Doug in here on occasion," Magic said.

"Me too," Kitten added.

"Did any of them ever approach you about doing anything other than dancing?" I asked.

"Not me," Fantasy said.

"Me either," Magic said. Kitten and Diamond shook their heads no.

"Was Candy a prostitute?" I asked.

"Hell no!" Diamond said.

"I dare you slander her name," Fantasy said.

All of the women leveled their displeasure at me in a stream of loud, vociferous protests that left me waiting to stem the tide. The door burst open and, to no one's surprise, Tony rushed in. I had assumed he was listening at the door.

"Alright, alright, let's settle down," Big Daddy said. The women did as he asked. "Maybe you'd better leave, Marshall."

Tony didn't scare me. No one did. It would do no good to anger anyone in that room any more than I already had. I gave a heartfelt apology. It was graciously accepted—not that I wouldn't do it again if I thought it necessary.

"Is there anything, anything at all, that you remember about last night that seemed unusual?" I asked the women. They thought for a moment. Diamond, Fantasy, and Magic shook their heads.

"Nothing," Kitten said. "You guys were well behaved as far as bachelor parties go."

"It's a shame, really," Fantasy added with a smile. Her smile seemed to spread to the rest of the women.

"That was a room full of good-looking men," Magic said.

"I wouldn't have minded being a little naughty last night," Diamond said, winking at me. The women laughed. Tony shot them a stern fatherly glare. They stopped laughing, shifting to mischievous grins and suggestive stares.

"Have you talked to Benny?" Diamond asked.

"She was still seeing that guy," Tony said with surprise.

"Unfortunately, yes," Fantasy said.

"Who's Benny?" I asked.

"Candy's sleazeball boyfriend," Kitten said with a sorrowful shake of her head.

"He puts the ooze in slime," Magic added.

"I told Candy to stay away from that punk," Tony said like an indignant father.

"We did, too," Kitten said.

"A lot of good it did," Magic added.

"He was her bad boy," Fantasy said.

"What's Benny's last name?" I asked.

"Higgins," Tony spit out.

"Has anyone seen Benny since Candy's death?" I asked.

"He's not welcome around here," Tony said. The women agreed.

"Do you have an address for this guy?"

"No, but I know someone who might," Fantasy said. Fantasy sent a text from her cell. Within a minute, I had the address of the sleazeball boyfriend.

"Thanks for your help, ladies," I said.

"Come back and see us anytime," Kitten purred.

"Day or night," Magic added with a wave.

I smiled and left with Tony, hearing their giggles but not looking back.

"If you find out that punk did this to Candy, will you let me know?" Tony said. As I said before, we're all capable of murder. I could see the bloodlust in Tony's eyes. It was my turn to get hardass.

"If I find out you've done anything to this Higgins guy, the police will be so far up your ass, you'll need a crane to get 'em out. Leave this investigation to me. Understood?"

Tony thought about it for a long, hard moment. "Understood," he said through clenched teeth.

"Good. I'll keep you posted if he's the killer. The Justice Department will take it from there."

"You do that," Tony hissed.

I left while I could still walk.

*　　*　　*

A man answered the Lower East Side apartment door after my third series of raps. He was as pale as a corpse. He wore a dingy, baggy terrycloth bathrobe that was too long for his thin five-five frame. The purple corduroy slippers that stuck out from the bottom of his robe were too big for his feet. The scraggly beard did not help his doughy face. His flat blonde hair reached just below his ears. His murky blue eyes were red, as if he had been crying. He smelled like vomit and the 750 ml bottle of Wild Turkey 101 he had nearly consumed.

What Julia Persons saw in this guy, I'll never know. Chock it up to another mystery of allure.

"What?" he said, fighting to maintain his balance.

"Are you Benny Higgins?" I asked.

"Who wants to know?" His speech was slurred. I'll bet his vision wasn't doing so well, either.

"My name's Marshall Freeman. I'm a private investigator. I'd like to ask you some questions about Candy."

"Her name is…" He dropped his head as if the weight of his words were too much to bear. "Her name *was* Julia Persons."

"I meant Ms. Persons," I said.

"You're too late. They caught the guy that killed her."

"That's what I'm here to talk to you about. I don't think they did."

He looked at me as if staring through a prism. "You think the bastard that killed my Julia is still out there?"

"Yes sir, I do."

Benny stepped aside and ushered me in with a lazy sweep of his arm. "Want a drink?" he asked, shoving the bottle at me.

"No thanks."

His place was messy, dirty, and smelled like a garbage dump. The roaches and flies were enjoying it. Benny plopped down on the couch without bothering to move whatever was there. I decided to stand.

"What'd you want to know?" he asked, as if words and thought were exhausting.

148

"How long have you known Julia?"

"'Bout a year."

"You were a couple?"

"I was going to ask her to marry me."

"You loved her."

"Yeah, I loved her." Benny took a swig of what was left in his bottle.

"Did she feel the same?"

"*What the hell's that supposed to mean?*" he asked, his grief belying his outrage.

"I mean, did she love you?"

"*Of course she loved me, you fuckin' asshole.*" Benny took another swig of his liquid comfort.

"Her friends at The Runway seemed to think differently," I said, waving away a couple of pesky flies.

"What the hell do they know?" Benny leaned forward in a drunken lurch. "They don't like me because I'm in the porn business."

"Are you?"

"I'm a producer. Let me show you some of my work." Benny attempted to stand.

"Don't bother; I'll take your word for it." Benny stopped moving with a heavy drunken sigh. "Was Julia in the business with you?"

"She was thinking about it."

"As a producer, director, writer, or actor?"

"All four. Julia had the talent. She needed time to decide if it was for her. I warned her that once you take that step, there ain't no turning back. She said if the thing at the bachelor party went okay, then she'd know if she was up for it."

"What thing at the bachelor party?"

"She wouldn't tell me. Julia said it was hush-hush."

"She left you hanging."

"Julia said she had something extra lined up at the party. If she could do it, then she could do porn."

That explained a lot. I needed to talk to Glen. I thanked Benny for his help. He nodded and finished off his bottle, sinking deeper into depression and heartbreak. I let myself out.

*     *     *

The afternoon was clear, but crisp from the autumn air. Glen looked remorseful. I walked in to find Rosie setting on the edge of the couch, appearing agitated. Today was supposed to be their wedding day. Instead, I imagined they had been discussing Glen's infidelity.

I apologized for the interruption. They told me it was okay and offered me a seat. I sat next to Rosie. Glen offered me refreshment. I declined. My presence had apparently forced a truce.

"I'll leave you two to talk," Rosie said, standing to leave. I lightly grabbed her arm and asked Rosie to stay. She curiously conceded and sat down, sliding back in her seat.

"If we say anything that makes you uncomfortable, please feel free to leave," I said to Rosie. "I think this is something you'll want to hear." Rosie nodded.

"Have you got something, Marshall?" Glen asked.

"What's the last thing you remember about last night?" I asked Glen.

"Laughing it up and enjoying the party ... drinking," Glen said. Rosie looked away. Glen kept his eyes on me.

"Do you remember any of us leaving?"

"Sure."

"Are you certain?"

"I remember that Diamond and Fantasy left first," Glen said.

"Right," I said.

"Then, you left after them ... then Magic ... Doug ... Harold and Kitten," Glen said. "It gets unclear after that."

"Is this really necessary?" Rosie asked.

"Just bear with us," I said, firmly but gently squeezing Rosie's hand. Rosie appreciated the gesture. With a nod of her head, we knew it was okay to proceed. "Unclear how?" I asked Glen.

"It was like I was in and out of consciousness."

"Do you remember when that blurred sensation started happening?"

"Not long after Harold left."

"I've know you a long time, Glen, and you can handle your liquor."

"True," Glen said with an agreeable nod.

"From what I recall, you were taking it easy on the booze because you wanted to be clear-headed for your wedding."

"'That's right." Rosie smiled briefly at Glen's thoughtfulness.

"Do you remember ever blacking out from drinking before?" I asked Glen.

"Not since I was a teenager," Glen said. "That's when I learned my lesson."

"What are you getting at, Marshall?" Rosie asked.

"I think Glen was drugged."

"*What?*" Rosie said.

Glen looked at me in total disbelief. "What in the world makes you think that?" he asked.

"I'm not sure."

"Do you think one of the strippers did it?" Rosie asked.

"I'm still working on that."

"Why?" Glen asked still stunned.

"That's what I'm going to find out. I thought you should hear this too," I said to Rosie. "Your fiancée was set up."

*    *    *

I returned to The Runway to ask Tony if he knew if the women who performed at Marshall's bachelor party were the only ones who were asked. Tony said he didn't know, but allowed me to nose around. A late afternoon crowd had shown up to pack the club. It took a couple of hours and two hundred dollars worth of tips, but I found what I was looking for.

I called Detective Powell to ask him to meet me to discuss Glen's case. He was hesitant. I won him over by agreeing to buy dinner.

Over an early dinner, I laid out for the detective my theory of how and why Candy's murder went down. He listened intently as we ate. I could tell we were on the same page by the time we were having dessert.

*       *       *

Dave invited me in. He said he had just gotten off the phone with Rosie, and that she wasn't doing so hot. He offered me a drink. I told Dave no thanks to the drink, but took the seat in the living room chair he offered.

"Dave, you know I'm working on Glen's murder case," I said.

Dave shook his head in sorrow. "I still can't believe it. Poor Rosie—poor Glen."

"I've come up with a theory that may exonerate Glen, but I need your help."

"Anything I can do, just name it."

"My theory is that someone else at the party murdered Candy."

"You're kidding?"

"I'm deadly serious."

"Who—it wasn't one of the strippers, was it?"

I took a deep breath before speaking. "It was you, Dave."

"*Me*? Are you out of your mind? Look, I know Glen's your best friend and we haven't known each other that long, but to accuse me of murder is insane."

"Do you remember Peaches and Honey?" I asked.

"Were they at the bachelor party?"

"They strip at The Runway."

"Their names don't ring a bell."

"They remember you."

"Could be," Dave said. "I go there often enough." His indignity was bowing to apprehension.

"They remember you because you made them an offer. It was a very specific offer of prostitution."

"*Excuse me*."

"You offered them twenty thousand dollars to have sex with Glen at his bachelor party."

"I don't know who you talked to, but you're nuts."

"Ten thousand up front, the other ten the day after the party."

"You're crazy."

I was beginning to smell fear. "They get money-for-sex offers all of the time, but offers that rich don't come along every day."

"You're delusional, Marshall."

"Candy accepted your offer."

"There was no offer."

"I forgot to ask myself the age-old homicide question: who stood the most to gain by Candy's death?"

"It was an insane reaction to a bad situation. Glen had too much to drink. He banged Candy. He became panicked that Rosie would find out about it and killed the stripper."

"That's exactly what you wanted everyone to believe."

"You're as crazy as Glen."

"You're in love with Rosie."

"We've known each other since grade school; of course I love her. She's one of my oldest and dearest friends."

"I've seen the way you look at Rosie. That's not a look of friendship."

"So what, if I do have deeper feelings than friendship for Rosie. That doesn't make me a killer."

"The bedroom closets of the Maple Leaf Hotel have operable wooden louver doors."

"So?"

"Someone could hide in the closet, and if they were quiet, could see without being seen."

"And?"

"On a tip from yours truly, I asked the lead homicide detective to have a forensic specialist dusts those louvers for fingerprints."

"There must be dozens of fingerprints on those doors."

"Not that many, but yours were amongst them."

"I was in the bedroom. I probably touched them at one time or another. You go through the bedroom to get to the bathroom. I don't remember. I was drunk."

"I doubt you were drunk at all. According to the forensic expert, the way your fingerprints were positioned could have only happened if you were inside the closet."

"Don't be ridiculous."

"Why were you in the closet, Dave?"

"I wasn't."

"There's something else."

"More insanity, I take it."

"The police lab tested Glen's gloves and they found traces of dried perspiration and skin cells that didn't match Glen's."

"What are you saying?"

"Someone else wore Glen's gloves when they strangled Candy."

"If that's true, why haven't the police figured it out before now?"

"The case looked open and shut. Drunken fiancée has sex with stripper, panics, and kills her in an attempt to hide his shame."

"That's exactly what happened. All of the evidence points toward Glen. I'm sorry, but Glen looks guilty to me, too."

"That's the way you planned it."

"Planned it? Planned *what*?"

"To frame Glen."

"This is a desperate attempt to save your friend. I'm not going to let you frame me to do it."

"Candy's real name is Julia Persons, by the way—but you already knew that."

"How would I know that—or even care?"

"Because the police found some of the upfront money you gave Candy back at her apartment in a brown envelope. Guess whose fingerprints were all over the envelope and cash?"

"Yours," Dave sarcastically said.

"Try again." Just when I thought Dave was about to go over the edge, a disturbing calm set in his eyes.

"This is all speculation. My lawyer will tear this apart. It'll never make it to trail."

"The whole doctor and pharmacist's story was b-s," I said.

"Pretty much, human suffering and dead bodies don't bother me at all. I simply enjoy being a pharmacist."

"Good performance."

"I thought so."

"You love Rosie."

"I've already stated that."

"I mean, you adore Rosie."

"What's your point?"

"You want to marry her."

"Rosie deserves better than that asshole friend of yours for a husband. She deserves me."

"*You*," I said.

"Yes, me. I've loved her since grade school and I've been waiting for her to recognize that she has the same feelings for me. And she was about to when that wannabe Casanova came along and blinded her to real love."

"Rosie and Glen love each other. Rosie sees you as a good friend—that's it."

"She'll come around; especially after that idiot fiancée of hers was caught cheating on her on the night before her wedding. Whose shoulder do you think she was crying on when she found out? Mine. Give her some time to get over that moron and I'll pop the question. Then she and I will be standing at the altar. Play your cards right and you might get an invitation to our wedding."

"You were in the closet filming Candy and Glen having sex."

"You're damn right I was. I paid Candy to have sex with Glen. And, let me tell you, she was worth every dollar."

"You drugged Glen to make certain it would happen."

"He would've done it without the drug inducement, but I wanted insurance. He performed well, I'll give him that. I have digital proof that I'll now have to destroy for the sake of freedom."

"Why'd you kill Candy?"

"She had a bout of guilt after it was over. She was sorry she did it, and didn't want to be the cause of breaking up a marriage. Candy said I could have my money back and that she was going to tell Rosie that the whole thing was a setup. I couldn't allow that to happen."

"So you killed Candy."

"I tried to reason with her. I even threatened her with the prospect of jail time for prostitution, but she didn't care. It wasn't right, and she said something else about the porn business not being right for her, either."

"Then you killed her."

"You keep saying that. Glen staggered into the living room after he had sex with Candy. I went in to check on him—"

"You mean, you went in to see how much of your conversation with Candy he might have overheard."

"Okay, if you insist," Dave said, a self-righteous smugness taking hold. "Your buddy Glen had passed out on the floor. When I saw his tie and gloves, the idea came to me—if Glen's in prison, there'll be no chance of reconciliation between him and Rosie. I did what I needed to do before I sent Glen on his way."

"What do you mean, 'sent Glen on his way'?"

"What do I have to do draw you a map? I got Glen dressed, out the door, and on the elevator. Once he got to the lobby, the doorman did the rest."

"You planted the gloves on Glen, but left the tie."

"The tie was the murder link. The gloves were his. They weren't a plant. To be honest, I never thought the cops would make the gloves connection."

"You stayed and waited until enough time had passed to call the cops."

"No, I left. I snuck out of a back entrance, through the alley, to my parked car a few blocks away, drove home, and waited."

"Why'd you go back to the hotel? Why not wait for room service to discover the body?"

"I thought of that, but then it dawned on me. What better way to divert suspicion from myself than to be the person to call it in. Good citizen bit and all."

"It also gave you a chance to stitch together your story any way you'd like."

"Now you're catching on. You're brighter than I gave you credit."

"You murdered that young woman for Rosie."

"Love is a powerful motivator. 'Make you do right, love'll make you do wrong.'"

"You're quoting Al Green, now?"

"Why not? It's appropriate. It was an easy setup for your dim-witted friend."

"You're a twisted fool."

"I'm in love. What about you?"

"You know I'm going to the police with this."

"Go ahead. By the time they get here, the evidence will be long gone and it'll be your word against mine. I mean, you are best friends with the prime suspect, and despised by a fair amount of the police department and DA's office. Who do you think will end up the winner?" Dave didn't wait for a response. "You can let yourself out."

I opened the front door. In walked Detective Powell with four uniformed police officers.

"What's this?" Dave asked. Detective Powell walked up to Dave.

"David Tenderloin, I have a warrant to search your premises." Detective Powell slapped Dave in the chest with the warrant. Dave's smugness twisted to anger as he took the warrant.

"You can't do that!" Dave shouted at the detective.

"I can and I will." Powell was nonchalant in both words and actions. He signaled for three of the four officers to begin their search of the house. "I don't suppose you're going to tell us where you're hiding the sex recording?" Powell asked Dave.

"I don't know what you're talking about," Dave said.

"Suit yourself." Detective Powell signaled for the remaining uniform to cuff Dave.

"What are you doing?" Dave protested.

"David Tenderloin, you're under arrest for the murder of Julia Persons," Detective Powell said.

"You can't arrest me. I haven't done anything." The uniformed officer spun Dave around and cuffed him. "I want my attorney," Dave said.

"Take him to my car, and don't forget to read him his rights," the detective said to the uniform. The uniform read Dave his rights as he led the loudly protesting criminal away.

Powell and I stood side by side, surveying the house interior as if evaluating a painting. "How'd I do?" I asked.

"You're ready for prime time," Powell said.

"The wire worked, I take it."

"Like a charm. This case is a slam dunk."

"I've heard that before."

"This time, it is."

"You know that Sikes is going to be mad at you," I said.

"I'll live. Thanks for your help."

"Can I get that thanks in writing, or better yet, on digital. Because no one is going to believe that a police officer from the 39th ever thanked me for anything."

"It'll be our little secret. You think your buddy Penshaw will defend Tenderloin?"

"Not him or anyone at his firm."

"Good to hear. What was up with that 'I'm going to the police' line?"

"Simply making the perp aware of my intentions," I said.

"If I didn't know better, I would've thought you were trying to bait him."

"Bait him for what?"

"Provoke him into attacking you so you could beat the crap out of him and call it self-defense."

"Just because he tried framing my best friend for murder and ruined his marriage before it ever got started? Why would I do that?" My bitter sarcasm wasn't lost on the detective. I handed Powell the tiepin, camera, and transmitter device and walked away.

"Where are you going?" Powell asked.

"To see a friend."

*     *     *

When Glen answered the door, he looked as if the world had been dropped on him.

"What's wrong?" I asked.

"It's over," Glen said. "Come in."

I waited until we were seated before following up with, "What's over?"

"Rosie and me. She got an anonymous DVD of what happened with me and Candy at the party. That's what we were talking about the last time you were here."

"Dave sent it."

"*What?* I thought it might have been one of the strippers."

I explained to Glen about Dave.

"I knew he was a squirrelly bastard, but I never imagined he'd do something like that," Glen said.

"Once Rosie learns the whole truth, maybe you two can work it out," I said.

"I hope so. Rosie's the only woman in the world for me."

"When the time is right, tell her that."

"I can't even look her in the eye."

"I know a relationship counselor who might be able to help."

"How in the world do you know a relationship counselor? You've never been in a relationship long enough to be counseled."

"I met her working on one of my cases—never mind. You just show up and do what she says."

"I'm up for that. I doubt Rosie is."

"Harold and I will handle Rosie. We'll bring her around."

"Harold can talk the spots off a leopard."

"What about me?"

"You just show up and do what Harold says."

I shook my head and smiled.

"Thanks for everything, Marshall," Glen said in a solemn voice. We stood shook hands and hugged.

"No problem," I said from the heart.

"I can't believe Dave set me up like that."

"Love will make you do crazy things."

"But, drugging me and murder … I can't get my head around that. If Rosie and I do reconcile, I think we'll elope."

"That's probably for the best. I know one thing for sure."

"What's that?"

"My bachelor party will be just the guys. We're going bowling, and the strongest drinks being served will be sodas."

"Make mine a 7 Up," Glen said. "Want some tea?"

"I could go for a cup."

"I've got a Tai blend I had made up just for you. I'll make us a cup."

We headed for the kitchen. "A sandwich would go nice with that tea, and maybe some salad."

"You know where everything is."

"So much for hospitality."

"Friends can make themselves at home, especially those as close as

brothers."
     I couldn't argue with that.

# GENE

My name is Gene Oliver Stanton. I'm the second of four children, sandwiched between two brothers and a baby sister. I'm fifty-six, independently wealthy, and African American.

I have short silver and black dreadlocks that at times I switch to cornrows (and, on occasion, a small neat Afro). My eyes are dark brown. My normal skin tones range from tan to copper, dependent upon my length of exposure to the sun. I have a clean-shaven, oval baby face framed with average ears. My Roman nose sticks out from the middle of my face and my full lips—when static—arc down toward a square chin. When I smile, I have deep-dish dimples and perfect white teeth. At six-three, I weigh in at 187. I'm in good shape for a man of my age due to my workout regimen and healthy eating habits.

As I've said, I'm African American. I don't sound or behave like the American entertainment stereotype we are constantly fed about who we're supposed to be. The impolite of my people might call me 'uppity.' That's their choice. I can handle that backhanded insult, just as it is my choice to refer to my detractors as 'ghetto' or 'ignorant.'

Frankly, it's rather disappointing. Poverty is a major deterrent to many things, but you do have an individual choice on how to conduct yourself. Uppity, I'm not. I am articulate and educated, and unashamed of either. If that brings out the worst in someone, that's his or her problem; not mine.

I didn't start out rich, but made my fortune over the years. I have a higher education and a real world expertise in both domestic and international commerce and economics, topped off with a penchant for profitable trends and stalwarts.

In short, I have an affinity for making money—which is interesting, seeing as I come from a household where my mother is a civil rights attorney and my father is a tenured sociology professor.

What sets me apart from many of my by-the-book colleagues is I have a knack—maybe even a gift—for knowing exactly what to do and when.

I'm not bragging; it's just fact. Early in my career, I earned big money for others. Then I wised up and did it for myself, as well.

I have four children. I love them all. In the game of committed love, I'm batting oh-for-four. In high school, I paid close attention during sex education classes. I even heeded the warnings of relatives, friends, and Unplanned Parenthood, taking the necessary precautions most of the time.

Love has a tendency to lull you into dropping your guard. Before you know it, a haymaker that you never saw coming floors you. My intentions for starting a family were simple and basic: marriage before childbirth.

Life has a way of making a mockery of your best-laid plans. While I managed to obtain my professional goals with relative ease, my personal objectives didn't quite turn out the way I imagined.

I remember the day we met. I had just moved to New York City from Harrisburg, Pennsylvania, where I was born and bred. I landed a job as a financial counselor with Haben Investments, a high-end investment firm in Harrisburg, right after graduating from Howard with degrees in Finance and International Business.

I moved up the ladder rather quickly. Besides my numbers-crunching acumen, my investment instincts were razor sharp. The firm was making money hand over fist from me, and they wanted to exploit my talents to the fullest before another firm snatched me up—or, worse yet, I ventured out on my own, taking my client base with me.

I wasn't doing too badly for myself at the time. My personal investment portfolio was growing by leaps and bounds, earmarking the secret of my success. Besides implementing the general investment philosophy of taking the long view on market cycles and keeping a sharp eye on risks, I never offered any asset advice to a client that I wasn't willing to commit to myself, no matter what brokerage properties we were told to push.

You have a tendency to be especially careful with what venture choices you're willing to make when your own money's on the line. You could call it ethical, but I can't see doing business any other way.

Haben transferred me to the New York office inside of a year. They wanted to fast track me up the ladder, so they sent me to the fastest track in the nation to learn from the best.

It was a blistering, humid summer day in late July. I'd only been in New York for a couple of weeks, and work was all I knew. There was no deer-in-the-headlights big city culture shock for me. I had visited New York City enough times with family, friends, and on my own to know the lay of the land.

She was walking down Wall Street toward me wearing a bright striped bikini top, cutoff jean shorts, white tennis shoes, and mirrored sunglasses. Her skin glistened in the sunlight like clover honey. My first thought was that she was gorgeous. If she were fine jewelry, royalty would wear her.

Her wavy dark brown hair was pulled back away from her face into a long ponytail, exposing her full round face, Castilian nose, and lush lips. I was so mesmerized by her beauty that it took me a moment to realize my right thumb had been in the cab door when I slammed it shut. A flurry of expletives later and a gradual dulling of the raging bolt of pain from my thumb, and I had met my first wife.

Her name was Carmelita Sarita Theresa Sanchez. I got my first peek at her delicious big brown eyes when she removed her sunglasses and hooked them into her sun-kissed glistening cleavage in order to examine my throbbing wound.

Her eyes were the same honey color as her skin, and radiated the kind of warmth that could tame a despot. I remember thinking *lucky shades* as she held my hand in her own; hands as smooth as silk and soft as cotton. I remember the chlorine smell of her hair hovering only inches away from my nose, along with the dulcet sound of her voice.

Carmelita had darted to my aide. When I say darted, I mean that literally. I later discovered that Carmelita had run the 100- and 200-meter track events in college. According to her friends, Carmelita was only a few tenths of a second away from making the U.S. Olympic team in both events: facts she modestly acknowledged.

Carmelita had maintained an athletic figure by continuing her college workout with a couple of distinct variances. She jogged instead of running dashes, and her gym workout was lighter than what she had done as a competitive athlete.

Carmelita was a licensed graduate nurse doing her internship at Daniel Hale Williams Medical Center. She was on her way home from the YWCA after enjoying some leisure time in their indoor pool.

Carmelita knew exactly what to do about my injury. She tightly wrapped my thumb in my white handkerchief and maintained firm pressure on it with her left hand. With her right hand, Carmelita flagged down a cab. In no time flat, I was admitted to the emergency room of Daniel Hale (or The D.H., as it's locally known), fixed up, and was ready to go. My angel of mercy stayed with me the entire time, turning my pain into pleasure.

Later that evening, Carmelita allowed me to thank her for her kind assistance by buying her dinner. Her hair smelled of apricots, that evening. It turned out to be the first of many dinners together to come. We liked each other from the start. We fell in love about a year after we met—or, should I say, for Carmelita, it took a year for her to confess it. For me, it happened in about three weeks.

When Carmelita told me she was pregnant, I was stunned. While we had discussed having children, her pregnancy was unplanned. We had used birth control in the form of various contraceptives, absent the pill. One side of me was elated at becoming a father. The other side kept thinking this wasn't supposed to happen until a couple of years after our wedding, which was still three months away.

For a devout Catholic like Carmelita, this was a moral dilemma. For me, it was merely a speed bump in our plans. I suggested we move our marriage up to immediate in order to quell Carmelita's religious concern. Carmelita felt that it wouldn't matter in the eyes of God. We married anyway.

Since we already had the license, we only needed to go to the justice of the peace. With her younger sister and my visiting younger brother acting as witnesses, we were married the day after Carmelita broke her pregnancy news to me.

Afterwards, we told our families about the shotgun marriage and the pregnancy. We also informed them that the wedding was still on. Everyone took it rather well. It wasn't until Carmelita received the full blessings of her grandparents and the Catholic Church that she found peace in our circumstance.

Our healthy 8lb, 4oz son was born on April 23 at 9:16 p.m. after fourteen hours of an intense natural vaginal labor in deliver room 1A at The D.H.

I had never known such all-encompassing happiness as I felt when I held Guillermo Valencia Connor Stanton in my arms for the very first time. My tears of joy wet my cheeks and salted my smile. My first-born child changed my life forever.

To everyone's surprise, when Guillermo was six months old, Carmelita announced she was leaving the Catholic Church. Carmelita said she no longer believed in God, and that being religious was not a requirement for being a good person.

While her new sentiments echoed my own, I never, to my knowledge, consciously attempted to influence Carmelita to adapt to my way of thinking. In fact, I had agreed to raise our son as Catholic out of respect for her beliefs.

Carmelita's family, of course blamed me, the heathen, for her change of heart. One thing seemed to lead to another, from religion to money to cultural differences and miscommunications, until one day a landmine exploded at the core of our connubial lives. My wife, my love, told me she wanted a divorce.

The news floored me. I couldn't sink any lower—or so I thought. I pressed Carmelita as to why she wanted to end our marriage. Once her paper-thin excuses were reduced to ashes, the woman in my life, the woman I loved with all of my heart and soul, confessed she didn't love me anymore.

Specifics on when and why that happened, she couldn't say. Carmelita told me that the day she'd found out she was pregnant was the day she had intended to reveal the truth and call off our Catholic wedding.

Had Carmelita not been a good Catholic, she would have had an abortion and put an end to it all. Her religion didn't allow her freedom of choice in the matter. Carmelita blamed both Catholicism and me for her plight.

When I couldn't talk Carmelita out of divorce, I tried offering other solutions, such as counseling or a trial separation. Carmelita wouldn't hear of it. When I tried convincing Carmelita to give me custody of our son, she went ballistic. While Carmelita may not have initially wanted Guillermo, our son had become the center of her universe. What love she no longer possessed for me, she harbored a thousand times over for our child.

Our divorce was finalized shortly after Guillermo's third birthday. It was an amicable affair, with Carmelita and me deciding on the terms before we approached our divorce attorneys.

Carmelita wanted little compensation from me. My love wanted my assurance that I would remain a constant presence in the life of our son. That was an easy promise to make. We agreed upon child and spousal support, with me giving Carmelita more than she requested.

Carmelita granted me ample visitation rights. I could spend time with Guillermo any time I wanted, as long as I gave Carmelita reasonable notice. It was a contingency I embraced.

In the early stages of our separation, Guillermo was somewhat traumatized, as many children are after a divorce. His fears were drowned beneath a tidal wave of love and support from his parents, grandparents, and the whole of his extended family.

I purchased Carmelita a three-bedroom house in an upper-class neighborhood. I bought a condo for myself a couple of blocks away. Carmelita had finished her residency and had become a fully accredited RN. By that time, she had established herself as one of the elite nurses at The D.H.—a stellar reputation that was making its rounds to other medical care facilities, bringing with it tempting offers to move on.

I wasn't the least bit surprised. Like me, Carmelita had a natural gift for what she did. I tried to convince her to become a doctor, but she wouldn't hear of it. As was her way, Carmelita graciously thanked me for having confidence in her ability to conquer medical school, but that was never her dream. She was content right where she was in her professional life.

I was extremely proud of Carmelita, not only because of her

professional accomplishments, but also for knowing herself so well.

Haben transferred me to Charlotte, North Carolina as part of an executive team to spearhead the branch office that was to be our gateway to the southern market. The new position came with a sizeable salary increase as well as other perks, such as a larger expense account, increased benefits, and a pork barrel portfolio.

Leaving my son was heartbreaking, not to mention that I still loved Carmelita and had fantasies of reclaiming her love. It's tough to say no when the woman you love is encouraging you to make the move. Guillermo was five when I left New York with over twenty million dollars in my coffers.

Leaving my first-born was the hardest thing I had ever done in my life up until that point. Carmelita returned to the Catholic Church, indoctrinating Guillermo to its precepts. I was never clear on what prompted her decision, but I suspect that making peace with her family had a great deal to do with it.

When Guillermo was a teenager, in private he confessed to me that he was doing the whole Catholic thing for his mom, but he really wasn't into religion. I made him promise never to tell anyone else about how he really felt. The last thing I wanted for my son was to be scolded by Carmelita's family in the same way I had been on that subject for much of our relationship.

Guillermo kept his promise. He was good at keeping his word, even as a teenager. My parents say Guillermo takes after me in that regard. I suppose. Now, as a man, Guillermo is making his own way in this world. It makes me chuckle to think that he's become a more devout Catholic than his mother ever was.

*      *      *

In New York, as in Harrisburg, I discovered a minority of people who held the same major principles of personalizing their investment choices as me. Interestingly enough, they, too, were lucrative. In both cases, I turned my client pool over to my kindred counselors.

In Charlotte, I had a major say in personnel hiring. As one quarter of the executive team, I did my best to stockpile our office with like-minded financial counselors. I was one-quarter successful. The other three-quarters reflected the diverse investment philosophies of our team.

Charlotte was quite a contrast to New York. It took some time for me to wind down from the hustle-and-bustle of The Big Apple to become accustomed to the more easygoing lifestyle of Charlotte.

Fortunately, Victor was there to show me the ropes. I stayed with my oldest brother and his family until I found a place of my own. It not only gave me a great opportunity to spend quality time with my brother and sister-in-law, Mia, but with my niece and nephew, Sienna and Noah, as well.

Victor was the principal architect for Prism, a multi-discipline engineering consulting firm. It was a successful company that he and three of his engineering pals started thanks to urging from yours truly for him to strike out on his own. Prism eventually grew from a respected high-demand local company of twenty-two employees to a national, then an international engineering consulting firm with 62 branch offices worldwide.

Mia was an office/personnel manager for a budding Henson rent-a-car company only marginally known throughout North Carolina. A few years later, it would expand like wildfire throughout the Carolinas, Georgia, and Florida, thanks to a brilliant expansion and marketing campaign heavily contributed to by Mia.

And yes, I gave Mia a few pointers along the way to help her out. As I said, I know how to make money. One of the ways to make a sizeable profit is to recognize platinum opportunities when they present themselves. For me, it's like a radar, honing in on those prospects, that never shuts down.

When I go to a restaurant, for example, I find myself evaluating it for whether it's making the most of its earning potential, as much as the quality of its service and cuisine.

Don't get me wrong. I'm a union advocate. I believe in a decent minimum wage, equal pay for equal work, and full benefits for all employees, including stock options, when available. No company or corporation should fatten its bottom line by dismissing employees, slashing benefits, and raiding pension funds. That, to me, is unconscionable. There's no reason we can't all sculpt out a decent living in this free market enterprise system.

Less greed at the top and more motivation at the bottom and that dream could be realized for all, in my opinion; but greed will never voluntarily relinquish its iron grip on anything. Its talons must be pried free like the Jaws of Life liberating accident victims from mangled wreckage.

Granted, I'm very careful with whom I share my personal opinions. In the circles I frequent, far too often, greed *is* good.

A few years after blazing through a number of states along the Eastern seaboard, Henson went national to become the second largest rent-a-car company in the nation, along with a smattering of success on the international front. They parlayed that major success into storage and moving equipment rental offshoots, a diverse move that would place them solidly at number two domestically, as well.

Mia would ultimately ride that success to a Henson presidency loaded to the gills with bonuses and stock options. Along the way, Prism and Henson offered public shares of stock in order to grow. Not only did I invest, but a number of Haben clients were convinced to do the same, and our bottom lines are all glad we did.

But, I'm getting ahead of myself.

In the early years before their tremendous professional and financial successes, needless to say, my big brother and sister-in-law had their hands full with the demands of their burgeoning careers, along with caring for two young children.

Even though I was busy myself, I was glad to lend a hand when I could. I was babysitting when Sienna asked me when her dad would be home to take her to dance class. I knew nothing about what she was referring to, so I gave her dad a call.

Sienna had her first dance class scheduled that Saturday afternoon. Victor was supposed to take his five-year-old daughter. My brother had an afternoon site visit scheduled with one of their biggest clients that he was obligated to attend.

I could tell, when confirming Sienna's class with Victor, that it had completely slipped his mind. There was no way he was going to be able to make Sienna's dance class.

Mia was in a similar situation. My sister-in-law was at the office, where she was most Saturdays, keeping up with the high demand working essentially two jobs required.

I volunteered. For me, it was no problem. I was my own boss, who made my own hours. Victor accepted my offer. Taking my darling niece to her first dance lesson was something "Uncle Gene" was happy to do.

I've always had an appreciation for the arts—an appreciation Carmelita and I shared. We often attended theater, museums, exhibitions, and performances of music and dance. If given a choice of going to The Garden to watch my favorite sport of basketball or attending a quality arts performance or exhibition, I would chose the arts every time.

I delivered my energetic niece to the Little Angels School of Dance. Little Angels appeared to be a modest affair with its handmade sign, red brick face building, and shiny storefront window. On that early summer day, the heavy curtains that covered the window were open. The owner and head dance instructor of Little Angels later confided in me that she preferred curtains to blinds because they reminded her of the stage.

The presumption of modesty of the Little Angels School of Dance was reinforced in the reception area. Parents (or guardians, in my case) were given the option to either drop off their children or wait in the rather snug reception area.

The dance studio was another matter, in regards to size. It provided ample room for students to warm up and perfect the rhythmic arts of modern, tap, and ballet dance. We weren't allowed inside the dance studio during class. I later learned the reason was so as not to distract or make the children self-conscious during their lesson. Since I had Sienna's equally energetic (just shy of two) little brother in tow that day, waiting in the reception area was fine with me.

Sienna's dance teacher was Judith Mitchell. Miss Mitchell (to her students) taught ballet and modern classes to kids ranging from ages 5 to 8, 9 to 12, and 13 to 18.

There were no fireworks when I first met Miss Mitchell. I couldn't deny that I found her striking. She was wearing the standard dance uniform of white tights, a black leotard, and dance shoes, as did all of the female students in her class. At five-nine, her sleek figure and slender neck made grace her staple.

Miss Mitchell had shoulder-length, pencil-thick black braids wrapped in a bun. Her satiny smooth skin was the color of hot cocoa. Her gentle demeanor and dark brown eyes emitted a sense of constant calm. I could gaze into her eyes for eternity and never tire of their light; their serene glow.

Miss Mitchell preferred to be known as a dance educator rather than a teacher or instructor, since she blended dance history with her physical and mental lessons of the art. To me, Miss Mitchell looked very much the part of a dance educator—not a grueling taskmaster, as dance teachers are sometimes depicted, but a firm, gentle coach guiding her students to their fullest potential.

The following week, I moved into a country-style mansion within striking distance of my brother. It had six bedrooms, six baths, and all of the amenities. One bedroom was mine. The second was for Guillermo when he came to visit. The rest were for guests.

Taking my niece to her dance class became our standing date. Sienna had so much fun when I took her the first time that she requested me as her permanent escort. It may have had something to do with her Uncle Gene indulging his favorite niece to choose where we ate afterwards. And fast food was out of the question.

Miss Mitchell always greeted everyone at the door with a welcoming smile and endearing repartee. I didn't take it personally. I've been in sales (so to speak) far too long not to recognize when someone is schmoozing her client base. But there was something about Miss Mitchell that was genuine. Something even the best of us couldn't fake. It struck me like a bolt from the blue on our fourth encounter.

Judith Mitchell loved what she did. She had a passion for dance and education that made her glow. Perhaps it was during that quixotic epiphany or illusion that I developed feelings for Judith (as she insisted I call her when we first met). It was also the day that I asked Judith out on our first date (out of earshot of everyone else, of course). Thankfully, she said yes.

A born and bred Southern girl marinated in the sauce of Southern charm. Miss Mitchell had studied in New York and Paris, professionally dancing with both ballet and modern dance companies once her studies were completed. It was during that professional period that Judith discovered her love for choreography, having had opportunities to choreograph original pieces for her dance companies. Her zeal for educating young dancers seemed to go hand and hand with the latter.

How we fell in love, married, and eventually divorced makes for the stuff of bittersweet memories, now.

We became engaged ten months after we started dating. Judith moved in with me a couple of months later. During our engagement, Judith believed in fate, not contraception, when it came to making love. If it was in the cards for us to have a child together, she was more than happy to accept that fate, no matter the time or circumstance.

My view was a lot more practical. There were risqué, passionate moments when we tempted fate. Fate decided, about five weeks before our wedding, to gift us a child.

Judith had her first major show a few months after we moved in together—'Kaleidoscope,' performed by the Charlotte Dance Company at the Magnolia Theater, a centerpiece of Charlotte performing arts.

Kaleidoscope was an innovative, daring, eclectic, and vibrant work combining ballet and modern dance with a diverse array of jazz and classical music. There was no middle ground with Kaleidoscope. It was either going to be a hit or a miss, and everyone involved knew it.

Judith was as nervous as investors around earnings season, to say the least, and was never truly relaxed until she read the reviews hot off the presses.

Kaleidoscope was a huge success, launching Judith into the realm of 'choreographers to keep an eye on' in Charlotte and ultimately beyond. My fiancée and I continued the late-night celebration at our place with more champagne that had begun flowing at the Concerto restaurant with supportive family, friends, and the CDC, as the locals referred to the Charlotte Dance Company.

We made ourselves comfortable on a white arctic fox fur rug in front of our inviting bedroom gas fireplace. The soft firelight magnified her beauty tenfold.

Judith still hadn't come down from her success high, and the effects of the champagne helped keep her there. I know what it's like to ride that buzz of remarkable achievement. I've been there many times. A moment of magic and lust overpowered us. We threw caution to the wind. I'm confident that it was on that night that our son Xavier was conceived.

A little more than seven months after we were married, Xavier came into our world: 9lbs 2oz of screaming joy. *Man*, that kid had a set of lungs on him.

We couldn't be happier. Carmelita and I had long since moved on. Guillermo was happy. He had a little brother to go along with the little sister that Carmelita and her second husband had given him.

Xavier was four when Judith asked for a divorce shortly after being offered the artistic director position of the Philadelphia Dance Theater. I was shocked Judith wanted to end our marriage. We'd both been busy with our careers. Neither of us had allowed that to effect the raising of our son or our marriage—or so I'd thought.

Judith complained that making money meant more to me than she did. I argued that this wasn't true, citing that she spent as much time advancing her career as I did making money.

My argument went up in smoke when Judith was able to prove that, on average, I spent 70 to 80 hours a week making money versus the 40 to 50 hours a week she spent choreographing, teaching, and overseeing stage and video productions.

The proverbial last straw came at her mom's surprise birthday party. A sizeable profit opportunity popped up at the last minute that I simply couldn't pass up for my clients or myself—an opportunity that required lightening-fast research and an urgent response.

Caught up in the whirlwind of commerce, I lost track of time. For the entire week, I had promised Judith I would be there. When I arrived three hours late, needless to say, my wife was furious. Judith managed to keep her rage in check until we were alone. In the back seat of our chauffeur-driven limousine on our way home, with tears in her eyes, Judith told me, "Making money is an addiction you will never break. For the last time, you've chosen the bottom line over our family."

Carmelita and I had become dear and close friends over the years. My first wife bolstered Judith's claims with her own. Carmelita admitted that she had never fallen out of love with me. She simply came to realize that she could never compete with my money fever.

By the time Judith asked for a divorce, I had amassed a personal fortune slightly over 300 million dollars. Our divorce was far from amicable. Judith wanted half. She got a settlement of 20 million dollars, along with a generous alimony and monthly child support payments.

Years after the dust cleared upon the battlefield of our divorce war,

Judith confessed she'd sought half my fortune out of spite for me having broken her heart. She was furious with me.

Her love had not been enough, or so she'd believed. It had hurt her to the core, and she wanted to literally make me pay.

To her credit, Judith didn't use Xavier as a weapon of revenge. My rights to our son were never in jeopardy. Judith knew without question that our son forever came first in my heart. It was my relentless pursuit of assets that Judith believed I coveted more than her love that was our downfall.

Haben became corporate. It was a logical move, since we were much too big to be a company any longer. The Charlotte office became the corporate regional headquarters for our southern branch, of which I had become president, just as our New York office became our regional headquarters for the northeast. The Harrisburg office became our main headquarters.

We were looking to branch westward. Corporate decided that I was the best person for the job.

I was offered an opportunity to transfer to Kansas to jump-start our corporate presence in the Midwest. After a few years of getting our Midwest region into full gear, Haben made me another offer to do the same in California in order to establish our West Coast presence. Each time, they managed to sweeten the deal so much, it could have given me diabetes.

Somewhere, Haben must have a psychological profile on me. It's the only way to account for knowing what buttons to push to offer me deals I couldn't refuse. It was no longer about money— I had plenty of that. It was the challenge—the challenge of being part of something bigger than myself.

It jolted me with an adrenaline rush that was an even greater high than making money; an insatiable thirst I could never seem to quench.

Judith was partially right. I was addicted to money, but I was also addicted to conquest. That was certainly true in financial matters. Maybe that was true in love, as well. Perhaps once I captured the heart of a woman, my interest waned. It didn't feel that way, but perhaps a part of me, the junkie part of me addicted to making money and conquest, refused to be satisfied with what I had.

Leaving Xavier and Judith was just as tough as leaving Guillermo and Carmelita. I was also going to miss my brother and his family. Still, off to Kansas then California, I went to tackle the major challenges of building something from the ground up.

*     *     *

Carmelita had become the ledger for the providence of my connubial life. In Kansas, I met my third wife. I was attending Kansas Grandest Rodeo. My first summer rodeo was an entertaining and eye-opening experience for a city-bred dude like me.

Try as I might to blend in with my roper boots, bolo, cowboy trousers, shirt, and hat, it didn't work. Your first thought might be because of my race. Not so, since there were a handful of African American cowboys and cowgirls present who didn't garner a second look.

In the same way that I could tell if someone was new to the city, was the same way the rodeo community could tell I was new to their neighborhood by just looking at me.

There are traits (some stark, some subtle) that are intrinsic to any culture that can't be faked. We humans are just like animals when it comes to picking up on those characteristics. My first rodeo could have made for an awkward experience had it not been for my native Haben hosts making me feel right at home.

They introduced this tenderfoot to some good people and showed me the ropes. Before I knew it, I was granted a visitor's pass into the rodeo world and was enjoying myself.

Logan Hawke, our Kansas accounting head, introduced me to her. Margaret Grace Boyle was a robust, five-eight, fresh-faced, radiant Midwestern wheat-blonde rancher with sparkling crystal blue eyes and a smile that made the worst of times melt away. She wore whitewashed jeans that accentuated her firm curves, tucked into her tan leather cowgirl boots, coupled with a heather-gray tank top and denim vest. A pink bandana dipped into her modest creamy white cleavage. From under her ivory-colored straw cowgirl hat flowed an over-the-shoulder side braid. Her quiet confidence masked her bold and adventurous outdoor spirit—a spirit I found intoxicating and easy to embrace.

Carnal sparks flew at our first meeting, although we did our best to hide it. Margaret insisted that everyone call her Maggie. I gave Maggie an open invitation to dinner under the thinly veiled ruse of wanting to discuss the advantages of allowing Haben to become her financial advisor. Maggie accepted my dinner invitation a few days after the rodeo ended. As they say, the rest is history.

Maggie educated me on the contributions of women in the West. She taught me horseback riding, hunting, outdoor camping, and fly-fishing, amongst other things. I taught Maggie about investment and marketing strategies, helped her cultivate a palate for fine arts, and showed her how to drive a Porsche, amongst other things.

Maggie was as comfortable in a cocktail dress at a highbrow function as she was in jeans with folk gathered around a campfire.

I asked Maggie how she managed to co-exist comfortably in both worlds. Maggie turned the question on me and asked how *I* did it. I thought for a few moments before answering, "Better to keep your mouth closed and thought a fool than to open it and remove all doubt." Maggie laughed. She practiced the same principal, but she added that she loved to learn and remained open to new experiences.

Margaret Grace Boyle never did sign with Haben—not even after becoming Mrs. Stanton. She preferred to handle her own financial affairs. My third wife had charisma, elegance, wit, grit, and brilliance. She was another amazing woman willing to commit to a lifelong relationship with me, that I managed to screw up.

*     *     *

Wife number four, I met in San Francisco. Her name was Chiyo Mayonaka Kimura. I overheard Miss Kimura asking at the front desk of our Haben Building about which elevator she needed to take her to the Haben offices. I politely introduced myself and offered my assistance.

Miss Kimura mentioned, as we rode up in the elevator together, that she had a scheduled appointment with Akira Ikeda. I knew Akira, and volunteered to escort Miss Kimura to his office.

When we arrived, I personally introduced Miss Kimura to Akira, giving Miss Kimura one of my business cards before we parted company with the usual mantra, "If there's anything I can do to be of service, please don't hesitate to call."

While I found Miss Kimura very attractive, my gestures were simply good business practices, and I would have done the same for any prospective client. A few days later, Miss Kimura called to invite me to lunch. I accepted.

At five-four, her petite figure was toned from regular exercise and a healthy diet. Miss Kimura had a clear, youthful complexion; a bright, adorable smile (when it suited her), olive skin, and straight raven-black, jasmine-scented, waist-length hair. Behind her hazel eyes seemed to dance perpetual amusement at the world.

On the day we first met, Miss Kimura was wearing pitch black (what I'd heard described as) comfort pumps and a crisp, neat, medium charcoal double-breasted woman's pencil skirt business suit that stated confidence, success, and professionalism.

On the day of our first lunch together, Miss Kimura was casual chic in a strapless red feather print dress with a matching belt at the waist and cork wedges, exuding more of a sensual assurance. In both instances, her make-up, nails, and hair were impeccable.

Miss Kimura bought me lunch at Marea Alta, one of the finest restaurants in San Francisco, as a thank you for my assistance. Over lunch, Miss Kimura (who insisted I call her Chiyo, and I insisted she call me Gene) raved about her Haben financial counselor. I wasn't surprised.

Akira Ikeda was one of our finest advisors and was a Haben star on the rise. I had trained him myself. Chiyo had sold her lucrative West Coast grocery chain to a conglomerate and was looking to cement her financial future with the proceeds. We discussed her investment portfolio for a bit before rippling out to other more personal subjects.

Chiyo had a private school and Ivy League education, excelling at both, plus a great childhood and wonderful college experience. Chiyo could effortlessly bounce from one subject to another, be it business, politics, religion, sports, poverty, education, economy, environment, nutrition, fashion, the space program, or something personal. You name it and Chiyo could astutely converse on the topic.

Successful business blood ran in her family. Her grandfather owned a thriving tire manufacturing company that he sold for a nice profit. Her grandmother owned a successful restaurant that she handed down to her oldest son, who turned it into a profitable chain. Her dad, the middle child, owned a handful of independent automobile parts and supplies stores that he sold to a corporate chain taking half the purchase price in corporate stock that made him quite wealthy.

Chiyo herself accepted startup capital from her parents to build a grocery chain from the ground up, demanding her family allow their sparrow to succeed on her own—which she did. It was a remarkable achievement for a thirty-three-year-old even if she was born with a silver spoon in her mouth.

Chiyo was a positive ball of energy that seemed to remain in motion even when she sat still. She mentioned being engaged twice, but had called off her weddings at the last minute. They were men Chiyo confessed to loving, but could not imagine spending the rest of her life with.

I felt compelled to tell Chiyo about my exes and my children—a fact you would think would warn off most women. Chiyo seemed intrigued.

Whether it was the company, food, ambience, wine, or ease of conversation, we both knew we'd be seeing more of each other as I escorted Chiyo to her car.

Femininity is a quality I cherish in women. It's a trait which, when administered properly, can mesmerize me. Add love to the mix and I'm reeling. Being the polar opposite of masculinity, I suppose that's to be expected.

All of my exes had that power over me to some degree when they chose to exercise it. Chiyo seemed to live in that zone. Some might describe Chiyo as a girly-girl. I'll confess that Chiyo possessed those properties when it came to her personal appearance, style of dress, and behavior, at times. Defining her as girly-girl would be going too far.

Chiyo could throw an internal switch to become as tough and direct as needed without breaking a nail. Her intelligence was never in question, even when she was being chipper—moments that predominately emerged when in the company of family and close friends. I would describe Chiyo as simply being one hundred percent comfortable in feminine skin.

Chiyo and I fell in love during our first year of dating. For me, I believe the feeling crystallized during our first real-world ballroom dancing experience. Chiyo had talked me into taking ballroom dance lessons. It was an ideal I was cool on, at first, but I did it for her. I found I enjoyed it as much as Chiyo did.

We were at a tango club, ready to test our abilities. We were nervously excited. The harder we tried, the more mistakes we made. We finally reached a point where the whole experience became hysterical. We started laughing at our mistakes.

Chiyo has a great laugh. It's like listening to joy manifest itself. We finished our first effort with a bumbling flurry, winding up laughing in each other's arms. I hate to draw on a romantic cliché, but it happened just that way. We were laughing as I held her close. We gazed into each other's eyes. Our laughter faded away right into a kiss. I don't know how long our kiss lasted, but it was enough to draw applause and whistles from onlookers. The rest of the evening was magic. Our dancing even improved.

A few months after our first dance floor kiss, I asked Chiyo to marry me. She said yes. I waited a month before asking Chiyo the follow-up question of how I could be certain she wouldn't bail on me at the last minute. Chiyo coquettedly said I'd have to wait and see.

Thankfully, Chiyo stayed the course. We managed five years of marital happiness and one of a rocky road before lightning struck again. Another extraordinary woman slipped through my fingers because of my money fever and conquest addiction.

If anyone could understand me, I was confident Chiyo would. It didn't work out that way.

While Chiyo could appreciate my drive and focus, she drew the line when it came to spousal neglect. From my unions with Maggie and Chiyo came two wonderful children, daughters Hailey Addison Stanton and Amaya Katsu Stanton, both also conceived just weeks before our weddings. While all of my children may have been conceived out of wedlock, they were born into a loving two-parent home.

*   *   *

I'm a fool when it comes to love. It's a curse I've accepted. My marriage to Maggie and Chiyo paralleled the pattern of my previous two. Each proclaimed me a workaholic whose adoration for money left little room for them. Each filed for divorce on those grounds under the heading of 'irreconcilable differences.' When the root of their displeasure with our marriage was exposed, it always came down to the same cause: I could not show them love in the way they needed.

What never penetrated my thick skull was that Carmelita, Judith, Maggie, and Chiyo had been stating their cases time and time again over the course of our marriage, and every time I vowed to change and failed to do so.

I will say this, in my defense. Making money is important to me. Conquest is important to me. Okay, they may even be obsessions. In my opinion, however, I was the same man after marriage as before the nuptials.

I've heard it said that women don't fall in love with a man for who he is, but who they imagine him to be. It begs to ask the questions of how much of me my exes really loved, and how much my money and power were the main attraction.

Did they ever truly love me to begin with—at least enough to make our marriages work? Didn't they have a clear picture of the man they were committing to before pregnancy and marriage vows?

My family says I'm nuts to ever doubt their love or commitment. Deep down, I know they're right. You can't lie to your heart. At times, I need such logic and the interjection of misgivings to help me cope. I don't regret what we had. Out of each union came an amazing child, and for that I'll forever be grateful to the loves of my life.

The biggest irony of it all is that it wasn't true. I never loved money or financial conquest more than Chiyo, Maggie, Judith, or Carmelita.

It's said that actions speak louder than words. Had I been more proactive in proving my love for them, then maybe at least one of my great loves would have stayed. The truth is, I didn't know how to marshal proof. I don't know that I've learned that lesson yet, to be perfectly honest.

I can see how my exes came to the conclusions they did. When it comes to making money and pursuing financial conquests, I have tunnel vision. I have a tendency to block out everything but the tasks needed to consummate the deals. My emotions are absent during such times. I'm in a pure financial logistics and intuition mode.

My nuclear circle and the majority of my extended family love and accept me for who I am. They know it's nothing personal. My children accept me as I am because I'm their dad. They were often bounced on my knee when they were young as I went about the art of the deal.

Knowing was not enough for my ex-spouses. They wanted me present with them more than I was able. I wish I'd had the insight I now have about myself, so I could have explained it to them. Perhaps we could have worked things out, or at least come to some compromise that would have salvaged our marriage.

Time instructs and takes away. There are often small windows of opportunity to take advantage of good deals in financial matters.

Marriage has offered me those same windows of opportunity in my life. I'm a genius in one area, a total dunce in another. I literally experience a dull headache whenever I think about my failed marriages for too long. It's the sweetest pain I've ever felt, in a twisted way.

At Haben, we developed an axiom. We don't follow Wall Street— they should follows us. We didn't follow Wall Street or financial services down the rabbit hole of economic disaster that they created.

Haben not only didn't need a government bailout or corporate welfare, but aside from a few expected bumps along the way, our investors emerged from the Great Recession even better than before the collapse. These are remarkable accomplishments that make me proud and make me feel good about Haben. I take pride in knowing that my motto of not advising clients to take asset risks you weren't willing to take yourself pumps through Haben's corporate veins.

I'm retired from Haben, after serving as CEO for a decade. I still keep a tight rein over my financial empire and occasionally advise Haben officers on asset matters, now and then. I'm constantly checking the books and making purchases and sales—pretty much doing everything for myself that I have done for clients throughout my career.

It's a snap to stay connected, with today's technology. While I travel the world, I spend most of my time in the States. I like to have easy access to my children, and them to me. Owning a couple of private jets doesn't hurt, in that area.

While my ex-wives were right about me in regards to neglect, that can't be said about how I feel about my children. I guess you could say my children fill the four chambers of my heart, right beside their mothers.

All of my exes have remarried at least once. We've managed to maintain or develop healthy, friendly relationships, with any animosity or bitterness having burned off over the years.

I've just finished traveling the country to spend quality time with my children and relatives, settling in from my family whirlwind tour at my house in Vancouver, Canada.

Guillermo, Xavier, Hailey, and Amaya have gotten to know each other. I'm proud to say they get along well as family. Along the way, I became a Canadian, Mexican, Ghana, and Portuguese citizen because I liked these countries so much.

I've traveled all over the world on many occasions, taking my children with me. I rather regard myself a citizen of the world.

The world is an amazing and sometimes depressing place. For my children and me, our travels (albeit predominately for pleasure) helped solidify my belief that we are connected members of the human family. Those of us most fortunate have a duty to help those in need. Being that my children have or will become multi-millionaires by the time they graduate college (college graduation with parental-approved degrees being a prerequisite for them to receive such inheritance), understanding the privilege and scope of that responsibility was something I wanted them to experience firsthand.

My fiancé joined me in the study where I was checking the New York Stock Exchange, NASDQ, The Dow, S&P, and the Federal Reserve online as a warm-up for my day of trading, buying, and investing. That's right: I'm in love again. Maybe the fifth time's the charm.

Her name is Aabharana Garati Sharma. She is a Canadian citizen by birth. My fifth fiancé has cinnamon skin, a svelte figure, luxuriant curly brown hair, smoky brown eyes, and a disarming, dimpled smile.

Aabharana had entered the study without saying a word, which was so unlike her. Typically, Aabharana announced her coming like the arrival of royalty. Being the only child of doting parents and a trained

Bharatanatyam dancer, that comes as no surprise.

Aabharana moved across the room as if she were floating on air. She was glowing. My fiancé walked up behind me, leaned over, and embraced me, as was her ingratiating habit when she saw me working. Her scents were honeydew and jasmine. Her cheek was soft, smooth, and warm against mine, her smile both playful and alluring. Aabharana could entrance a king cobra with her smile.

"Hello, sweetheart," I said in my usual flat voice when my thoughts were elsewhere.

"Hello, my darling," she whispered into my ear, her words as comfortable and soothing as a pleasant dream.

"I have something wonderful to tell you," Aabharana whispered.

"Um-hmm," I said, half-listening, assuming it was going to be another update on our wedding in a few weeks. Aabharana kissed me again on the cheek, her smile broadening. "Honey ... I'm pregnant."

# THE LAST SERIOUS MAN

The year was 1978. The Alman Brothers drafting/design employees stood in a scraggly single-file line, impatiently awaiting four-thirty on the company timeclock.

At the head of the line, facing forward, stood steadfast and erect the senior man of the department, Franklin Stern, a tall, svelte man with large hands resting by his sides, his cinnamon face a portrait of his last name. His steely-brown, slightly uneven eyes periodically glanced at the eternally slow-moving timeclock.

Franklin had changed a fair amount over the past seventeen years, albeit at a gradual forward march of time. His wavy hair was as natty as ever. Its only difference was its harmonious mix of distinctive silver, immaculately wedded to jet-black. A youthful, muscular face populated by a few worry wrinkles added to his tapestry of age. His aquiline nose still stood proud; his chin was dimpled, square, and strong. His ten-year-old tan cashmere coat fit just as it had when he had bought it. Regular workouts and a keen eye on his diet had helped maintain his physique.

While Franklin would not admit it, he took great pride in himself more to please his daughter than to satisfy himself. For Rosie's summer visits, he wanted to look and feel his best.

As was usual for Fridays, the narrow, moderately lit, green-walled hallway was flooded with anxious voices ready to embark upon their hard-earned weekends. Mr. Stern rarely participated in timeclock chatter, for he'd found that his co-workers seldom discussed anything worthwhile. When they did, someone eventually belittled the subject by making light of it.

Franklin Stern saw nothing amusing about anything meriting discussion from him. He viewed people who did as taking life too flippantly for his taste. Having displayed such an attitude for the better part of the last two decades, his co-workers thought it best to minimize his participation in all general conversations.

Franklin observed silliness all around him, be it at the expense of world leaders or persistent socioeconomic iniquities. People seemed to laugh at anything if presented with an "I'm just kidding" or "It's just a joke" tag. Nothing was sacred, so nothing had value outside the realm of a good punch line. Life was mere grist for the comedy mill, as if wringing out any seriousness from misfortune or genuine pain made otherwise grim subject matters presentable to an ever-increasingly desensitized public. It was times like these, when he was the only one who did not laugh at an apparent joke, that made Franklin Stern feel like the last serious man on earth.

Mr. Stern rarely looked behind him at the all-too-familiar faces of his fellow nonexempts. Listening to them gibbering away about their minuscule weekend plans was bothersome enough. So patterned were their conversations that he could practically predict verbatim what each would say.

Johnny loved to brag about snow-skiing, even though he had done it only twice. Carl, Peter, and Maurice always boasted of their big weekend together of beer-drinking and sports-viewing. Jeffrey and Alice swapped family itineraries. Kevin talked about boating. Barbara talked about fishing. Erma just talked. For Mr. Stern, these people made the last five minutes of his day seem like an eternity.

Ermine Kleinstied—or Erma, as everyone called her—was, in his most generous opinion, an unattractive airhead. She always laughed (which sounded more like cackling) loudest at any joke or riddle, even when it was at her expense. Her most salient feature, according to Mr. Stern, was her smile. Although, at one time, he would have described it as cute, her loss of two upper and three lower front teeth obliterated its memory.

From his perspective, one would think such a jack-o-lantern grin would discourage jubilance. But not Erma. She was quite the opposite, always laughing and smiling. For the life of him, Franklin Stern was stumped as to why.

Now and then, to pass time while awaiting liberation, Franklin would choose one of his co-workers to characterize. He believed himself capable of writing an in-depth dossier on each of them. Today Ermine Kleinstied would be his subject.

He noted, as he had on multiple occasions, how Erma had changed over the years. When she first came to work at Alman's (nine years ago come next Tuesday), her appearance had borderlined on immaculate. Her jet-black, shoulder-length hair had always been neat and clean; not dowdy, as it was now. She had worn attractive dresses, skirts, blouses, and pants of a more feminine flare instead of the rugged jeans she sported these days. Her voice and manner had been pleasant and charming, and she'd laughed only at things she found to be genuinely amusing. Her fresh face, which once had only wee bits of near-undetectable makeup, now appeared dry, wrinkled, and painted. Her language ranged from gracious and articulate to vulgar and obscene.

Even her once-firm body exhibited no history of its formerly wholesome frame. Now her unkempt, five-foot-seven-inch physique and slattern visage could be desirable only to one of the downtown winos loitering in darkened doorways mumbling to themselves.

Franklin peered at the clock before continuing his train of thought. It was not until her husband died (struck by lightning, of all things) a bit more than four years ago that Erma changed for the worse. While he could sympathize with her tragic loss, he could not accept that as reason enough for the total lack of disregard she now displayed. *After all, life goes on,* his mind callously stated.

A loud burst of laughter—led by Erma, of course—caused Franklin to glance back at her. He instantly realized his mistake. At times, she would attempt to draw him into the group's conversations. This worked on occasion, but this was not one of those times.

After ignoring her calling him "Frank"—as did most people, which he quietly disliked—Franklin answered her question about what his weekend plans were with a curt "Nothing." He ignored the comments and ribbing his response sparked in his co-workers. As anticipated, they ceased their good-natured attempts at getting Franklin to participate and just ignored him.

Franklin glanced down at the clock. *Two minutes, and I'll be rid of these babbling imbeciles for the next two days*, he thought. *Thank God for small miracles.*

Despite Erma's numerous faults, Franklin maintained that she still had one physically endearing trait: two wonderfully deep-dish, girlish dimples graced the ends of her now-depleted smile. Even her unrefined use of heavy makeup could not dissipate the charm of those dimples.

*My wife has dimples like those*, he thought—*ex-wife, that is*. Evelyn's memory brought with it a twinge of melancholy, one that an undertow of distress about the divorce washed away.

The Sterns' divorce was an exercise in hostility. Evelyn and he had fought over their daughter, the house, the car, plants, furniture, finances, and more. Nothing was spared. Franklin won a few battles. but lost the war. The biggest defeat by far did not appear on their divorce papers—it was inscribed on his heart. The departure of his mate, the woman he had promised to protect and love until death do them part, left him branded with the stench of a burning failure he had yet to shake.

Not death, but change, severed their relationship. The erosion began without words—a chiding silence of two people growing apart. Marriage counseling did not help. Even the birth of Rosetta did not change Evelyn's feelings toward him.

At his best, Franklin knew he was not a good lover. He had known that even before Evelyn pointed it out to him. But she loved him for other reasons: he was a good provider, trustworthy, and steady as a rock. "Quality characteristics," she conceded during one of their counseling sessions. Notably absent were passion and romance—two things for which Evelyn had developed an insatiable appetite.

Evelyn had been attending night school at the local community college. She became interested in art, literature, dance, and men who had an appreciation for such things—not like Franklin, a man who believed that technology ruled the world.

He was a bore, she told him. His life was one huge technical manual, and she and their daughter were simply chapters in that dreary book. He was too tedious and too serious, in her opinion—a condition ripe for a corpse, not a living being—or, at least, not the man in her life.

The final round of the fight to salvage their marriage began when they stopped having sex, though Franklin and Evelyn had stopped making love years before then.

Their daughter was only nine months old when the divorce was finalized. Now, as a teenager, Rosie—as everyone called her—had grown to be a lot like her father: serious-minded and technically skilled. She had already chosen to major in mechanical engineering.

His daughter, the engineer—there was a certain poetic justice in that. Evelyn hated Rosie's choice of majors, which made it all the sweeter—a sort of nerd victory, if you will; an ironic swerve in a deserving twist of fate, as far as Franklin was concerned.

Franklin rarely smiled since his family left.

He remembered when his family had left him for good. It was an overcast, humid spring day. Everyone was quiet. Even Rosie did not so much as whimper or gurgle, and her silence chimed into the stagnant remorse filling the air.

Evelyn had decided to return to live with her parents until she could get on her feet. Oregon was far from Pennsylvania, and thus, so permanent a move. He and she stood face-to-face in the living room at the center of their vacated house. The judgment had required them to sell everything and equally divide the proceeds. They'd dutifully complied.

As part of their divorce decree, Franklin would pay Evelyn child support and alimony. He never missed a payment—a case for reliability and stability, as he saw it—two qualities Evelyn might cite as humdrum and predictable.

As hard as they fought with each other during the divorce, when they stood facing one another on the threshold of their divide, exhausted and worn to the bone, Franklin knew without question that he would always love Evelyn.

She told him she loved him, but not enough for a lifetime. He remembered thinking, *How does she know? What internal meter does she have that measures the voltage required for a lifetime's worth of love?*

Evelyn traced Franklin's brow with her smooth fingertips, moving down along the bridge of his nose, along his cheek, and holding his face in her hands. It felt strange to him, this gentle affection—awkward only because he did not know how to respond. Years of marriage had not taught Franklin how to open himself to display his feelings. He had them. Was that not enough?

Evelyn kissed his cheek, and then his lips, before leaving without another gesture or word. He smiled. It was actually more of a grimace to fight back the flood of pain that threatened to overtake him.

He did not wave goodbye to the taxi shuttling his family away to Pittsburgh International Airport. He did not watch it cruise up the street they had lived on for five years and vanish around the corner, carrying its tearful fare and somber child, routinely ferrying away the only joy he would allow himself to know from that day forward.

A quick burst from the fire-alarm bell raised a cheer from behind Franklin. He eased his yellow-and-white time card in and out of the punch-clock, which signaled its approval with a thump. After checking his time card for the black ink marking of *4:30 P.M.*, he gracefully slipped it into the dark gray metal card slot labeled 645 among the bank of metal card slots hand-numbered and mounted on the wall.

Franklin casually made his way to the end of the hall, turned left, took four steps that funneled him to the third-floor lobby, and pressed the 'down' button. His co-workers stampeded down the stairs. For them, the elevator was much too slow. Franklin Stern was grateful they had such feelings.

He could hear the elevator grinding as it struggled up to the third floor. Metallic gray doors cranked open. The metal cabin patiently awaited its next command. Mr. Stern entered and pressed the black plastic button painted with a white L. He listlessly stared out at five large glass display cases arranged in a semicircle around the bland third-floor lobby. Inside each case was tidily grouped the company's entire line of automobile products.

A tickle of pride rushed through Franklin, stemming from the knowledge that he'd had a part in the creation of almost every item in those cases. He was tempted to smile a prideful smile. The urge passed with the closing of the elevator doors.

Their flat, polished surfaces provided a gray mirror in the soft white light. Poised in the center of the elevator, his large hands resting by his sides, he carefully examined his reflection, which was divided in half by the black seam where the doors met. His examination left him with the thankful conclusion that he was the man he envisioned himself to be.

The elevator doors parted. Franklin's image vanished much more rapidly from his eyes than his mind. With bold strides, he stepped off the elevator and walked through the bright first-floor lobby. Automatic glass doors slid open without his having to break his pace, inviting him into the crowded Wilkinsburg street nicknamed 'The Avenue.'

Icy winds reminded Franklin that it was winter. He fell in with the rest of the crowd scurrying up The Avenue. Since he did not live far from his office, he made it a habit to walk to and from work, which was quite a feat for a man who preferred the natural serenity of his country youth to the bustle of the city.

But there were times when he did enjoy the noise and calamity of Wilkinsburg. For the most part, those times existed in the other three seasons. Winter seemed a bitter trek home, no matter how fast he walked.

Turning up his narrow lapels, he held them in place with one leather-gloved hand while the other hand, also gloved, was nestled deep inside his coat pocket. Halfway home, the crowd completely dissolved. Heavy vehicular traffic crawled up and down The Avenue, but that was to be expected.

The wind seemed harsher than earlier, reddening his face. He had forgotten his hand-woven woolen scarf that morning, which did not help. Mr. Stern switched hands, giving the numbing other an opportunity at warmth. Among the row of buildings to his right, a sign appeared just ahead, painted in large, black, Middle English-styled letters on a smooth white brick surface: *221B BAKERS ST.*

Pushing open one of two heavy wooden light-blue doors, Franklin Stern stepped inside. After taking a moment to remove his gloves, stuff them into one of his coat pockets, and unfold and align his lapels, he sauntered over to one of the black vinyl padded barstools, vigorously rubbing his hands together all the while. Before sitting, he unbuttoned his coat. Sitting upright on the stool, he firmly planted his feet on the cylindrical brass footrest that ran the length of the bar and waited for the bartender to take notice of him.

Behind the oak bar, a large man with brown freckles, flat, piercing greenish-brown eyes, and short reddish-brown hair was talking to a pudgy, disheveled-looking man sitting on the stool across from him.

Mike, the bartender and half-owner, glanced in Franklin's direction. He brusquely excused himself from the conversation and confidently strolled toward Franklin Stern.

"The usual?" Mike asked in a tone reminiscent of a perfunctory song he had played a thousand times. He placed a white paper napkin printed with the likeness of Sherlock Holmes on the bar.

"Yes," Franklin answered.

"Is it snowing outside?"

"Not yet."

"We're supposed to get a blizzard tonight," Mike went on to say. Franklin Stern shrugged his shoulders, emphasizing his disinterest in Mike's weather update. Mike took the hint. "Here you go, Frank: a nice, tall glass of dark lager." He set the pilsner's thick round bottom squarely on the face of Sherlock Holmes. "That'll be two-fifty," he concluded with a rehearsed bartender's smile that did nothing for his face.

"Where's Carmen?" Franklin asked as he took his gold money clip out of his pocket.

"You mean Mattie, don't you?"

Her full name was Madison Haiden Meaghan Kern. Mattie was Mike's sister and the other half of 221B Bakers Street. Kern was her maiden name, which she reclaimed after each of her divorces. None of her marriages had "blessed her with children," as Mattie had phrased it, but Franklin did not press as to why. She was captivated by Franklin, and all of the regulars knew it.

Over time. she had offered up personal portions of her life from their symbiotic interactions, just as Franklin had his. Why a vibrant, desirable woman such as Mattie was attracted to a crabby man eight years her senior was the riddle of the bar.

"Since you brought her up, where is your sister?" Franklin asked.

"Where Mattie is at the moment, I don't know. Carmen is out sick, in case you're really interested."

"What about Kate?"

"She's running late."

Slipping three dollars from his clip, Franklin fanned them face-up on the bar. "Keep the change," he said dryly, looking Mike in the eye.

Sweeping the money up with his portly right hand, the bartender half-heartedly thanked Franklin and deposited the bills in the antique-styled cash register on his way back to his disheveled friend.

Franklin Stern had not known the love of a woman for over sixteen years. He had begun to question the whole concept of two souls united as one. He doubted that unconditional love even existed. He had occasional bouts with romance along the way, but nothing came of them—they became neither friends nor even acquaintances after their brief time together.

Since Franklin was not good at small talk, his dates seemed to amount to intellectual sparring matches or juvenile battles of will. His last date told him he had a fear of flying. When he asked her to elaborate, she said that love frightened him: "You've been hurt, and now you're afraid to ride the fickle winds of love."

"Who isn't?" was Franklin's stoic response. His date glared at him with a look of exasperation, as she had a number of times that evening—as had all of his dates before her at various times during their engagements. She accused him of being cold and cynical and demanded he take her home. He nonchalantly disagreed with her assessment of him and did as she asked. He did not mind. He was not enjoying her company anyway.

Franklin had repeatedly passed by 221B, as everyone called it, for years without ever exploring it. He had resisted any curious inclination to drop in, excusing it as only another bar where nothing good could possibly happen.

Due to a forced invitation by his then-department manager—who insisted Franklin be there to help him celebrate his ten-year anniversary with Alman Brothers—Franklin Stern received his first glimpse inside 221B. That was when he first saw Mattie Kern.

Mattie turned his head at the virgin sight. Her copper skin was as smooth and radiant as polished silver. Curly, reddish-brown hair collared her shoulders and outlined her round face. Brown freckles flecked across her nose and cheeks. When Mattie looked his way with her greenish-brown eyes flickering in the unflattering bar lights, he was as dumbfounded as a boy infatuated by an older woman. Her full, sensual smile gave him butterflies.

She was the type of woman you could look at and tell that she worked out. She had tight round hips, muscular legs, a narrow waistline, and small breasts on a powerful upper frame. Being somewhat of a gym-rat himself, Franklin could tell she was all woman—no steroids.

Although Mattie was married at the time (he had noticed the telltale band on her finger), Franklin believed he spotted a glint of interest toward him in her beautiful eyes. That belief was substantiated, in his opinion, when Mattie took his order.

"And what can I get for you…?" She waited for him to fill in the blank. He told her his name. She introduced herself to him. The rest of the party all took notice. Franklin hated being the center of attention. Not knowing what else to do, he placed his order. Mattie did not make matters easier for him by saying, "Coming right up, handsome." The table roared at her comment.

He wanted to vanish from embarrassment as Mattie waited on the rest of the party. Nothing more was said between them the rest of the evening than would not normally transpire between a food server and customer, which was quite a relief to him at the time.

Franklin was tempted to dismiss Mattie's behavior as harmless flirtation. When he saw she did not treat most customers with the same familiar attention he had received, he gave into the idea that a genuine attraction existed between them. He could feel it.

Erma noticed it, too. She pointed it out by nudging Franklin and whispering in his ear, with smelly beer breath, that she thought Mattie was sweet on him. He tried to defuse Erma by informing her that their server was married.

"So?" Erma said it like a question. "Marriage don't stop feelings, Frankie. Sometimes you just gotta grab a moment of passion when it presents itself."

"In a crowded bar, where do you suggest we do it? Right here on the table?"

"Works for me," Erma guffawed, as if she had just heard the funniest joke in the world. To make matters worse, she stood up and waved her hands over the table, as if attempting to shove everything off. "Clear the table!" she shouted. "Frankie needs room to do the nasty!" When everyone else wanted in on the joke, Erma clued them in. The razing became so bad that Franklin stormed out, much to the chagrin of his co-workers and manager.

The latter let Franklin know of his displeasure at his subordinate's temperamental departure the following day. He did not bother mounting a defense. He knew his manager well enough to know that it would fall on deaf ears.

Just as Franklin knew, his manager resented that he had been the company's second choice for the position. Franklin had been their first. He had turned down their offer only because he enjoyed his current position and did not want the responsibility of managing the productivity of others.

While taking a swig of beer, Franklin reflected upon the question Mike had asked about the weather. He considered it foolish for Mike to include the word "outside" in his question. Had it been snowing, it most certainly would have been doing so outside. But he had learned to expect such thoughtless oversights from his fellow man.

Franklin leaned forward onto the bar, idly glancing about the establishment, enjoying his cold beer. He bypassed Mike and his seedy companion, moving along the rose-colored wall hand-painted with crisp Holmes paraphernalia.

His eyes paused to observe the activities of three men gathered around the electric pinball machine that had a colorful portrait of Holmes and Watson on the scoreboard glass. The early-thirty-something men looked like factory workers in weathered jeans, battered work boots, and plaid flannel shirts. They were guzzling bottled beer and laughing uproariously in spurts. *They're probably laughing about something uncouth,* Franklin reasoned before continuing his survey of the place.

His eyes settled upon a couple sitting at a small table near the back wall beside the ultramodern jukebox that played songs Franklin never recognized or liked. A quick evaluation found them to be typical of hundreds of moonstruck couples he had seen over the years, always laughing and kidding and ending each jocund outburst with a rugged hug or tender kiss.

It pleased Franklin to see people in love, but one would never know it by looking at him. He surmised that if people spent half as much energy pulling together as they did to remain separated, then love (or at least a reasonable understanding) among humankind could be achieved.

Turning his back on the couple, Franklin immediately dismissed that thought as one of a foolish middle-aged man. *In the real world, nothing as simple as love will change things*, a voice bellowed up inside of him. *By now, you've realized that love is the only justifiable grounds for anyone to be mindless. All other matters of man should be handled with logic and tact, if possible. That is the seed of respect from which flowers of harmony can blossom.*

"Oh, well," he mumbled. His mind finished what the mumbling had begun: *Either way, it makes no difference in the world which philosophy I believe will work, so I might as well stop thinking these ridiculous thoughts.* Mr. Stern did as his mind suggested and sat quietly, drinking his beer, no longer thinking about the world.

In the beginning, he returned to the bar only a couple of times per month. His excuse was to have a cold one before he settled in for the evening. At times, he took his meals there. Then it became once a week, a few times a week, and finally Monday through Saturday, except when Rosie was in town or on holidays when they were closed.

He and Mattie talked more and more each time he came in. Franklin helped to navigate Mattie through her divorce, her third in ten years. She became his shoulder to lean on. She would spend her break time with him, and every slow moment she could steal away. He would not allow what he accepted as a friendship to progress beyond the bar. It was safe within the confines of 221B. He did not want to take any chances in possibly destroying what little affection she brought into his daily life by asking her out.

Rosie changed his mind. While his daughter had his reasoning and technical mind, she also had her mother's zeal for life. Rosie was always badgering her father to be more social, attempting to educate him on the subtitles of romance and dating. She told her dad that not having a woman in his life was unhealthy.

When his daughter asked if he were gay, he was shocked and appalled. He mentioned Mattie in an effort to put an end to the topic, but Rosie was persistent. She wanted to know more about "this woman." Rosie made him open up on how he felt about Mattie. The things he said surprised even him.

Rosie made her father promise he would ask Mattie out on a date. Franklin could refuse his daughter nothing. Simply thinking about asking Mattie out made his knees wobbly. He didn't know where he would find the courage, but he was a man of his word.

After glancing again at the young couple in the corner, Franklin turned back toward the bar and removed a sealed envelope from his breast pocket near his heart. He had hoped to leave the letter with Carmen to give to Mattie. On the front of the envelope, he had written "Madison." On the inside was a handwritten letter to Mattie, asking her out to dinner.

The letter had been his contingency plan in case he lost his nerve. As the time drew near, the letter had become, in his mind, his only feasible action.

Carmen was nice and had grown to either like or accept him for who he was. She tried to encourage Franklin, after Mattie's last divorce, to "make a move," as she put it. Carmen finally gave up after months of both subtle and direct prodding.

Kate rarely had much to say to Franklin, or anyone for that matter. Married and the mother of two young children, Franklin was under the impression that Kate was often exhausted and didn't have the energy or desire to become involved in other people's business. Now that the Carmen option was off the table, Franklin was left with no choice.

He called to Mike, who ambled over. "Want another?" he asked.

"Yes." Franklin polished off the last of his beer and peeled off a five from his money clip as Mike stepped away to serve up another pilsner. When he returned, Franklin said, "I want you to give this to Mattie for me," and attempted to hand Mike the envelope along with the five-dollar bill.

"What's in it, a *love letter*?" Mike said, loud enough to embarrass Franklin. The presumed factory workers and the man at the end of the bar snickered. The couple mooned over how cute it was.

Franklin was not deterred. "It's personal."

"Aren't you man enough to give it to her yourself?"

"I'm man enough to do a lot of things. Mattie's not here right now, and I'm asking you for a favor. Are you going to give Mattie this letter, or not?"

Mike stared at Franklin for a few tense heartbeats before putting out his hand.

"Thank you," Franklin sincerely said as he handed Mike the letter and money. "Keep the change."

"Yeah, yeah," Mike said, walking away. He deposited the money in the till and jammed the letter between other papers on the side of the cash register before helping newly arrived customers at the bar.

The after-work crowd gradually filed in. To Mr. Stern, that signaled it was time to leave. He finished his beer with a deep, satisfying swallow. Rising from the stool, he turned and faced the big blue doors across the room. Mattie seemed to appear out of nowhere.

"Hi, Frankie," Mattie said with a sexy tone and sensual smile. He loved it when she called him "Frankie." It had a certain intimate ring to his ear, coming from Mattie. "How are you, sweetie?"

"Fine, Mattie. Yourself?" He was glowing inside. He had never heard her call anyone else "sweetie" in all of the time he had been coming to 221B, unlike the full-time servers who did it to create an air of familiarity in hopes of fattening their tip. Mattie meant every syllable of the word, melting like butter on his potato.

"Good," she answered. "Leaving so soon?" She tried to mask her disappointment, but her eyes betrayed her smile.

"I have to go before the weather gets bad," he responded.

Her disappointment broke through her facade. Franklin did not know what to say.

"How do you like my outfit?" Mattie asked him, stepping away from him enough to model it for him. The tight wool skirt reached just above her knees and accentuated her impressive lower body. The peach cotton blouse did the same for her upper body.

"You look great," he softly said.

Mattie smiled. Anyone who knew Franklin knew he never said anything he didn't mean. "You don't think this skirt makes my hips look big?" she asked him as she turned to give him a good view of her hips.

Franklin tried not to gawk. He wondered if Mattie was wearing that outfit just for him. Mike was waiting on a customer two seats away from Franklin, and out of the corner of his eye he saw a sly smirk on her older brother's face. He supposed it was for their little show.

"Mattie, millions of women would kill for your hips," Franklin said.

"So would millions of men," said one of the men Mike was waiting on. Everyone within earshot laughed except Franklin and Mike. Franklin thought it was a crude thing to say, and he said as much to the man who made the remark. The man lazily waved his hand at him, as if shooing away an annoying insect.

"You look beautiful, Mattie," Franklin said once the laughter had fully died.

"Thanks, sweetie," she responded. "What's that on your cheek?"

"Where?" He turned his cheek to her for her to have a better look. She kissed him.

"Just my lips."

Franklin blushed, fighting back a boyish grin. Mattie wiped her lipstick from his cheek with a cocktail napkin. He loved having her that close—close enough for him to feel her warm breath on his face and to smell the fragrance of her hair.

Mattie apologized for making such a mess. Franklin assured her it was all right.

"Be careful going home, honey," she said, her dismay more evident than ever.

"You, too." After a hard swallow and a deep breath, he said, "If it's really too bad outside when you leave work, you're welcome to walk over to my place."

"Really?"

"Yes, anytime. I mean—the weather doesn't have to be bad, or anything."

"I may take you up on that, Frankie."

Mattie moved closer to Franklin. He could smell the gentle sweet scent of her perfume and feel the electricity of her stare. It took every ounce of courage he could muster to say it, but it came out: "I left a letter for you. It's up there"—he pointed with a shaky finger—"next to the cash register. When you have a chance, read it."

"Wait! I'll read it right now." She ran around to the cash register.

"Mattie!" Mike barked with an edge. "We've got customers!"

She ignored her brother. "Where is it?" she asked Franklin as she rummaged around the register.

"I'd prefer if you didn't read it—I mean—it can wait."

Mattie found the letter. She stopped herself from opening it. *She's reading me,* Franklin could tell. She walked up to him. "You are a shy one," she said, attempting to ease his discomfort.

"I think I'm more bashful than shy."

"I think it's sweet."

"Hey! Can we get some service over here?" A group of suits had claimed two tables. The one who shouted at Mattie looked as ornery as any hard-time ex-con Franklin had ever seen.

"Mattie!" Mike yelled.

"Why can't you wait on them?" Mattie said over her shoulder, not turning away from Franklin.

"Because I'm tending bar! At least *one* of us is working!"

"All right, already, in a minute!" Mattie's voice returned to that sultry lilt that could send Franklin into erotic fantasies. She turned back to him. "I've got to go, Frankie. Customers are waiting."

Franklin surprised himself when he kissed Mattie. It was no more than a peck on the lips—nothing more than a boy stealing a kiss from a girl he liked. She licked her lips, as if tasting the last morsels of a delicious dessert. He stared into her twinkling eyes. His stomach turned somersaults. He felt something deep, fiery, and alive inside—a sense of bliss he had never experienced before.

Even with Evelyn, it had been a gradual evolution: it began with a liking, then comfort, until finally rolling over into a sedentary love. With Mattie, it felt more like—dare he think it—*passion*.

"My address and phone number are in the letter," he said, to ease his fascination.

She wiped his mouth clean of lipstick with another paper napkin. "We'll talk later," she said.

He smiled. He didn't mean to; it just happened: a bright grin, accompanied by a rosy rush of warm light, danced all through him— one he could not contain or control.

"What a smile you have, Frankie," she said, smiling herself. "You should show it more often."

"I'll try. See you later, Mattie."

"Yes, you will," she said before making her way over to take orders from the suits. Franklin watched her walk away, as did most of the men in the bar. He was as dumbstruck as a lovesick child caught in a fantasy come true.

En route to the blue doors, Franklin took a last look at the loving couple and imagined himself and Mattie in their place. He was smiling. It felt as though everyone in the bar saw him and was smiling back. Everyone except Mike, that is. Franklin left the bar feeling as if he were floating, his steps light as air.

He was greeted by the whispering silence of cold, as quiet and piercing as the first winter breath of God. Daylight was gone. Furious winds whipped large, bountiful snowflakes in all directions, forcing Franklin to use one hand to shield his eyes while the other grasped his lapels as he scurried homeward.

After battling the freezing elements for a few minutes, he arrived at the corner of The Avenue and Willow. Making a sharp right onto Willow, he thought, *almost home.* At the next corner he made another sharp right onto Pride and proceeded at a half-trot up the hill into the howling face of the white wind.

His hands and face had become numb. Thoughts of Mattie helped block them from his mind. Tonight was the beginning of the rest of his new life. For the first time in a very long time, he was looking forward to the days ahead. He could not wait to tell Rosie about this new development.

At a third of the way up Pride, he pivoted right, vaulted up a set of wide cement steps, and halted in front of two eggshell-white wooden doors. He searched awkwardly through his pants pockets for his small collection of keys.

He stared anxiously through the diamond-shaped peep-glass into the long, vacant hall of Manor Arms Apartments. The crystal chandelier suspended from the French ceiling emitted just enough light to enrich the hall with an enticingly warm glow.

His fingers had lost more feeling than he'd realized. While he saw the keys outlined in his pocket, he could not command his numb fingers to grasp them. "Come on!" he urged, becoming both angry and frustrated with himself.

After a few desperate attempts, he managed to work his insensate fingers around the elusive keys and ease them out of his pocket, making certain of their abduction with his eyes. Identifying a gold round-headed key, he clumsily separated it from the others. Using both hands, he inserted the key and turned it until he heard the definitive thud of the deadbolt coming undone.

Franklin Stern rushed inside to the heated refuge of the vacant hall, relieved to have escaped the bitter cold.

# MIST

Matt patiently waited at the King County Metro bus stop. The morning mist brushed his skin like a lover's eyelashes in the August dawn. Gray toyed with sunlight as clear blue sky found an occasional peephole through the dense white cloud cover. Matt searched three lanes of oncoming traffic for his bus. It was nowhere to be seen. His mind nestled into the previous night like a puppy into its favorite resting spot.

His first year of marriage to Monica was magical. Their passion seemed bottomless, their affection divine. Sleep had fallen on Matt like a soft cotton blanket after the exhaustion of their fervid lovemaking. His last conscious recollection was hearing the footfalls of dreams amidst Monica's voice. Her words became sweet murmurings pooling at his doorstep of mystic lullabies, wrapping him in a tranquil shroud of celestial serenity.

The distant cry of seagulls rippled through the morning mist like a mantra chant. Matt took a deep breath, then another. The cool mist felt refreshing, filling his lungs like a satisfying cool drink of water on a hot summer day.

His smartphone rang. He hoped it was Monica calling to tell him that she missed him and to wish him a good day at the office. He checked the display before answering. The caller ID said, "EX-WIFE."

*This can't be good*, Matt thought. He answered.

"What in the world are you doing, Matt?" Vicki had a mid-ranged nasal voice that annoyed most people. His friends and family never understood why it didn't bother him. "Love," was his answer. For years, Matt found his ex-wife's voice one of her endearing qualities, like her hiccup laugh and her insidious sense of humor. *When did I turn the corner and find those qualities grating?* Matt asked himself. *Was it a gradual turn, or did I reach that conclusion at breakneck speed, like falling off a cliff?*

"What are you talking about, Vicki?"

"You know what I'm talking about?"

Another characteristic that went from endearing to grating was Vicki's zeal for asking open-ended questions.

"If I knew, I wouldn't be in the dark."

"Child support payment, *late*—ring a bell?"

Vicki was right. Matt could not believe he had forgotten to mail his child support payment. He'd only realized his mistake when he discovered the addressed-stamped envelope to Vicki while rummaging through some papers in his briefcase. Matt had put the payment into his briefcase two weeks ago, intending on mailing it that morning. The path of good intentions had just arrived at that burning road to Hell, and Vicki was ready to drive him all the way to the fiery end.

"I'm sorry, Vicki. I sent the check Priority Mail on Saturday. You should get it today—tomorrow at the very latest."

"None of which are the seventh of the month," Vicki protested.

"I forgot, alright? I apologize. What do you want, blood?"

"It's the third time this year. I want you to consider that I am still the mother of your two children, *Mr. Newlywed*. Paul and Michelle— remember them? Your eight-year-old son, and five-year-old daughter who miss their daddy very much."

"If you would allow me to direct deposit the child support into your checking account like I wanted, then this sort of thing wouldn't happen at all."

"I don't want you anywhere near my finances. No telling what you might do with that kind of access."

"I wouldn't do anything but deposit my child support payments. I'm not a thief and you know it."

"There's a first time for everything."

"Don't start, Vicki."

Matt knew Vicki didn't need his money. Vicki had recently been promoted to vice-president of Mason Bank. She made in a week what Matt took home in a month. Matt knew for a fact that Vicki deposited his child support payments directly into savings and investment accounts that she had set up for their children.

Her motives were emotional, not financial. Vicki leapt at any means she could find to irritate Matt. For the moment, a tardy child support payment was her ammunition.

"A new wife does not give you license to neglect your children."

"Her name is Monica, not 'new wife,' Vicki."

"This may come as a shock to you, *Matt*, but I don't give a damn what her name is. What I *do* care about is taking care of *our* children."

Matt listened and inwardly agreed. Wedded bliss had made him forget what day it was, sometimes. His new marriage should not interfere with the welfare of their children, although he knew his ex-wife's accusation was bogus.

He would never neglect his children. As much as he loved Monica, his children came first in his life. He didn't attempt to voice his assertion to Vicki. He knew she had not called to listen. *Apologize and hope for the best*, is what he thought.

"You're a good mother, Vicki, and I—"

"We rely on that money, Matt. When it's not here on time, it screws up my accounting system. That means bills don't get paid in a timely manner, some of the children's needs are placed on hold, and I have to explain it to everyone involved about how my ex-husband is slacking off on his legal financial obligations."

"It won't happen again."

"You're damn right it won't, because if it does, your open visitation rights just might get closed."

"You wouldn't do that," Matt said, not believing his ears.

"Married to me for ten years and you still don't know what I will or will not do. Of course I would!"

"Go to hell, Vicki."

"Been there. I was married to you, remember? Did you send the full amount?"

"Have I ever not?"

"Just remember your fatherly duty next time, without me having to remind you."

"*Remind me—*"

"You promised Paul you would take him to his Little League baseball game on Thursday," Vicki interrupted.

"I remember."

"Maybe you should jot that down in your Day-Timer so you don't forget and break your son's heart."

"*Now, wait a minute!*"

Vicki hung up. Matt stared at the phone as if he could crush it in his hand. He wrestled with his impulse to star 69 his EX-WIFE.

*Breathe in…breathe out…breathe in…breathe out.* Monica's voice floated to the forefront of his thoughts. Matt did as she instructed. Monica was a part-time yoga instructor and was damn good at it, if Matt said so himself.

*Think calm thoughts…serene thoughts…a lake…a meadow…a breeze…the infinite expanse of a clear sky.*

The seagull chants echoed along the mist. Matt looked up. Five geese flew by in a ragged chevron formation. Some clouds had moved on to allow the blue of sky to see more of the world.

*Let that place become your center…breathe in…breathe out.*

His heart and blood pressure steadied. The tension raced from his body like steam from a kettle. He embraced the calm and put his phone away.

A half-filled bus arrived. Matt wished the disgruntled-looking bus driver a good morning and made himself comfortable at a window seat. Matt had turned off the ringer on his cell phone and set it to vibrate. It vibrated against his chest. A text message read, "Wish you were here. Love, Monica."

Matt thought again of last night. A warm smile he could not stop fell into place on his face as he gazed out of the bus window, imagining Monica everywhere he looked.

*       *       *

On the evening Matt met Monica, her Ananda yoga class was filled to capacity. Matt had been fortunate enough to get the last spot. The class had come highly recommended by a co-worker. The co-worker claimed it had helped him relieve stress, increased his focus, and had done wonders for his body—all the things Matt felt he needed help with, at the time.

Work was work. Matt could handle that. Vicki was his real stress point. Since the divorce, Vicki had badgered Matt mercilessly about any and everything she could. Matt mostly took it. He had assumed her resentment and bitterness would eventually burn away, and that something workable between them would remain in the ashes. Only, it continued to fester like a boil that grew larger, but refused to pop. Matt had to do something to stop it from infecting his life.

People were quietly pleasant in the class, warming-up with a variety of stretches. The airy instrumental music was melodic and tranquil. A hint of vanilla incense was in the air. The room itself was pristine, with no furniture or wall decorations—only a small Bose stereo system right-center of the front wall.

The lighting was soft and warm. Matt felt immediately at ease.

Matt unrolled his new yoga mat and sat down to watch his fellow students. The studio could comfortably accommodate thirty students with room for everyone to stretch out. There were bodies of all shapes, sizes, and colors. No one spoke a word. Everyone's focus seemed to be inward. Matt respected their space. Matt lay on his mat and closed his eyes.

The music was silenced. A firm, gentle voice said, "Good evening."

"Good evening, Swami," a few students responded.

Matt opened his eyes and quickly looked around. Everyone had gotten into a sitting position, of resting their butts on their heels with their hands placed on their knees or upper thighs. Matt scrambled to get into that same position. When he looked up at his Swami, her beauty stunned him.

A tall, brown-skinned woman stood with unassuming confidence at the head of the class. She had the combination body of a runway model and a dancer, long and lean and gracefully powerful. Her breasts seemed large for her frame, but her movements suggested she was at ease with them. What drew Matt deeper into her personality was her face. Her dark brown curls framed her smooth round face and brought a warm sparkle to her medium-brown eyes.

There was an aura about her—a genuine poise and confidence; a gift that cannot be manufactured. It drew Matt to her like a magnet. Judging by the mesmerized looks on the faces of many of his fellow students, he was not alone.

"My name is Monica, for those of you who are new to my class," she announced. "Today we have both intermediate and beginning students with us. I apologize to my beginner students in advance. My beginner's class is full at the moment, so I invited those interested in learning the practice of yoga into this class as an introduction. We may cover some yoga positions that beginners might find daunting. Do not let that discourage you. Do what you can.

"This is not a competition. We are here to learn and grow as human beings. I will be starting a second beginner's yoga class next Tuesday at this same time. There is a signup sheet for that class, in the reception area. I hope you will find this class informative enough that you will pursue yoga as a wonderful addition to your life."

Then Monica smiled. Matt found himself feeling the same way he had in fourth grade about his music teacher, Mrs. Fletcher. Infatuation was what it was called, then. He remembered thinking if that definition of his young feelings still applied to middle-aged men.

Matt barely survived the intermediate class. He signed up for the second beginners' class.

Matt would prepare for Monica's yoga classes as if he were going out on a date. He took an extra shower, shaved again, combed his hair, flossed, brushed his teeth, and gargled.

He was one of the first students there. He was not only smitten by her beauty, but was impressed by her ability as an instructor. Monica explained everything to such a degree that it made perfect sense.

Why they posed as they did. How to breathe, focus, and meditate. Monica made life make sense in a way that Matt had rarely thought about. She linked the physical with the spiritual, simplifying how they embraced each other.

Matt made it a point to talk to Monica after each class. He kept his questions focused on the practice of Ananda Yoga. Monica was pleased to answer them. Matt thought he saw something else in her eyes. It was something more than a mere willingness to aide an eager student, but he failed to muster the courage to act on his belief.

After six weeks, Matt finally found the nerve to ask Monica out to dinner.

"I make it a policy not to date my students," Monica said to his request. "But in your case, Matt, I'll make an exception. Six o'clock Friday okay with you?"

Matt was speechless.

"Don't worry about the restaurant," Monica said. "I'm open to all sorts of food."

"Six o'clock on Friday will be fine," Matt managed to babble.

"Good." Monica walked over to her gym bag. Matt followed her like a love-struck child.

"Here's my number." Monica handed Matt one of her yoga business cards. She had written down her personal number on the back. "Give me a call if something comes up between now and then, or if you just want to talk."

"Un-huh," was all Matt was able to say.

"I have to run. I'm having a dinner party at my place to celebrate my parent's fortieth wedding anniversary. You're welcome to come, if you like."

Matt declined. He didn't feel comfortable meeting Monica's parents. Matt was barely holding it together that she had said yes to his dinner invitation.

"I'd better not," Matt said. "I've got some work to catch up on." Which was true. He did.

"No worries." Monica kissed Matt on the cheek. "See you on Friday."

With that, Monica turned and left in the same way a ballerina exits the stage to a resounding roar of applause after a brilliant performance. Matt held her business card aloft as if it possessed some form of magic. Matt looked around the studio. He was alone. The studio was quiet. Matt gathered his things and left in a giddy haze.

*   *   *

It was a hot clear Saturday afternoon at the tail end of July. Matt had been cruising in his brand new emerald green Mustang convertible with the top down for the last two hours, enjoying the sun and wind. Matt was bare-chested, wearing leather sandals and a pair of shorts that matched the color of his Mustang. His hair was close-cropped, his baby face clean-shaven, and his dark brown skin radiated in the sun.

'Long and lean' was how people described Matt. He had run the mile in high school and college as a walk-on. He was an average runner, but he enjoyed the competition and camaraderie. His mother was fond of saying, "It kept him away from the wrong crowd." Maybe she was right. Matt kept his workout regimen going after college. It kept him fit.

Matt was free and single and was loving it. He had earned a B.A. in Business Management in three years in his rush for what he called "liberation." Matt wanted to be on his own, and not because he didn't like living with his parents. A burning desire had revealed itself in him to be free once his older brother showed Matt his bachelor pad.

As much as Matt was awestruck by the décor of his brother's townhouse, he envied most of all the fact that his brother had the freedom to come and go as he pleased.

Matt had been yearning for that from his parents. They would not budge on his midnight curfew, no matter his age. Matt agreed to attend college locally and reside at home to lessen the financial burden on his parents.

His parents wanted him near so they could keep an eye on him. Matt realized that. He used it as motivation. The rush for independence was on, and a college degree offered him the key.

Matt spied a Dairy Queen about a half-mile up the road. A banana split with all the toppings sounded good to him.

He noticed her as he pulled into a parking spot. She was wearing low-cut sneakers, tight white shorts, and a peach-colored halter top that matched the hue of her skin. Her natural black curls flowed over her shoulders like mink. She and two girlfriends were standing near a blue Honda Civic, enjoying ice cream cones. Matt wasted no time ordering his banana split with all of the toppings before joining the women.

"I'm Matt." His greeting was primarily directed at the woman in the white shorts. Charmaine did the honors of introducing herself and her friends, Charity and Vicki.

"Nice to meet you," Matt said to all. They were smiling at him. His world narrowed to Vicki. Her eyes were a sparkling brown, her lips full, her nose prominent, she had round cheeks and chin, and her smile burst upon her face like a sharp beacon of light through pitch-blackness. Her breasts were small, but firm. Her stomach was as flat as an ironing board. Her body filled her clothes like an American gymnast, compact and powerful.

"Nice to meet everyone," Matt said.

"Nice to meet you," Charity said.

"Vicki," Matt said, "do you have a boyfriend?"

"We all do," Charmaine answered. All of the women laughed. Vicki had a laugh that was more like a hiccup. Her laugh made Matt laugh with her, not at her.

"Why do you ask?" Vicki said.

That was the first sampling Matt had of what would constantly be described as Vicki's reedy voice—a voice Matt immediately liked. "I wanted to know because I'm interested in you," Matt said.

"My boyfriend and I are pretty tight," Vicki said.

"Then I have my work cut out for me."

"What makes you so special?"

"I'm not, but you are. That's why I'm here. To try to get to know you better. And I hope you want to get to know me."

"What makes you think you have a chance?"

"Chance is something we all have. Opportunity is a lot more fleeting."

"Good one," Charity said, as if she were rating Matt's performance.

"Tell you what, Mr. Opportunist," Vicki said, folding her arms across her chest. "I'll give you five minutes to tell me why I should leave my boyfriend for you."

"This ought to be good," Charmaine said. All of the women laughed.

"The clock's ticking," Charity said, looking at her watch.

"I'm not asking you to leave your boyfriend."

"You're not?" Vicki said, looking at Matt askew.

"Nope."

"Then what do you want?"

"I'm asking you to invite me into your life."

"As what?"

"An acquaintance, a friend—whatever suits your purpose. It doesn't matter. Because, in the end, I'm going to be more than your man; I am going to be your husband."

All of the women let out a gasp.

"You're moving pretty fast, aren't you?" Charmaine said.

"I didn't mean we would get married today," Matt said to Vicki, "or tomorrow, or even this year. But someday, when the time is right..."

"You're certainly sure of yourself," Vicki said.

"What I'm certain of, Vicki, is fate. You and I are meant for each other. Time will prove me out on that point."

"Really," Vicki said.

"No doubt." Vicki and her friends stared at Matt. Matt ate his banana split. They licked their ice cream cones. Matt knew they were trying to determine whether he was sincere.

"Give the man your number, Vicki," Charity said.

Vicki smiled. Matt inhaled her smile. Charmaine reached into the glove compartment of the Civic and handed Vicki a pen and notepad. Vicki wrote down her telephone number, ripped it out, and handed it to Matt.

"Don't lose it," Charity said.

Matt put Vicki's number in his wallet. "I won't," Matt said with a smile so broad his brother would have described it as dorky.

"That's your Mustang?" Charity asked.

"Yep."

"Nice," Charity said with a few nods of her head. Vicki and Charmaine agreed.

"We have to go," Charmaine said. "I promised my mom I would have her car back by six."

"No problem," Matt said, dimming the wattage on his smile. "Nice meeting you, Charmaine, Charity, and especially you, Vicki."

"Likewise," Vicki said with a warm smile. Matt had meant what he said to Vicki. He was already planning their first date before the Civic pulled away.

"Matt!" Charity yelled out of the car. "If it don't work out with Vicki, give me a call! My number is 363—"

Matt could see Vicki put a hand over Charity's mouth. Vicki said something to Charity. Charmaine and Charity laughed. Matt watched the Civic until he could no longer see Vicki staring at him through the back window.

*     *     *

Matt and Monica had been dating for one year, much to the chagrin of his ex-wife. Their relationship had aged well with time. As in all vibrant relationships, Matt had learned both superficial and illuminating facts about Monica during their time together.

Monica was a dental hygienist who had never been married, although she had been proposed to half a dozen times. Monica played high school soccer. She'd danced for three years with the Pacific Northwest Ballet until she broke her ankle in a pickup weekend soccer game with friends.

Her favorite color was red. Her favorite flowers were chrysanthemums and tulips. She loved dancing, soccer, music, reading novels, yoga, board games, puzzles, and spending time with family and friends.

Inside of the woman with a long, lean, powerful figure and an ingratiating smile, Matt discovered a person of boundless energy and infinite optimism.

Monica housed a surprising competitive fire quelled primarily by the quiet strength and wisdom of her yoga sensibilities. She was a great debater who preferred to utilize her verbal skills on important matters. Her laugh was sophisticated. Her jokes were horrible. Her journey to become the best person she could be was constant. Her dream was to contribute something positive to the world, although she had not concluded what that contribution might be.

Then there were her big beautiful brown eyes that could lead one into the abyss of her soul when she allowed you to enter. It was a region Matt had visited on a number of occasions. The most powerful moments were when they made love.

The flesh knows heaven in those rare moments of complete shared surrender. All of those things, and more, Matt had come to appreciate and at times adore in the lady in his life.

To celebrate their one-year anniversary together, Matt wanted to do something special for Monica. Matt trolled the internet in search of bed and breakfast inns in Western Washington. His criteria for a desirable getaway were: romantic, secluded, and luxurious with good, wholesome food and in natural surroundings.

Based on their website descriptions, six bed and breakfast resorts were chosen. Matt personally investigated each retreat.

All six resorts were impressive. Only one retreat inspired Matt. He felt it the moment he drove onto the grounds.

As in all the bed and breakfast inns Matt had visited, he was encouraged to look around. What Matt saw was twenty-five acres of rapture nestled in the foothills of the Olympic Mountains. There was an abundance of waterfalls, ponds, lush plant life, wildlife, and gardens almost everywhere he ventured. Absent from the pristine landscape were unnatural sounds, air pollution, and crowds.

A warm energy embraced Matt in a way he could not explain. It was a haven that Matt knew Monica would love. Mystical Gardens was his choice.

Convincing Monica to take a week off from work was easy. Convincing her to surrender her yoga classes for a week was tough. Matt made it happen somehow.

Monica thought they were going to spend a relaxing week in the quiet coastal town of Newport, Oregon. When Matt took the Bremerton Exit off I-5 South, Monica knew he was up to something. It took all of Matt's willpower not to give in to her battery of questions. Her face lit up like a child observing a glorious wonder when they arrived. 'Perfect' was how Monica described Mystical Gardens once they had settled in.

It was a Wednesday morning in early summer. Monica and Matt were hand in hand, taking their early morning stroll around Tulip Pond before breakfast. A thin gray gauze of the early morning fog remained. It was wet and cool and lingered on and around the emerald surface of Tulip Pond like an intimate friend who did not wish to leave.

Monica and Matt spoke in hushed voices. Anything above a whisper seemed sacrilegious at such a sacred moment. They felt like the only humans left in paradise. Matt turned to Monica. His gaze settled upon her face. She was not only beautiful, but she looked so serene. A tranquil aura surrounded her being. Matt was in awe.

A few geese and ducks swam along the surface of the pond, minding their own business.

"Did you want to say something, Matt?" Monica asked.

Matt continued to stare. The words came softly without thought, but with full resonance of what Matt felt. "I love you, Monica."

Monica smiled. "I know, honey," Monica said with quiet confidence.

Monica kissed him. Matt kissed her back. The call of the geese broke their kissing spell. Monica took Matt's arm and laid her head to rest on his shoulder. They continued their stroll in blissful silence until the fog burned away.

"Will you marry me?" Matt asked.

It happened like a hug from God filled with warm affection and electric love. The question surprised Matt a lot more than it did Monica. Matt was unprepared. He had not purchased an engagement ring. He had not intended to propose. The question had fluttered from his mouth like a butterfly.

Matt stared into Monica's beautiful brown eyes. Her face was as calm as the morning. Matt could no longer imagine a world without her. Monica smiled at him. His universe stopped. He could not think or move. Time held its breath.

"Of course I'll marry you, sweetheart," Monica said, as if it were preordained. "I love you and I want to spend the rest of my life with you."

Time took a deep breath. The universe preceded its motion. Matt was ecstatic to the point of being paralyzed. Monica kissed Matt. Matt swept Monica up in his arms.

"What do you say we have breakfast in bed," Monica said after their long, passionate kiss. The geese and ducks sounded their approval. Matt responded with a nod.

The weekend following their return home, Matt and Monica went shopping for an engagement ring.

*　　*　　*

Ivory linen tablecloths winked like stars against the blue velvet of a clear summer night under soft lighting. Crystal clear chamber music flowed from a gothic ceiling decorated in vivid High Renaissance-style hand painted, romantic, idyllic scenes. Elegant place settings and décor, delicious French cuisine, and accommodating servers made La Amour a lover's paradise for fine dining.

La Amour was filled with Friday night couples imbibing in the romantic ambiance of the restaurant. It was a unique place for Matt and Vicki, an intimate dining place they reserved for special occasions.

Vicki loved French food. It was their third year dating anniversary. Matt used that knowledge to sway any suspicions Vicki might have that something was amiss. By convincing Vicki, he wanted to show his lady how much he loved and appreciated her by taking her to her favorite restaurant.

Matt had worn a navy blue chalk-stripped designer two-button suit, a pale blue designer tennis-collar shirt, and a silk blue tattersall designer tie. His Italian black leather shoes were spit-shined. A crisp white silk pocket hanky stood majestically out of his breast pocket like a four-pointed crown. He was clean-shaven, as always, and his black hair was brushed back in uniform silky waves, completing his elegant look for the evening.

Vicki had followed suit in the department of elegance. She was wearing a designer black silk paisley, form-fitting V-neck dress bordered by solid velvet at the hem that fell to her knees and hugged her gymnast body in all of the right places. A short string of white pearls—a birthday gift from Matt that year—shone against her peach-colored skin like pale moonlight.

Vicki often wore her hair pulled back in a curly ponytail because she considered her thick brunette curls (which Matt liked so much) unmanageable. That evening, her hair flowed over her shoulders like a lion's mane made of lamb's wool. Her make-up highlighted the fullness of her lips, her sensual brown eyes, and her smooth, round cheeks.

How Vicki looked that evening underscored what Matt thought of her appearance most of the time. *Amazing*, was what Matt thought when he first saw Vicki that evening. From the stares Vicki received from other men, he was not alone.

Matt checked his right jacket pocket for the thirteenth time during dinner. The black velvet ring box was still there. He had gone to the bathroom three times; once because he needed to, twice to rehearse his lines.

Matt found himself isolated with Vicki. While Vicki's family and friends accepted him, the same was not true of Vicki in regards to his family and friends. They didn't want to be around Matt when he was with Vicki. His friends did not like her laugh, voice, or personality, and described her appearance as "all right."

"She's obnoxious, self-centered, materialistic, and vain," his mother came out and told Matt when he pressed her for an opinion about his girlfriend. "I don't trust her," was all his father would say on the matter. His brother described Vicki as an "opportunist" who would use Matt for what she could get, then dump him when something better came along.

Matt never doubted that Vicki was the one for him. He had grown to dismiss what his family and friends thought of her. The Vicki he knew was intelligent, focused, driven, sweet, sensitive, caring, and, above all else, loved Matt as much as he loved her.

Their conversation had been both light and serious—moods controlled mostly by Vicki. They were in the middle of a delicious dessert of Poire Belle-Hélène when Matt drew in a deep breath, whispering to himself, "Here we go." Matt pushed back his chair to stand.

"Vicki, I have something to say," Matt opened with, if he didn't say that Vicki would not be quiet long enough to let him finish.

"Vicki, we've been dating for awhile, and it's been the best time of my life. I knew when I met you, and I know even more now, that I love you. I need you, and I want you in my life forever."

Matt stood before Vicki. He fumbled the ring box out of his jacket pocket. There had been a buzz of conversation, and motion throughout their dinner that seemed to shut down as Matt continued. All eyes in the restaurant turned their way.

"Vicki," he said, dropping to one knee while he plucked the ten-thousand dollar diamond ring from its satin seat. "Will you marry me?"

Matt held the ring before Vicki as if presenting her majesty the queen with a humble offering. There was a hush in the restaurant. Vicki was in awe. Her face and eyes glowed. A force of unfettered joy exploded behind her words. "Yes, yes, yes, sweetheart. I'll marry you!"

Vicki leaped into Matt's arms with such force that Matt dropped the ring. Vicki repeatedly kissed Matt on the lips, saying yes between each thrilled kiss. There was applause and a smattering of congratulations hurled their way.

"It's not official," someone said, silencing the enthusiasm. "He has to put the ring on her finger."

Vicki regained enough composure to be seated, although she could not stop fidgeting in her chair. Matt found the ring. Vicki presented Matt with her hand. Matt polished the engagement ring with his pocket hanky, then slipped it onto Vicki's ring finger.

The ring stopped at her knuckle. Both Matt and Vicki could see it was too small. A few futile attempts were made by Matt to force the engagement ring onto Vicki's ring finger. At the suggestion of the food server, they tried ice, butter, and olive oil. Nothing worked.

"Oh!" was the collective cry in La Amour when it became clear the ring would not fit.

"How could you not know my ring size?" Vicki said, loud enough for all to hear. Matt was asking himself the same question.

"I can get the ring resized tomorrow, honey," Matt said, unable to mask his dismay.

"Or buy me a new one." The twinkle in Vicki's eyes burned laser hot.

"Come by my jewelry store tomorrow," a neat gentleman with a thick white mustache said from three tables away. "I'll resize the ring for free." Matt thanked him with an uneasy nod, using that opportunity to look away from Vicki.

Vicki wrested the ring from Matt and placed it on her left pinky finger, standing triumphant and waving her hand in the air like a beauty queen saluting an adoring crowd. There was applause, laughter, and congratulations all around.

Matt plummeted from embarrassment to humiliation. Everything about that evening but placing the ring onto Vicki's finger had gone as planned. He stood and brushed off his pants, trying to mask his shame.

Vicki locked her arms around his waist and squeezed Matt tight. Matt squeezed back. They kissed.

The applause and cheers stopped once they sat down. Matt's humiliation evaporated during their acceptance of the adoration of the crowd. Both were too excited to finish their desserts. Vicki decided they would go to Matt's place to celebrate. The restaurant manager who mentioned the restaurant catered weddings as he gave them his card personally delivered a complimentary bottle of champagne to them. Vicki and Matt took the champagne with them back to Matt's place, where they consummated their engagement all night long.

The first thing after breakfast, Matt was having Vicki's engagement ring resized by the man with the neat, thick, white mustache with Vicki by his side.

*    *    *

Monica and Matt's union was a backyard wedding in the second week of August beneath a clear expanse of deep blue sky and brilliant sunlight. In many ways, it was a traditional white wedding ceremony embodied with all of the sacraments and ritual preparations.

There was a holy man from an established religion who presided over the proceedings from a makeshift garden chapel. To the left of the holy man, family and friends of the bride were seated in handmade stained and padded wooden pews staked to the ground. To his right were seated family and friends of the groom in handmade stained and padded wooden pews staked to the ground. Directly before the holy man, an aisle of green grass was the procession way for the wedding party.

The wedding included a maid of honor, a best man, bridesmaids, groomsmen, a flower girl, a ring bearer, ushers, and a junior bridesmaid.

The bride wore a traditional white gown and veil as well as something old, something new, something borrowed, and something blue. The groom wore a traditional tuxedo (albeit not black, but turquoise). Wagner's "Bridal Course" played as the bride made her entrance and processional march to the altar, escorted by her adoring father. The bride and groom recited their personal wedding vows, placed symbols of their union on each other's ring fingers, and sealed the deal with a kiss. All of it went off without a hitch. How their wonderful wedding ceremony came together was memorable and somewhat unique.

Matt learned from Monica that she had never dreamed of having an expensive wedding. Her only dream was to marry the man she loved. Monica felt that spending an exorbitant amount of money on a wedding was wasteful and foolish. That money could be used more practically, such as for a down payment on a home; or it could be invested or saved.

Just as Monica insisted, Matt spent no more than two thousand dollars on her engagement ring. The amount of money spent on a ring was not synonymous with the volume of their love, Monica believed.

Matt had to restrain himself from spending ten times her ceiling. With Monica by his side, resolved in her parsimonious conviction, it was easier for Matt to throttle back his desire to splurge.

Monica took that same prudent and pure love approach to the planning of their wedding. To quote Monica, "It is the thought behind a gift, rather than its value, that gives it meaning." Monica wanted her wedding to come from that place. It echoed in the theme that she gave their wedding ceremony, "A Common-Sense Affair."

Monica laid out her vision of their wedding to an intimate gathering of family and friends at their engagement party, given by Matt's parents. Matt's family and friends adored Monica, a feeling they shared with Monica's family and friends.

Everyone was so impressed by Monica's ideas that they all volunteered to do something within their area of experience or expertise.

Monica had that way about her. People wanted to do things for her. Matt believed it was because Monica was quick to help others in their times of need. Karma was being fulfilled, in his opinion.

As a self-appointed wedding planner, Monica coordinated and developed all aspects of her vision for their impending nuptial. Matt didn't care about the details. Whatever ideas Monica brought to Matt regarding the wedding, Matt pretended to give the matter some thought, then unequivocally agreed with his bride-to-be's opinion.

Monica's parents volunteered the use of their spacious backyard for the ceremony. Monica's dad owned a chain of popular floral boutiques. He agreed to supply all of the floral needs for the wedding. He also brought Monica his ideas on how to decorate their backyard for the ceremony. Monica heartily approved.

Matt's dad was a successful contractor. His major contribution was providing the pews for the outdoor reception at no cost to the couple. He refused to tell how much they cost, and took any attempt at reimbursement as an insult. Monica could also rely on Matt's dad to provide any manual labor she might need for free, as well.

Monica's mom had been an aspiring fashion designer before changing course to become assistant dean of the Northwest Art Institute. She volunteered to design and make Monica's wedding gown and Matt's tuxedo. The veil was the same one Monica's mom wore at her wedding.

All of the guests were encouraged to come casual. Their presence, not their wardrobe, was all that were important to the bride and groom. All wedding invitations were e-mailed and gifts were optional.

The wedding guests ignored the casual dress code Monica had suggested. Family and friends came dressed in their best, their collective excuses being that their casual clothes were still at the cleaners. The bridesmaids and groomsmen pleasantly surprised Matt and Monica by wearing coordinated outfits, a request that neither the bride nor groom had made.

Vicki made it a point to dress her own children for their wedding. "No children of mine are going to look like castoffs at your bohemian affair," Vicki told Matt. Besides having their children exceptionally groomed, Vicki dressed their son in a tailor-made, five-piece tuxedo, cummerbund, crisp wingtip pleated shirt, satin bowtie, and calfskin leather shoes.

Their daughter wore a designer flower dress, lace gloves, ivory ruffled socks, calfskin leather shoes, and the pearl necklace that Matt had given to Vicki as a birthday gift years ago.

Matt's parents volunteered the use of their home for the reception. Matt's mom was a therapist by profession, but she had a flare for décor and decorations that flourished during major holidays and family celebrations. She put that skill to good use by coordinating an elegant reception that Monica found outstanding.

Matt's brother was a chef. Monica requested that the food at their reception be healthy, but delicious. Matt's brother prepared a menu that, with a few minor adjustments from Monica, she approved. Matt's brother took on all catering responsibilities, calling on favors, including one from a baker buddy to make a four-tier wedding cake complete with a traditional bride and groom on top.

Monica's old music teacher, who remained a friend of her parents, played the wedding music. A close professional disc jockey friend of Matt's handled music at the reception. Both refused payment for being a part of something that gave them so much pleasure.

The only drama during the entire wedding planning process was Vicki. Vicki was invited to attend their wedding despite deep reservations from Matt. Vicki refused. Vicki also refused to allow their children to participate as ring bearer and flower girl.

It wasn't the fact that their children thought the world of Monica that made Vicki defiant. Nor was Vicki concerned that Matt would try to steal their children from her. Vicki never attempted to hide her disdain for the fact Matt was remarrying. The person he was marrying was insignificant.

Matt had anticipated his ex-wife's stance on that issue. As much as he hated to put his children through an arduous legal ordeal, Matt felt it would be best for the children, in the end, to prove to them how important they remained in his life. He asked his attorney to set in motion a plea to force Vicki to allow their children to be a part of his wedding.

Their participation fell within Matt's legal rights, especially since his wedding date fell on his normal weekend of having full custody of his children, as outlined in their divorce decree. Vicki claimed to be taking the children to Disneyland that weekend. Matt positioned himself to have a court order issued for his children.

Vicki finally recanted, but not because she feared a court battle or a loss. Matt later discovered that his children had told their mother that if she did not allow them to be a part of their dad's wedding, they would run away.

Vicki knew her children possessed the same stubbornness and determination as their mother. Vicki also knew that if they followed through on their threat, it could bring into question her fitness as a parent.

Better to come off as the bigger person and allow the children to participate, was her conclusion of necessity. Her absence would be her silent boycott against the affair.

Family and friends filled in whenever and wherever they were needed. Most times, it felt more like a party than a chore. The day came, and all was in ready. Matt believed that the brief but heartfelt vows he said to Monica at the altar summarized the entire spirit of their nuptial:

"On this day, let it be known to all we encounter that my love for you is infinite in scope, and eternal. The life we step forward in together, bathed in the love and best hopes of our family and friends, is blessed by their belief, as well as our own, that we are forever grateful to the universe for this union.

"Love is the word I use to summarize my feelings for you and those that share this precious moment with us. It is a word, an emotion, which skims the surface of the depth and breadth of what I feel. May this day, that in the days to come be known to us as our wedding anniversary, be cherished by Monica and I forever.

"Let us not forget those who gave so much of themselves to make this day come to pass in such splendor. With all that I have to give to you, Monica, I am forever yours."

*  *  *

What Matt remembered most about his marriage to Vicki was that it was a lavish affair attended by more than 300 guests, most of whom Matt did not know.

*  *  *

The bus carefully maneuvered its way around an accident scene involving a woman driving an SUV and a man who had been riding a bike. The bicyclist's leg was clearly broken. The driver was on her smartphone, appearing frightened. A police cruiser pulled up.

The driver launched into a frantic tirade that indicated how the accident was the bicyclist's fault. One of the officers attempted to calm her down while the other went to check on the bicyclist. An emergency medical team was attending the man with the broken leg, who writhed in considerable pain. Matt could see tears on his face.

The bus maneuvered, as if in slow motion, around the troubling scene.

*     *     *

Ten years and two children after their nuptial, Matt had given up on being happy with Vicki. He would settle for contentment. The professional focus and drive he had admired in her had ballooned into an obsession that dominated their lives.

Vicki wanted to be president of Mason Bank in twenty years. It was clear to Matt that Vicki would make any sacrifice to achieve that goal. From her taxing work hours to her constant networking, it was all part of her master plan to achieve her professional objectives.

Time with him and their children was not top priority on her list, except on those few occasions when Matt would put his foot down. Even then, Vicki grudgingly conceded.

When Vicki was promoted to regional manager of Mason Bank, Matt had hoped things would get better. He had hoped Vicki might take a breather from her professional aspirations and pay attention to their children and him for a while.

Matt had intended on surprising Vicki with one of her favorite meals as a celebration for her promotion. Maybe rekindle some of the lost romance in their marriage in the process. He left work early, picked up all of the fresh ingredients he would need, and got home around noon. That gave him plenty of time to prepare everything before he had to pick the children up from school.

The first thing Matt noticed when he attempted to pull into their two-car garage was a black Hummer parked in his space. Matt didn't recognize the vehicle. He entered his home with caution, concerned it could be some sort of home invasion.

Carefully, Matt looked around downstairs. The only suspicious things he encountered were two used wine glasses and a near-empty bottle of merlot.

Matt made his way upstairs to the master bedroom. No one was there. Remaining alert, Matt quietly slipped past his children's bedrooms to the guest bedroom at the far end of the hall, trying his best not to allow his imagination to lead the way.

The door was closed. He could hear the sounds of sexual passion coming through the closed door. Matt recognized Vicki's voice. For a brief moment, Matt considered walking away. He considered confronting Vicki about her infidelity later, or even suppressing that information at the likelihood of a divorce. Anger ruled. Infidelity was one thing Matt could not tolerate in his marriage.

His anger erupted in him like a volcano, boiling over with rage. Matt tried the door. It was locked. Matt stepped back and kicked it in. Vicki was in the cowgirl position on top of her lover, facing him. Matt rushed them. He grabbed Vicki by her shoulders, lifted her up, and threw her against the wall behind him.

Matt recognized the man. He was the president of Mason Bank. The bank president attempted to rise, but Matt hit him with a right hook that sent his head bouncing off the pillows. The bank president grabbed his eye with both hands, screeching a painful expletive.

Matt punched him in the stomach and ribs to get him to drop his hands from his face. The sparring matches he'd had with his father and big brother were paying big dividends.

A chaotic calamity of pounding flesh and frantic voices filled the room. The bank president swung wildly at Matt. Matt blocked his attempts and hit him with a furious flurry of precise punches to the head and body. Vicki screamed at Matt to stop. The bank president tried to shove Matt away with his legs, to no avail.

The vicious onslaught left the bank president defenseless. Matt was blind with fury. He heard Vicki's screams, but they didn't quell the inferno devouring his gut.

Vicki leaped onto his back. Matt was prepared to hit the bank president again, his fist drawn back and shaking with rage; but the act of Vicki holding him even as an act of restraint, her hot breath on his neck, had a momentary eerie calming effect.

Matt straightened, dropping his hands by his side. The bank president, black, blue, and bleeding, reeled in pain from the beating Matt had given him.

"Are you crazy?" Vicki screamed into Matt's ear.

"Get off me," Matt calmly said to Vicki with a voice hissing with ferocious intensity. Vicki did as he commanded. Matt stalked out of the room.

Matt waited downstairs, pacing back and forth, attempting to quell his fury. Vicki helped the battered man walk. The bank president's expensive rumpled clothes hid his bruised body.

Both stared at Matt with fear. It was the first time Matt had ever seen that look in Vicki's eyes. The bank president stared at Matt from the eye that had not swollen shut. What Matt had done to his face, only time and plastic surgery would heal.

Matt paced back and forth in the middle of their spacious living room, glaring at them, his fist and jaws clenched. He kept his distance for fear he might kill his wife and her lover. Without a word, Vicki helped the bank president out of the house through the garage entrance.

Matt heard the Hummer startup. He listened to the vehicle pull away. Vicki didn't come back inside. Matt looked out of the window. Vicki was driving the Hummer. Matt later learned that Vicki had accompanied the bank president to the local hospital emergency room.

After they left, Matt looked at his hands. There were mild bruises and razor cuts everywhere. Blood from the bank president's face stained his hands. Matt stared at his hands as if they belonged to someone else. He knew he had to wash them and seal the cuts before he picked up his inquisitive children from school.

*  *  *

No charges were pressed against Matt. In an effort to protect his marriage and career, the married bank president claimed he had been mugged and beaten: a story Vicki supported for the same self-serving purposes.

Vicki attempted damage control on their marriage. She suggested counseling, promised to be faithful, and pleaded for forgiveness, an act Matt believed she was incapable of.

Matt knew his wife well enough to know when she was being sincere. Her attempt at mending their fractured marriage was more for professional appearances than concern over him. Divorce was the only honorable solution for them, as far as Matt was concerned.

Matt was shocked at the number of affairs Vicki had that his divorce attorney's investigator uncovered. Five that they could confirm, and another three that they suspected. Matt looked over the list of lovers Vicki had had over the years.

All but one man on the list Matt knew could help Vicki get ahead in her career (the one outstanding affair, Matt assumed, was simply for pleasure).

While infidelity was the agent that dissolved their marriage, the largest problem the divorce dredged up in Matt's mind was what they sought in life.

Vicki lusted for luxury, power, and wealth. Matt desired to live contentedly within small means. Vicki was willing to sacrifice just about everything to achieve her goals. Matt placed family above all else.

Their chasm of beliefs was too great a bridge to cross. For Matt to follow Vicki, he would have to sacrifice his soul. For Vicki to fall in line with Matt, she would have to deaden her drive. It would have been easier for each to give up a limb than part with their true selves.

Their divorce was surprisingly amicable on most issues. Matt suspected Vicki wanted a quick and quiet end to their marriage for appearances' sake.

Matt fought for custody of his children, but not to the point that he would allow his attorney to attack Vicki as an unfit mother. Matt did not ever want his children to think of their mother in that way. Matt believed Vicki had instructed her attorney to do the same, since his fitness as a parent was never broached at any time during their divorce proceedings.

Matt lost the battle for custody of their children. He did win one custody weekend a month and open visitation rights (with proper notification beforehand to his ex-wife). Vicki had no problem agreeing to those terms.

Why Vicki may have placed her professional aspirations ahead of him and the children, Matt never doubted Vicki loved their children as much as he did. Ironically, their divorce made Vicki an attentive mother.

Since Vicki made four times more money than her husband, and her infidelity was ruled as grounds for divorce, Matt was entitled to alimony. Matt rejected the offer. He insisted on paying child support. His mother thought him foolish. His father and brother understood. It was a male ego issue.

A man that pays his own way in this world was the kind of man he was. It was the kind of man he wanted his daughter to respect and expect; the kind of man he wanted his son to be.

When a final ruling was handed down on their divorce, there was disheartened relief between Matt and Vicki. There was a moment, as they signed their divorce papers, when their eyes met, unshielded by any contempt for the other.

For an instant, Matt felt the love between them that had somehow been kidnapped. He was reminded of the Vicki he had fallen in love with, the love of his life.

Vicki's smartphone rang. It was her office: a call Vicki had to take. Matt left that meeting already missing his children, but not their mother.

*　　*　　*

Matt's moments of connection and reflection passed. The bus arrived at his work stop. It was a grand morning. Matt decided to walk down to the waterfront instead of heading into the office. His job could wait for a little while.

Matt sat on a bench that allowed him to look out over The Sound. Mantra chants from seagulls filled the air. A Puget Sound ferry cut a clean swath through the bright sun and calm emerald surface of Elliot

Bay.

Across the bay, a crown of gray mist hovered above the homes and trees of Bainbridge Island. Matt's phone vibrated. He checked the phone display. "EX-WIFE" it read. Matt thanked the tech gods for caller ID, turned off his phone, and put it back into his pocket.

# THE CASE OF THE MISSING TEENAGER

It was summer. The temperature had reached eighty-eight degrees in Portland, with an uncharacteristic seventy percent humidity.

I had just nailed a scam artist who had bilked several insurance companies out of 20.5 million dollars over the last six years. The case had been grueling, requiring around-the-clock surveillance for two months.

He was smart. He was careful. In the end, he proved human. When I linked the con man with half a dozen aliases to half a dozen fraudulent insurance claims, that knotted the legal hangman's noose. Allowing him to move forward with his latest scheme had put the noose around his neck.

His newest venture involved a severe back injury while working as a garage mechanic. The garage owner was in on the scam. He had a physician and chiropractor on his payroll, as well.

I had photographs proving his back injury claim was bogus. No sooner did he have the insurance check in hand, than he was arrested. The check was made out to Philip King. His real name was Edgar Fox.

I was ready for a vacation when Scott Wright walked into my office, a clean-shaven, chubby dark brown man with short dregs, large hands, and perfect teeth. Mr. Wright had been referred to me by the love of my life, Destini Pendleton.

Destini is also a Portland Police Department homicide detective. She had clued me in that Mr. Wright would be dropping by. I tried wriggling out of it.

The Wrights were friends of the Pendleton family. Destini and Scott went to high school together. Destini had the highest regard for most of her fellow police officers. She was also aware of how swamped with cases they sometimes got. She recommended Wright talk to me for additional help in finding his sister Dana. How could I refuse?

"My sister's been missing for five days," Scott Wright said, his face drawn with worry. "I'll admit Dana's on the wild side, sometimes. Mostly she disappears for a day or two and then shows up at my parent's house as if nothing happened. This time is different. I can feel it."

"Is it because of the time span?" My eyes narrowed on Wright's face. My face was drawn as tight as my lips.

"That, and something in my gut tells me Dana's in trouble. Normally Dana telephones me or Jackie, my wife, to let us know she's okay. We would let my folks know Dana had called. My folks would gain comfort from knowing Dana was fine."

"Why doesn't Dana contact your parents herself?"

"Teenage rebellion stuff, I suppose. She's coming up on her senior year of high school. My parents have been riding her to decide her future—college and all of that. Dana doesn't want to hear or think about it. My sister believes in living in the moment. Tomorrow will take care of itself."

*Most teenagers think that way*, I thought. *Too bad adults are so anxious to rob them of that gift.*

I heard a note of disdain in Wright's voice when he spoke of his sister's belief in living in the moment. My investigator instincts told me it was a matter I needed to explore. "How do you feel about Dana's attitude, Mr. Wright?"

"Huh? About what?"

"Your sister's philosophy about living in the present?"

"It's her life. She should be allowed to make her own choices."

"Did you think as Dana did when you were her age?"

"No way. I had planned my life to college and beyond. That's just how I am."

"How are those plans working out?"

"About fifty-fifty."

"If Dana goes to college, who will pay for it?"

"My parents, myself, student loans, grants—somehow, the money will materialize. Why are you asking me about this?"

"I'm just trying to get a snapshot of Dana's mental state. In her absence, those closest to her can help fill the void." What I didn't say was that I was also ascertaining Scott Wright's mental state, as well.

I had seen many perverse and sad situations in my years as a DEA field operative. Those experiences hadn't made me cynical—they had prepared me to expect the unexpected. Just because Dana was his sister didn't make him any less of a suspect in her recent disappearance.

"She's a typical middle-class teenager," Scott said.

"So it would seem."

"You'll take the case?"

"Are you certain you don't want to wait a while longer to see if the police find her first?" I felt that, if given enough time, Dana would come home, or the police would find her. If the latter happened, I hoped that she was alive and healthy when they did.

"I would feel better knowing someone was working exclusively on finding my sister and not have her be only one of a cop's caseload."

*Suit yourself*, I thought. "My fee is $300 a day, plus expenses. I'll need an advance deposit for one week." His being Destini's friend didn't entitle him to any discounts in my book. Business is business.

Scott whistled. "Man, that's steep."

"There's always patience."

"No, no, I'll rest easier knowing one of the best detectives around is on the case."

"I'm a private investigator. Law enforcement has detectives."

"Sorry."

"No problem. Thanks for the compliment. Do you have a picture of your sister?"

Scott handed me a color print of a young woman with box braids, a full round face, a diamond stud in her right nostril, and a deep dimpled smile. She had her brother's complexion.

There was a hearty gleam in her dark brown eyes that not only spoke of joy, but defiance. Like her brother, she also had perfect teeth.

I studied the print for a moment. I didn't see anything in the photo that made me regard Dana as a wild child. Her eyes kept drawing me in. *What are you up to, Dana?* That was the question that immediately came to mind.

"I'll need a list of her friends and acquaintances," I said. "A boyfriend you might be aware of, places she might hang out, clubs she might frequent—that sort of thing."

"No problem. I'd like to keep my parents out of this, if you don't mind."

"Why?"

"They're worried enough as it is. If my parents know I've hired a private investigator, they might assume the worst."

"Are you, Mr. Wright?"

"Excuse me?"

"Assuming the worst."

Scott swallowed hard. I supposed it was the first time he had allowed his worst fears to manifest.

I had gone too far. I should have let the matter drop. Having my vacation plans interrupted had knocked my bedside manner out of whack.

"I don't know," he said in a distant whisper. "And I don't want to think about it."

"Don't worry, Mr. Wright. I'll find her. It's probably just like you said—some rebellious teenage thing."

My injection of hope was too late. Scott Wright told me about everyone and anything he could think of regarding his sister. I jotted down key persons and places I would check out. Ten minutes after Wright left my office, I was out in the field.

*     *     *

I decided to cut to the chase. Teenager, missing. Most likely reasons: love, drugs, or liberation. The boyfriend would be the best place to start, from the list of people her brother had supplied me.

It was late morning. I knocked on the front door of Raymond

Tisdale in an upscale community of pruned yards and three-story homes. A teenager of about five-ten with a sinewy build and cropped hair, who reminded me a lot of Lenny Kravitz, answered.

His visible tattoos were a tribal war band wrapped around his right bicep and a phoenix around his left forearm. He had a diamond earring in his left ear. In his right ear, he wore a ruby. His platinum chains and hip-hop gear made him look like he had just stepped out of a rap video.

I asked for his parents. He said they weren't home. I identified myself and asked his name. He told me with an attitude. He turned out to be just the person I was looking for.

Ray, as he insisted on being called instead of Raymond, asked me what I wanted. I told him that I had been hired by Dana's brother to find her. Ray's face went from badass to frightened child. I reassured him that anything he told me was confidential, and that no blame would be placed on him. I asked him to step outside so we could talk. He invited me in.

"What'd you want to know?" His belligerent tone had returned.

"Where and when was the last time you saw Dana?"

Ray averted his eyes. Was that nerves, or a reflex reaction to lying? "At a party," he said with a slight tremor in his voice.

"Where was the party?"

"At my dog's house."

"Was this dog a friend of Dana's, too?"

"No. Dana knows him, but that's it."

"Does this dog have a name?"

"Yeah," Ray said, as if that were the end of it.

"Care to share?"

"Not really."

"Did you leave the party with Dana?"

"No."

"Did she leave alone?"

"Nah—I mean, ah, yeah, Dana was by herself." Ray looked away when he answered, and the tremor was back. It was definitely a lie reflex.

"When Dana left, was she in a clear state of mind?" I asked.

His jaw tightened. His eyes fixed on mine. "If you mean was Dana sober, the answer's yes. Dana doesn't drink."

"Does she get high?"

"Hell, no!"

"Are you certain?"

"Yeah, I'm certain!"

"How do you know?"

"She's my girlfriend, and Dana don't get down like that," Ray stated with belligerence.

"Wives keep secrets from their husbands all of the time. What makes you think girlfriends are any different?" I was goading him to see where it might lead.

"I know Dana. She wouldn't be caught dead with drugs. She hates them."

"Do you?"

"Do I what?"

"Hate drugs?"

"I thought you were here looking for Dana."

"Forgive me if I seem to get off track. Even people who don't use drugs can be acquainted with those who do. With a few degrees of separation between them, one innocent acquaintance can evolve that could get them into unintentional trouble."

"What?" Ray said, clearly confused.

"Somebody she knows could have gotten in trouble behind drugs and involved her."

"Oh," Ray averted his eyes. "No, that didn't happen."

"Did Dana say where she was going when she left the party?"

"Home."

"Did she leave alone?" I asked the question again to check his previous response.

"No—I mean, yeah." Again, Ray averted his eyes.

"Are you sure?"

"I'm sure," Ray said, determined to sell his lie.

"Did you notice anyone or anything suspicious at the party who might have meant Dana harm?"

"Man, you're paranoid. No, I didn't notice anyone or anything suspicious at the party."

Ray had told me all he was going to. Needling him anymore wasn't going to break his silence. He knew more than he was saying. He had told me a couple of things without knowing it. Drugs were involved, and Dana did not leave alone.

"Who else was still at the party when Dana left?"

"You're kidding, right?"

My silence answered for me.

"A bunch of us. Dana left early."

"How early is early?"

"Around ten."

"Why didn't you leave with her?"

"I wasn't ready to go."

"I take it that means she had her own transportation."

"Yeah."

"Who threw the party?"

"Puffy."

"As in P. Diddy?"

"No, as in Lee Griffin. He goes by the name of Puffy."

"Address and telephone number, please."

"Why?" Ray asked, apprehension turning his look askew.

"I'm going to need to talk to Puffy."

"About what? I've already told you everything," Ray said, squaring his eyes to mine.

"Maybe he saw or heard some things you didn't, or he knows someone who did."

Ray was quiet.

"No problem. I'm sure your parents will be more cooperative."

"*Alright, man.*" Ray gave me Lee Griffin's address and telephone number. When I left, Ray was as nervous as an athlete using illegal steroids on drug testing day.

I circled the block and found a good spot where I could observe the Tisdale house. Ten minutes later, Ray raced out, talking frantically to someone on the other end of his cell. Then he jumped in a new tomato-red Ford Mustang and raced off.

*   *   *

Ray was driving so fast. we were both lucky Highway Patrol didn't pull us over. An hour later, I found myself following Ray on some quiet back roads through a mix of Oregon backwoods and farmland. Finally, we came upon a clearing.

Ray parked in the back yard of a single-story farmhouse that was well off the beaten path. I watched through my binoculars. Ray entered the house through the back door.

I locked my car and jogged around to the front of the house, assuming the occupants were congregating toward the back. The front windows were boarded with plywood, making me confident that my approach had gone unnoticed. I slipped onto the squat front porch without a sound. I checked the front door. It was unlocked. I opened it and walked inside. They were standing at the end of the short entry hall. A plump young woman of about five-five and Ray were kissing.

Dana Wright. I recognized her from the photo.

Dana saw me first. Ray rushed me, attempting to land a wild right hook. I caught him by his right wrist, spun him around, pinned his right arm behind his back, and then shoved him hard toward Dana.

Ray stumbled and fell to his knees. Ray was on his feet like a shot, with full intentions of tearing me a new one.

"Don't even think about it, son," I said, pointing a stiff index finger at him like a warning shot. Ray continued his march, spurred on by my threat. I was ready to hurt Ray enough to discourage him but not render any serious physical harm.

Dana bolted between us. Ray stopped. Dana edged Ray back a few steps with her hands firmly on his chest, Ray glaring at me the entire time. They weren't alone. Another young woman had stepped into the picture from the family room.

"Please, close the door," Dana said, having turned to face me. She held out her arms, keeping an irate Ray at bay like a basketball player attempting to block out an opponent.

I did as Dana asked, after which, I moved closer to the teenage trio. I could see most of the family room from where I stood in the short hallway. On one side of the family room were three rolled-up sleeping bags. On the other side were three upholstered metal folding chairs, collapsed and placed upright against the wall. A gasoline-powered generator, along with a portable space heater, was against the same wall as the folding chairs.

I ordered the young people to stay put. There was no reaction on their part. Dana had made herself a human roadblock between Ray and me. They looked scared. Even Ray's bravado didn't hide that fact from me. That was good. Fear and doubt would keep them rooted long enough for me to do a quick sweep of the house to make sure we were alone.

The farmhouse was comfortable, considering the weather. A portable A/C unit in the family room was the reason why. Its hardwood floors were pitted from neglect, except for the bathroom and kitchen. They were peach-colored vinyl. The walls were discolored by time.

In the kitchen was another portable gasoline-powered generator powering the refrigerator, stove, and a box fan. There was plenty of bottled water and canned goods on the kitchen counter and table, along with an assortment of nutritional supplements. A few dated furnishings probably left behind by previous occupants had been cleaned up and made functional. The kitchen and dining sets were part of that era.

There were clean supplies of women's underwear, sweat socks, shirts, and jeans neatly ordered in the bedroom closet. That suggested to me that Ray did not stay with them. The smell of bleach and disinfectant was everywhere. The plumbing was working. So was the hot and cold running water. Modern touches, such as a couple of laptops and a smartphone on the plain wooden coffee table, brought one back to the present. Besides a few flourishing houseplants and strategically positioned flashlights, there was little else to see. The place was sparse, neat, and orderly. They had all of the basics covered, and enough creature comforts to set up house.

I didn't know where these middle-class teenagers learned their survival training for this circumstance, but they had it down pat. The farmhouse was empty except for those three.

I returned to find Ray standing beside Dana, who had her arms wrapped tight around the taller unidentified girl's waist. The mystery teenager was trembling.

"How'd you find this place?" I asked.

"How'd you find us?" Ray asked.

"I followed you." Ray's jaw tightened. Dana touched his shoulder, as if to let Ray know it was okay.

"Who are you?" Dana asked.

"He's that detective I was telling you about," Ray answered.

*Private investigator*, I thought, but kept my mouth shut. "Anyone want to explain to me what's going on?"

My question was met with unblinking stares and silence. I waited a few moments to see if any of them would break. Once that didn't work, I moved on. Maybe a little misdirection would loosen their tongues.

"Who's your friend?" I asked Dana.

Dana hugged the girl closer. "This is Kimberly Wilson. She's my best friend."

"Looks like she's trying to kick a bad habit."

"She's doing better than trying. She's doing it!" There was strength and pride in Dana's voice. Kimberly stopped trembling and perked up with resolve. Ray moved to Kimberly's other side, hugging her about the shoulders. All of the hate for me drained from his eyes, replaced by warm compassion for his friend. "Ray and I are going to help her through this, and nobody's going to stop us."

"You never told me how you found this place."

"We noticed it when we came to a rave out this way," Dana said.

I wasn't buying it. An out-of-the-way abandoned farmhouse is not the kind of place someone discovers in passing. You have to scout it out. I decided to let it go.

"We checked it out and liked what we saw," Ray said, his lie reflex betraying him.

"It's the perfect place for an out-of-the-way rehab center," Dana added. Dana was clearly their rock.

"Nobody came by to see what you were up to?" I asked.

"Nope," Ray said with conviction.

"Not a single visitor," Dana said, "which made it all the more perfect."

Kimberly hadn't said a word. She stood stock-still, as if willing herself invisible. Her healthy complexion was most likely cinnamon. The third party was as pale, as if much of the melanin had drained from her skin. Kimberly stared at me with eyes that were sad, tired, and desperate. A child resurrected from death.

Her going through a major narcotic withdrawal would explain the heavy use of disinfectant and bleach. Dana and Ray had probably sanitized the farmhouse before initial occupancy, and maintained it as needed. My years with the DEA had left me witness to far too many scenes of people trying to kick narcotics addictions. They were always brutal. Some ended in triumph, others in tragedy. As I looked into that frightened teenager's eyes, I prayed for victory.

"What makes you think anybody would try to stop you from helping Kimberly?" I asked Dana.

"Kim got hooked on crack," Ray said.

"So?" I said.

"You obviously have not been keeping up with our legal system," Ray said. "Being a crack addict is the same as being a criminal. If Kim asked for help and it got back to the police, she could wind up in prison for being nothing more than a user."

Ray was right. The laws on drug users and addiction had become lopsided to increase the number of people classified as criminals and not aide victims.

"What about Kim's parents?" I asked.

"There's just her mom," Dana said. "She doesn't know."

"Or care," Ray said.

"*Ray*," Dana said.

"Sorry, Kim," Ray said. His apology was sincere. "We wanted to help Kim clean up before she told her mom."

"Is your mom looking for you, Kim?" I asked.

"I guess," Kim said. Her voice was hoarse, probably due to the rigors of physical withdrawal. "My mom's gotten used to me being gone. She thinks I'm doing it to get under her skin."

"I'll bet your mother knows and cares a lot more than you're giving her credit for," I said.

Kim shrugged, "Maybe."

"Why don't you try talking to her and find out."

Kim looked at Dana. Dana nodded in agreement.

"I'll try," Kim said.

I applauded what those young people were doing to help their friend. That fact could not be severed from the concern of their parents. It was a tough call, but I had to make it.

"It looks to me like you've gotten through the worst part," I said to

Kim. "You'll need to tell your mom what you're going through so she can help. Give me a call once you do. I'll do what I can, as well."

I didn't mention that crack cocaine addicts suffer physical withdrawal symptoms, on average, for a week. The more significant challenge is overcoming the psychological cravings. That could take months.

They all nodded in acceptance of my offer. I handed each of the teenagers one of my business cards.

"Dana, you need to call your parents and let them know you're okay and that you are on your way home," I said. "You might want to give your brother a call, as well."

Dana said that she would.

"Ray, make sure these ladies get home safely."

Ray nodded.

"I'm entrusting you with this responsibility, Ray. Don't disappoint me, or I'll finish what you started here."

Ray repositioned himself behind Dana and Kimberly, placing a hand on each of their shoulders. "Consider it done," Ray said with complete confidence, appreciative of the opportunity.

"Kim," I said, "I know some drug counselors who would be more than willing to talk to you, if you'd like. Of course, they'll keep things quiet. Would you be interested?"

Kim looked at Dana. Dana nodded. Kim looked at me and nodded.

"Good. You've all got four hours to get home. I'll check up on each of you. If you're not at home, I'll haul your asses into the police station myself."

Dana gave me a slight smile, then let it drop from her face. She was sharp. I could tell by the look in her eyes that she wasn't the least bit intimidated by me. Dana would make the choice she believed was in Kim's best interest without hesitation, damn the consequences.

At that moment, I disagreed with something Scott Wright had said to me about his little sister. Dana Wright was, far and away, not your typical middle-class teenager.

"Will we get into trouble with the police?" Kim asked.

"For what?" I said, "Nobody here is going to say anything to them, right?"

Their smiles were nervous, as were their measured laughs.

"The clock's ticking," I said before I left.

I made sure they saw me drive away—an act of trust or faith; call it what you will. I checked on each of them just as I said I would. My gamble paid off.

There was a message from Scott Wright on my answering service the next day. Dana had told her parents everything. I supposed the children had decided to come clean. They were more adult than some adults I know.

I called Scott Wright back. I told him I had ripped up his check. I asked that he put the money toward Dana's college fund—if she decided to go. He agreed.

They say Aruba is lovely this time of year. I wondered if Destini could swing a week off from work to join me.

# FOGBOUND

My name is Jace Harris. I am six-three and a svelte one-ninety that can be contributed more to genetics than exercise. I keep my black African hair cut scalp-short, my eyes are marble brown, my lips are full, my nose is philistine, and my ears are small. When I smile, my eggshell-white teeth shine against the backdrop of my copper skin. That is the physical me in a nutshell.

Who I am as a man, I would prefer those who love me to define. I am college educated and behave in a manner some would derisively call bourgeois. I am not materialistic or conservative and am only somewhat conventional.

Those facts don't matter to those who'd rather operate with labels rather than substance. Their primary intent is to put me down in order to uplift themselves. It never works. When focused on destruction rather than building, then negative waters are where you swim.

Val is also college educated and has been accused of being bourgeois, which she is not. Val is five-six. I was never allowed to know her weight, as I now refer to her as adorably chubby. Her skin is the hue of and is as smooth and shiny as tanned leather. Her shoulder-length hair is dark brown and naturally curly. Her lips, too, are full, her cheekbones high, her nose a petite wide, and her eyes a clear brown. Despite her weight, she moves with the grace of a dancer.

My family is considered affluent, since we do not work for our money but have it work for us. Val chooses to work. It's in her blood. Riding the gravy train never set well with her. It seemed to undermine her independence.

That's one of the qualities I love about Val, the woman I still prefer to call my wife. In a way, her independent work ethic has gotten us to this place.

My parents never liked Val. Neither did my sister. My father didn't trust her. My mother saw her as loose. My sister questioned Val's motive in marriage, bluntly stating to me that she believed Val was after my money. My mom expressed her feelings to me a little more than a year after she was unable to derail our wedding plans:

"Beware the woman who would rather be a whore in your enemy's bed than a queen in your own." When I caught Val with another man, my mother's words proved prophetic. Had it not been for our children, I would have ended it with Val right then and there.

Shay and Cera mean the world to me. For them, I would at first endure, then move to a middle ground with Val, if possible.

There were no clues I could see that Val was having affairs (yes—*affairs*). Val didn't have any complaints about our sex life even after we'd separated. What she couldn't do was keep her panties on.

My wife apparently required a variety of lovers to keep her sexually satisfied. One was not enough, no matter how good they might be. For a man in my position to have that attitude would garner him the polite label of Player or Playboy.

For a woman—even in these modern liberated times—she is branded a whore, slut, hoe or, a gentler term, promiscuous. For a man to crave variety in his sexual partners is regarded as natural. For a woman, it's considered taboo.

Men, of course, established these definitions. I personally believe women have as much right to sexual liberation as men. I don't happen to believe those sexual freedoms extend to husbands and wives.

We had been married twelve years. During that time, we made ourselves a marvelous home and brought into the world two amazing children.

There had been occasional rumors along the way that Val was being disloyal. Even my parents, sister, and a few of my friends warned me that something was amiss. Since no one ever had proof of infidelity—and Val turned out to be an excellent liar—, I continued to trust the woman I loved.

I was en route to Home Depot to order what materials I needed to construct a greenhouse I'd been considering building for Val in our spacious backyard.

Yes, I do manual labor when it suits me. In fact, I enjoy working with my hands and am rather good at it. I was driving past a house about three miles from where we lived when I noticed a car parked in a driveway that looked exactly like Val's.

My wife is a real estate agent. Staked in the front yard was one of the generic sales signs of the real estate agency in which Val was a controlling partner.

I wouldn't have thought twice about it, except my wife had mentioned she would be showing a mansion to a prospective buyer on the other side of the city. I had wished her luck with a firm hug and a passionate kiss. The traditional red brick, mid-size ranch-style home was not only in the wrong location, it was a far cry from being a mansion.

I made a U-turn and parked on the street in front of the house. I took a closer look at the car in question. It was Val's, all right. I thought I'd pop in and surprise her. I had done so on several occasions, and Val never seemed to mind.

Have you ever had one of those queasy feelings in the pit of your stomach that something was not quite right? I had that feeling as I approached the ranch house. The question I asked myself was: did I want to go inside to discover what may have caused it, or should I drive away and try to put the whole thing out of my mind? Anyone who knows me could have given you the answer to that question.

The queasy feeling became stronger as I walked up the red brick steps onto the narrow porch and faced the front door. I took a couple of nervous breaths and rang the doorbell. I waited. There was no answer. I rang again, and there was still no answer. *Maybe no one's home*, I thought.

The idea came to me that the person who lived there might also have been the same person in the market for the mansion. Perhaps Val left her car and went with the potential buyer in his car to see the property. That wasn't an unusual scenario for realtors and clients.

I decided to leave. As I stepped off the porch, I looked back at the house. Through a bay window gauzed by sheer white summer drapes, I saw a man wearing blue boxer shorts come into view. I recognized him immediately.

Hudson Walker and I had played football for rival high schools. Hudson went to Yale. I went to Harvard. We played four years for our prospective college football teams as walk-ons. We faced each other mostly on special teams.

Hudson and I made a beeline for one another on the football field whenever possible, trying to knock the crap out of each other. It was safe to say we had a steaming hatred for one another, yet aside from being football rivals, I knew next to nothing about the man.

We went our separate ways after college. Occasionally an old high school or college teammate would relay something they had heard about Hudson. Aside from those rare reports on my gridiron nemesis, I hadn't given Hudson much thought over the years.

Hudson stood near an entrance I could only assume led to a bedroom, staring at the front door as if it were an intruder he was concerned about approaching. Val joined him, wearing nothing more than her black lace panties and bra.

My first thought was to crash through the bay window and kill Hudson. Murdering Hudson was what I was thinking when I marched up to the front door and kicked it in.

I'm not certain whether it was merely the shock of someone kicking in his front door, the sight of me, or both that caused the startled expression on his face.

*"Jace, what the hell are you doing?"* Hudson screamed at me. Val was frozen with shock.

"You son-of-a-bitch, you're fucking my wife!"

"What the hell are you talking—" before Hudson could say another word, I was on the bastard like a linebacker on an unprotected quarterback. We fought, with Hudson trying to reason and me kicking his ass. With Hudson flat on his back, reeling from a clean right hook I had landed to his chin, my eyes hunted for Val.

My wife had used our fight to slip away and get dressed. I caught Val tiptoeing through the family room toward the unobstructed front door with the splintered doorframe. I bolted in front of her, thwarting her escape.

"Hi, honey," Val had the audacity to say with a nervous smile, as if she had only been caught executing some misdemeanor crime. "I can explain."

"I'm listening."

Val stared at me as though she were about to puke and pass out at the same time. She was not looking defiant, as some women might in a similar circumstance, ready to condemn their husband as the root cause of their betrayal. Val looked as ashamed as a proud strong woman who looked everyone square in the eye. Even in my outraged state, I found that pitiable and disarming.

I moved to stand in front of her. When I did, her big brown eyes widened with fright. Val flinched when I crossed my arms over my chest. If Val knew me at all, she should have known I would never lay a hand on her, even under those excruciating circumstances. Even with my blood boiling.

Hudson staggered to his feet, rubbing his chin. "What the fuck did you do to my door?" he asked, as if he'd had one too many drinks.

"You were *fucking* my wife." Val winced. I could only assume it was due to the crass word spewing out of my mouth.

"Of all the people you chose to mess around with, you choose him."

"*She's you're wife?*" Hudson said, sounding more clear-headed as he walked toward me.

"Don't act like you didn't know."

"I didn't."

"I'm so sorry," Val said, "but I have a problem—*an illness.*"

"You're damn right you do," I said to Val. "And I know just the cure for cheating wives."

Standing next to us like a cleric about to make the pronouncement *you may now kiss the bride*, Hudson said, "Man, I honestly didn't know."

It was at that moment that I realized Hudson was telling the truth. Val used her maiden name of Church for all of her business dealings. She said it helped her maintain an independent persona separate from the wealth she had married.

I grabbed Val's left hand. Her platinum cobblestone wedding band set with diamonds was missing, replaced by a concave sterling silver ring of equal width. Val also wore a sterling silver Elsa Peretti wave five-row ring on her middle finger next to where her wedding band should have been.

I grabbed Val's right hand while still holding her left. She wore an 18k gold Paloma Marrakesh ring on her right middle finger. On her right ring finger was a green jade Elsa Peretti Cabochon ring set in 18k gold; all of which I recognized as heart-felt gifts I had given Val for one occasion or another. They were rings Val had said she preferred not to wear because she never wanted anyone to be distracted from her most cherished possession.

"Where's your wedding band?" I growled. We stood still for a moment, holding hands, staring into each other's eyes, projecting the illusion of two people fiercely in love. Val attempted to move her hands. I didn't realize the firmness of my grip.

I released her hands with a show of disgust. Val slipped off the concave silver ring and dropped it into her purse. From the same purse, she extracted her wedding band. Before Val could slip her wedding band back onto her finger, I snatched it away from her.

"Don't bother," I said, shoving it into my pants pocket. Val started hyperventilating.

"Look, Jace," Hudson said. "I didn't know she was married—and I especially didn't know she was married to *you*."

I glared at Hudson. He took a couple of steps backward. I returned my attention to Val. Val tightly closed her eyes and took a couple of deep asthmatic breaths. As much as I hated Val at that moment, I could not help but still love her when she appeared so vulnerable. I wanted to take her in my arms and calm her fears.

I glowered at Val, who had inched closer to the front door. "You didn't tell him you were married, did you?"

Val nervously smiled. "He didn't ask, and I didn't tell." Val let out a heavy sigh, as if finally resigning herself to the truth. "He didn't know I was married, Jace. It's not his fault. It's mine."

"This is your slut cover," I said, "setting up phony real estate deals?"

Shaking her head, Val said, "*No, it's nothing like that.*"

"Then what the hell are you doing here, besides fucking Hudson?"

Again, Val winced.

"Hudson is selling his house and is looking to move into a bigger place," Val said.

"I only bought this house as a temporary dwelling," Hudson said, sounding very businesslike. "I always intended to scale up to something larger once I was satisfied I wanted to settle into the area." Again, I glared at Hudson. Hudson took another step backward.

"Hudson—Mr. Walker—contacted our agency to handle his real estate transactions, and I assigned myself to make it happen."

"And this is your way of consummating the deal," I said.

"No, Jace, you've got it all wrong," Val said. "I didn't know anything about the history between you and Mr. Walker, or I would have given the assignment to someone else."

"Instead of screwing Hudson right now, you would have been off fucking some other *client?*"

Val's only response was a look of shame.

"Is this how you close all of your real estate deals? Or is this special treatment reserved for only your high-end clients?"

"This had nothing to do with the real estate deals," Hudson said. I stepped toward Hudson, ready to pick up where we left off. To my surprise, Val stepped between us and grabbed me firmly by my wrists.

"It's true, Jace. Mr. Walker signed the papers for the mansion last month. It's a done deal."

Now I was speechless, stewing in my own fury.

"Look, Jace," Hudson said. "I didn't know she was married. Now, I know we've had this long running football feud going for reasons I can't even remember, but that's all it ever was. If I'd known Val was married—even to you—I would have never allowed this to happen."

I stared at Hudson for what seemed an eternity. I knew he was telling the truth. The evidence was right there on Val's hand.

Reason prevailed long enough to roadblock my rage. I faced Val, who was still holding my wrists. When I looked at Val, I'd always had a warm, comfortable feeling that resonated through me even during our most vexed moments.

That feeling had turned ice cold. I despised Val at that moment. Val later confessed she had never before seen me so angry. I never told Val that what she had witnessed could have been described as the death knell of my love for her.

The police arrived to find us where we stood. Hudson refused to press charges. Instead, he kept apologizing to me for what happened. Val chimed in with Hudson, when necessary, to help alleviate any possible criminal charges that might have come my way. The officers left us to sort it out, chalking it up to a domestic dispute.

I made Val leave before me with a promise she would head straight home. Before I left, Hudson again offered his sincere apologies. I had nothing to say in response.

The children were still in school when I got home. Val had arranged with a dear friend of ours to pick them up, rather than me, which was our normal routine.

My wife confessed she suffered from hypersexuality disorder (more commonly referred to as sex addiction). It started in college, and she had struggled with controlling it ever since. I scoffed at the notion as being a ridiculous scapegoat tactic to exonerate her adultery. That was, until Val showed me the bills from a therapist she had been seeing.

The bills dated back two years. When I asked Val if she had been unfaithful all of the time we had been together, she confessed she had, more times than she was willing to admit. I was furious, both with Val for being untrue and with myself for being such an idiot as to not to have seen it sooner. My wife was a sex addict and I'd had no clue.

The next couple of months were intense in our household, to say the least. The sight of Val made me fume or sink into yearning. The latter made me angry with myself, for feeling that way for someone who had committed the ultimate betrayal, in my book.

We shielded our children from our tension as much as we could. That amounted to me minimizing my hostility toward Val when the children were around. We wrestled with getting a divorce—me pro, Val con. The stench of divorce hovered in the air between us like smog over a garbage dump.

To my surprise, my family and most of my friends allied with Val. They believed her sex addiction defense and strongly suggested I accept her explanation. Val repeatedly vowed to defeat her disorder and pleaded for the opportunity to prove she could be faithful. The pressure became too great for me to make a choice. I moved out.

The topic of divorce lingered even after our voluntary separation. I had to know more about the depth of my wife's adultery. I hired a team of investigators to root out what they could of Val's affairs. They uncovered a couple dozen liaisons since we'd been married. None was long-lasting, but were more like trysts.

Val confirmed every one, emphasizing they meant nothing to her. They were only a means by which to satisfy her compulsive sexual behavior. When I pressed Val if she'd had any affairs with co-workers or anyone we knew, she emphatically said no. That aspect of her addiction, she managed to keep away from our professional and social circles Hudson Walker being the accidental exception.

A couple of my friends believed that the time for counseling had passed. If Val had come forward and confessed her affairs and condition before she was caught, they reasoned, then maybe we could have worked our way through it.

The fact I had to catch my wife cheating before she was willing to confess her treachery was something they couldn't imagine forgiving. They asked the question I asked myself: if I hadn't caught Val, would she have ever come clean?

With each passing day of our separation, I found I missed Val and our children more and more. In discussing Val's condition with a psychiatrist friend, she conferred everything Val had told me about her disorder.

She pointed out that Val was an addict. Like any addict, they would do whatever was necessary to satisfy their craving. Most addicts are ashamed of their situation. They will go to great lengths to hide their habit from the people whose love and respect they most covet. My psych friend also emphasized that, with proper therapy, Val's condition could be controlled and ultimately eradicated. She also maintained that it would take the full support of the people closest Val in order for her to overcome her hypersexuality disorder.

To weigh my legal options, I discussed with my attorney my chances of gaining full custody of our children, should I follow through on a divorce. When pressed on whether Val was a fit mother and good wife, I could only answer yes to both questions.

Val was a great mom, in fact. The children couldn't ask for anyone better. As a mate, up until the time I discovered her sex addiction, I would have said I was a very fortunate man to have such a remarkable woman as my wife.

My attorney mentioned there was a slim possibility of full custody if I wanted to push the compulsive sexual behavior angle. We would have to prove that because Val could not control her sex addiction, it in some way impeded the wellbeing of our children.

My attorney speculated that Val's attorney would parade a team of experts before the court to testify that Val suffered from a condition that rendered her helpless from being faithful to any one man, but which in no way jeopardized her ability to parent, as proven by the superb job she had done thus far.

My attorney also stressed that such a strategy could force the children to testify on behalf of one parent over another. The court would, at most, order Val to seek counseling for her addiction, which she already had done. That particular outcome, along with the fact that the last thing I wanted to do was place my children in the middle of a divorce firestorm, left that option off the table.

In short, the sex addict offense angle would probably be a bust.

The tastefully furnished, five bedroom, two-and-one-half bath, four-car garage country house I live in is nestled in a quiet valley that has yet to be overrun by modern civilization. I had this vacation home built on this plot of land for that partially secluded reason. It is far enough off the beaten track for privacy, yet close enough to the creature conveniences my family and I am accustomed to and enjoy.

The morning fog felt cool as I stepped out onto the stone column wraparound porch with a fresh cup of Venetian-roasted Sumatra coffee in hand. I drank the coffee from a deformed clay cup covered with pink hearts and the rainbow-colored words "Daddy's Girl" crookedly sprawled across its face.

My daughter made that cup for me in first grade. It is my favorite cup. My morning coffee always tastes best when I drink from her cup. It was the perfect way to begin my day.

I love this place—or rather, I used to. It is now more a residence of necessity rather than choice. Val, Shay, and Cera have remained in our family home in a plush section of the city. The place I now call home served as an eerie reminder of teetering love and sorely missed children.

A couple of wooden planks creaked under my weight as I moved toward the edge of the porch. The mild squeaks were comforting sounds, like the velvety speaking voice of my grandfather or the warm embraces of my parents. Shay called the house noises 'voices.'

Today marked the one-year anniversary of our forced divide. The whole separation thing had happened with a bang rather than a whimper. I'm still not certain what to make of its origin.

My marriage had been relative bliss until the quake that caused our separation. Due to its dreadful anniversary, that agonizing day brought into sharp focus the moment that hurled my family life into a stalemate. Even now, I question whether it really happened, or was a resonating nightmare.

None of my servants or gardeners had arrived. The house was quiet. So was the valley. As I said before, my country home is isolated. I happen to know that a major development plan is in the works by bottom-line property investors that will turn this peaceful valley into a place teeming with modern homes, filled with modern families.

I will have moved and roosted in a land minimally spoiled by our kind before they had dug their first new sewer line.

A thick gray mist covered the valley floor. Foggy mornings were a constant here, their gray gossamer pillow a cool cushion for quiet heads to give flight to dreams and nightmares. My lungs filled with the dewy mist.

One of the wooden planks moaned as I took a couple of steps into the grayish haze of daylight. My dad has an expression: "Not every closed eye is asleep, and not every goodbye is farewell." I'm not certain how that applies to my situation, but it felt appropriate.

I'm waiting for Val to drop off our children. The way I caught Val cheating was karma, kismet or fate. Take your pick. I couldn't deny I still loved her. Val has told me she felt the same about me.

Val is in therapy, trying to get a handle on her sex addiction. In order to prove her sincerity in working toward a cure, Val asked her therapist to give me candid reports on her condition and progress. The reports were to be confidential between her therapist and me. Val's analyst agreed to do so.

The classified weekly reports have been very encouraging. If the therapist is to be believed, Val is well on her way to liberation from her hypersexuality disorder. Now, if I can find a way to heal my bruised ego, then perhaps our future together could be resurrected.

Val agreed to forfeit her career for me. Part of the reason she had become a real estate agent was it kept her in the field, giving Val opportunities to act on her sexual impulses without ever giving me pause to suspect a thing. It worked. I had seen no signs of her adultery over the years. I'd had no indications from our children that they had, either.

I told Val that if we reconciled, she wouldn't have to quit her job. We would work something out. She smiled. Her smile unlocked the vault to my heart. Val caressed my face in her hands and kissed me. We made love. When we are together, I find it difficult to believe there was ever anyone else. I find it hard to forget there wasn't when we're apart.

We never suffered in the bedroom. From what I'd heard from other married couples with children, our sex life was to be envied. While I didn't share our sexual experiences with anyone (for me, intimacy is personal), I couldn't agree more. During our separation, Val and I have made love forty-two times. Somewhere in the back of my mind, I have asked myself: is Val actually making love to me, or needing to satisfy her addiction?

For some men, that conundrum wouldn't matter. It does to me. I have accepted the fact that I can't resist Val. She remains the love of my life, despite it all. If we are forced to part, I may need to seek therapy of my own.

I finally mustered the courage to ask Val about it after one of our times of estranged lovemaking. Val empathically stated that her condition played no part in the love we made. She stressed that it was what we had that made it clear to her she was suffering from a condition she later learned was hypersexuality. Reports from her therapist confirmed that what Val said was true.

I've run into Hudson a couple of times since the illicit affair. He could barely look at me. At most, Hudson said a hasty hello and darted off in another direction.

Based on our history, I would have thought Hudson would have gloated over the sexual conquest of my wife. Rub my nose in it, so to speak. Instead, Hudson seemed to regret what had occurred. When I caught him staring at me from the corner of my eye, he appeared ashamed. In spite of what happened, while I haven't developed any friendly feelings toward Hudson Walker, I don't hate him anymore. I wonder what my psychiatrist friend would draw from that conclusion.

My sister told me the past needed to be released in order for me to be free to move on. I knew she was right. Time had forged chains that weighed me down with bitterness and shame—the bitterness of having discovered my wife had been a chronic adulterer, and the shame of having been the last to know I was married to a sex addict.

I had been able to let go of my loathed past with Hudson Walker within a few months. It had taken me almost a year to find a place of peace and acceptance I had heard so much about, in regards to Val.

It was a tremendous relief when I saw a glowing set of yellow headlights knifing through the gray mist along the only paved road leading to my house. It was too early to be anyone else but Val. I had called to let her know it would be all right to wait until the fog cleared before bringing the children. Val was insistent on giving our children an opportunity to spend as much time with their father as possible. Since the children agreed, how could I say otherwise?

As the car got closer, I could make out its silhouette. It confirmed what I alleged. I couldn't wait to see my children. They were going to spend the weekend, as they did twice a month since our separation. It seemed that every time I saw them, they had become smarter and gotten bigger. Our children had adjusted well to our separation. They were great kids.

The last report I received from Val's therapist stated she believed Val had her condition under control. Her therapist was going to suggest Val no longer require counseling, but would leave the door open for discussion if Val ever felt a need to talk. Val had yet to discover her therapist's conclusions. Her therapist intended to break the good news to Val at her next session.

I had planned to invite Val to stay, for the first time—at least until the fog cleared. I've heard it said that without fear, there is no courage. An invitation to Val was as much courage as I could muster.

I had wrestled with the idea for days leading up to the moment of their arrival. The question lingered. Should I ask Val to stay? My heart screamed *yes,* agreeing with the opinion of most people closest me to stop being foolish and try to work things out. My ego shouted *no,* urging me to remain obstinate about an unpardonable sin. Which would have the final say?

I found myself constantly missing Val. I expected I would feel that way about our children, but was surprised to discover how much I missed my wife. It wasn't only in the bedroom that much was predictable.

I missed her voice and her smile, and the sexy way she walked even when she wasn't trying. The way she would laugh uproariously at something funny, then cover her face as if embarrassed at having done so. I missed the faraway look in her eyes when she witnessed something she perceived as magical. I missed our intellectual jousts on philosophy to politics to art and science and everything in between.

It had been one long year since our separation and our near-fatal divorce. In all of that time, I had never stopped longing for her. Was I that deeply in love with Val all along, or was I falling for the old adage "Absence makes the heart grow fonder"?

The car pulled into the gravel driveway, its tires crunching a path to my porch. The lights gently struck me like a candle in the dark. The fog parted. I could clearly see the warm, glowing faces of my family. They made me glad. They made me proud.

Courage spoke. *Ask Val to stay.*

Val turned off the engine. My children—our children—rushed from the car to show me their love. Their words came in a jubilant rush. I listened and responded when required. Val trailed them, stopping at the bottom of the steps and watching with warm eyes and a gentle smile as the moment unfolded. There were no bags to cart inside; I had everything our children needed in their second home.

"Go inside," I told Cera and Shay with a smile. "I've got a couple of presents in your rooms. But they're hidden, so you'll have to find them."

"*Presents,*" Cera said.

"What are they?" Shay asked.

"If I told you, then they wouldn't be surprises." Shay and Cera looked at each other, as they often did, before they made a joint decision. Then they rushed off inside, leaving the front door open behind them.

"You're going to spoil them," Val said with a smile.

"That's the plan." I smiled back. I walked down the steps and stood before her. Val's smile dropped from her face like a scared little leaguer trying to catch her first fly ball. The warmth raced from her eyes, replaced by fear.

I'm certain Val wasn't expecting me to take her into my arms and kiss her. When our lips parted and our eyes met again, I could tell she was glad we'd kissed. I knew at that moment that I wanted Val back under any flag of feelings and by any capacity that would make our relationship work.

"Can you stay the weekend?" I asked. It was my wish that Val would welcome it as a first step to either reclaiming the blissful relationship we had prior to discovering her sexual promiscuity, or moving forward into a future of accepted doubts.

"Sure," Val said, a slight nervous tremor in her voice. "I can do that. Is there any special reason why?"

"I'd like to talk to you about me coming home," I said.

Val was speechless. That was quite a feat for a woman who had something to say about practically everything. Her eyes welled with tears. Val placed a hand over her mouth, grabbed my face, and kissed me. The heart had won. My ego found a dark place in my conscious mind to brood.

"*Do you mean it?*" Val asked after our kiss.

"Yes," I said. We hugged. Shay and Cera were standing in the front door, staring at us. They noticed us hugging each other. Most of all, they noticed their mother crying, even if they were tears of joy.

"What's the matter?" Shay asked. Cera put her arms around her brother's waist. My daughter looked frightened. Shay hugged Cera about the shoulders.

"Your mother and I are talking about getting the band back together," I said.

Shay understood and smiled. "For real?"

"As real as real gets," Val said.

Cera looked up at her brother for an explanation.

"Mom and Dad are getting back together," Shay said.

"For real," Cera said.

"Yes, honey," I said. "This family's been apart far too long. It's time we all got back to where we belong."

Our group hugs and excited exchanges lasted a while at the foot of the steps. We decided to move our celebration inside. We went into the kitchen to make breakfast and finalize our plans.

Our children were so excited by the news, they forgot about their presents. I would like to believe it was because we gave them the best gift they could ask for.

On the way inside, the thinning morning fog still felt cool against my skin. I took a slow, deep, soothing breath, its ethereal embrace a dewy mist that filled my lungs with effervescent hope.

# CONVERSATION

*Skin the color of Kiwi seeds, with flesh as soft and supple as its fruit.*

*"Love does not defer lust in a relationship."*

I rolled over in the bed I shared with my wife, facing the pillows where she normally laid her head. The scent of her apricot shampoo greeted me. Her small, round face, wistful brown eyes, and soft lips were absent, but the recollections of her balmy breath and the silkiness of her chocolate skin remained.

For a moment, I ached for her; to have her near; to embrace her. That is how we welcomed sleep. What movements our bodies made during our dream-gorged slumber is anyone's guess. Jordan was forced to abandon me for her job.

Today, this Tuesday, begins my weekend. Otherwise, the bed would have been made and vacant of hungry memories.

*Instead of an alarm clock awakening me, I would prefer it be the orchestra of birds returned from winter vacations, warm breezes rustling bright green leaves.*

*"Dream as if you'll live forever. Live as if you'll die today."*

*"There's nothing like a cold toilet seat to get you going in the morning."*

We're newlyweds, according to our marriage certificate, but we had been a couple for four years before its signature date. I met Jordan in my junior year of college.

A junior as well, Jordan transferred to Carnegie Mellon University from Pitt out of preference for CMU's poetry program. When I first saw Jordan, she reminded me of the divine Lauryn Hill when that talented singer first arrived on the music scene with The Fugees. Killing me softly with her sensual smile and sultry eyes, Jordan easily attracted the leer of most men.

Why Jordan chose me to kick it with, only she knows. I've never asked Jordan what she saw in me that made me her preferred choice of male companionship, and she never volunteered an answer. I'm only grateful of her verdict.

*"I've never believed in love at first sight. To me, that was folklore, like werewolves or finding children in a cabbage patch. Then I met your mother and she changed all that. One look into those soulful brown eyes and I knew everything there was to know. I was deep in the big muddy. God does have a sense of humor. So I did what most men do when their nose is wide open. I tried to run."*

*Just because I desire your body doesn't mean I don't respect your mind.*

Upon getting to know Jordan, she immediately engraved her own identity in my psyche, staking out her individuality over her musically gifted twin in my heart. The journey from infatuation to genuine affection that caused me to slip on the greasy banana peel of mind-blowing love took all of about three months. To make Jordan fall as deeply in love with me, I'd say that was more like three years.

*"We listen to the modern media expel hordes of obnoxious cynical banter, traversing conflicting camps of our political sphere without lending feasible results for those most in need."*

*"I hear your voice and it feels like flying."*

*"You call my name and it feels like home."*

My dear wife loves to talk. Since she has what I would describe as a melodious voice, listening to her speak is literally music to my ears.

That doesn't mean she's always agreeable. Jordan is never afraid to speak her mind. We've had our fair share of loud discussions, arguments and fights. Most, I've rather enjoyed. Guess that says something about me, exposing the combative side of my nature. Debating is something I'm rather good at. That doesn't mean I pick fights for the sake of it. I'm simply no pushover when one arises.

*A plume of steam rising in a clear night sky;*
*trust is a migratory bird that may flee in the throes of bad weather.*

Being talkative does not mean that my wife's without her quiet time. Jordan is a good poet. During her most contemplative moments, when she nests deep within the cradle of her muse in search of innovative charmed offerings, she is as silent as candlelight.

We can occupy the same room in contented coexistence without breathing a word for hours. We're comfortable in that place—as comfortable in our silence as our dialogue. Most couples I know are not. They need something to burst the silence, chatter to fill the empty voids. Without the constant rustling of speech, corrosion may seep into their space and rust the chains that bind them.

*"There are no more hallowed halls of learning free from consumerism."*

*"An illusion of an open economy, social justice, multinational corporations, hype, corporate driven science, moral champions, immoral despots, salvation, New World Order…"*

*"Capitalism is not democracy. They are not pseudonyms. They do not operate under the same principles. Hence, when it is said that we live in a democratic society, and we live in a capitalist society, it's not true. You cannot have both."*

*"International banks and corporations are the real powers behind the thrones. They run this."*

Two creative souls vying for crumbs in the great capitalist continuum was a recipe for starvation. Fortunately, for us, Jordan's practical side balanced her choices. Despite her talent as a poet (and encouragement by those in our literary circles to pursue such a gift), Jordan functioned under no illusions that she would be one of those blessed few capable of earning a stable living at her passion.

Jordan wasted no time, after securing her master's in English, in getting her teaching certificate. She lucked up and landed a full-time position as a grade school English teacher with union benefits and everything. A career at teaching was her second and more realistic path toward stability.

*"Life is to be lived, not controlled, and humanity is won by continuing to play in the face of certain defeat."*

*Walking on a tightrope, backwards, blindfolded, and going uphill.*

I, on the other hand, fully embraced the notion of living off my royalties as a novelist after acquiring my master's degree. After a couple of years of working dead end jobs, often for little more than minimum wage and no benefits, I landed at Starbucks.

Working at Starbucks was supposed to be a temporary gig until my big break, which I imagined would be barreling around the corner at any minute.

Minutes eclipsed into days, weeks, and months. I never intended to stay long enough to become store manager. I still believe my liberation day will arrive, catapulting me into my destined artistic career. My soul wouldn't have it any other way.

*Writing, at its base, is a craft. At its pinnacle, it's art.*

*"The central objective of any artistic work is to locate that resonance of meaning, that core extension that is stimulated whenever we unveil kindred recognitions articulated within the efforts of another."*

*"Perfection is not required of art or craft, but it's great when it happens."*

While I have a thick paragraph of short story publication credits in a host of high profile and respected literary magazines, that has done little to procure me a seat at the real world, big picture round table of novelists. For one, it more brands me as a literary writer—which, in these times, *ain't* good in the eyes of large publishing houses.

I am a literary writer and I'm damn proud of it! We, who were once appreciated for infusing social, political, and historical commentary with exquisite storytelling, have become print pariahs, squeezed out and discarded like dregs, reportedly due to our lack of salability. That's corporate speak for 'we deal in widgets, not art.'

*"It was the truth. That was all I needed to know."*

*"Talent is an ambiguous gift, I'm told. Culture is not."*

*"Education is both a reward and a privilege."*

*"Ignore the messenger. Pay attention to the message."*

My agent has been asking me to keep the faith regarding my global warming novel (that also happens to be the working title). Nicole's my third representative, and is by far the best of the bunch.

She's been pitching my latest manuscript for the last few months, with no takers thus far. Nicole believes in me. She reminds me of that fact even more than Jordan does. Nicole and I have been together for a couple of years. She claims that the global warming novel has a real chance of making it into the hands of a large publishing house.

Global warming is a hot topic. It's that aspect of the novel that Nicole had me focus on when writing my synopsis.

She emphasized that I should not mention the other left-wing causes of combating human trafficking and poverty, corporate greed, or the government takeover by the top one percent that was challenged by other characters in the novel.

When I asked why I should neglect to mention them in my synopsis, Nicole told me, in her most reassuring tone, "Let's focus on getting our feet in the door before we feed them too many details."

I refused to accept her reasoning and pressed her to be more specific. She was. "You need to stop championing liberal causes in your novels. At least, do a better job of disguising or minimizing their presence in your work.

"You're a novelist, not a reporter or a crusader. It's extremely difficult for freshmen literary talent to break in as it is, without having to deal with someone who is constantly promoting a political or social agenda."

When I asked Nicole why she wasn't pitching my novel to college or university presses, she chuckled and said, "You want to make money, don't you?" Statements like that reminded me that while her heart fully supported the arts, her mind was stonily focused on business.

*Most people are like water. They take the path of least resistance.*

Perhaps I'm a fiction prude or a creative writing zealot, but I understood what Nicole was trying to hammer home. I needed to be low key; deal in less abrasive topics. I didn't argue with her professional assessment that time, nor have I done so since.

That so-called political agenda Nicole spoke of is the fiery inspiration that stokes my muse. They are the seeds that provide me with the impetus to write novels in the first place.

I keep moving ahead with new writing, remain conscientious about my job, and try not to think about what could be. The novel I'm currently writing does as Nicole suggests.

It's not as innocuous as she might like, but I am doing a better job of masking and minimizing my characters' liberal activism in the hopes of not raising any elitist publishing hackles.

*"Some people will only digest their version of the truth. No other points of view matter. These are typically the most dangerous humans."*

Last night, Jordan read to me fragments of her latest poem that had yet to honor her with a title or lucid direction.

"I give my sermons in the cemetery

An empty bottle of Thunder Bird laid to rest in a withering bed of
flowers
   A discarded black hair net
   A forgotten brown leather glove
   Beanbag philosophy
   Shrimp étouffée speckled the vomit
   I cut myself shaving and think of the song 'Only Women Bleed'
   She screamed at the moon
   He grappled with mountains
   No more crying! No more suffering! No more hunger!
   No more fools yelling insanely out on street corners
   In the incredible eye of time
   There is a spec known as our universe
   Another negative love song
   My hope incinerated
   Burnt out candles
   Lumps of melting wax."

*"It has been written by some science fiction writers that computers could take over the world in a diabolically aggressive manner. Computers have taken over in a much more subtle way. Humans are required to adapt to technology, not the other way around."*

*"Modern technology has become the primary component in creating the sweatshops of the new millennium."*

I learned, early in our relationship, to offer my opinions only as to whether I liked or disliked Jordan's work. Jordan required no other input from me regarding its content or structure or substance and the like. Writing poetry, for her, was truly an organic experience, being drawn from the deep well of her emotions, nurtured through her intellect, and honed by her craft. It was an experience she preferred to have alone.

I, on the other hand, seem to distance myself from my work without effort, as if viewing the entire event through someone else's eyes. It's an almost cerebral or clinical exercise, if you will.

Unlike life, where emotions are valid for me, my writing life is a written exercise aimed at eliciting particular responses from the reader. In order to accomplish that result, I find it best to detach myself from the material. Odd for a literary votary, I know, but it's what works for me.

Jordan's input is always welcomed at any point during my creative process.

*"How would you like to be remembered?"*

*"I did my best, and my best was good enough."*

*"That's what's wrong with the world today. Everybody's thinking about themselves."*

*"I've got a newsflash for you. That's what's always been wrong with the world. Generation after generation, century after century, motivating attitudes, egos, and people haven't changed much. And that's the problem."*

*"World's coming to an end. See you on the flip side."*

*"I love children. They make you realize that you still have far more questions about our universe than you do answers. And that's a good thing."*

*Fighting is easy. Love is hard.*

A fly has swan-dived into the warm milk of our marriage. Jordan doesn't want to have children. I do. Jordan believes it would be stupid and selfish for us to bring a child into this dark world, leaden with bleak prospects.

I believe anything created out of love is amazing, a light capable of casting out the darkness, and I look forward to cultivating a life and battling for a better tomorrow.

It's an issue that has rocked the foundation of our perfect union, at times. Jordan is three weeks pregnant. We haven't told anyone. When I found out, I wanted to shout it from the rooftops. Jordan made me promise to keep it a secret. She hasn't decided whether she wants to keep our child.

We've talked about it. We've argued about it. Jordan is as obstinate on the subject of children as she is a talented poet. If Jordan decides to abort our child, I don't know what I'll do. That could create a strain in our relationship that might never be healed.

*"Everything old was once new."*

I rose from our bed and opened the winter curtains. The thick beige carpet tickled my bare feet. I looked out of our second floor bedroom window of our rented home. Our once-decent, blue-collar, middle-class community had raced downhill in dire economic times to become a dilapidated neighborhood that appeared cursed.

A steel gray sky spit cold rain on the potholed and cracked streets and everything else in between. Battered indehiscent trees and shell-shocked grass pleaded for death and to never be resurrected. Carnivorous weeds and their dissipative rat and roach cousins thrived. Abandoned and neglected properties wallowed in their self-pitying misery. In the distance, a weed-choked lot had become a depository for discarded items belonging in a junkyard or the city dump.

The metro bus shelter across the street, once a clean and bright haven for public transporters, had been gutted, scarred, and branded as a war zone. A refugee camp was blighted with local gang markings, the trash receptacle next to it overflowing with garbage.

Amongst the debris, littering in and around the bus shelter, were a handful of abandoned or lost disposable lighters, crack vials and pipes, cigarette and marijuana butts, crumpled fast food bags and candy wrappers, a jumbo soda tub with a cockeyed straw poking out of the center of its plastic lid, a soggy newspaper, and an open bottle of malt liquor filled a third of the way with what I hoped was its original contents.

Sometime today, I'll take it upon myself to clear away the garbage and trash. No one will help. No one will care.

*"Bask in the glory of that which is nature."*

*"Nature is everything we are and everything we will be and everything we know."*

*"The phrase 'man against nature' is a joke. There is no competition. No matter the outcome, nature never loses."*

*"Save The Planet" above the logo and words of the "Hard Rock Cafe" below "Orlando," on the back of a black leather jacket: amusing contradictions."*

The ground looked saturated from cold rain, nature preparing it for the snow I was certain was soon to come. A pigeon pecked at the entrails of his dead relative.

I took a few moments to take it all in. Aside from sporadic vehicles wandering through, there wasn't a person in sight. It felt like the calm before the storm; a strange and eerie peace that had settled over the land before the inevitable shelling of discord began.

We're looking to move to a better neighborhood now that this one has gone to pot. Still looking to rent, not buy. Jordan and I had scoped out a few places, but none of them seemed quite right. We decided to put off our search until after the New Year.

*"For us, they're laws. For them, they're suggestions."*

A couple of sharp barks pricked my ear. I could hear our adopted dog pound mutts playing downstairs. Adam and Eve were abnormally independent, for dogs. Unless they needed or wanted something from us, they didn't hang around their caregivers much.

Jordan believes they were domesticated felines in a previous life, and maintained those independent personalities in this one. It didn't mean they didn't love us. It simply meant they weren't clinging vines like most dogs.

Jordan must have already fed them and taken them for their morning constitution. Otherwise, they would have been upstairs now with longing eyes, either their feed bowls or leashes dangling from their mouths.

*"Why is it that no one shuts up anymore?"*

I like to listen. That's not true. I love to listen. Whenever given the opportunity to eavesdrop, I leap at it like a hungry predator at its prey. Being a writer, listening is a good thing. I do more than listen with my ears. I listen with my eyes, my skin, my nose, my tongue, and my heart.

It's a constant state of existence for me—has been since I was a child. My grandmother saw me as an old soul returned for unfinished business. I see myself as a quintessential inquisitive child born anew, in search of comprehending the complexities of the human condition from every level and at every turn.

*"Arrogance is one thing, intelligence another. So often, they are believed to be proponents of each other. Usually that mistake is made by the person who misinterprets their arrogance as superior intelligence when precisely the opposite is true."*

*"I believe much, but know little."*

*"Encyclopedias of ignorance."*

*"Racists: can't live with 'em, can live without 'em."*

I don't write down whatever I encounter. Instead, I carry them with me in my memory, perhaps even my subconscious; filed away like random index cards earmarked in card catalogues, extracted when I need them to help shape my fictional mold.

*"Don't take it so seriously."*

*"What's not serious about it?"*

*"You think you're something."*

*"Yes, I do: for what is a man who thinks himself nothing?"*
*"You're a liar."*
*"What did you call me?"*
*"You know what that is. You see one every time you look in the mirror."*

While I often remember who said what, even when and where, it becomes of little significance, even when the musings are my own. The words are all that matter. Words shift into place in the context that suits the narrative.

*"We're not taught to compete, in America. We are taught to win at all cost. That is the subliminal and direct message promoted throughout our society. Hence, it's part necessity for an imbalance in how society operates, a balanced playing field being a myth. To maintain the status quo, to thwart undesirable cream from rising to the top, to keep legitimate competition from winning too much or too often, they must be handicapped."*

*"When one is clearly focused on a positive objective, that will serve you far better than a distorted obsession of competition;"*

*"Wall Street collapse, bank bailouts, Tea Party, lynch mob mentality."*

*"Refusing to run a civilian down with a tank when ordered by his superior officer, the soldier was faced with a court-martial. He still refused. When asked why, he replied, 'I'm a soldier, not a murderer, sir.'"*

*"There are some heartless bastards in this world. Hopefully they don't make it to the next."*

I dropped by a college buddy's house to see what he was up to, the other day. What I stumbled upon was an attempted bonding session with a group of his co-workers whom he had invited over for beer and pizza.

With no video games or acceptable sports to watch—those being football, basketball, baseball, hockey, soccer, tennis, track and field, boxing, or mixed martial arts—and mutual interests nonexistent, my buddy took to channel surfing and came across a PBS documentary that immediately grabbed our attention. The documentary covered the Vietnam War era.

His guests wasted no time mocking the period when they weren't spellbound by their smartphones. They went out of their way to belittle peace and love and understanding, bashing their cosmic quest and spiritual values as if they were silly pipe dreams that only wimpy fools could believe.

It was quite a sight to witness beer-guzzling modern thinkers smirk at what they considered useless, trite, or incidental behavior.

Philosophies and agendas had evaporated in importance because we had become enlightened in our age of preemptive wars, corporate takeovers, extravagant excesses, and the mania to bear arms.

Those tie-dyed freaks and longhaired hippy weirdoes' visions were frivolous. Nonviolent battles were absurd. The questions and ideas of such groups were child's play, and grownups knew better. They cackled at their music as a joke rebellion and equated dropping out to turning on idiot banter.

Fighting the establishment was for simpletons and wise men who accepted the realities of our volatile world, realizing the necessity of such a credible presence in order to defend and protect our privileged stature on the world stage. An establishment was more than willing to take on that responsibility for a startling price.

It was as if modern America had discovered the answers to those mystifying questions in their prefab homes, gas-guzzling SUVs, space age technology, acres of malls and superstores, and online shopping (or their fragile jobs that provided them enough survival ingredients for the moment, if they had one).

They comprehended what actually mattered and kissed it full on the mouth, slipping in a little tongue when prevailing forces demanded.

My friend bowed to their unrelenting badgering to find something worth watching. He channel surfed from the Vietnam War documentary until he found a show that drew praise from the crowd— a sitcom packed full of humor for a juvenile mind.

*Education—of the best intentions—in and of itself does not, will not, dispel ignorance, racism, sexism, prejudice, or the like. That light must be ignited from an unshakable desire from within.*

I kept quiet. I listened, observed, and took mental notes. I knew my friend well enough to know that he couldn't wait to be rid of those people and had come to realize the mistake he had made trying to bond with them. Once the last exited, a heavy groan bellowed from deep in his chest. I stayed to help clean up and chat about what had occurred.

An art graduate working in a brokerage firm was far from idyllic for him. I tried convincing him it was only temporary until his real career got underway. My persuasive attempts were unsuccessful, especially since I couldn't lead by example.

He looked depressed when I left, as if all he believed, all he held sacred, had been scraped from his soul, stuffing the womb of his dreams with bramble and sawdust for them to subsist.

*"What happens to a dream deferred?"*

I prayed he'd be okay.

*A lot have much to say after the fact, their voices silent when their opinions matter most.*

*"A simpleton's view of the world is that of one who listens to an exquisite piece of music, reads a master work, or eyes brilliant art and brutishly discards its wonder. They usually belong to the tell-you-how-to-live-your-life tribe."*

*"Many are experts outside of their fields."*

*At times, it's not easy playing the fool. Other times, it comes naturally.*

I need solitude to write, not isolation. It is the life-blood of my creative heart, the fabric of my imagined worlds. Those who love me accept my antisocial mood swings even if they don't fully understand their basis. It is most important to me; as vital as a mind to a philosopher, opposable thumbs to humans, and wings to a bird.

*The anchor for the local evening news thanked the weatherperson for the sunny day she'd forecasted for tomorrow ... as if the weatherperson was personally responsible for the outcome of the weather.*

As I said earlier, I don't only listen with my ears. Experiences are filed away in the same manner.

Like the time Jordan and I had been waiting in frigid winter weather for a metro bus headed our way, for nearly an hour. We had gone to see Othello at the Pittsburgh Playhouse that evening. The blizzard that struck was predicted, but had come a day early.

We walked into the theater faintly dusted with mild flurries and emerged three hours later to a storm-strangled city. It was as if someone had dumped a gigantic hopper filled with snow.

Our car was in the shop, having its winter checkup and being fitted with snow tires, nonetheless, so we had decided to take the bus.

I was dressed for winter, including a black wool overcoat, and sat on the bus shelter bench. Jordan sat on my lap. Jordan was equally prepared for the weather with her tan wool overcoat. We were alone.

It was rare we saw anyone about through the wickedly beautiful snowfall that had the city by the throat. The metropolis looked comatose, as if forced into hibernation.

*Time slows in the arctic expanse of winter, as if cold affects it like blood circulating through a frigid body.*

*"Lost in their overcoats, waiting for the sunset…"*

*"Preserve your memories; they're all that's left you."*

Jordan had lost her mittens earlier in the day and we hadn't had a chance to replace them. I gave her my gloves to wear. She asked if my hands were cold. The same hands attached to the arms that hugged her close as she sat across my lap.

Yes, I have an ego, and have exhibited my fair and unwise share of male bravado in my day. Of course, I denied it. My hands were practically numb. Jordan repositioned herself so that she sat on my lap with her back facing me. She turned at the waist so that she could put her arms around my neck and then told me to put my hands into her coat pockets. I did. I was still able to hug her close, still able to kiss her and rub noses when she allowed.

Eventually, an off-duty taxi happened by which was gracious enough to take us home at the going rate. They were small things, perhaps even insignificant in the greater scheme of our lives, let alone the world. But it was real life, real magic; the spirit of which found its way into a chapter of one of my unpublished novels.

*"Survival takes precedence over any romanticized, preconceived notions one might have about their commitment to a cause or a person or art."*

*"Guess you would have to have lived to know the truth in that statement."*

The gas furnace kicked on with a thud. I could hear the hot air being forced through the open floorboard vents. Adam and Eve barked at one of the downstairs vents, as if ordering it to keep quiet.

I took those occurrences as my queues to begin my day. Before I got started, I would check on Adam and Eve—make certain they weren't into anything they weren't supposed to be. Then I'll shower, shampoo, shave, eat, floss, brush, dress, take my mug of steaming hot Sun-Dried Ethiopia Harrar Joe to our second bedroom that serves as our study, and pick up where I left off on my latest novel.

I'm attempting to make this manuscript simply entertaining without any political overtones or rebellious shadings. It should be commercially viable once it's finished. If I'm going to make a decent living doing what I love, I need to consider selling out.

If Jordan decides to keep our child, it'll make the traitor gruel a lot easier to swallow. Hell, I'll even do some ghostwriting, if I have to, in order to help support our family.

*His right eye involuntarily twitched when he got angry. The angrier he got, the more it twitched.*

*A lean black man strutted into the bar, eyes large and searching, discovering what he sought with a grin. He patted a bearded white comrade drinking cold beer from a clear long neck bottle on the back before taking the empty bar stool next to him, mentioning, "My throat's dry as the Sahara."*

*A man and a woman share a wooden toothpick.*

*Warped trees are robbed of leaves, but strong of branches, trunks, and stems.*

*The foul smell of sewage was so strong you could taste it.*

*Her expression exceeded having a bad day. She appeared to be having a bad life.*

*They were the type of couple that, when you looked at them, you could never imagine having sex.*

*His skin felt like gauze.*

*Tanja—another spelling for Tanya—a tall woman with thinning bleach blonde hair, blue eyes, fleshy fingers, heavy make-up, a bright red sweater, and large saggy breasts.*

*"There will always be people looking over your shoulder. That's okay. They're the ones who are behind."*

*The appetizing aroma of fried pork chops.*

*A teenager on the metro bus reading "A Death in the Family" on a hot summer day, a vibrant rush of variant external noises sweeping through the open windows on the seldom-quiet bus.*

*Clouds ahead, behind, above; mountains and oceans and forests and plains and streams; cities and farms and rivers and lakes; humans pricking the planet landscape; distant and short commutes; long and brief walks; pockmarked blacktop, paved gray roadways; steam billowing from the roof of a building; rain kissing my skin; puddle rainbows; deep fried catfish and barbequed ribs.*

*Community; gunshots; children; guile and innocence; running; scurrying; escaping; cars racing for shelter; anguish and physical pain; sirens ripping the night; silent snow; deafening blood; curious crowds eying tragedy as entertainment while discussing their reviews amongst themselves; prisons; ghettos; gated communities; poverty; prosperity; austerity; bitterness and bliss; dark brackish water; life and death and struggle and humanity and faith; ostentation; achievements and failures;*

*technology; power; limited resources; energy; diversity; pollution; evolution; sweatshops; modern slavery; possession and loss; concrete balustrades akin to chess pawns; putrid carcasses of shame; polished statues of glory, courage and cowardice; gruesomeness and grace; fate chasing chance; religion and politics; apathy wrestling passion, joy and pain; commerce versus art; a barge knifing downriver creasing the dawn; love; hate; concrete island; people smile and laugh and cry and sing and sin, worship and commemorate, celebrate and survive; a metro bus turning into downtown; a pale green handrail paralleling white marble steps; the decent into hell; the ascent toward heaven; stepping from public transport into the vein; going to work and praying.*

*"Each of us has the capacity to become a saint."*

*"He had a tendency to make a short story long."*

# ABOUT THE AUTHOR

Michael's passion for literature inspired him to devour everything from contemporary novels to classical prose. As a high school student, he wrote poetry for his enjoyment. That joy blossomed into a zeal that would not be contained. Composing poetry rippled into writing short stories, novels, and screenplays.

Michael has studied English Literature and Creative Writing at Point Park University, Sonoma State University, and Portland State University to improve his craft. He has written creatively for more than four decades and has had poetry and short fiction published in numerous literary publications.